The following transcript was discovered among the papers of the late Henry Blaine Barton, Commander, Imperial Navy Reserve. Between the time of his retirement from active duty and his death at the age of seventy-nine, Commander Barton added to his military honors by distinguishing himself as the Empire's foremost expert on Sauron Phenomena.

Critics have pointed to a certain lack of objectivity (some say fanaticism) on the part of Commander Barton regarding Sauron "survivors" that might have escaped the destruction at the second Battle of Tanith and the following Sack of Sauron, spreading throughout the Empire as sort of a "genetic fifth column," claiming that Barton's wartime experiences clouded his judgment. In Commander Barton's defense, it must be pointed out that his knowledge and expertise concerning the Saurons, gained though it was by sifting through the ruins of their society on Sauron, was far superior to that of any of his ͏   a point conceded by the more honest o͏͏͏

Thus, while his warni͏   ͏   ͏auron can be seen (in the ͏   ͏   ͏ughout the Empire͏   ͏   ͏uld be a mistake to ͏   ͏   ͏erhaps the danger is less͏   ͏ ͏on than from twisted individual͏   ͏erate societies seeking to emulate the͏   ͏t it might be a danger, nevertheless. . . .

WELCOME TO WARWORLD

CREATED BY

JERRY POURNELLE

**With the editorial assistance of
John F. Carr and Roland Green**

WAR WORLD II: DEATH'S HEAD REBELLION

This is a work of fiction. All the characters and events portrayed in this book are fictional, and any resemblance to real people or incidents is purely coincidental.

A Baen Books Original

Baen Publishing Enterprises
P.O. Box 1403
Riverdale, N.Y. 14071

ISBN: 0-671-72027-9

Cover art by The Stephen Hickman Studio

First printing, December 1990

Distributed by
SIMON & SCHUSTER
1230 Avenue of the Americas
New York, N.Y. 10020

CREATED BY
JERRY POURNELLE

VOL. III:

WAR WORLD

DEATH'S HEAD REBELLION

With the editorial assistance of
John F. Carr and Roland Green

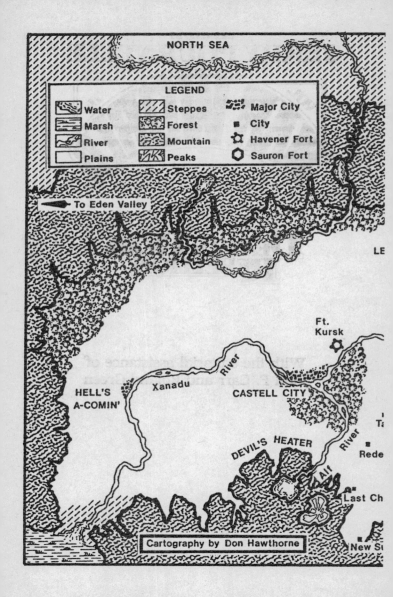

Chronology

2032   *Captain Jed Byers of the CDSS Ranger discovers a planetary sized moon of a gas giant and names it Haven. It is not so much a niche as a loophole for life.*

2037   *Garner Castell buys the license to establish New Harmony settlements on Haven*

2038   *Sauron is discovered by Avery Landyn, a survey pilot for 3M. World is rich in radioactives and heavy metals.*

2040   *CoDominium Bureau of Relocation begins mass out-system shipment of convicts and undesirables. Colonization of Sparta and St. Ekaterina. First convicts arrive on Haven.*

2046   *Two thousand American miners sent to Haven after the Great Lakes Iron Revolt. When they discover the strict laws prevailing in Castell City, they found their own town, Hell's-A-Comin'.*

2052   *Shimmer stones are discovered on Haven. Word leaks out by tramp ship and miners begin to flock to Haven.*

2058   *CoDominium sends a brigade of Marines and an ambassador to Haven. The new viceroy lays the foundation for Fort Kursk.*

2079   *Sergei Lermontov becomes Grand Admiral of the CoDominium Space Navy.*

2098   *Saurons evict the CoDominium and declare their independence. They begin to build their own space navy.*

2103   *Great Patriotic Wars. End of the CoDominium. Exodus of the Fleet.*

2250   *Leonidas I of Sparta proclaims the Empire of Man.*

2258   *Seventy-seventh Division ("Land Gators") of the Imperial Marines is commissioned on Haven. Principal duties, garrison and peacekeeping on Haven. Mobile Reserve for Twelfth Army.*

2250–2600   *Empire of Man enforces interstellar peace.*

2434   *First Cyborg is created on Sauron.*

2603   *St. Ekaterina is nearly destroyed by the Saurons. Secession Wars begin.*

2613   *Lavaca is liberated from the Saurons during the Lavacan Campaign.*

2618   *Third Imperial Fleet is nearly destroyed off Tabletop.*

2623   *Seventy-seventh Division is withdrawn from Haven along with all Imperial officials.*

2637   *Sauron supported Secessionist armada and Claimant fleets fight to a draw at the Battle of Makassar.*

Table of Contents

THE FACE
OF THE ENEMY
DON HAWTHORNE

First there was the CoDominium, an uneasy alliance which kept the peace on Earth, but at a cost greater than many were willing to bear. Then came the Alderson Drive, which gave mankind the stars; and those who hated the CoDominium could leave, and many who did not want to leave the Earth were exiled.

Mankind had the stars, but not wisdom; and when a hundred worlds were settled, the CoDominium could no longer keep the peace. CoDominium became chaos, and from that rose the Empire, built on dreams but held together by the Navy. And the Empire grew its own seeds of destruction, to dissolve into the Secession Wars.

Through it all Haven endured. Then the Saurons came.

THE FACE
OF THE ENEMY

DON HAWTHORNE

The Universe exists in chaos;
  Man is the measure of the Universe.
The ultimate chaos of man's existence
  Is the human endeavor called War.
By mastering War, we master the Universe.

> *Children's song taught in Sauron*
> *primary schools, Translated by*
> *Colonel Nigel McKeegan, Direc-*
> *tor of Imperial Forces of Occupa-*
> *tion, Secession Wars Historical*
> *Task Force, 2643*

"What are we?"

The question was directed toward a viewport of the Sauron heavy cruiser *Fomoria*, but was addressed to the figure behind the speaker, who blinked in surprise at the words.

The officer at the viewport stood with hands clasped behind his back, watching the immensity of interstellar space before him as if he might actually discern something amid all that blackness. If any human-spawned eyes were capable of it, his were. Vessel First Rank Galen Diettinger turned from the viewport and fixed the young Soldier before him with a piercing stare. "I asked you what we are, Fighter Rank Severin."

"Your pardon, First Rank, but the question is out of

2

context. Are you referring to this ship and her crew, or to you and me, or is the nature of the question metaphysical?"

Diettinger nodded slightly, seeming satisfied and disappointed at the same time. "The context is immaterial, Fighter Rank Severin. You have answered the question." Diettinger took his seat at the desk. "Sit," he ordered. Severin sat. "You commanded the reconnaissance flight to Tanith System this morning. Report your impressions of the situation there."

Severin remained impassive, but inwardly he was disapproving. He was part of that group of younger Saurons, born since the start of the Secession Wars, who believed personal interpretation of data to be at best an outdated tradition and at worst a dangerous indulgence. Accurate information, in sufficient quantities, made it unnecessary to "read" the enemy's intentions; whatever his *intentions* might be, his *actions* would be dictated by the actions of the Saurons.

But Diettinger was of an older school, one that thought prudence to be as crucial as boldness, an idea Severin's generation could barely understand, let alone embrace. The First Rank even had an Old Earth antique in his office, something called a "sampler" from the Peninsular Campaigns of the Sauron role model, Wellington, which read: "Discretion is the better part of valor." Whatever *that* meant.

"First Rank, enemy fleet dispositions at Tanith are three *Chinthe*-class destroyers, the light cruisers *Strela* and *Konigsberg*, and the Imperial battlecruiser *Canada*."

Diettinger waited until the silence began to discomfit the Fighter Rank. "Ground force deployments," he said.

"Deployments, sir?" Severin was confused. "Sensors indicated one battalion of mechanized infantry, one of heavy armor, and four of foot infantry, with assumed attendant support units and an unidentified concentration presumed to be a special operations brigade, standard for Imperial ground forces of this size."

"You seem unconcerned, Fighter Rank."

Severin shrugged. "Their lack of armor support or infantry vehicles suggests overall poor combat readiness."

Diettinger's face remained blank. "How low was your reconnaissance pass, Fighter Rank Severin?"

"Low, sir?" Severin was taken aback; doctrine directed that reconnaissance ops be conducted from high orbit, to allow the maximum spread of the sophisticated sensor gear aboard the fighters. "Standard, First Rank, 150 kilometers."

Diettinger almost smiled. "While you were optimizing the scanning equipment on board your fighter, did you make any use of the scanning equipment in your head?"

"First Rank, Tanith is under almost perpetual cloud cover, I saw no reason—"

"Tanith is under such cloud cover, Fighter Rank, because it is hot, extremely so. It is a veritable jungle in every place above sea level where it is not swamp, or sheer cliff, or broken ground. That is the reason for the low vehicle-to-infantry ratio. With very few exceptions, armored vehicles are worthless on Tanith, while infantry with airlift support, and particularly special forces groups, comprise the dominant forces in battle. Your failure to provide accurate disposition of these enemy forces has endangered the success of our mission and the lives of hundreds of your fellow Soldiers."

"But, First Rank, they are only human norms!"

Now it was Diettinger's turn to be surprised. Recovering, he stood and looked down at Severin. "What have you learned since release from your training *creche*, Fighter Rank? Have you forgotten that it has been 'human norms' across known space who have bled Sauron white in this war?"

Severin went cold; this type of conversation was perilously close to treason. Sauron reverses in the last few years of the war could clearly be attributed to manpower and materiel superiority of the enemy forces;

even at that, such Imperial victories as had been won were, to say the least, pyrrhic. The situation at Tanith was a classroom exercise; the Sauron heavy cruiser which could not utterly destroy such a meager opposing force as Severin had reported was not worthy of the name.

"Your squadron will immediately make secondary reconnaissance sweeps and report directly to me. These will be low altitude passes, 100 *meters* or less, with augmented visual recording gear. If your second report is satisfactory, you and your squadron will not be remanded to combat overwatch during the battle. Dismissed."

Diettinger watched the young Soldier leave.

The new ones arrive filled with the invincibility of Sauron, he reflected. *Their historical training is being neglected, or they would know that only losing armies do that to their young warriors.*

Diettinger reviewed his orders once more. "Massive quantities of pharmaceuticals on Tanith awaiting convoy for off-shipment," they read, and then one word: "Secure."

Pharmaceuticals on Tanith meant one thing: borloi. An addictive vice among the human norms that comprised the Empire, borloi in its most concentrated form was the only drug capable of anesthetizing a Sauron for surgery. With the fearful weapons both sides were employing in this war of secession, more and more Soldiers were being wounded and maimed, and while their superior healing ability and resistance to trauma increased their survivability *vis à vis* their Imperial counterparts, they couldn't grow back lost limbs or organs without help.

At least, Diettinger thought, *not yet. And until the Breedmasters perfect that capability, we can't fight the Empire with paraplegics.* Regeneration might be an exact science, but grafts and regrowth implanting were not painless, particularly for burn victims. Sauron needed that borloi, and Diettinger's ship was the closest to Tanith for the mission.

He accessed data on the vessels Severin had reported in orbit: three destroyers, two light cruisers, and the original of the *Canada* class of battlecruisers. The *Canada* would be over fifty Standard Years old; perhaps the Empire was straining in this war, as well.

Sauron ship designations were derived from weaponry and mission profiles, rather than tonnage, but the *Fomoria* was more than a match for the Imperial BC. The other ships would be dangerous inasmuch as *Fomoria* would have to ignore them while she engaged the *Canada*, during which time all the Imperial vessels would be firing on her, attempting to overload her Langston Fields with energy weapons and slip missiles past her point defense systems.

Though space was the only battlefield where the Imperials could engage Sauron forces on something like an even footing, Diettinger himself had developed tactics to redress that problem, tactics which were now standard procedure wherever the Saurons faced the Imperial Navy. The naval aspect of the raid was thus the least crucial. The problem was the raid on Tanith herself.

Library data gave him the general layout of Tanith's main spaceport, but it was accurate only to ten years ago, making Severin's reconnaissance update crucial; still, until he knew more, the First Rank would work with what he had. After a few minutes' planning he had arrived at what he felt was an acceptable battle outline.

He scheduled the Staff meeting for one hour after the return of Severin's squadron.

Captain Will Adderly of the INSS *Canada* and commander of the Tanith Patrol Fleet launched his pen across the room toward the dart board for another bull's-eye. It was something he did to relieve tension, and it was almost second nature to him now.

Design Notes:

The *Chinthe*-class destroyers (Type D-76) were originally designed by Prabash and Beng, Ltd., of Makassar, as fast merchant vessels. However, at the time of their design the possibility of a breakdown of the Empire had apparently occurred to certain people in the firm.

So the ships (designated the P-8 Class) were given high speed, a limited self-refueling capability, compartmentation to military specifications, oversized computers, and a number of compartments that could easily be converted to weapons' mountings or ammunition storage.

The result was a ship with limited armament for its size (greater than most light and some heavy cruisers) but high speed and (when lightly loaded) exceptional range. These qualities became valuable from the early days of the Secession Wars, as hostile forces disrupted the Imperial Navy's network of bases.

Consequently, an order was placed for twenty-six P-8's with a built-in armaments suit. . . .

—From *Jane's* ALL THE GALAXY'S WARSHIPS 19th Edition (Sparta, 2645)

He read the reports again, hoping they would say something different this time, but it was not to be. The *Talon*-class Sauron heavy cruiser *Fomoria* was still out there, a ship as fearsome as the reputation of her commander. Sauron heavy cruisers were designed to be all-purpose vessels, carrying fighters, ground troops, and far more armament than their Imperial Navy counterparts. They were an Admiral's dream, the first ships in human history truly able to "outfight what they couldn't outrun, and outrun what they couldn't outfight." Adderly launched another pen. Unfortunately, the very flexibility of such a ship made it impossible for him to guess what it might be doing here. A force of transports and battleships meant siege and invasion, a force of carriers meant a strike, but one heavy cruiser only meant trouble.

The Saurons had arrived in-system three T-weeks ago. As usual in this war, they had been preceded by automated bombs, high-yield nukes on simple clockwork timers, sent ahead along the Alderson Point tramline to soften up anybody waiting on the other end. The disorientation effects of Jump Lag made such a tactic mandatory, since all humans, even Saurons, were so debilitated by the phenomena that a monitor waiting on the other end could destroy them with ease if it happened to be close enough to the tramline's exit point. Computers fared worse, but even Jump Lag couldn't disrupt a spring and a handful of gears.

Immediately upon recovery, they had engaged the converted asteroid sentry base, still recovering from the Sauron nukes, that guarded Tanith's Alderson Point. In less than a day, it was reduced to rubble.

And since then, nothing. The *Fomoria* still had made no move against his meager task force and he still did not dare engage her until the convoy arrived with its escort to reinforce.

The Saurons had been probing this sector off and on for about four years now, and despite being bloodied in three major naval engagements, they were far from beaten. It was only by grace of the travel times between Alderson Points that the Empire had survived the initial Sauron victories of the war at all. The decades following were filled with the constant struggle to push the Saurons and their allies back. Now it seemed as if the Saurons were on the wane.

But twice since the tide had turned in the war, the Imperial General Staff had launched offensives against Sauron strongholds, and twice the carefully garnered reserves and precious resources of men and ships had been obliterated, when everything in the Staff plans had predicted otherwise.

Now they were at Tanith, one of the crossroads into the heart of the Empire. From here it was only a short trip to Gaea, or Covenant; even Sparta, the Imperial capital, would be in range of a Sauron Fleet based at Tanith. If the enemy got a foothold there . . .

Adderly's constant requests for reinforcement had gone unheeded. He had been promised that a portion of the convoy escort would be turned over to his control, but he couldn't leave the *Fomoria* out there, unmolested, to welcome the convoy when it arrived, helpless in the throes of Jump Lag.

Adderly recalled the old military adage from over a century ago, when Sauron still provided loyal troops for the Empire, before the Secession War: "No battle plan survives contact with a Sauron." Too true. Perhaps even more so of *this* Sauron. Adderly rechecked the slim intel file on Galen Diettinger, commander of the *Fomoria.*

At least it's an old warhorse like me, he thought.

One problem with being at war for generations was that details on the enemy's up-and-comers became almost impossible to get. There simply were no Sauron defectors, and human norms who tried to impersonate them rarely succeeded.

It wasn't all that tough for a Sauron to tone down his

abilities and pass for a human norm. Rumor had it they did not look all that different. For all the "racial supremacists" bilgewater the Imperial Propaganda Committee put out about them, the Saurons varied in physiognomy as much as human norms; they were, after all, "purpose-bred people." And they possessed enough human norm worlds as allies from which to draw their espionage community. On the other hand, there seemed to be no end to the petty thieves and bureaucrats willing to betray the Empire for a few feeble promises of neutrality or special treatment, or just plain money.

And what did that say about the state of the Imperial society he was risking his neck to preserve? Adderly dismissed the memory of his wife's voice. Alysha would never understand. Alysha never had, although she had promised she would. They had married during his midshipman days at the Academy—when no one had yet dared to label the Empire's ongoing skirmishes as the Secession Wars—he promising to join her father's merchant fleet as soon as those skirmishes were resolved.

But the Saurons had emerged to lead the Secessionist cause, and the skirmishes had become a war. His four years of required service became a lifelong career, despite his influential father-in-law's offers to get him out of the Navy for "critical civilian services." His refusals had led to battles with Alysha that rivaled those with the Secessionists.

Adderly sighed; at least this Diettinger was a more or less known quantity. The file called him resourceful and innovative, with a flag at the last word. Sauron discipline and aggressiveness tended to make them somewhat predictable, but they possessed their share of daring commanders. And, being perhaps the ultimate military pragmatists, they were quick to place these exemplars where they could do the most good.

Adderly read of engagements in which the *Fomoria* took part under Diettinger; none of the accounts gave him cause for rejoicing. The *Fomoria* typically had been used to engage numerically superior forces, once even here during the Battle of Tanith.

Soon to be renamed the First *Battle of Tanith, no doubt,* Adderly mused.

Diettinger had one of those records that a Civilian might have chalked up to mere genius, but Adderly knew better. No action Diettinger commanded had ended in defeat for the Saurons unless he had been relieved by the appearance of higher ranking officers. The man was not just good, he was lucky.

It was a rare Sauron who claimed a consistent record of naval victories. Ship to ship, the Imperial Navy was equal to anything the Saurons could muster. It was all that was winning the war against them. It was also why Sauron ships were built to be twice as powerful as any opposing vessels of their type.

If the Sauron moved before the convoy arrived, Adderly knew that any battle plan he could come up with would be only the first casualty.

He decided it was time to confer with the commanders of the light cruisers *Strela* and *Konigsberg,* and called his First Officer's duty station. "Jimmy, get Captains Casardi and Saunders on line for a briefing in two hours. Thank you."

Will Adderly had been in the Navy for twenty years, all of them at war, all fighting Saurons or their allies, and he had developed a smell for trouble. He looked at the holo of the Tanith system above his desk.

It stank.

"The enemy convoy is due in-system at any time. We may expect heavy support in addition to the transport ships. The issue is therefore to be resolved as a raid, with rapid deployment of ground forces to the spaceport to determine the location of the borloi, secure it, and maintain the perimeter against local counterattack while the material is being up-loaded to the *Fomoria.*"

Diettinger turned to the commander of his ground force complement, Deathmaster Anson Quilland. "Status?"

"All forces at operational strength, First Rank. Heavy anti-armor unit outfitting now, heavy antiaircraft units will be ready in one hour."

"The Imperial force deployments indicate they are moving their ground units to reinforce the spaceport, evidently to secure it from our attack, but only two enemy infantry battalions have reached it as yet. Augment your force with twice-normal anti-personnel weapons. Use captured projectile weapons as they become available. It will add to the enemy's confusion if he sees non-energy weapons like his own firing from within the spaceport."

Quilland smiled; he considered himself fortunate to be in Diettinger's command. The First Rank was crafty and thorough, and under him, Quilland had been promoted quickly. No one else of his *creche* had yet attained the rank of Deathmaster, the authority to decide whom among their Soldiers would be committed to large battles, and thus who would live, and who die.

"All means at your disposal are authorized to secure the perimeter. The enemy must be aware of our presence in-system and cannot fail to eventually guess your objective, but the longer we keep them believing that an invasion bridgehead on Tanith is our goal, the less difficulty we will have in off-shipping the borloi." He looked to his left. "Speak."

"What are loss parameters for the operation, sir?" Second Rank was compiling the database necessary for the coordination of the plans by her Staff department.

"None." Diettinger acknowledged the reactions of the other Soldiers with a nod. "High Command's orders were to secure that borloi. No options were indicated." Diettinger turned to the massive form at the end of the table. "Cyborg Rank Koln."

Heavy facial bone structure, little subcutaneous fat and the short, lank hair of the Cyborgs gave Koln the look of a hungry skull. Diettinger had heard that human norms called the Cyborgs "death's heads," after the crossed bars and skull-shaped nuclear cloud of the Pathfinders' insignia. He had begun to suspect that was not the only reason.

"Your Pathfinders will, as usual, precede the first landings to mark and secure the drop zones and, most importantly, locate the borloi. Your forces will have to split up sufficiently to maintain pressure on the spaceport until reinforced, however."

Koln shook his head. "No difficulty, First Rank. Four Pathfinder Cyborgs can locate the borloi while the rest of the force maintains the feint."

"Be aware that we cannot risk the nuclear pre-strike standard in your operations; the borloi is useless if radioactive."

"Understood."

"Very well. In four hours the *Fomoria* will move to engage the Tanith patrol fleet. Finish your operational plans and coordinate with Second Rank; she will have your timetables for you in ninety minutes. Dismissed."

After the others had left, Diettinger turned to Second Rank. "The convoy will be escorted with additional Imperial warships. Double the density of mines at the Alderson Point. Detach a squadron of heavy fighters to engage and delay anything that gets through." Diettinger considered the improved quality of the latest reconnaissance. "Give the command to Fighter Rank Severin."

Second Rank raised her head. "Comment, First Rank."

"Speak."

"Will not all fighter squadrons be required to engage enemy spacecraft?"

"Hopefully not, because your next task is to dispatch an emergency distress buoy through the Alderson Point back to Second Fleet. Tell them that we are encountering heavy and unexpected resistance, with more enemy ships arriving daily, and to dispatch all available reinforcements."

Second Rank's eyes widened. "But . . . First Rank . . . that's not true!"

Diettinger looked at her. "No, Second Rank, it is not true. Today. Nor may it be true tomorrow. It may in fact *never* be true, but I am not willing to take that chance."

"First Rank, if word of this gets back to High Command, you will be executed for misuse of resources." Diettinger did not notice that her voice was trembling.

"Second Rank, the Imperials will receive reinforcements when their convoy arrives. They will certainly request more as they engage us, if they have not already; that is standard Imperial procedure. We, too, will request reinforcements as *they* escalate, that is standard *Sauron* procedure. I am simply moving up the timetable. I will have that borloi for Sauron, Second Rank, and I will take no chances that it be lost because our Fleets are on standby, waiting to rescue one of our more incompetent allies from their own blunders. Dispatch the buoy, dismissed."

He watched her go, back stiff. How she could be so concerned with procedure at times like this was beyond him.

Couldn't they see, any of them? After two decades of war, the pattern I described to Second Rank is now set in stone. Sauron has lost the ability to seize the initiative, to make the enemy react to us; the Imperials now know what *we will do; not in detail, we still hold that tactical advantage. But in procedure, that field where battles may be lost but the war still won.* Diettinger ran a hand through his hair, straight, white and, he realized, thinning.

The Imperial commander at Tanith knows what I will do. My only hope is to deceive him as to how I will do it.

"And the hell of it is, gentlemen, that I haven't the faintest goddamned idea of what those Sauron sonsofbitches are going to do, nor when, nor how, nor even *why*!"

Adderly had been throwing his pens at the dartboard for the last ten minutes; there was a cluster of them grouped around the bull's-eye, each later makeshift dart driven in deeper than the last. He was now starting to pitch them hard enough to bury them in the plastic of the wall behind the board, and it was doing no more to relieve his tension than when he'd started.

Captain Edwin Casardi of the *Strela* leaned back in his seat and spread his hands. "Will, take it easy; they haven't moved yet. If they wait until the convoy arrives, they're hopelessly outnumbered. If they hit us now, we only have to hold, harass and withdraw. One Sauron heavy cruiser against Tanith Starports Langston Field won't amount to a pisshole in a snowheap."

Adderly stopped to look at him, then to Casardi's opposite number, Saunders. "Is that what you think, Colin?"

Saunders was a red-haired Gael from New Scotland, fair skin and freckles making him look eternally young. The freckles almost disappeared when he was angry, as he was now.

"Like bloody hell. Sir." Saunders did not like Casardi, and made no secret of it. The *Strela's* CO was too confident for Saunders' taste, and too easy on his crew by half. Saunders' own *Konigsberg* boasted the best readiness record of her class, if not the Navy. Now here was a chance for that readiness to be proven, and this lazy wop wanted to run!

"This *Fomoria* is a heavy cruiser, by their rating, a heavy battlecruiser by ours; she outguns *Canada* and either of our light cruisers; but she canna' outgun all three ships and the *Chinthes* t'boot! We know she's out there, and if she's preparing to hit us, as you say, then I say she'll ne'er be more vulnerable. Let's take all we've got and run the bastard t'ground!"

Adderly rubbed his face with his hands. "I'm amazed, gentlemen; you agree on something." He looked up at both of them, scowling. "And you're both dead wrong.

Pull out, or attack; either way we leave Tanith to fend
for herself. Christ, men, we're the bloody *Navy*! What
if we guess wrong, Colin, and don't find her, and she
slips in the back door with a load of thermonukes, and
Tanith gets slagged in a terror bombing while we're out
beating the bush? Or say we pull safely out of range,
Ed, and wait for the convoy to pull our asses out of the
fire, and suddenly, *wham*, the Sauron drops a division
of marines through the Field and into the spaceport just
in time for *their* reinforcements?"

"Will, there's almost two-thirds of a full-strength Division down there!" Casardi sounded offended. "They'd
outnumber a Sauron Battalion by six-to-one!"

After twenty years of being kicked around by the
Saurons and their Coalition of Secession, Adderly knew
that the Navy's ranks had been winnowed mercilessly,
leaving men who had been fighting in this war long
enough to become shrewd, dedicated and skilled in
judging their Sauron foe.

I wonder where those men are? he thought, rubbing
his eyes. "Ed, Sauron Battalions are *designed* to engage
Imperial Divisions; engage them and defeat them."

Casardi almost snorted. "Maybe twenty years ago,
Will, but they're on the run, now, everybody knows it.
It's only a matter of time."

"Aye," Saunders snapped. "So you'd as soon avoid
putting your neck on the line and let somebody else do
the dirty work?"

Casardi's eyes flashed. In her first engagement three
years previous, *Strela* had been rammed amidships in a
battle off Kennicott, losing half her crew in an instant.
Twice since then she had suffered heavy losses, once
when her fighter cover had strayed, exposing her to
attack, and again when a missile bay had taken a freak
hit through a flaw in her Langston Field. The *Strela*
was now marked; an unlucky ship.

"My crew has seen combat, Captain Saunders. I con-
fess I would like to try to spare them further unneces-

sary "glories" which less experienced officers might find welcome."

Adderly had heard enough. "All right, that's enough, both of you. When this is over I'll officiate at a sanctioned duel if that's what you want but until then, and I mean this, *gentlemen*, I will relieve you both if you don't put your personal differences aside and start working together immediately. Is that understood?"

The short silence that followed before Adderly's order could be acknowledged was shattered by the battle alarm.

"NOW HEAR THIS. NOW HEAR THIS. BATTLE STATIONS. BATTLE STATIONS. ENEMY WARSHIP DETECTED AND CLOSING. CAPTAIN TO THE BRIDGE."

"Ah, Christ on a crutch," Adderly groaned. "You two get back to your ships; Ed, I'll want *Strela* in squadron with *Canada*. Colin, *Konigsberg* stands back at reserve distance until further notice."

Saunders was too well trained to object, but the bitterness couldn't be kept from his: "Aye, sir."

Casardi only looked at Adderly. "Right," he said, thinking: *three destroyers, one light cruiser and a half-century old BC against the* Fomoria. *This is it for* Strela; *our hoodoo's caught up with us, at last.*

Adderly caught his look, pretending to ignore it as he ushered his officers out and raced for the bridge. He knew the *Strela's* reputation for hard luck and he knew Saunders' temperament; he'd chosen Casardi's ship to accompany *Canada* for those very reasons. Casardi would be prudent in the engagement, while Saunders might prove reckless. And when the inevitable reinforcement was called for, Saunders would throw his ship into the battle with all the fury he'd built up waiting on the sidelines.

If the Navy wouldn't give him geniuses, he'd have to try and use what he had with brilliance.

*   *   *

"Enemy ships closing, First Rank. Three *Chinthe-*class destroyers, the battlecruiser *Canada* and the light cruiser *Strela*. Engagement range in fourteen minutes."

In contrast to conditions aboard the Imperial ships, the Sauron bridge was quiet. No klaxons blared. No stations reported readiness levels; they were always prepared for battle. Only deficiencies were allowed to interrupt the First Rank's concentration, and aboard the *Fomoria* there were none.

Strapped into the acceleration couch, Diettinger watched the display on the battle screens. Tanith's surly orange bulk crouched on the bottom left while five red circles tracked slowly about the middle of the view. "Marine status."

"Standing by, First Rank." Diettinger's personal modification to space combat was ready; no doubt the Imperials were prepared for it, but there was really no way they could prevent it.

The three smaller circles moved away from the larger two, moving down and to the left, across the face of Tanith.

"Destroyers flanking to port, First Rank."

Weapons half-turned in his seat; the First Rank often waited to raise the Langston Field until the last moment, but he was taking even longer than usual.

"Enemy systems locking on us."

"Target the *Canada*."

"Done."

The smaller circles were at the lower left edge of the viewscreen. "Destroyers off port bow."

"Visual to 360."

The walls disappeared. There was now only the ceiling, the floor, and around them Tanith space.

Weapons' finger hovered over the Field activation pad. "Destroyers to port," he called. "Coming about and closing on bearing 225. Destroyers have activated their Fields."

"All enemy Fields activating." The red circles had changed to solid squares of black with red backlighting.

"Targeting stations, abort fixes on *Canada*," Diettinger said. "All batteries switch to and engage the middle destroyer. Activate Field."

Weapons' finger stabbed fire pads and the Field key almost simultaneously. "Torpedoes away; lasers firing."

Aboard the *Canada*, Adderly's bridge crew had locked down their own acceleration couches into the circular floor plate surrounding the combat hologram. Adderly wanted them prepared for violent maneuvering, in the hope that the *Canada*'s agility might not be known to the Sauron.

The black bubble of *Canada*'s Langston Field was charged to maximum, ready for the initial enemy salvo. Adderly wanted to buy time for the destroyers to get in and unload on the Sauron; the *Chinthes* were a new design, greatly over-gunned for their size, and he was hoping they could charge the *Fomoria*'s Fields with more energy than could easily be dissipated before *Canada* started firing.

"The Sauron's lost her lock on us, sir!" The weapons officer's elation turned to puzzlement. "Wait, she's locking again—*gods*, they're fast!—right; now she's firing, sir."

"Engineering, stand—" Adderly watched the traces in the combat hologram reach out and enfold the lead *Chinthe*-class destroyer. That ship, too, had her Field at maximum, but it was not so powerful as the *Canada*'s, and was never intended to absorb such a flood of energy at one blow. The *Chinthe*'s Field went from black to red and up through the spectrum to violet almost too fast for the eye to follow. White sparks danced over its surface as the *Fomoria*'s battleship-killing lasers burned through with insulting ease. The Field collapsed abruptly and the *Chinthe* was obliterated.

"The sonofabitch is going for easy kills," a helmsman cursed. "Cowardly Sauron bastard."

The other two *Chinthes* cut hard away from each other, one preparing to pass to the rear of *Fomoria* and the other to go below her.

Adderly was grim. "Don't kid yourself; he's working strictly by the numbers. That's one less ship to help overload *his* Field." *And I needed her.* "Time to impact of torpedoes?" he snapped.

Langston Fields on the big ships didn't go quickly like those of destroyers; they absorbed lasers and proximity-detonated nukes in prodigious amounts, becoming supercharged walls of missile-eating energy. The time to get torpedoes in was now, before their own beams turned the Sauron's Field into a free line of defense against them.

There were all sorts of wrinkles to this line of work.

"Ninety seconds, sir."

"Helm, lay in thirty degrees port, five-G emergency burn and stand by." Five-G was more than human norms could be expected to suffer for any length of time, even with the acceleration couches, but Adderly was sure they'd prefer it to being vaporized by the Sauron.

"Thirty degrees port, five-Gs emergency laid in."

"Signal *Strela* to go positive two kilometers and fire all lasers at will."

"*Strela* acknowledging."

"Incoming torpedoes, First Rank."

"Target the *Canada*." The black square representing the middle *Chinthe* was gone from the viewscreen. Excellent. Diettinger's Intelligence officer had estimated that this class was very heavily armed for their size, and the enemy commander's commitment of them at such close range confirmed it. Destroyers usually hovered at the fringe of battle, launching missiles to aid in overloading enemy Fields. Only if they had great laser capability would they be worth risking close in against a ship like the *Fomoria*.

And now an alarm did sound, but it was a soft, triple chime from Weapons' console. "Point defense penetration, First Rank; one torpedo incoming." Weapons completed targeting the enemy BC rather than anticipate the missile impact; there was nothing to be done about that.

The *Canada*'s torpedo detonated inside the *Fomoria*'s Field. Much of the energy was still absorbed by the back side of the screen, but the rest poured into her hull, vaporizing plates of reflective armor, exposing the true outer hull and in places even burning through that. Superheated air and coolants burst within the *Fomoria*'s skin, rattling the heavy cruiser with a sound like bad plumbing in winter.

"*Chinthes* slowing; holding positions aft and negative. They're firing, First Rank."

"Assess and report," Diettinger ordered. "Torpedo damage status?"

"Combat efficiency unimpaired."

"*Strela* at two kilometers positive, First Rank. Opening fire with lasers; locking torpedoes. *Canada* closing, firing again."

"*Chinthe* assessment, First Rank."

"Speak."

"Main laser batteries in the C-gigawatt range, tens-kiloton thermonuclears in torpedoes, but light salvo indicates small load same."

Diettinger was glad he'd killed one early; the *Chinthes* were armed with the firepower of a light cruiser. The *Fomoria* now had enemy ships pouring fire into her Field from five of her six aspects, leaving only one free for shifting power into areas of the Field that might require it. The trap was obvious. "Aft and ventral batteries; engage destroyers and continue firing until destroyed. Dorsal batteries, engage the *Strela*. Weapons."

"Weapons ready."

"Mixed ordnance, heavy salvo, on the *Canada*."

Mixed ordnance was the proverbial kitchen sink. The *Canada* would receive fusion torpedoes, particle beams, visible lasers and X-ray cluster bursts in an attempt to both burn through her Field and roll back her point defense systems. Weapons' fingers flew over the keypad; this was, after all, what he had been born to do.

"Engineering, six-Gs in one minute. Deathmaster Quilland."

"Quilland here."

"Have your Marines stand by."

"Acknowledged."

"Sir, *Chinthes* report their Fields going into the green."

"Tell them to just hold on for a few more seconds. Signal *Konigsberg* to engage; she's to take up our position as soon as we've cleared and unload on the Sauron with everything she's got. Gunnery, prep starboard batteries for enhanced charge and stand by." Adderly watched the hologram; if they could keep up the punishment to the Sauron's shields, and not lose another ship, this might work. The Sauron should soon have to shunt power from the starboard, non-engaged sector of his Field to those being bombarded and, hopefully, weakened.

Then, if he knew Saunders, the rabid Scotsman would be in their position almost before they left, allowing Adderly to bring *Canada* across the Sauron's bow and hit the enemy's thinned starboard Field sector with the battlecruiser's full broadside. He wouldn't get a Field collapse out of it, but he might get a few burn-throughs, and that could provide him with the edge he needed.

"*Konigsberg* at two hundred thousand kilometers and closing, sir."

"Speed?"

"Speed of . . . this can't be right—uh; he's coming like a bat outta hell, Cap'n."

Adderly grinned. *Good old Colin.*

"Helm, execute. Gunnery, stand by."

"Thirty degrees, five-Gs emergency, aye."

"Gunnery standing by." The Gunnery officer's last word was wrenched out of his lips as the *Canada*'s main and maneuvering thrusters roared into life at five gravities' acceleration.

"Engaged Field sectors moving into orange, First Rank."

Diettinger had activated the overhead viewscreen, and was watching the *Strela* in his positive aspect rain its lasers into them. "Enemy status?"

"*Chinthe* shields moving into violet. *Canada* and *Strela* shields moving into the green."

"Weapons, fire mixed salvo on the *Canada*. Engineering, accelerate to six-Gs. Marines, launch pods."

Fomoria and *Canada* leaped toward one another at a forty-five degree angle. *Fomoria*'s mixed salvo savaged the Imperial battlecruiser's starboard side, piercing her Field with a dozen burn-throughs. *Canada*'s starboard batteries, overcharged for Adderly's planned enhanced broadside, blew out over half their capacitors, destroying the weapons and turning the surface of the Imperial battlecruiser into ragged foil.

On the heels of the mixed salvo, *Fomoria* disgorged dozens of pods and hundreds of chaff dispensers. The pods were torpedoes, their payloads removed and modified with internal maneuvering controls, and each carried one of Diettinger's picked EVA Marines.

A third of the pods sped past the *Canada*, effectively out of the battle until they could be retrieved or turned around. Perhaps a dozen were hit by point defense, despite the chaff, or caught in the ragged salvo the *Canada* yet managed to generate from her ruined batteries, a volume of fire that vaporized chaff and pod alike. But the rest pierced the battlecruiser's shredded Field, losing some kinetic energy to the Field's effect but not enough to keep them from intercepting the *Canada's* hull, where they maneuvered into position and disgorged the bulk of Sauron marines in powered battle armor, who regrouped on the hull within seconds and began planting breach charges.

The *Canada's* own salvo was much reduced, but still effective. *Fomoria's* acceleration carried her out from between the combined beams and missiles of the *Strela* and the two *Chinthes*, and directly into the path of the oncoming *Konigsberg*. Saunders had everything the light cruiser could bring to bear firing on the Sauron, and the Field shifted to meet it.

Canada's broadside burned through the *Fomoria's* weakened starboard Field sector at three points, disabling two batteries and breaching the hull at a hangar door.

"Proximity alert."

The *Konigsberg* and the *Fomoria* closed at a combined speed approaching thirty kilometers per second; respectable even at the distances normal in space battles.

"Roll starboard 180, negative five hundred meters. Ventral and port batteries maintain fire, fire for effect."

Diettinger's orders made little sense to anyone until the moment the *Konigsberg* and the *Fomoria* passed each other. Narrowly avoiding collision, Diettinger's maneuver had kept the distance between the ships to less than four hundred meters, putting them inside one another's Fields.

The ventral and port batteries of the rolling *Fomoria* were firing blindly, but it was impossible for them all to miss. The *Fomoria's* lasers, with no Field to stop them, raked across the belly and port-low aspects of the *Konigsberg*, opening her to space like a gutted fish. As if to add insult to injury, the two ships' intersected Fields "bubbled," combining as they passed and distributing the stored energy in the *Fomoria's* Field evenly between the two. The *Fomoria*'s screens dropped from yellow back to dull red; all Adderly's work from the beginning of the battle was lost.

At the time, however, Adderly was too busy to notice.

"Damage Control! Helm, hard about, come to 170, slow to one G." Adderly was coughing as the air filled with smoke. He tried to pick out details on the bridge. The battle hologram stood out brighter than ever in the haze, but now he could no longer see the crew around it. "Helm, acknowledge, dammit, I know you're not dead, I can hear you bleeding."

"Hard about 170, aye," the helmsman hacked out a reply. "Slowing to one G."

"Damage report."

"Starboard batteries out, sir; Field intact, but . . ." He fell silent for a moment. "Captain, I'm getting weird signals on my board, looks like multiple hull breaches."

"What?" Adderly directed his acceleration couch to the Damage Control Officer's station. "What's the location?"

The DCO shook his head. "Everywhere, sir, mostly toward the rear of the ship, but spread out in pockets— there goes another one."

"They must have gotten something inside the Field, but what would do—"

He suddenly recalled Diettinger's file: the product of a race of soldiers who yet had never lost a naval engagement when in full command. An innovator. To Adderly those two facts meant Diettinger's successes stemmed from chances he took that the regular Sauron High Command would never have allowed.

"I will be dipped in shit." Adderly whispered. "Helm! Emergency stop, all engines reverse full."

"Reverse full, aye, emergency stop."

The next instant, the klaxons went crazy, followed by the voice of the *Canada*'s Security Officer on the emergency address system.

"ATTENTION ALL DECKS. ATTENTION ALL DECKS. INTRUDER ALERT. INTRUDER ALERT. ENEMY MARINES ON DECKS ONE AND THREE, SECTIONS FIVE, SEVEN, EIGHT, NINE AND TWELVE. NUMBER UNKNOWN."

Adderly keyed in the Security Officer's station. "What the hell is going on, mister?"

The SO was a young Imperial Marine, Lieutenant Harris, struggling to get into his battle dress and talk at the same time; Adderly could hear small arms fire in the background.

"Saurons, Captain, some kind of EVA Marines. They're using breach charges and coming in through the hull. We're losing atmosphere up there and half my men can't get to their suits."

"What's their strength?"

"Unknown, sir. There's at least a dozen of the bastards inside; they aren't even trying to secure an airlock, they're just burning their way in—" Harris suddenly looked confused, then startled, and finally shocked. Adderly realized he couldn't hear the background noise any more, understanding only when he saw the lieutenant's cheeks turned pink and his eyes red as he began frantically groping at the wall. Finding an emergency oxygen hood, Harris was pulling it on when an impossibly broad shape appeared in the doorway behind him.

"Harris—" No use; there was no atmosphere to carry the warning, and Harris wasn't wearing a headphone. The armored Sauron's weapon probably killed Harris; it certainly destroyed the communications plate. The screen went dark.

"Engineering, seal off decks one through four."

"Which sections, sir?"

"All of them, stem to stern! And seal deck five as well. Then flood them with whatever you've got, and I don't mean gas. Use coolant, use fuel, use *plasma* if that's all you've got, but do it, and I mean *now!*"

"But . . . Captain Adderly, there are still men up there . . ."

The look in Adderly's eyes told him that he knew that; that, in fact, he was not likely ever to forget it.

"Entering Tanith's gravity well, First Rank."

"Cut velocity, enter orbital path." Diettinger had heard nothing from Damage Control, meaning they were on the job. *Fomoria* was now at 87 percent combat effectiveness, well within acceptable limits. "Deathmaster Quilland: status of EVA Marines?"

"Assault Leader Bohren reports top six decks secured, First Rank. Imperials tried flooding the decks with liquid hydrogen from their fuel cells, but the Marines reached the sixth deck before it was sealed off."

"Excellent." The EVA Marines were on their own for a while, at least until *Fomoria* emerged from the other side of Tanith. "Communications: enemy status?"

"*Strela* is coming alongside *Canada*. Both *Chinthes* are firing controlled bursts into the upper decks of the *Canada*, igniting pockets of fuel in the flooded sections."

Diettinger turned in his seat at that. "What?"

Communications was just as bewildered. "It is apparently intentional, First Rank. I am getting fragments that indicate the Imperials think they have trapped the EVA Marines up there and are trying to finish them off."

Diettinger thought about what that implied. *Can they be that irrational? Could any race of men hate another so much?*

"And the *Konigsberg*?"

"Fired engines at maximum reverse, First Rank. Acceleration now .001 G, drifting. Field erratic; I'm picking up sporadic communications that indicate severe internal damage."

Diettinger nodded, satisfied. It had all gone surprisingly well. The opportunity to fire at the *Konigsberg* from inside her Field had decided the battle. He realized Second Rank was looking at him.

"Speak."

She stood against the now three-G acceleration with little effort and approached Diettinger's chair. "The message buoy, First Rank."

"Yes, Second. The one I ordered you to send. I presume you did so."

"Of course, First Rank; but . . ."

"But now you are concerned that it was unnecessary."

Second Rank said nothing.

"Recall, Second, that we have not yet secured the borloi, and we may yet have to deal with an enemy convoy and its reinforcements." He turned back to the screens. "And, in any case, what is done is done. Return to your station."

"Entering Tanith orbit, First Rank."

"Time to spaceport?"

"Twenty-three minutes."

Diettinger accessed Drop Bay Three. "Cyborg Rank Koln."

"Koln here."

"Stand by for drop in twenty-three minutes."

"Affirmative."

The featureless cloud cover of Tanith revealed nothing of the surface beneath to the naked eye, but the screens projected the outlines of continents, islands, inland seas, overlaid with the traceries of man's marks on the face of the jungle world. There were not many of those.

At one minute before the drop point, Diettinger turned control over to Koln. Sixty-one seconds later, Weapons' panels read green.

"Pathfinders away, First Rank."

"Deathmaster Quilland. Prepare your men for drop on the next pass."

"Affirmative."

Forty-five minutes later, Koln signaled the spaceport

sufficiently secured for reinforcement, and the *Fomoria*'s drop tubes opened again. Diettinger's full complement of ground forces was now committed to Tanith's spaceport. "Take us out of orbit. Make for the *Canada*. Stand by to retrieve any EVA Marines who have not reached the enemy ship."

Seeing the *Fomoria* closing on them again from Tanith orbit, Adderly ordered the *Strela* and the two *Chinthes* to try and get any survivors off the *Konigsberg*. The *Canada* was beyond help.

The Sauron EVA Marines had not been caught in the upper decks as was hoped. *Canada's* marines had been killed to a man by at least fifty Saurons, probably more.

Adderly had given the order to abandon ship, forcing his bridge crew off almost at gunpoint, finally demanding they leave as his final order. He had then tried to initiate the scuttle codes, but found he couldn't access them. Either the Saurons had done something to the ship's computer or it had been damaged when the *Canada* took the mixed salvo from the *Fomoria*.

Whatever the cause, Adderly had been frantically trying to run a manual self-destruct program when the Saurons had blasted their way onto the bridge.

The next thing he knew, figures in powered armor were shoving him into a space suit. He was prodded down the corridors ahead of a wicked looking energy weapon and hustled into his own shuttle. A Sauron waiting there put cable ties about his wrists while another one piloted the shuttle out of the bay.

He looked out the viewport, hoping for some sign of the *Strela*, but it was nowhere to be found. Instead, the dagger-shaped Sauron heavy cruiser grew in his sight. His shuttle landed in a hangar bay that could have held all three *Chinthes*, and the rush began again.

The Saurons always seemed to be in a hurry, but Adderly found that he didn't really mind; he was beyond caring. No one taken prisoner by the Saurons had ever been heard from again, and he doubted that he would be any exception.

Adderly wound up in a room with a desk, a viewport and a conference table. The two guards in powered armor who'd brought him in the shuttle stood behind him on either side. Incredibly, he found himself reading a sampler on one wall, looking impossibly ancient, and reading in Anglic: "Discretion is the better part of valor."

After a few moments, the door behind him opened, and a distinguished-looking man entered. Tall, with sharp features, his straight white hair yet failed to make him look old. He went to the desk and sat down.

The helmet was suddenly unlatched and jerked from Adderly's head, and he blinked despite the lighting of the room, subdued, comfortable.

The man at the desk frowned at the cable ties on Adderly's wrists and said something to the guards in a strange language. One of the guards was about to pull Adderly's wrists apart to break the cable tie, but the man stopped him with a single word. The guard instead broke the tie with his fingers.

"You are the commander of the *Canada*," the man said.

Adderly frowned. "I am. Captain Will Adderly. May I ask who you are?"

"Vessel First Rank Galen Diettinger, commanding the *Fomoria*."

Adderly's jaw dropped. "What?" He looked over his shoulder at the huge forms behind him. "But . . . this is a Sauron ship!"

Diettinger looked puzzled. "Yes. Is it surprising that a Sauron ship should be commanded by a Sauron?"

One of the guards guided Adderly to the chair opposite Diettinger's desk.

"But you . . . you're *human*. At least, you *look* human."

At that, Diettinger actually blinked. He leaned forward, frowning. "What did you expect, Captain Adderly?"

Since the Secession Wars had begun, interstellar trade had ground to a standstill. Imperial propaganda had been stronger every year, and Imperial paranoia over Sauron eugenics had grown more strident with each passing day. It had suddenly struck Adderly that he had been fighting Saurons for twenty years, yet this was the first time in his life he had ever actually seen a Sauron.

These were the people who were bringing six hundred years of interstellar civilization crashing about his ears; who were breeding themselves for war, fine-tuning their genes to create a race of human Warrior Ants. The people who had sterilized almost a dozen worlds in half as many years.

Somehow, this Diettinger's obvious humanity and apparent decency made it all even worse than it already was.

"I expected . . . something different. What do you want?" Adderly asked, his voice dead.

"I had you brought here not as a prisoner of war, but for a parley. My marines are taking the *Canada* as a prize ship, but you have my word that after this meeting is concluded, you will be released for retrieval by another ship of your task force. Captain Adderly, I am here at Tanith on a simple raid, not for this world's conquest."

"You must think I'm an idiot," Adderly said. "Tanith's Alderson Point routes are old news. Her tramlines reach into Secessionist as well as Loyalist space. And Tanith system has a mucking great gas giant for cheap refueling. That makes the whole system extremely attractive."

Diettinger nodded. "Obviously. But there are many other ways into the Empire, and securing Tanith is the last one I would choose. It should be obvious, however, that more than a single heavy cruiser would be assigned to the task. In any case, that is not my decision." Diettinger leaned forward, watching him for a moment.

"And if I thought you were an idiot, Captain Adderly, you would not be here, now."

He doesn't blink, Adderly thought, though he knew it had to be his imagination. He suddenly realized that this was the first time in his life he had ever been confronted by someone with a discernible force of will. *Charismatic bastard, I'll give him that.*

"I have a proposition for you that can save a great many lives, both Sauron and Imperial." Diettinger said.

I would have said "both Sauron and human," Adderly realized. He smiled a tired smile.

"This should be good. Let's hear it."

"I want the exact location of the borloi awaiting shipment by your convoy. I have Pathfinders looking for it now; I believe you call them 'death's-heads.' They are supporting Marines who are securing the spaceport for shuttles to ship it to the *Fomoria*. While this situation persists, both your forces and the citizens of Tanith will be subject to heavy loss of life."

"Borloi—" Adderly said, almost sagging in the chair with relief, but caught himself.

They're here after the borloi? Why? Suddenly he remembered what Diettinger had said about Tanith: *"There are many other ways into the Empire."* Had he meant routes, or tactics? Were the Saurons going to try to destabilize the Empire by flooding it with the drug? It didn't make sense, nobody had time or money for vices in this kind of war, but . . . He wracked his brain, trying to think of the military applications of the drug.

None came to mind, but the Saurons did nothing without a reason, usually military, and they were no slouches in the chemical warfare department. Still, if the borloi *was* their target, that meant they didn't know the real reason the convoy was coming.

Adderly waited a long time before answering. "All right," he said finally, defeated. "Give me something to write with."

Diettinger smiled. "I have an excellent memory. You may simply tell me the location."

Adderly shook his head. "What good would it do? How old are your maps of Tanith? Sure, the borloi's at the spaceport, but where? There are a lot of storage chambers, most unmarked, and all of them underground."

Diettinger considered a moment, then handed him a writing stylus of some heavy Sauron alloy. "Very well. Please don't embarrass me by trying to kill yourself with this, or yourself by trying to harm me. I promise you that neither your speed nor your hand-to-hand combat skills are a match for mine or those of my troops."

Adderly grunted and began to draw. Rectangles, circles, landmarks, roadways; all neatly labeled, all pure fiction. He was flirting with treason to buy time for that convoy, so he was determined to be convincing.

He had almost finished when he noticed Diettinger had turned to the viewport, looking out at the wreckage of the *Konigsberg*. Something twisted in Adderly's chest at seeing this Diettinger smugly reviewing his defeat of Adderly's task force.

Another one for your record, eh? It was hopeless anyway; he had never entertained the notion that Diettinger's promise to release him had been sincere. He added a few more notes to the fraudulent map while he waited for Diettinger to start to turn around again. The Sauron's reflexes might be superhuman, but he couldn't react to what he didn't see coming, and they *had* to be as vulnerable as humans somewhere. He only hoped the pen was heavy enough.

Adderly made shaking motions with the pen. "I thought these things were supposed to work in low gravity."

"I'll get you another." Diettinger began to turn to his desk, and Adderly extended the motion into an over-handed throw.

The pen was a centimeter away when Diettinger saw it—and caught it, Adderly realized with a shock—but almost too late. The makeshift dart had penetrated deep into the Sauron's left eye.

Diettinger's head snapped back and cracked against the viewport. Instantly Adderly felt a hand close about his throat and lift him off the floor. The guard holding him began shaking him like a rat.

"No!" Diettinger said. He had pulled the pen out, and was holding a hand to his ruined eye. The other guard was speaking rapidly into an intercom device, probably summoning medics to treat Diettinger and carry away what would be left of Adderly.

"Congratulations." Adderly thought he heard him say, unsure of anything as his vision darkened; the guard hadn't killed him, but he hadn't put him down, either.

At a signal from Diettinger, the guard drove Adderly to his knees against the deck. Adderly watched the Sauron commander's blood fall slowly to the floor before him, then stop. He looked up; Diettinger's face was close to his, the ruined eye darkened with clotted blood, no longer bleeding.

Fast healing, Adderly groaned inwardly. *They would be . . .*

"I cannot understand you. I brought you here because you conducted yourself like a soldier, and I wanted to offer you something I thought you valued, the chance to save lives."

The guard was holding Adderly down, crushing his throat; he could breathe, but only a little. He cursed through clenched teeth, gasping: "As if you bastards ever cared about that!"

Diettinger remained impassive. "In point of fact, Captain Adderly, I do. Though we do not see death the way you do, I am human, after all."

"You're a gooddamn traitor, then—" The grip tightened. Adderly desperately wanted to lose consciousness —he had no desire to see the end the Saurons would provide for him after this—but his brain stubbornly refused to shut down.

Diettinger rose. "I serve a race fighting for its independence from a regime that does not understand our motives and cannot possibly appreciate our goals. That makes me a patriot, Captain Adderly. You serve that regime, enforcing its will on hundreds of planets, regardless of whether they want you there or not. What does that make you?"

Adderly glared at the Sauron. "Patriot? Freedom fighter, maybe? Like hell; you think you're the first ones to trot out that old saw? You started your 'war of independence' by an unprovoked attack on St. Ekaterina! A billion people, Diettinger! You think you can justify that? Go ahead, give it a shot!"

Diettinger appeared honestly puzzled. "We don't 'justify' our actions, Captain Adderly, any more than you explain your motivations to the family pet. Sauron is the cradle of the ultimate expression of the human race; and that is a far greater responsibility than suffering public censure over the removal of a threat like St. Ekaterina, or an inconvenience like her mongrelized population of convicts, thieves, and other non-productives."

"Inconvenience . . ." and for the first time since being captured, Adderly was truly afraid. Not for his life, or any of his crew that might also have been captured; not for the convoy, or even the Empire. He was suddenly very afraid for all mankind.

The Saurons were making a ruin of the Empire, and they were *losing the war*. What would they make of humanity if they won?

"I will assume this map to be useless, of course," Diettinger said, "so we will carry out the battle, and people will die on both sides; a waste, since the population of Tanith is regarded as genetically promising. But understand, Captain Adderly, it is immaterial to me whether their casualties are one or one hundred million, I will have the borloi, you have my word on it.

The outcome is decided. I merely wished to give you the opportunity to decide the means."

He gestured to the guards, who lifted Adderly to his feet. "See that his spacesuit is intact. Provide him with a rescue beacon and put him out the airlock."

Adderly was stunned. "What?"

The Sauron looked back at him with his remaining eye. "I have given my word to you on two counts today, Captain Adderly. I want you to see that I am reliable on the one, so that you will not make another mistake by doubting the other."

One of the *Chinthes* picked him up a few hours later.

Diettinger was back on the bridge, the left side of his face hidden in bandages.

How could I have been so stupid? Haven't I seen the evidence of their hatred for us a thousand times? Didn't I see it again, today, when they were willing to risk a conflagration aboard their own ship just to finish off Saurons they thought were already trapped, and probably dead?

Diettinger found the idea of such hatred difficult to credit, and impossible to justify. Saurons were trained from birth to accept the nature of the human species as being emotional, rational, predatory, dominant. To these and the dozens of other adjectives summing up the Sauron version of the human condition, the race that called themselves "The Soldiers" had added a final qualifying virtue: efficient. The level of passion which human norms applied to their activities in general and their relations with Saurons in particular was, Diettinger felt, conspicuous in its lack of appreciation for that virtue.

There was something about them that made personal dealings difficult, diplomacy impractical and surrender for either side impossible, and Diettinger found it all . . . what?

Wasteful, he realized, but the confusion and distaste he felt was not so easily summarized as that.

And yet the degree of the human norms' hatred for Saurons was no more than the Saurons' degree of contempt for them; *probably less*, Diettinger thought.

Some Sauron commanders in the Secession War regarded the conflict as one of extermination; Diettinger was not one of these, but gingerly probing the wounded side of his face, he wondered if all human norms might not be.

His depth perception was gone, of course. Adderly's throw had been very strong, and the optic nerve itself had been ruined. Damned nuisance; it would mean at least a week in regeneration therapy, but there was nothing for it; he couldn't very well wear an eyepatch like some ancient pirate captain.

Fomoria was in high orbit off Tanith again, now accompanied by the *Canada* as a prize ship. Tanith spaceport's Langston Field was on, and with an atmosphere and plenty of ground water to dissipate energy into, it could hold off against a dozen *Fomoria*s indefinitely. Laser communications antennae lofted by Quilland's unit pierced the Field in a dozen places to establish contact with the Sauron warship. Fighting for the spaceport was reported heavy, but indecisive. Despite the numerical superiority of the Imperials, the large ratio of Cyborgs augmenting the already potent Sauron force prevented them from mounting any assault that would not require leveling the spaceport, and this they were understandably reluctant to do.

"Cyborg Koln; status on the objective?"

"Material located and secured, First Rank."

Splendid; an eye lost for nothing. Diettinger sighed. *Ah, well. Live and learn. . . .*

"Deathmaster Quilland; enemy anti-aerospace strength?"

"Marginal, First Rank; the Imperials have been arriving piecemeal, disorganized. We assume this is a result of poor surface transportation network and low airlift capability, compounded by inclement weather."

Diettinger looked again at the solid mass of orange

clouds over the surface of Tanith. "It all looks inclement from here, Deathmaster."

Quilland chuckled, a rare moment of humor, which meant events planetside were going very well, indeed. "Affirm. Weather data being up-loaded now, First Rank; shuttles should have no difficulty."

"Spaceport status."

"Currently eliminating pockets of Imperials still within the spaceport perimeter. The spaceport's Langston Field generator has been captured intact."

"Very good. Be advised that INSS *Canada* taken as war prize; her shuttles will also be engaged in the off-shipment of material. Expect first wave—"

"Emergency break in." Communications cut through.

Diettinger changed orders in midbreath; no human norm mind or tongue could have switched tracks so quickly, or completely.

"Speak."

"Fighter Rank Severin at the Alderson Point, First Rank; large force Imperials emerging from Jump at three second intervals. Squadrons engaging during Jump Lag."

Standard Imperial convoy Jump procedure, Diettinger recalled. *No nuclear precedents; why should there be? They think they're coming into a friendly system.*

"Force mix." The answer surprised him.

"Enemy battlegroup . . . first wave, all capital ships; four battleships, one carrier, six heavy cruisers . . ."

This was no ordinary convoy; this was a Fleet. Diettinger whirled on Second Rank. "Lay in course for the system asteroid belt at seven Gs acceleration. Download data for same to autopilot on *Canada.* Quilland: Enemy fleet arriving in system, stand by for composition. Deploy for siege. Under no circumstances are you to lower the spaceport's Field."

While Quilland set Diettinger's orders in motion, the First Rank returned to Fighter Rank Severin. "Enemy fleet status?"

"Capital ships' Fields have gone up." An automatic and expected result of a ship being attacked while her crew was still in Jump Lag. "Enemy ships still emerging, First Rank . . . ten light cruisers . . . twenty destroyers . . . six troop transports . . ."

Six troop transports? His force on Tanith could not hold out for long against that level of reinforcement; without *Fomoria*'s aerospace support they would inevitably be overwhelmed. *Unless* . . .

"Fighter Rank, break off attack on capital ships and engage transports. Override the targeting sensors on half of the mines and guide them to the transports."

"Affirm."

There was nothing to do but wait, now. In minutes, the human norms aboard the first wave would be recovered sufficiently to evade the mines and launch their own fighters. Severin's voice came back a moment later.

"All enemy Fields up, First Rank. First wave maneuvering into fleet ops formation. Second wave beginning to maneuver. Enemy fighters emerging from carrier."

"Mines."

"Closing on all ships; capitals taking hits . . . transports evading, First Rank."

Evading? Then it hit him: Of course they were evading; they bore no cargo to reduce their maneuverability. They were not coming for the borloi; the drug's medicinal value to norms was so potent that there was more here than they could use in centuries; it was all simply surplus. The real cargo of value on Tanith was the two divisions of trained fighting men, desperately needed by the human norms, perhaps to fight the Saurons, perhaps to hold their crumbling Empire together as world after world used the war to declare their independence.

"Fighter Rank Severin, break off and rendezvous at asteroid belt sector five. Do not attempt to engage."

Diettinger made contact with Quilland once more and apprised him of the situation. "We will make a supply pass to your forces before removing to the asteroid belt. Until our own reinforcements arrive, we can only mount harassment attacks. You may expect greater effort on the part of the Imperials to seize the spaceport. Whatever happens, the borloi must be retained."

"Understood." Diettinger broke the connection.

He turned to Second Rank, who was watching him with an utterly indefinable look.

Well, Diettinger thought, *at least now my request for reinforcements can't be called misuse of resources. That ought to make her happy.*

The Imperial fleet was less than an hour behind as *Fomoria* finished her supply drop at Tanith and prepared for the seven-G dash to the safety of the asteroids.

"Status of Tanith patrol ships," Diettinger said abruptly.

"One *Chinthe* shadowing us, First Rank. *Strela* and second destroyer rendezvousing with Imperial Fleet."

"And the *Konigsberg?*"

"Still drifting at .001 G, no emissions. Effectively dead in space, First Rank."

Diettinger nodded. "Good, Make for the belt; fire on the *Chinthe* until she's vapor or driven off."

For two days, the Imperials hunted the *Fomoria* and her prize, the deadly game frustrated each time by the asteroid belt. On Tanith, the Sauron troops and their Cyborg support unit held off the Imperial ground forces with almost insulting ease. The Tanith troops were far from inept. It was simply that there were so many Cyborgs. Imperials usually encountered the Super Soldiers as special forces units, or *ad hoc* groups integrated with Sauron allies for support duty, or with regular Saurons for a breakthrough; and regular Saurons were bad enough.

But as Adderly knew, Sauron heavy cruisers were special operations craft, and carried four times the number of Cyborgs in their troop complement as any other capital ship. On Tanith, no less than a hundred of these "death's-heads" had been deployed, and the Tanith military simply could not bring sufficient force to bear to root them out without orbital strikes from their fleet, which, in piercing the spaceport's Field, would doubtless destroy the facility as well as the Saurons, and maroon the Imperial troops for weeks or even months.

So, far above the orange clouds of Tanith, the Imperial Fleet circled, and waited, laying siege.

"First Rank, massive radiation readings at the Alderson Point; Sauron-wavelength precedents."

"Enemy presence at Alderson Point?"

"INSS *New Chicago*, three squadrons Imperial Heavy Fighters."

"Current overwatch?"

"Two *Chinthes*, sir; twenty thousand kilometers positive. The *Strela* is holding at fifteen thousand kilometers negative."

The Imperials were searching for them, but the asteroid field blocked their view; *Fomoria* and *Canada* had merely to extend passive sensors out from behind their asteroid hiding place to know when their "shadows" were getting too close.

"Five thousand kilometers negative, make for the Alderson Point at three Gs. *Canada* to mirror our maneuver after three minute delay." The Imperial light cruiser would have to choose whether to pursue from above or below the belt. Whichever way she took, she was outgunned. "Weapons."

"Ready."

"You have discretion here and for *Canada*. If the Imperials pursue either ship, concentrate fire and destroy them, priority to the *Strela*."

"Affirm."

*   *   *

Will Adderly stood on the bridge of the *Strela*, and cursed the luck that had let him live.

The arrival of the Imperial convoy to pick up Tanith's troops had secured the system from the Saurons and trapped their troops on the planet, but it had also brought Admiral Sir Owen Kellogg, whose relationship with Adderly quickly became as inimical as Diettinger's. The Admiral's reaction to the loss of *Canada* was cold fury. Within an hour of the task force's arrival, Kellogg had summoned Adderly to his quarters aboard his flagship, the *Aleksandr Nevsky*. After listening to Adderly's report, Kellogg had dismissed his secretary and launched into a tirade.

Adderly's report of the EVA Marines substantiated several rumors that Imperial Intelligence had of new Sauron naval tactics, but Kellogg dismissed their importance. Instead, the Admiral raged that their effectiveness could only have been the result of Adderly's incompetence . . . or worse.

Kellogg brought up the matter of Adderly's capture and, incredibly, release, compounded by his claim that the Sauron commander had asked about nothing more than the borloi.

Adderly had exploded at the implication, and Kellogg's retorts had culminated with the notification of a full board of inquiry as soon as Tanith system was secured.

But the most the Admiral could do now was pull rank. He couldn't afford to relieve Adderly, so he had deposited him and the other survivors of the *Canada* debacle aboard the *Strela*, leaving Adderly in command of the remnants of the Tanith Patrol. These Kellogg dispatched to hunt for the *Fomoria* in the asteroid field. They were forbidden to engage, only to shadow the Saurons and their prize and alert the *Aleksandr Nevsky* immediately upon sighting them.

Adderly scowled as he stared at the combat hologram. *And here I can be the first to see when my ship, which I lost makes a run for it. Good old thoughtful Admiral Kellogg.*

"Son of a bitch," he murmured.

Casardi looked over. He could feel Adderly's strain, the desire to conn the *Strela* himself; but he knew he would never usurp Casardi's authority. Knowing it, Casardi respected him all the more for it. And as far as Casardi was concerned, Adderly would never have to usurp him.

If Adderly had told Casardi to fly them into Tanith's sun, he'd have done it in an instant, knowing he had a reason, and that the reason would see them through.

For Adderly was the man who had led *Strela* into combat, against a Sauron heavy cruiser, and brought her out unscathed. The hoodoo was lifted, and every man jack aboard knew it; an unofficial party had gone on for thirty hours, until every shift had its chance to participate and toast the Old Man's name. Secretly, of course. Neither Casardi nor his men would have embarrassed Adderly by saying anything to his face. Adderly's former bridge crew, however, was another story; they were nursing hangovers that would be weeks in the forgetting.

The First Mate turned to them: "Captain, I have multiple nukes at the Alderson Point; ships on station there report very high-yield precedents." He listened for a moment, then continued: "*New Chicago* reports heavy damage to her fighters, recalling them now . . . Fields going to . . . sir, Fields went straight into the violet, one of the precedents was a direct hit on *New Chi*'s field, at least a hundred megs!"

Casardi met Adderly's eye.

"This is it," Casardi said.

Adderly nodded. "They'll move, now; signal the *'Nevsky.* Tell them we're preparing to shadow the Sauron and—her prize." He just couldn't bring himself to say it.

.

*   *   *

The INSS *New Chicago* had backed off from the Alderson Point, her batteries out of range, watching as the Sauron reinforcements emerged from Jump. Admiral Kellogg had ordered *New Chi's* commander to hold his position until relieved, so the carrier had recalled her surviving fighters, refueled and rearmed them, and sent them out again.

"*Fomoria* still accelerating, Captain."

"Where's the *Canada*?" Casardi asked his own boards.

"There, sir; *Canada* going five thousand klicks positive, matching speed and maneuver on the *Fomoria*."

The first Sauron ship through the Alderson Point emerged with her Field activated, spewing more precedent nukes; few ships carried large enough Field generators to do so with impunity, but this was one of them.

The commander of the *New Chicago* immediately ordered his flight controllers to warn off the fighters, but it was too late for half of them. The rumor that Saurons recovered from Jump Lag more quickly than human norms was apparently true, for the batteries and missile launchers of the Sauron battleship *Leviathan* began sweeping *New Chi's* fighters from space.

Kellogg had his fleet closing on the Alderson Point at four Gs, but *New Chi's* skipper knew that it would not be enough. *Leviathan* was deploying thousands of perimeter mines, clearing the way for the reinforcements which must follow her. *New Chicago* was forced to open range as the *Leviathan* continued to advance, but her screens still picked up the arrival of at least a dozen Sauron warships in the first wave.

Aboard the *Strela*, Casardi's communications officer turned from his board. "Sir, the *Fomoria* is in contact with the Sauron battleship; I think it's the *Leviathan*, sir."

Casardi and Adderly shared a look. The *Leviathan*

had been the vanguard of the Sauron invasion force that had captured Meiji over three years ago; nothing had been heard from the Imperial world since, and the Sauron battleship had been on hand for most of the Empire's disasters that followed. To say she possessed a fell reputation in the Imperial Navy was to damn her with faint praise.

"More Saurons emerging, Captain . . ." The commo officer began calling off ship types and identification estimates, and as the list grew, Adderly's spirit died.

God, we haven't a prayer; we've got half the Eleventh Fleet here, but there's just so many of them.

"Captain Casardi, please have your communications officer patch me in to the bridges of the *Chinthes* accompanying us. Secure beam, if you would, and I'll make the contact in my cabin."

Casardi carried out the request instantly. But he spent a long time looking at the door after Adderly left.

"*Chinthes* and *Strela* shadowing the prize ship, First Rank," Weapons announced. "Activating *Canada's* batteries now, firing on the *Strela*."

Diettinger maintained his own communication with the commander of the *Leviathan*, Vessel First Rank Vonnerbek. They had worked well together in the past, and he was confident they would do so now. As the commander on the scene, Diettinger was placed in charge of the *Leviathan* and her attendant forces for the duration of the mission; in this case, the securing of the borloi. Vonnerbek waited until Diettinger had finished relating the tactical situation to him before speaking.

"Thank you, Diettinger. Be advised that the First Fleet is arriving this location in nine days."

Diettinger was thunderstruck; only iron discipline kept the shock from his voice and features. "Do you have information regarding this, Vonnerbek? Is the High Command planning to invade Tanith, attempting to secure it permanently?" He remembered what he had told the human norm, Adderly, regarding routes into the Empire, and with good reason. Tanith lay at several tramline exit points, true, but each one in Empire territory was an Imperial Naval base! The jungle world was industrially worthless and militarily untenable.

Vonnerbek spoke freely; there was no known way to tap into modern communications lasers. "Affirmative. The First and Second Fleets together represent the majority of Sauron's remaining naval strength. Our planners indicate that if we secure Tanith, even as no more than a refueling stop, and move before the Empire can react, then the next stop could be any or all of those bases, even Sparta itself."

Diettinger held the other First Rank's gaze. "That will not win the war, Vonnerbek."

"That is High Command's estimate as well. But Socio-Ops are convinced that such action against the cattle,"—it was the Sauron term for non-combatant human norms, not an insult—"will result in vast civilian backlash against the Imperial military, possibly forcing a peace."

Diettinger arched his right brow, the one not covered by bandage. "I see. Socio-Ops is not my field," he said simply.

"Nor mine," Vonnerbek agreed. In fact, both of them considered it a waste of personnel, talent and resources. But both were Soldiers, and that meant both followed orders. "And of course," Vonnerbek concluded, "*Leviathan* is carrying special Occupation Breedmasters."

Occupation Breedmasters were the "eugenic shock troops" of the Saurons; supplied with a hundred thousand fertilized ova from Sauron females, they implanted these in selected human norm "Breeders" who would then carry the Sauron fetuses to term. The genetic quality of these walking wombs would have no appreciable effect on the resistant proto-Saurons they bore, and freed female Soldiers for more important war duties.

Diettinger nodded, but the idea did not sit well with

him. The use of Occupation Breedmasters signaled total commitment on the part of the High Command, and he doubted if they were aware of the growing fanaticism among the human norms against the Saurons. They had not seen the enemy's *Chinthe* destroyers strafing their own *Canada* just to kill a few Sauron Marines.

"I wonder what Socio-Ops would make of my interview with the human norm, Adderly," Diettinger added.

Vonnerbek shook his head, and for a member of a race known for an inexhaustible supply of willpower in the face of adversity, Diettinger thought he had never seen such a look of hopelessness in his life.

"I strongly doubt they would take any lesson from it, Diettinger."

Diettinger nodded; he and Vonnerbek were agreed.

We have lost, and in this last stage of the war, we are trying to regain the initiative against the enemy military with diplomatic tricks dreamed up by warriors, and genetic terrorism conceived by diplomats.

Still . . . if the war had taught him anything, it was that anything was possible. Perhaps the Imperials could be forced into a peace of sorts. And in that peace, Sauron could rebuild.

Unlikely, but we may yet survive, somehow. That will be up to diplomats, however; perhaps the Breedmasters can create a species of Sauron devoted to that art. It will not be up to Soldiers like me.

"*Strela* and *Chinthes* breaking off."

Diettinger acknowledged Second Rank's update and returned to the conversation with Vonnerbek. "Very well. Prepare task force status for transfer to *Fomoria*'s tactical computer. Secure the Alderson Point and stand by for Staff meeting on our arrival. Diettinger out."

Adderly waited for the skippers of the *Chinthes* to digest what he had said. Both were on private linkups to him, but each had to know the other was being consulted. He had ordered them not to be influenced by that fact, but he knew that would do no good. Finally, each one signaled him that they were willing to try.

"Thank you both, gentlemen. Godspeed, and good luck."

I'm asking them to commit mutiny, he thought. *But I can cover for them if I'm wrong, and if I'm right, I won't have to.*

There was another if, of course . . . if the *Chinthes* were destroyed, by Adderly's order or the Saurons. But there was no point in thinking about that.

"Sir, Admiral Kellogg's force is closing with the Sauron fleet."

Casardi looked to Adderly, but the Old Man simply stared at the screens. "Helm, port fifteen, make for the fleet," Casardi said quietly. "Signal the *Chinthes*—"

"Belay that." Adderly turned to Casardi. "Conn the *Strela* as you will, Captain Casardi. The *Chinthes* have their orders."

The Imperial and Sauron Fleets clashed like ramming icebergs; an initial impact, formations interfacing and locking as ships began pouring energy into one another's Fields, then the slow dance, as each side probed the edges of the enemy's formation for weak spots, spreading out the concentration of ships in three dimensions, the rainbow-hued Fields connecting in a lattice of green and red lasers and streaking torpedoes. Inevitably, amid the flares of the thermonuclears and the brilliant laser batteries, there came the brighter flashes of collapsing Fields, as outmatched or outgunned ships died.

Unnoticed in the first minutes of the carnage, two *Chinthe*-class destroyers dove through the center of the Sauron formation, Fields at maximum, lasers firing and torpedoes dropping through their Fields to engage targets of opportunity. Far richer targets were available to the Sauron gunners, and the destroyers were ignored.

In the confusion of the battle's early moments, their fate was indiscernible.

Kellogg's Operations Officer knew only that they disappeared into a maelstrom of Sauron lasers somewhere near the Alderson Point. The Saurons probably knew what had happened to them, but they weren't telling.

Eventually, a series of lucky hits burned through the Fields of the largest Imperial warships. The Imperial Fleet broke off, but the Saurons were in no position to pursue; all their Fields were into the violet, and Diettinger was determined not to throw away half the remaining Sauron space forces unnecessarily.

Instead, he ordered the Sauron fleet to skirt the system in a wide arc, toward Tanith, to relieve their ground forces and get what he, at least, had originally come for.

"Admiral Kellogg on the line, sir." Casardi's commo officer had managed to refine his "sirs" so that Casardi knew when he meant him and when Adderly. It was for Adderly, this time.

"Adderly here."

"Adderly. I see you've lost the rest of your destroyers."

Adderly said nothing. Kellogg couldn't make much of that anyway; half the fleet's destroyers had been lost this day. But the mood on *Strela's* bridge went brittle as cold iron. Adderly heard one of the middies mutter an oath, tactfully directed toward his screens.

"Your pardon, Admiral, but we have casualties here, and damage control has us pretty busy. What can I do for you?"

It was insubordinate, of course, but Adderly didn't really give a damn. It would be worth it to watch Kellogg's face.

"Well, I have good news for you, mister," the Admiral almost sneered. "The *King George V* lost her bridge crew in that last salvo from the Sauron battleship *Wallenstein*. Captain Lester, his First Officer; all dead.

I can't afford to have the *KGV* out of action and I haven't anyone to spare from the Fleet."

Adderly felt the floor rock beneath him and knew it had nothing to do with the *Strela*. *A second chance? Or was Kellogg really just desperate? And what difference did it make either way?* "My bridge crew from the *Canada* is intact, Admiral. I know they'd be eager to serve."

Kellogg lost control, slamming his fist against his desk. "Goddamnit, Adderly, don't make me ask! We've been *mauled* in this engagement, but that's nothing like the worst of it. This mess is holding up an entire relief operation; *we need to get those troops off of Tanith!*"

Adderly felt his face redden. Somebody was being a stupid, selfish bastard, and it wasn't Kellogg. "I'm sorry, sir. We're on our way."

Kellogg raised a hand, which he then put to his brow, like a man who'd thought of something he'd been trying to remember all day. "I've just seen the reports on *Strela*'s performance in the engagement, Captain Adderly." He sighed, wearied at holding the words back "My compliments to you and Captain Casardi. You've both been mentioned in despatches. Signal me when you're aboard the *KGV*. Kellogg out."

The connection had not been broken one second when Casardi gripped his hand. "Congratulations, Will." He grinned and snapped off a salute as he delivered the traditional Navy farewell to a departing Flag officer.

"And good riddance. Sir."

Adderly smiled back, but he was not thinking of the *KGV*, not even the *Canada*. As he had since giving them their orders, he was thinking about the *Chinthes*.

Over the next five days, the Sauron and Imperial Fleets kept the planet between them while they re-formed, tended their wounds, and spaced their dead with the ceremonies respective to each Navy. Neither pursued the other aggressively, but the Saurons doggedly drove off any Imperial attempts to bombard the spaceport, and the Imperials made it clear that they were not about to allow the Saurons to retrieve their forces from the planet's surface.

Maneuvering so close to Tanith put both Fleets deep within the planet's gravity well, where high-speed accelerations would result in ships being slingshot out of the action almost before they could engage. Caution and patience became the watchwords as the opposing fleets circled Tanith warily, waiting for an opportunity to destroy one another.

Between those fleets, Tanith turned under her changeless skies, the ground battle having reached a stalemate. The Sauron and Imperial troops were both unsupplied, but the Saurons were too outnumbered to venture out of the spaceport, and the Imperial troops were not about to storm the gates and go hand-to-hand with a force containing over a hundred Cyborgs.

The enemies waited, and planned.

The *Fomoria* was mated by docking sleeves and umbilicals to a fleet replenishment vessel. Combat and personal supplies were transferred between the ships, preparing them for the next engagement being planned even now by Diettinger and the other commanders of the Second Fleet.

Second Rank was delivering the Fleet status update from the *Fomoria*'s briefing room; the other commanders were tied-in by message laser.

"Casualty reports 10 percent in our favor, plus a variable advantage conferred by the destruction of an estimated 75 percent of the *New Chicago*'s fighters."

"Status of the enemy capital ships?"

"Estimates only, First Rank," she said. "Our reconnaissance cannot close sufficiently for accurate observation."

Diettinger pressed a switch that cut off their signal to

the other ships. "Then give me the estimates, Second; an apology for circumstances beyond your control is pointless and time-consuming." He had slept little, his temper was as short as their time for resolving this conflict, and Second Rank's habit of overclarification was becoming annoying.

Second Rank did not look up from her screen as she read. "*Aleksandr Nevsky*, *George Washington* and *Garibaldi* suffered moderate but reparable damage. *King George V* suffered burn-through to her bridge section by an X-ray laser; 95 percent probability of complete command crew fatality."

Diettinger listened to the rest of the report, struck by the similarity in casualties taken on both sides. Except for the lucky hit on the *KGV* and the destruction of the enemy fighters, losses were approximately equal. On impulse, he asked Second Rank for specifics about one ship.

"Status on the *Strela*."

"No damage, First Rank, despite its engagement of four of our ships at different points in the battle. The *Strela* is evidently conned by an extremely capable commander."

Diettinger smiled, allowing himself to notice for a moment the dull ache in his face where his left eye had been. *Capable*, he thought, *or highly motivated; just what did happen to that Adderly fellow? And what happened to those two* Chinthe *destroyers that were headed for the Alderson Point at five Gs? Did that last salvo get them both, or only one?*

"Very good." He turned to face the images of the Fleet element commanders. "As you know, the First Fleet will arrive here in four days. This will precipitate a conclusive battle for control of Tanith space and the invasion of the world itself, necessitating heavy planetary bombardment. The borloi is still there, and must be removed from the surface of Tanith before such bombardment destroys it.

"First Rank Vonnerbek; the *Leviathan* will lead the first element of the Fleet against the Imperial force. You will maneuver around Tanith and attack from over the north pole of the planet. First Rank Lucan; the *Wallenstein* will lead the second element around the equator with a five-minute separation from Vonnerbek's element. First Rank Emory; the *Damaris* will lead the third element over the north pole as well, with a ten-minute separation from Vonnerbek's element.

"Between the time task force *Wallenstein* engages and task force *Damaris* departs, *Fomoria* and the combined shuttles of the Fleet will enter geosynchronous orbit over the spaceport and begin simultaneously resupplying the troops there and lifting the borloi. *Fomoria* will then proceed immediately to the Alderson Point to Jump to Sauron. Task Force *Damaris* will accompany us as escort and to secure the Point for the arrival of the First Fleet. Questions?"

Emory spoke. "Deployment for the initial engagement, First Rank; would it not be more effective to engage the Imperials from a third flank, thus spreading their forces?"

"Negative. Once the second element of the Fleet engages, the Imperials will perceive a pattern and begin shifting forces to meet the third attack you suggest. Human norms choose patterns in their tactics—orienting their naval ops parallel to the plane of the ecliptic, reacting to sequential maneuvers in a clockwise pattern —it is a trait of which even they are seldom aware. As a result, there is an even probability that they will shift their forces, either toward the south pole, or away from Lucan's equatorial thrust with task force *Wallenstein*, thus further weakening their position for your reinforcement of Vonnerbek's initial thrust."

Emory nodded in admiration. There were few Imperials who could boast Diettinger's mastery of naval tactics, and almost no Saurons.

"Proposition, First Rank." Vonnerbek this time. "The

Fomoria's ground troops have been on-station for almost two weeks; troops of the First Fleet *en route* and those aboard our own ships were designated for invasion ops before departure and are heavily supplied for same. They could assume occupation duty of the spaceport while your troops were returned to *Fomoria*."

Diettinger considered the offer; the moment the borloi was secured, he would be expected to make for Sauron, and any delay to recover his own troops, in the face of the current Imperial presence, could well prove fatal.

He nodded. "Excellent, Vonnerbek. Thank you. Your shipboard Deathmasters may coordinate with our own Quilland and my Second Rank."

"Casualty parameters, First Rank," Lucan asked. Quiet, low-keyed, even for a Sauron, Lucan was widely referred to as "The Phantom." Under his command, the *Wallenstein* had led a charmed life: more than two dozen major engagements, seven enemy capital ships and merchants without number destroyed, all without the loss of a single crewman.

Diettinger smiled. "Let's see how it goes, shall we?" He was confident; these First Ranks were the finest naval officers of Sauron; the First Fleet now on its way would have many more ships, but no commanders of their caliber. "The situation will very likely present unexpected opportunities."

There were no more questions after that, only satisfied acknowledgments from the other First Ranks. "Commence task force formation." Diettinger finished the meeting. "Operations commence in twelve hours."

The bridge of the *King George V* was eerily intact. No equipment was damaged, the acceleration couches showed no blood; there was even a bulb of cold coffee floating idly in the corner. It looked as if her bridge crew had all simply stepped into the next room and would return at any moment. There was nothing to indicate they had all died within seconds of one another.

A squad of Imperial Marines standing guard at the bridge had presented arms, their corporal delivering a mournful Taps before a Navy bosun piped Adderly and his own crew through the hatch.

A little late, Adderly thought. There had been no such ceremony in the confusion of his arrival, but he had demanded it before he would set foot on the *KGV's* bridge. He would not explain whether the decision arose out of respect or superstition, but whatever his reasons, the Marine and the bosun would carry the word to the surviving crewmen that the new skipper was a man who did the right things.

"All right, Jimmy," he told his First Officer, calling up the *KGV's* status report at his command station screen. "Let's see how the lady's feeling."

Adderly's new command had come to him with more woes than an empty bridge, but most damage-control reports were into the green already, the status lines reflecting the work of an excellent repair crew. Adderly saw that while several lines were still amber, only one remained red: BRIDGE CREW.

He frowned, tapping it with a knuckle, a habit as ancient as it was pointless. Finally he called upon the Damage Control Section and informed them of the error.

"Sorry, sir. We show green for the bridge throughout the rest of the ship; probably something bollixed by that X-ray laser hit. Might have burned the sensors into that setting. Let me try a few tricks at this end."

But despite the DCO's efforts, the status line would do no more than flicker briefly into the green before stubbornly returning to red.

Bad luck, that, Adderly thought, trying to make it humorous but not succeeding. He noticed that even with a full and busy crew, the bridge was quiet. Men carried out their duties with subdued conversation, if any, and remembering the *Strela's* crew, convinced of their own ill luck, he wanted to avoid any such rumors aboard the *KGV*.

Put the dead to rest, Adderly thought; sailors as a rule were a notoriously superstitious lot. The other half of the old saying suddenly came to him. *And God grant they lie still* . . . Evidently Captains were no exception.

He had barely finished reviewing the repair operations when the Fleet alarm went off.

Adderly's headset was patched into the Fleet Communications Net before he was strapped into his acceleration couch. His fingers stabbed the acknowledgement codes into the commander's terminal. *Captain Lester was doing this less than a week ago,* he suddenly thought, wondering what sort of man the *KGV*'s former skipper had been.

FleetComNet was chattering in his ears, giving him force deployment and formation orders; his officers who needed all this were getting it too, but everything in the Imperial Navy went past the Old Man as well.

The faint voices of acknowledgements were overlaid with the signal of Kellogg's Fleet Operations Officer, Commander Sakai: *"—reconnaissance report enemy fleet elements approaching from over north pole of Tanith . . . one-fourth estimated surviving strength enemy Fleet in task force, Sauron Battleship* Leviathan *identified as core vessel . . . Task Force* Washington, *shift to Tanith-positive aspect and prepare to engage . . . Task Force* Garibaldi, *stand by . . . Task Force* King George V, *status report . . ."*

KGV's Damage Control Officer relayed the necessary information while Adderly ordered all shipboard systems to full alert; any repairs left for the *KGV* or the ships with her would have to wait; doubtless there would soon be more to go with those she already had.

Admiral Kellogg's image suddenly appeared on all command screens, abruptly breaking through the cacophony of voices.

"Sorry, gentlemen, but the Saurons aren't giving us

much time for a battle briefing. This first wave coming over the pole means they'll probably send the successive waves from opposite directions along the equator and under the southern planetary axis. We can expect this attack to be typically Sauron-thorough; they rarely leave loopholes in their maneuvers that aren't traps. Keeping that in mind, there is little excuse for us to fall into one. All Task Forces are to maintain strict cohesion; no one will engage until ordered to do so, and all activities are to be coordinated through myself or *Nevsky's* FleetOps officer, Commander Sakai. Kellogg out."

Adderly sighed. *This is twice now they've moved before we were ready for them.* This Diettinger really was the innovator the intel dossier had labeled him, which disturbed Adderly; the report had also noted that Diettinger had never lost an engagement of which he was in command.

"Terrific," he said aloud. The *Strela* crew's fatalistic streak had attached itself to him.

"Sir?" The First Mate looked up.

Adderly shook his head. "Nothing, Jimmy. Signal the task force to come into formation." *At least this time there's plenty of backup. . . .*

Task Force *KGV* was ordered to stand by in reserve for *Washington's* move against the Saurons. Adderly found himself anxiously watching the combat holo, listening for the engage order, checking and rechecking the straps of his acceleration couch. Every part of him ached to close with the Saurons, fight them, hurt them, smash them.

He looked around at his bridge crew, survivors of the *Canada*. They were still quiet, but now it was not respect for their predecessors; now they looked less reverent than grim. Revenge for the *Canada* was at hand, and they couldn't wait.

Adderly looked to the First Mate. "Blood in the water, eh, Jimmy?" he asked quietly.

The First mate smiled thinly. "Aye, sir."

"Well." Adderly addressed the bridge crew in a low voice that carried to every station. "Let's keep our heads even so, shall we, gentlemen? The day is wrong, but the toast fits: *'A willing foe, and sea room.'* I think it's safe to say that we're all getting that wish. Just remember that this foe is all *too* willing, and any mistakes we incur in our eagerness can benefit only him."

"Imperial task force *Washington* engaging the *Leviathan* element, First Rank. *Wallenstein* element accelerating and moving to engage."

"Signal *Damaris* element to delay engagement until notified." Diettinger amended the timetable; the human norms might sometimes be predictable, but they were also more flexible in their thinking than most of the rigidly-trained Soldiers. Their adaptability could surprise you. "Lay in course for the spaceport, standard ground force retrieval maneuvers."

He turned toward the sound of furious activity at a command station. "Weapons; status?"

"All systems operational, First Rank." Diettinger smiled at the strain in the officer's voice.

Saurons were masters of remotely-piloted vehicle technologies; the *Canada* was now an R-P platform, its actions dictated by the First Rank, but initiated by Weapons, who still retained all his duties aboard the *Fomoria*. Weapons was carrying out his task admirably, but the *Fomoria* and *Canada* were both formidable ships, and even Saurons could only do so many things at once.

Task Force *Washington* engaged *Leviathan*'s group with all the subtlety of a train wreck. The Sauron line held against the initial onslaught, but even the Soldiers were surprised by the ferocity of the Imperial attack.

At first, Vonnerbek wondered just who was attacking whom, but the engagement leveled off just as the

Wallenstein force rounded the equator. The Imperials dispatched TF *Garibaldi* to meet the new threat, holding the *KGV* and *Aleksandr Nevsky* in reserve, waiting.

Aboard the *KGV*, Adderly watched the screens, demanding continuous updates on the ships engaged. He did not have to ask where the *Fomoria* was; the moment the Sauron Heavy appeared, every officer on the bridge would shout it.

The Fleet Communications Net kicked in. "Task Force *KGV*, this is FleetOps; proceed with all speed, negative aspect, to southern pole sector Tanith, prepare to engage Sauron third wave."

Adderly frowned. "Say again, FleetOps? *South* pole?"

"Affirmative, *KGV*. Tactical analysis indicates Saurons attempting envelopment maneuver, you are to cut them off on far side of Tanith, engage and hold until relieved or recalled."

Adderly looked at the combat holo. The tactical analysis made sense; the guess of a Sauron envelopment *sounded* right, but . . .

He sighed. "Acknowledged, FleetOps. Helm, you heard the man. Communications, signal the rest of the Task Force we're moving out."

Both officers looked at him blankly. "Speed, sir?" the helmsman finally asked.

Adderly scowled. *All speed*, the FleetOps had said. He turned to the Engineering Officer. "What have we got, Mr. Rostov?"

"Engines are fine, Captain; we can make safe maximum with no problem."

That would be four-Gs, Adderly thought. *Tough on the crew, but bearable for the short time involved. And we will go a long way in that short time*.

"Two-Gs, helm." He noticed his First Officer's warning glance; the whole Fleet knew that Adderly was in dutch for the loss of the *Canada*. His caution now would not sit well with Kellogg. "And lay in an emergency course-change: three-Gs at 045, initiate on my order only, no prior notification to the Task Force."

The midshipman at the helm looked to his older, more experienced counterpart. Seeing no reaction there, the middie helmsman also complied without comment. *He's the Captain,* he told himself. *He knows what he's doing, I guess.*

It was as comforting a lie as any other.

"*King George V* group moving toward the Tanith south pole, First Rank."

Diettinger instinctively made a gripping motion with his hand. "Signal *Damaris* element to engage *Washington* group. Make for the spaceport." Expressive for a Sauron, his tone carried a sense of elation that puzzled some among his bridge officers; they had only fooled human norms, after all.

KGV and the ships of her task force were beneath Tanith's equator, the mass of Tanith's south pole looming above them, when the FleetComNet crackled with a stray signal:

"—nder *Nevsky*, this is *Washington*, third Sauron element joining the *Leviathan*. We are severely outnumbered, requesting permission to break off . . ."

"Commo, tie-in to that, I want to hear Kellogg's response."

"Sir, I don't know if—" the commo officer began, but Adderly cut him off with a shout: "*Do it, mister!*"

A moment later FleetOps officer Sakai's voice came through; Adderly noticed it had lost none of its cool detachment.

"Negative, *Washington*, do not, repeat, do not break off. Task Force *'Nevsky* moving all speed to your sector now, hold position and wait for reinforcements."

Adderly ground a knuckle into his forehead. He'd expected something like this, but he hadn't been sure. The Saurons had duped them; now what?

His First Mate cursed quietly beside him. "The *Fomoria* must be headed for the spaceport." He suddenly grinned. "That's why you plotted the forty-five-degree course change!"

Adderly nodded, once. "Yeah. Helm."

"Standing by, sir."

"Clear that course change from the board. Put us at four thousand meters and compensate for speed of one point five-Gs total. We're hitting those Sauron elements from the rear."

The First Mate looked puzzled. "But, Captain Adderly; the spaceport . . ."

Adderly nodded, staring at the combat holo. "That's right. The Saurons will get away, or it'll fall, whichever they choose to do." He turned to the First Mate. "I'm getting a little weary of doing what this Diettinger wants me to do, Jimmy. The Saurons can stand two full gravities' acceleration higher than we can; by the time we match orbits to engage whatever is at the spaceport, they'll be long gone." He turned back to the holo. "But if we can put three three Task Forces against the Saurons where they're expecting two, we can grind the bastards down to dust."

I hope, he added to himself.

Diettinger watched the viewscreens, scanning with his eye for information that could only be hoped for on sophisticated sensors. *Where was the enemy? Would they get here before the operation was completed?*

Before him, the troop ships turned over to him by *Leviathan, Wallenstein* and *Damaris* had moved into position and begun sprinkling points of light toward the black expanses of the planetary Langston Fields. The lights were assault boats launched by the hundreds amid broad-band interference decoys deployed by the thousands.

Dozens of lasers reached up from the surface of Tanith to intercept them, and where a laser hit, a light went out, but there were too many lights to extinguish them all. The decoys attracted the lasers, wasting the defenders' shots.

The *Fomoria* tracked the planetary lasers, firing to eliminate their sources before the more valuable shuttles would join the cloud of decoys.

Finally, the pinpoints reached the surface of the spaceport's Field, to disappear into the artificial night beneath, out of sight and out of communication. The planetary defense lasers ceased firing. There was nothing to do now but wait.

The bridge seemed silent for a long time before Communications, monitoring the ground troops, made his report. "First Rank, Cyborg Koln reports 83 percent of relief force arrived intact and regrouping at the spaceport."

"Resume suppressive fire on enemy ground lasers. Deathmaster Quilland, dispatch shuttles and begin retrieval. Weapons, interpose the *Canada* remote between the main concentration of ground batteries and the shuttle flight paths."

"*Wallenstein* element is holding against the *Garibaldi* group, First Rank. *Damaris* and *Leviathan* elements breaking through the *Washington* group, *Aleksandr Nevsky* group is moving to reinforce same."

"And the *King George V*?"

"Beyond the south pole of the planet; continuing on course for equator."

Diettinger called up the data to his own screen. Any moment now, they should be breaking off for the spaceport; but they were not. They were *allowing* the Saurons to take it? What was worth such a sacrifice to the Imperials?

"Communications, signal *Leviathan* and *Damaris* elements that the *King George V* group may attack their rear."

"Your pardon, First Rank, but planetary field interference very heavy, and no line-of-sight for message lasers at this time."

"Then put the *Canada* up and relay message lasers through her, immediately."

Either way, we get the borloi, Diettinger thought. *And the spaceport is secured for the arrival of the First Fleet, with more troops for the subjugation of Tanith itself. The Occupation Breedmasters will follow, and we will have a back door into the Empire.*

His mission was nearly complete, and with it, his status as Fleet First Rank. The Second Fleet had been his official reinforcements for securing the borloi, and so was under his control. The First Fleet would bring a new commander with a mission of his own.

Just as well, he considered. *This damned eye is becoming a nuisance.*

Aboard the *Leviathan,* Communications Fifth Rank Boyle strained to catch the lock-on signal of a message laser.

"Message from *Fomoria,* First Rank Vonnerbek, via *Canada.* Enemy group closing on our elements from the equator."

"Status *Washington*?"

"Multiple burn-throughs all ships *Washington* group."

Vonnerbek considered. All the *Leviathan* elements' Fields were into the violet, but there were no burn-throughs as yet, and thus no serious damage. The Imperials would have to preserve their Fleet to have any chance of defending their borders once the Saurons had Tanith. The *Washington* groups would be forced to break off at any moment.

And the *Aleksandr Nevsky* was closing to reinforce the *Washington* now. Vonnerbek's intel sources had identified the *'Nevsky* as the command flagship.

The human norms put great stock in such things, he remembered.

"Fight us through to the *Aleksandr Nevsky* group.

Signal *Damaris* element to go about and guard our rear. Maintain fire on the *Washington* group until it disengages."

Saurons were the product of hundreds of years of genetic engineering for the perfect soldier, whose defining personality trait was an utter subjugation of the ego to the goals of the Battle Plan. Vonnerbek was too perfect an example of the eugenicist's art.

What he himself did not possess, he could not conceive of in others.

"Last shuttle secured, First Rank. Full complement recovered, cargo intact."

Diettinger actually sighed in relief. Now, to resolve this battle before—

"First Rank, enemy group *King George V* is engaging *Damaris* element. *Wallenstein* element is breaking through *Garibaldi* group. *Leviathan* element is fighting through to engage *Aleksandr Nevsky* group."

"Status enemy forces."

The report did not bode well for the Imperials: only the *KGV* and '*Nevsky*'s ships' Fields were not in the violet. All those in *Washington*'s force had suffered burn-throughs, several were destroyed. It was nearly over, now.

"Dispatch all attached forces to return to respective elements and reinforce. Bring *Fomoria* and *Canada* into position to reinforce *Leviathan* element. Engage *Washington* group as *Leviathan* disengages. Signal all element commanders to prepare to break off engagement."

The naval part of the mission was over. When the First Fleet arrived, Vonnerbek could rack up all the victories he wanted.

"Emergency signal from the *Leviathan*, First Rank."

"Clear."

"*Fomoria*, this is Communications Fifth Rank Boyle. We have massive damage here, request immediate relief."

Fifth Rank? What had happened to the bridge? "Fifth Rank Boyle, who is in command?"

"Unknown, First Rank. One of the enemy Fields collapsed—I think it was the *New Chicago*—we were too close when she went, our Field was already in the blue. It caught the released energy and overloaded. We have heavy internal damage here, no response from bridge or forward weaponry."

"Status on enemy ships?" Diettinger asked Second Rank.

She was frowning, unable to resolve what she saw with logic. "No change, First Rank; the *Washington* group has no Field that isn't violet but they aren't breaking off."

Diettinger went cold. *Of course. They wouldn't.* In that instant, the entire character of the war changed for him: as a Sauron, a Soldier by breeding, training and perspective, he had seen it as a conflict between industrialized nations, an inescapable result of the dynamics of evolution. The Empire was in the way of Sauron's advancement; Sauron represented the next step in human evolution, therefore the Empire must go.

That the Empire would resist going was axiomatic. But that it would do so suicidally had been an extremely low probability consideration. Or so Sauron military philosophy had proposed.

But they are wrong, he suddenly realized, and unthinking, his hand stole to the ruined scar that had been his eye.

It is not, as Sauron philosophy has supposed, simply a war of evolutionary imperatives, not to the Imperials. To them it is a war of extermination.

"Stand by, Fifth Rank Boyle; signal the crew to initiate evacuation procedures." *A Fifth Ranker!* "And try to find some officer of command rank."

"First Rank, the *'Nevsky* is in range of the Leviathan; she's firing now."

"Make for the *Leviathan*, use maximum acceleration

allowing gravitational enhancement. All batteries and
Canada to fire on the *'Nevsky.'* He considered the
wording of his next order. "Communications; signal all
commanders. No break-off. Continue to fire on all enemy forces until destroyed."

"Standard pursuit options, First Rank?"

Diettinger shook his head. "Pursuit options unnecessary. The enemy will not attempt to disengage."

Ever again, he thought. But perhaps he could change
their minds; today, at least.

"Weapons. Prepare the following modifications to
Canada."

Commander Sakai, Kellogg's FleetOps officer, felt he
was becoming a part of his console. "Admiral, the
Fomoria and the *Canada* are closing with us, bearing
150, our heading, speed of five Gs."

Kellogg was staring at the combat holo unblinkingly.
The *'Nevsky's* Captain Harbour was carrying out his
orders to the letter. The *Aleksandr Nevsky* poured destruction into the *Leviathan*, burning through her Field
again and again. *Washington* had bought them all a
chance with her and *New Chi's* sacrifices; those sacrifices were not to be in vain.

"Who's on station there?"

"Heavy cruisers *Montpelier* and *Vladivostok*, Admiral, with a destroyer screen of seven *Chinthes.*"

Kellogg grunted. "Hm. Not much against the *Fomoria*
and a captured battlecruiser. Tell them to engage and
hold the Saurons until we've finished off the *Leviathan.*"

The FleetOps officer complied, then stared at his
screen, confused. "Admiral, I have the *Canada* making
seven Gs now, and still accelerating."

"Saurons can stand more than nine Gs with acceleration couches, Commander." Kellogg informed him, mes-
merized by the sight of *Leviathan's* death throes.

"Yes, Admiral, but . . . Admiral, the *Canada* is at
nine Gs now, and still accelerating . . . the *'Nevsky's*

gunnery officer is saying she has locked all weapons onto us."

"Our shields will hold, Commander," Kellogg remained cool. *Canada*'s purloined torpedoes would be impossible to evade when launched at that speed, and most would probably get through their Field; but *'Nevsky* was unwounded as yet, and Kellogg would not lose the chance to destroy the *Leviathan*. "Unless you're afraid they are going to ram us?" he added dryly. At nine Gs, the *Canada* could not hope to correct for any evasive maneuver taken by the *Nevsky*.

He went back to watching the holo. Every part of him was directed toward destroying the Saurons; even the mission that required Tanith's troops was forgotten.

"Admiral—"

"What the devil is it, Commander?"

"The *Canada*, sir; she's reversed heading and firing full thrust—she's maneuvering like a fighter plane."

At that Kellogg did turn away from the holo. Eighteen Gs aboard the *Canada* would flatten anything, Sauron or not. "What's happened to her weapon lock-ons?"

"Holding, Admiral, but her Field is going into the violet and she's still closing."

"Who's firing on her?"

"*Montpelier* and *Vladivostok* report scoring hits, but not enough for that."

Kellogg's instincts overrode all bloodlust and most of his training. *She's firing into her own Field* . . . "Cease fire on the *Leviathan*, signal all ships in the vicinity to break off and take evasive maneuvers."

FleetOps officer Sakai had patched in to all the commanding officers of Task Force *Aleksandr Nevsky*; he was about to pass on the Admiral's commands when he died.

Canada's last attack was a marvel of coordination possible only for a suicidal crew or a very good remote controller. Converted by Weapons' expertise into a fortythousand ton missile, her Field opened, and every intact torpedo port launched on the *'Nevsky*. As Kellogg had guessed, *Canada*'s lasers had been directed against the inside of her own Field, the stored energy then augmented by scuttle charges, and the Field capacitors themselves disengaged.

Canada's Field collapsed while she was only three kilometers from the *Aleksandr Nevsky*, even as her torpedoes drove the Imperial flagship's Field up through the spectrum to blue-green. The released energy from *Canada*'s resulting immolation proved more than the *'Nevsky* could take.

Aboard the *KGV*, Adderly watched the destruction of the *Aleksandr Nevsky* in mute horror. When he regained his voice, it was to answer his commo officer's announcement of multiple signals coming through.

"Hold them, commo; get me senior commander of the other battleships, first, whoever that is."

Jesus. The 'Nevsky *gone; eighty thousand tons of battleship, just* gone. . . .

"Captain Adderly," the commo officer almost whispered. "The other bridges say that Captain Lester of the *KGV* was senior commander after Admiral Kellogg and Captain Harbour—sir, *they* all want to speak to *you*."

He suddenly found it difficult to breathe.

Sweet Jesus . . .

Rescue of the *Leviathan*'s survivors was simplified by the break-off of the Imperial Fleet. The Communications Fifth Ranker who had contacted *Fomoria* had, indeed, managed to find someone of Command Rank. The Occupation Breedmasters aboard Leviathan had demanded priority for the fertilized Sauron ova they had brought for the subjugation of Tanith. In Sauron society, Breedmasters carried more influence than Cardinals of the Inquisition, so the first things that came aboard *Fomoria* were seventy suitcase-sized environment boxes; all that had survived of the one hundred that had been sealed away safely at the center of the *Leviathan*.

The Breedmasters complained that less than half might still be viable, but Diettinger ignored them. There were more important things to consider; the Sauron First Fleet had arrived.

"Congratulations, Diettinger," Fleet First Rank Morgenthau was speaking from the bridge of the fleet battleship *Sauron*. Pleased at the status report of the spaceport and the damage inflicted on the Imperial Fleet, he was less enthusiastic over the use to which Diettinger had put the *Canada*. Morgenthau was of the same *creche* as Fighter Rank Severin, Diettinger noted, though higher caste, of course. Young, but bred specifically for the job of a Fleet Commander.

"It was an older design, Fleet First Rank; little could have been learned from her that we did not already know."

Morgenthau seemed about to comment, but stopped. "Well done," he said finally. "We will isolate the remainder of the Imperials from the Alderson Point and hunt them down before leaving. The *Damaris* will escort you there now and accompany you back to Sauron."

"We are still carrying several hundred crew from the *Leviathan*, along with the Occupation Breedmasters and their equipment."

"Immaterial. The *Leviathan* crew should be returned to Sauron for treatment and reassignment. The Occupation Breedmasters as well; we have more than enough of them here with the First Fleet."

"Fleet First Rank, I request permission to stay in the Tanith sector and aid in the hunt for the Imperials; I feel I have gained a particular insight into their nature."

"Request denied. The borloi is required immediately on Sauron." Something flickered across Morgenthau's face. "There have been . . . severe reverses . . . elsewhere, First Rank."

Can that be why he reacted as he did to the loss of the Canada? *Diettinger thought. Are we reduced to using the enemy's captured ships now, as well as their captured females?*

"Understood. Then may I call special attention to the portion of my report that deals with two *Chinthes* which may have escaped early in the battle—"

"So noted."

"Fleet First Rank, I stress the danger of reinforcement which those ships present to—"

"That danger has been assessed, First Rank. Rendezvous with *Damaris* and return to Sauron."

Disciplinary action among Saurons was rarely needed, and thus so rarely encountered that Morgenthau's calm reiteration of Diettinger's orders was the equivalent of a physical blow.

Diettinger acknowledged and broke the connection.

"Make for the Alderson Point, Second Rank. Coordinate with *Damaris* for simultaneous Jump sequences to Sauron."

Adderly watched the combat holo with growing hopelessness. The glowing sphere with its ships and navigational aids had filled his vision for the last T-week, undergoing a bizarre apotheosis as it did so. No longer mildly hypnotic, it seemed now to *be* Tanith, and the space surrounding it, and the ships which lived and had died there. *This* was reality for Adderly and his bridge crew; not the smell of burned metal, the sight of burned flesh, or the wreckage that had been filling Tanith space on an almost daily basis since the Saurons had first arrived.

Now, over two hundred vessels surrounded Tanith, Sauron ships of every size and function. Messages from Tanith had continued, but the troops there had retreated from the spaceport; they had no hope of retaking it now.

By seniority of commission, Adderly was now Commander in Chief of the Imperial Fleet. The survivors of Kellogg's force, from destroyer on up to the *King George V* herself, numbered less than fifty. The original mission, to pick up Tanith's garrison for use in revolt supression at New Hibernia, was forgotten. Instead, hopelessly outnumbered, the Fleet had fallen back to the asteroid belt, where less than two weeks ago they had hunted the *Fomoria* and her prize, tending now to their own wounds, and praying for a miracle.

The Sauron Fleet invested Tanith, and had not ceased its bombardment in seventy-two hours. The city's Field could not hold out indefinitely, nor could her troops hold off against the planetside forces the Saurons had deployed.

Sighing deeply, Adderly turned his gaze back to the holo. As he watched, two of the lights representing the Sauron Fleet detached themselves, heading for the Alderson Point.

"Jimmy, can you give me an ID on those ships?"

"One's the *Damaris*, sir. Sauron heavy battleship. Huge drives, their IR signature alone is enough to give her away. The other one . . ." The First officer's face screwed up in concentration, then, eerily, smoothed out to match the lack of emotion in his voice. "The other one is the *Fomoria*, Captain," he said quietly.

Why were they leaving? Could it be that Diettinger's cock-and-bull story about the borloi had been true all along? Adderly realized suddenly that he didn't care. He felt a weight drop from his shoulders, and at that moment he knew what had happened.

Relieved, he thought. *Diettinger's been relieved.* And despite the irrationality of the thought, despite the fact that he *knew* it to be irrational, he found himself feeling like a man who dreamed he'd died, only to awaken safe in his own bed.

Vessel First Rank Galen Diettinger, the only Sauron who had never lost a naval engagement which he commanded, was leaving. At the moment, Adderly didn't know if he'd gone crazy or not, nor did he care. The idea bubbled up in him like a suppressed laugh in a graveyard, shocking, liquid, bright. It was past his lips before he knew it.

"We can't lose."

The First Mate blinked reddened eyes. "Sir?"

Adderly passed a hand over his face; stubble. Small wonder, he'd been living on the bridge the past two days. He laughed.

"I said, Jimmy, that we can't lose. Signal the Fleet. Pursue the *Fomoria* and *Damaris* to the Alderson Point. Come on, let's get cracking!"

The First Mate, now the Fleet Operations officer, relayed the commands to Adderly's new subordinates.

"Captain Adderly; they want to know the battle plan for the intercept."

"Plan? No plan, Jimmy. No plan at all."

"First Rank, I show multiple drives activating in the asteroid belt, bearing 090 our heading."

"Good. Fleet First Rank Morgenthau now knows where to find the Imperials. Accelerate to seven Gs and plot the Jump."

Navigation looked up in horror. The Alderson Points that began and ended tramlines between stars were by no means large; standard procedure called for them to be entered at less than a tenth of a G, since finding them was by no means an exact science. Diettinger's order could just as easily carry them so far past the Point that they would be weeks realigning for the Jump. Still, Navigation did the best he could.

"We'll never catch them, Captain Adderly."

Adderly watched the combat holo; fully half the Sauron combined Fleet had left Tanith orbit, and was bearing down on Adderly's force. "I don't care if we do, Jimmy. The *Fomoria* and *Damaris* are heading for the Alderson

Point. At their speed, they'll likely miss it. We, however, will not."

"Sir? We're *leaving*?"

Adderly's look would have dropped snow on Tanith. "You haven't heard me order a general retreat, have you? Now get back to your post, mister."

"Status on mines at the point?"

Second Rank checked her screen a second time before answering. "Unchanged, First Rank."

"Unchanged? The First Fleet didn't renew the seeding left by the Second?"

"First Rank, the *Second* evidently left no new minefield."

Diettinger was losing his temper; as rare an event as one could hope for. "Get me the monitor at the Alderson Point."

Second Rank shook her head in offended awe. "There *is* no monitor, First Rank; the Alderson Point has been left unguarded."

"Navigation, status on the Jump plot?"

"Complete, First Rank; comment."

"Speak."

"At seven Gs acceleration, we and the *Damaris* have less than a fifteen percent chance of accurately entering the Alderson Point when activating our Jump Drives."

"Thank you, Navigation."

"Enemy ships, First Rank," Second cut in, stumbling over the words. "First Rank, I have massive readings of enemy ships at the Alderson point; there are . . ." Her voice faded. Diettinger turned his acceleration couch enough to see far too many figures marching up her console screen.

"Estimate, Second Rank?"

"Approximately two hundred fifty to three hundred enemy ships, First Rank."

"Signal Morgenthau aboard the *Sauron*."

The return was agonizingly slow in coming. "What is it, Diettinger?"

"An enemy reinforcement fleet has—"

"We know that, First Rank. We will deal with the threat. All the required information is being coordinated now."

"*Morgenthau, there are almost three hundred Imperials coming in, and you didn't even mine the Jump Point!*"

Incredibly, Morgenthau smiled. "Our combined Fleet is statistically capable of inflicting break-off losses on twice that number, First Rank. Mining the Alderson Point would only have left the Imperials more prepared."

"Statistics? You inbred fool, don't you understand? Didn't the destruction of *Leviathan* teach you anything? *There won't be any break-off!* It took sacrificing the prize ship *Canada* to win the last one, and it will *be* the last one. The Imperials will press the attack beyond all rational military considerations, they will destroy themselves to destroy the Combined Fleet. And you've just divided your forces!" Diettinger's rage had him leaning out of his acceleration couch against seven gravities; cords stood out on his neck, and the wound beneath his bandages had opened. Blood soaked the dressing, streaking down his jaw in the artificial gravity to splash audibly against the floor.

Morgenthau's face went blank. "You have your orders, *First Rank*. Evade the enemy fleet and return to Sauron with the *Damaris*. *Sauron* out."

Diettinger didn't ask Second Rank for an update on the enemy fleet; the look on her face told him all he needed to know.

"Alderson Point in two minutes, First Rank." Navigation usually gave the warning time in seconds, but at seven Gs, minutes seemed more prudent.

"Evasive action, First Rank?"

"None. We'll be at the Point before they recover from the Jump Lag. Status on *Damaris*."

"Matching velocity and heading with us."

"Jump coordinates coinciding?"

"Affirmative."

Diettinger sat back. One minute and forty-five seconds to go. "Weapons. Set wide pattern mine release at thirty seconds to Jump. Disable seek and maneuver programs on mines and set fuses for simple proximity. Signal *Damaris* to match deployment." It was all he could do.

The *Fomoria* streaked between the Imperial Fleet ships still recovering from Jump. Her lethal shadow, *Damaris*, narrowly missed colliding with an Imperial dreadnaught, but passed through without other incident. Helpless as the enemy was, the Saurons could do nothing; they were simply going too fast.

With any luck, we'll miss the Jump Point and have to rejoin the battle, Diettinger thought.

He had not reckoned with the quality of his navigation officer and engineering crew.

Navigation counted down the last seconds to the Alderson Point, pausing at ten seconds with: "Engage Alderson Drives," and finishing at "zero" with "Jump."

The *Fomoria* winked out of existence; the *Damaris* followed.

Diettinger's report on the battle of Tanith would hardly have been credited by the High Command were it not for the corroborating testimony of Vessel First Rank Emory of the *Damaris* and those few survivors who later limped back to the Homeworld.

Finally facing the loss of the First and Second Fleets, the High Command recalled all forces to defend Sauron against "probable imminent attack." Diettinger and Emory were both promoted to Fleet First Ranks, despite the fact that their "fleets" at the moment were composed almost solely of supra-orbital fighters.

That would change, they were told. All nonvital industry on Sauron, both her moons and in the system's asteroid field, was changed over to military equipment production.

Which, for Diettinger, was the crowning irony. The borloi was downloaded to Sauron and placed in cold storage. No industrial facility could be spared for its processing. Soldiers on the operating table would have to get along without it, High Command informed him. They could stand a little suffering, couldn't they? They were *Saurons*, after all.

What is to become of us all? Diettinger wondered in his cabin. He had just received the date for his first regeneration session. It was unlikely he'd be able to keep the appointment; too much to do. It would be weeks, perhaps months before the Empire's Fleets arrived at Sauron to finish the work begun at Tanith, but they would come. High Command thought they could be forced to a negotiated peace. After all, they had argued, the Empire was hurt just as badly at Tanith as was Sauron; they would not recklessly strip their frontiers to pursue simple vengeance—their citizens would not tolerate it.

Perhaps they are right. Perhaps we can make the price of defeating the Homeworld a butcher's bill so great that even the Empire will see reason. He didn't think it likely.

He thought it far more likely that the Empire would stop killing Saurons only when there were no more Saurons left to kill.

And if that happens, what? Perhaps some of us somewhere will survive, to go on, to rebuild.

Rebuild.what, Diettinger didn't know, and with characteristic professionalism, he put the thought out of his mind. He couldn't concern himself as to whether or not Sauron or the races she had spawned would survive.

It wouldn't be up to him to decide, either way.

The result of the last Imperial reinforcements to arrive at Tanith system was summed up by the Fleet commander in one word: "Murder."

Imperial Navy Command had received word from the surviving *Chinthes* of the original Tanith patrol, dispatched by Adderly on their almost suicidal run for help. Incredibly, the Naval Staff had acted boldly; and seized an opportunity, stripping ships from every available operation and redeploying them to Tanith with one goal in mind; the destruction of the Sauron Second Fleet. Upon finding the Sauron First Fleet waiting for them as well, the battle had, as Diettinger anticipated, become a man of extermination.

Ship after ship of the Saurons died, their commanders unable, or unwilling, to believe that the losses the Imperials were suffering would not eventually force them to break off.

None did. By the end of the third day of continuous battle, ramming was not uncommon. By the end of the fourth day, the Imperials controlled Tanith's orbital space.

The Saurons occupying Tanith spaceport were dealt with in summary fashion: the spaceport was obliterated. A nearby city complex which the Saurons had captured after landing was officially designated "unsalvageable," and likewise erased from the face of the planet. No demands for or offers of surrender were issued by either side.

Adderly watched all of this, participated in most of it, understood little and could justify less.

By the end of the sixth day, the remnants of a mighty Fleet, bled white and ruined, reduced to less than thirty ships, broke for the Alderson Point to escape. Less than two dozen made it.

Adderly had been part of that, too, and he had stood on the bridge of the *KGV*, engines at last reduced to a merciful one-and-one-half Gs of thrust. They had tried to go to a standard gravity, only to find the crew overcompensating and bumping into things. More tools were broken, and more bones, living at One Gravity than during the last week of living between three and four.

Adderly had watched the ruined hulks fight their way to the Point, most making it, but some not.

Adderly had canceled the final attack, seconds before the last Sauron had Jumped, but he could not say why; only that he had been unable to give the order to shoot.

And therein lies a tale, he thought, waiting outside the offices of the Board of Inquiry. He'd been waiting an hour when a young officer came out to collect him, accompanied by two Imperial Marines. The officer looked like he had eaten something bad. The marines just looked like Marines.

"Captain Adderly; I'm Commander Jackson Harold. It's a pleasure to meet you, sir."

Adderly shook his head. "You might regret saying that."

Harold shook his head. "I doubt that, Captain." He looked over his shoulder, back toward the doors of the office where the Board sat. "I always enjoy meeting a fine officer as opposed to a scoundrel in uniform. And if I ever had any doubt of the difference, today it was dispelled."

Adderly looked at Harold for a moment. "Commander Harold, you look like a man with something unpleasant to say. I wonder if we should be heading somewhere while you say it."

Harold tried a smile; it almost worked. "Let's cross the grounds, shall we? Marines."

The sky of Tanith was characteristically orange, overcast, sodden and hot. Their tunics clung to their backs within ten paces, but it was *air*, by God, and Adderly allowed that he had never tasted any so sweet.

Lieutenant Harold walked slowly. "It's all falling apart, you know."

Adderly nodded. "Yes. The Sauron Fleets are wrecked; the next Navy push will be against their Homeworld. No more battles at the fringes. This one will be for the war. And after that . . ." Adderly shrugged. "The Coalition of Secession can't hold up without the Saurons for backbone. Their Unified State, their Trade Bloc, None of it will—" Harold was staring at him. "What's wrong?"

"I was speaking of the Empire, Captain Adderly. Ours."

Adderly took a deep breath. "Ah. Yes, I guess I knew that, too." But he wondered. *Had* he known? Or, more to the point, wouldn't he have been far happier *not* knowing?

"You're right about the Saurons, of course," Harold went on. "But it won't end with them. The Outies have been pushing everywhere, any place we've ignored or stripped to deal with the Saurons. The Coalition of Secession is gone, but the damage is done. Now there's another crop of Claimants. Did you know that we have three nobles who can prove—*prove*, mind you, the legitimacy of their claim to the purple? To listen to them, you'd think everybody and his brother were qualified to be Emperor. Right now they're screaming in the Senate for a 'council of emperors' based on their contributions to the war. Can you imagine what kind of hydra *that* would be?"

Could he? Adderly didn't know. In truth, he didn't care. The sky of Tanith was beautiful, in its way. This whole world, that he'd fought for and lived on and given everything to save, was at this moment the most glorious place he'd ever seen.

"Anyway, Captain Adderly—"

"Call me Will. I'll call you Jack; or do you prefer Jackson?"

Commander Harold's expression went from uncomfortable to downright miserable. "No, sir, Jack is fine. All right; Will. The loss of *Canada* was bad enough, to say nothing of the part it played in the loss of the *Aleksandr Nevsky*. Still, few of us have ever run into that EVA Marine tactic; the same might have happened to anyone. It's the borloi that's got them. That and the fact that the Saurons had you and let you go. That's never happened before, Will. *Never*. And your suggestion as to why it should have happened to you did not go over well with the Board."

"I stand by it. Diettinger conducted himself like an officer and a gentleman." *And I returned the compliment by trying to kill him, mutilating him instead.* But he hadn't told them that. They wouldn't have believed him, anyway.

"Yes, well, be that as it may, there is still the matter of the borloi drug. The board simply will not accept that the Commander of an Imperial Planetary Patrol Task Force, who lost a battle to a single Sauron heavy cruiser, should be entertained for a time aboard that cruiser and then released unharmed." Commander Harold thought he heard Adderly begin to laugh, and rushed on. "Particularly since you yourself claimed that the Saurons wanted nothing more than the location of huge planetside stores of the Empire's most profitable illegal drug." Harold now saw that Adderly *was* laughing, but the humor got lost on the way to his eyes. "That's their reasoning, anyway. The Tanith spaceport was nuked a dozen times over, so there's no telling if the Saurons got the borloi out of it or not. But they've had so many dealings with Outies and smugglers, to say nothing of traitors in—"

The Commander's voice died before he could say: "the Navy."

"The worst part, Captain Adderly, is their motives. Those bastards want to hang you not because you lost, but because you *won*. A Planetary Patrol Commander holds off two Sauron Fleets for a fortnight. That's bloody magnificent work! There's a lordship in that sort of thing these days, and those fools will fall to squabbling amongst themselves for it when you're gone."

Harold continued on past the officers' quarters and led Adderly and the Marines to the left-hand path that cut across the compound and past the gallows. "The Empire is dying," Harold said in a low voice, "and the jackals are killing each other for the bones."

Adderly shook his head and smiled.

So, in the end, Diettinger's triumph is total. Kellogg got his Board; the obvious, most convenient conclusion was drawn, and that is the end of William Daniel Adderly, Imperial Navy.

His guilt or innocence hardly mattered, nor did the avarice of the men who judged him; at this stage of the war, treason was a charge whose barest whisper would kill a man, if not physically, then certainly professionally.

The Empire's attitude toward the Saurons had changed. They were no longer the enemy, they were evil incarnate. Adderly had seen it growing in his men; he'd seen it in himself, the day he met Diettinger. He had seen it again in Kellogg's single-minded attacks, and finally in the Fleet's pursuit of the remaining Sauron ships to the Alderson Point.

That attitude would consume more than the Saurons, he knew, but they would be the first to go.

They had reached the stockade.

"I'm sorry, Captain Adderly. Will. But under the circumstances I think it's obvious what the verdict will be if you receive a court martial."

Commander Harold had stumbled over the word, but Adderly had caught it. *If.*

He looked at this young man; so very, very young. But not too young to know that the Navy would take its peculiar care of one of it's own. The brotherhood among Naval officers might not be able to save Adderly, but it could send a young volunteer—it was *always* a volunteer—like Commander Harold to show it had not abandoned him.

"If there's anything I can do . . ."

"As a matter of fact, there is. My wife Alysha. She's living on Gaea. Our address is in the records. Tell her all this, if you would. The real story, not the official one."

"I understand. I'm sure she'll be very proud."

"I'm not. But she'll be—justified, I think. That's very important to Alysha. I suppose it's important to a lot of people, these days." Adderly turned at the top of the steps, where two more Marines opened the door. He looked up at the clouds.

"It's funny, but I can't stop thinking about them. The Saurons, I mean."

There being nothing to say, Commander Harold listened.

"They're dying," Adderly went on, almost to himself. "And they can't understand *why* they're dying. They think they've been outfought, and they have, but they'll convince themselves it was some flaw in their battle plan. It will never occur to them that the cold logic of the ultimate Soldiers was simply no match for the heart of the Beast."

He turned and held out his hand. "Goodbye, Jack."

The two men shook hands, and Adderly felt the expected packet pressed into his palm.

"The men of the *King George V* wanted you to know they appreciated what you did for Captain Lester and the bridge crew." Harold swallowed. "Goodbye, Captain Adderly."

Adderly smiled. "Will."

Adderly had turned when Harold called him back. "Will?"

He raised an eyebrow. "Yes? Something?"

"Captain, I'm twenty-two years old, and I'm a full commander. It's not hard to guess why, and knowing why, it's not likely I'll see twenty-three. It's what you said, about how Diettinger treated you. I'd like to know: What are they *really* like? I only know the propaganda ministry stuff; but you've seen them up close, *talked* to one. What's it like to actually look into the face of the enemy?"

Adderly turned and looked at the jungle-choked hills in the distance; rife with some of the most dangerous predators in known space. He had hunted there once, on an absurdly dangerous dare. Closer in, on the far side of the compound, was the building that held the

Board of Inquiry. He almost laughed aloud, thinking of
how much safer that jungle looked to him, now.

The beasts have come down from the hills. . . .

A flagpole in front of the Board's offices bore a tired
banner, its faint movement in the sultry Tanith air
reminding him of some dying bird. Adderly saw it was
the flag of the Empire of Man.

*Dying; already dead? Or is it too much to ask that it
might just be asleep?*

Adderly said nothing for a very long time. Finally he
turned his gaze back to meet Commander Harold's.

"With enemies like them, Jack," he said quietly,
"you don't need friends." Then he went back up the
stairs and into the stockade, a Marine on either side to
escort him to his cell.

"For God's sake, let it go!"

Albert, Baron Hamilton of Greensward, smiled thinly. "Let it go. Major, if it would help ex-terminate the Saurons, I would personally burn Whitehall to the ground. It wouldn't, though." *Nothing will, but I can't say that to one of Gary's officers.*

Major Hendrix looked around the paneled study, with its high ceilings and ornate tapestries. Such elegance had always been rare on Haven. Now, after the widespread destruction brought by the Sauron invaders, it was unique. "Saurons. Why us?"

"I've wondered that myself. We're the arse end of the Empire. Maybe that's why. Maybe the Saurons are losing the war, and this shipload of the bastards is trying to hide."

"God, I hope so," Hendrix said. "And the Fleet will be back. It will."

"It might be a while. And meanwhile we hang on, and ruining Whitehall won't help."

"I don't want to ruin Whitehall, I want you to take our refugees."

"Same thing, really. If we take in everyone you send, we won't last a season. Better that some sur-vive than none."

"And what do you think you accomplish by the mere act of survival?"

Hamilton shrugged. "Possibly nothing. But I can try. Maybe the horse will sing. I want to save Whitehall, because losing it won't make any difference, and if we're here we can help rebuild. Major, if every one of those monsters drops dead tomorrow we'll be generations away from a civilization!"

"But, the Empire—"

"Major, I doubt the Empire will return. Ever. They abandoned us before the war heated up. Even if the war is over now—and we don't know that—Sparta has its own rebuilding to do. They don't care about us. Never did, really."

"Then you won't help us."

"Major, I can't help you, not with anything that will do you any good. House Hamilton can't even meet obligations to our own. We're turning out relatives of our own liegemen. Do you think I like that?"

"No, of course not—look, can you do anything? Anything at all?"

"I can take in your family. Yours and the General's. No more. And I can send you a hundred volunteers, reasonably well supplied and equipped."

"No more than that—"

"You can't feed more than that," Hamilton said. "Well supplied means they aren't starving. It doesn't mean we can spare a month's rations."

"Damn it, that's no help at all! Your grandson promised us more—"

"John does not command here." There. I've done it. Disavowed my grandson's pledged word. And there may be hell to pay for that. Hamilton suppressed a wry smile as he watched Major Hendrix. It was all too easy to see what Hendrix was thinking. Hamilton's Whitehall militia was scattered, and Hendrix had his own platoon of escorts. And John had already promised. One bullet, and there would be a new and more tractable Baron at Whitehall. I think he may try it.

Hamilton whistled, a short trill tone. One of the elaborate panels opened to reveal three militiamen. The sergeant touched his cap in salute. Hamilton nodded acknowledgment.

"Yes, Baron?" the militia sergeant asked.

"Please send word to my grandson that I wish to see him."

"Yes, sir." The panel closed again.

Hamilton sighed in relief. Good. Hendrix didn't have time to do anything he needs to apologize for. Maybe he wouldn't have anyway. Maybe.

"If that's all you will give me," Hendrix said.

"All I can give you," Hamilton corrected.

"Can. I don't agree, but I suppose I should take what I can get." He hesitated. "Also—I will be sending up my family. Ruth Hendrix, and the two kids."

"I will keep them as safe as I keep my own," Hamilton said formally. "Tell Gary Cummings the offer applies to him as well."

"Yes, sir. We—have a plan."

"I'd be amazed to find you don't. I hope it's damned successful, and damned bloody. Go kill some Saurons for me."

DEATH'S HEAD PATROL

ROLAND GREEN
AND
JOHN F. CARR

Roger Boyle knew he wasn't a real Soldier. In normal times he wouldn't have been admitted to the ranks, much less the War Academy, but the past decade hadn't been normal times. So many of the elite were dead, and the technical work still had to be done. Then, suddenly, training nowhere near completed, Boyle was Fifth Rank. But only a Tech. Not really a Soldier, not now, not ever, and the others would never let him forget even if he could. He'd never have graduated from the Academy. He shouldn't have been there at all—

It didn't matter. The Academy was radioactive dust. So was the Home Planet. Boyle watched it die. It writhed like a live thing, and from its ashes marched an endless stream of Imperial soldiers. When *Fomoria* fell from the skies to Haven's barren plains they laughed, and now they marched toward the wreckage, legions of them, death in their eyes. Soon there would be no more Soldiers. The marching column grew and grew until it filled the skies, and endless ships poured from the Cat's Eye, and the universe was filled with their noise—

Boyle found himself on the floor. *What was that?* Whatever it was had thrown him out of his bunk, and caved in half the wall. There were shouts, and men running. He stood groggily. Others did the same. For a

87

moment the barracks room was confusion before they sorted themselves out and began putting on their equipment.

"Ranks. Any Ranks here?" Boyle shouted.

"Aye aye, Assault Leader Roxon here."

"Fifth Rank Boyle. Who's senior?" There was no answer. He'd known there wouldn't be. "Fifth Rank Boyle assuming command," he said, as he'd been taught, and as he'd always known would happen some day. But in his fantasies when he took command he did great deeds, and High Command was proud of him. Now it was real.

Now what?

"Roxon, take two and see what's happening outside. Who's closest to the comm line?"

"Tareyton, sir."

"Does it work?"

"Checking. No, sir. No static. Dead, sir."

"Right."

There were sounds of combat outside. Small arms fire, and artillery. Boyle pulled on his jacket and fingered the sleeve unit. "Boyle calling anyone. Anyone, this is Boyle." Static. At least it was working. He hadn't expected more. "Help the wounded," he said. And nothing to do but wait—

Roxon came back in. He tried to keep his voice calm, but there was a nervous tremor to it as he said, "Mushroom cloud over Headquarters, sir. High explosive rounds dropping on barracks area. Delta one took a direct hit. I saw no other damage to barracks, but it's lethal in the open out there. There's still a lot of A-P falling among the bunkers."

Anti-personnel munitions peppering the bunkers. Harassment, it wasn't likely to do much damage. The barracks were solidly built, concrete bunkers protected by earthworks, and all of Firebase One was built like a Roman fortress, critical targets scattered, each defensively self-sufficient. But where the hell were the Ranks?

His orders were to survive. As the only officer present that was mandatory, until another Rank showed up.

More sounds of artillery. "That's ours," he said, and regretted it. They'd all know, same as he did. "What's the status of Communications Central?"

"Bunker looks intact," Roxon said.

"We'll go there as soon as it quiets down." *Which ought to be soon enough, with our counter-battery fire.* "When we move out, Roxon, you'll lead."

"Aye aye, sir."

"Who's had advanced med tech?"

"Here, sir. Swenson."

"Good. All troops, if you can't walk, stay here. We'll send Medical for you when we can. Swenson, do what you can, and listen on Channel Four."

"Aye aye, sir.

Outside was quiet. Counterfire had done its work. Boyle waited, watching his sleeve timer. Minutes passed. Still quiet. Long enough, anything on the way had got here. "Move out, and make it smart. They'll shift positions and fire again."

Twenty-eight men. Out of fifty in the barracks. Twenty-eight in the dim light, with the Cat's Eye hanging above, laughing at them.

Explosion. Another. Then—

He was thrown to the ground. Everyone dove for cover as debris rained down. Then another explosion. Not cluster bombs this time. High explosive, and they'd detonated something. *Fuel and ammunition supplies,* Boyle thought. *Has to be those. So what have we got left? Damn little.*

We have US. The Cyborgs, and the Soldiers. First Ranks. High Command. While we live, Sauron lives. Even if we breed with the cattle. Sauron lives here. Sauron rules here. And one day we will return to rebuild Homeworld.

*   *   *

The communications bunker hadn't been hit. An island of calm order in a sea of explosions.

"Fifth Rank Boyle here, reporting for duty. Who's in charge?"

"Communications Technician Landau acting in command, sir. Do you relieve me?"

"I relieve you. Report."

"Headquarters heavily damaged, may be destroyed. Radiation level stabilized at forty-four millirem, projecting sixty-five in two hours. There have been two attempts by small units to infiltrate the barracks area. I have increased surveillance to maximum. Standing by for further orders."

"Report change of command here to High Command, and carry on."

"Aye aye, sir."

At least he was among friends, who were no more Soldiers than he was. *We can play at being Soldiers. In fact, we damned well better. Go by the book. What else can we do?*

"Screens up," someone called.

The wall screen lit to display a terrain map. Two specks moved across it. Robots one and two, moving toward what High Command assumed was the enemy's Headquarters. Boyle watched in fascination. They moved inexorably, toward Fort Kursk.

"Kursk is ours," Boyle muttered.

"Not any more," Landau said. "Cummings and his militia took it half an hour ago."

Took it. From Soldiers. Kursk was held by Cyborgs!
"The cattle can fight," Boyle said grudgingly. He remembered the Academy professor, the odd one who had said they must never speak of the enemy as cattle, because "that term creates distorted expectations that might affect decisions made on the battlefield, and certainly after victory." *And this time even High Command underestimated the enemy.*

The dots moved slowly on the screen, toward Kursk. Toward General Cummings.

"Get Cummings and the war is over," Landau said excitedly.

"You address me as 'sir.'"

There was a laugh in his voice as Landau said, "Aye aye, sir." But the tone changed suddenly. "Apologies, Roger. Sir."

On the screen the dots converged on Fort Kursk, then wheeled away. Weapons launched—

There was a flare, the large jagged-edge red pattern that indicated a nuclear explosion. Ten megatons.

The men cheered.

"Silence in the ranks."

"We got him," someone shouted. "The butcher's dead."

Along with how many of our own? But it was worth it. Cummings who had killed Fomoria. Cummings was a goal worth dying for.

"Enemy message traffic, Fifth Rank. Coded. A lot of it."

"Identification?"

"Pattern indicates enemy High Command."

So we didn't get him after all. But the day isn't over, and the Hawks are still flying. "Locate and notify Firebase Two."

"Aye aye."

Cummings, we're after you. Just stay there a little longer—

"Nothing but static, sir."

"You're sure it's static, not jamming?" General Cummings asked.

Sergeant Alice Hoskins shook her head. "Just the bomb plus Haven's usual conditions." A month ago she'd been a civilian tech in the Communications Ministry. Now—

"Carry on, Sergeant."

"Yes, sir, but—when are we going to move?"

"When I'm done!" Cummings looked at his watch. It had stopped. EMP, probably. *One more damned thing to worry about.*

At least she didn't have to worry about delayed radiation effects. Dosages that threatened to kill him before the Saurons did were another matter. *If we had been an hour closer to the Fort . . .*

Cummings looked downhill to where the last of the rubble was being shoveled on to the graves. Eighteen militiamen. The rubble was as much of a grave marker as they'd ever have. Ten times more were part of the dust cloud where Fort Kursk had stood.

It was cold comfort that most of them had died before the bomb hit, killed in retaking the Fort and reactivating its weapons systems. But forty of the best would have seen the fireball. Or worse. *At least we hurt them. Enough?*

Last month it had been Major Seastrum and his company, drawing the Saurons away from the missile team that destroyed the ship. *Next month it will be someone else. But I swear by Laura and the girls' memory that I will never get used to it.*

"We're ready to move whenever you give the word, sir," Colonel Anton Leung said.

Cummings nodded. The nervous attentiveness in Leung's Tartar eyes reminded Cummings of how he himself watched over Marshal Blaine during the liberation of Lavaca. Had old age caught him already, at seventy-three?

Well, maybe not old age, just long service. He'd spent his whole adult life in uniform, at the Marine Academy on Freiland, then in the Imperial Marines, then as Marine Commandant of Haven, and finally these last eighteen years as Commander-in-Chief, Haven Militia.

That's one post I won't be retired from! A joke, because militia commandant was a retirement post. He

should have been a gentleman farmer, close to Whitehall, raising lettuce. For amusement he could shoot
stomachsnouts, and hoist a glass or two with Albert.

Cummings chuckled at the thought. Sure he'd be
welcome at Whitehall! With every Sauron on Haven
looking for him. Some friend, to carry that scent . . .

Now the Brigade was scattered between Redemption
and the Miracle Mountains. With intensified Sauron
surveillance, it was best they stayed in small groups.

"Colonel, send Charlie Company on ahead to New
Survey. We'll veer west, to Greensward. I have to warn
the Baron about what we've unleashed here today."

"What about a tight-beam message?"

Cummings jerked his thumb toward the site of Fort
Kursk. "The equipment's back there. This time, we're
really on our own."

Leung shrugged his broad shoulders with the weary
resignation of a man who has seen it all, but is willing to
see it all again if that's what his C. O. needs.

Cummings continued. "We'll send out scouts as we
march, to trade ammunition for drugs and mounts. I've
heard of some remarkable things done with local plants."

It was Leung's turn to point at the plateau. "Anybody
who helps us could be risking that."

"Some of them won't care. Others—we'll put on a
convincing 'bandit' act for them. Let *them* tell the Saurons
we scared them witless." *Maybe it won't be an act.*

Leung laughed sharply. The laugh turned into a bark-
ing cough, and the cough into a siege that left him bent
over and gagging.

"Are you all right?"

"Nothing that a T-year in a warm, moist climate
wouldn't cure, General."

"I'll buy you a ticket to Tanith as soon as I can find a
travel agency."

Colonel Leung wiped blood-flecked lips and grimaced.
"The Saurons may not believe we'd be willing to rob
our own people— "

"You don't know, Colonel Leung, what the Saurons will believe about what they call 'cattle' until you've been on a Sauron-*pacified* world. On Lavaca—oh never mind, that was years ago. Let's stick to the problems we have. I want to avoid another engagement."

"No word from Cook yet?"

Leung's tone wasn't entirely professional, but then his son and daughter-in-law had gone in with Cook's company. His wife hadn't lived to see the coming of the Saurons, only the breakdown of order on Haven after the Imperials left. His other son and his family died with Castell.

"Nothing since they told us to expect an air strike," Cummings answered. The picked company with short-range rockets and demolitions to follow up the strategic strike had reported themselves in position. Operation Shutoff had worked as planned, cutting off key communications and detection equipment just before the strike. Cook had reported initial results, including the destruction of one fighter and the ammunition dump.

There hadn't been a word since. Cummings refused to believe that 180 picked troopers could have gone into the bag without a peep. They had to be busy.

It didn't help, either, that Cat's Eye was not only up but having a first-class radio storm. At times like this, even if a message got through, it needed a couple of repeats before you could be sure you had an ungarbled version.

"They'll turn up, one way or another," Leung said.

More likely dead than alive, probably—but not without leaving their mark.

"Com gear's packed," Alice called.

"Right." Cummings turned to Leung. "The Com section has a spare muskylope."

Motorized vehicles weren't extinct on Haven, but driving one outside Sauron-occupied territory was asking for trouble. A vehicle's heat signature was guaranteed to be picked up by a Sauron bombardment satellite, leading to a hypersonic crowbar rammed up your exhaust.

After six weeks of the Saurons, Haven was a long way back toward the Dark Ages. Baron Hamilton had known what he was doing, when he fortified Castle Whitehall and put his men into durasteel long johns.

Even the muskylopes and horses that gave the strike force what mobility it had were mostly for weapons and equipment. Officers were the only unwounded troopers mounted when they turned their backs on the plateau.

This was the first time Roger Boyle had ever attended a staff meeting. But then, it was also the first time he had seen senior Communications Rank available.

Communications Fourth Rank Davis was still alive, but Haven stone was hard enough to break Sauron ribs and dent a Sauron skull. He would be in bed for at least a T-week, on light duty for several more.

For anyone from the Citadel, it was a two days' journey to Firebase One, through guerrilla-infested country. The Saurons' aircraft had more important work than ferrying staff officers. One job: following up suspicious heat signatures picked up by the three low-orbit satellites that covered the Shangri-La Valley. That might put them on the trail of Cummings' Brigade. Even learning where they had been could help; a few raids on Cummings' sympathizers might reduce their sympathy.

Or at least their numbers, much good that may do us.

It was only an unlucky coincidence that this thought came to Roger at the same moment his eyes met those of Cyborg Rank Koln. The Cyborg's eyes were large, apparently unblinking, and pale gray. They made one believe the rumor, that Cyborgs were telepathic, never mind what the manuals said.

Had Koln just read a defeatist thought out of Boyle's mind?

First Rank Diettinger took the chair.

"The Haveners have shown complete disregard for their own casualties when afforded the opportunity to kill our troops," Diettinger said. "All soldiers are therefore to be secure in their respective posts before truenight." Having established that the meeting was to be brief, the First Rank nodded to Deathmaster Quilland. The senior staff Rank rose and stepped before the electronic map display.

The Deathmaster's legendary brevity made a complex subject no simpler, nor did his ability to see opportunity everywhere make bad news any better. That was Boyle's firm opinion, and considering the twenty-odd long faces around him he wasn't alone.

Cummings' missile strike had destroyed formidable percentages of the Sauron's remaining special weapons, strategic delivery systems, fuel stockpiles, and other irreplaceable items. Personnel casualties had been surprisingly light, thanks to the limited manning of the above-ground facilities, but Breedmaster Caius still had to make a final assessment of potential genetic damage.

The Haveners had clearly reoccupied Fort Kursk, either bringing in strategic delivery systems by covert means or more likely activating stored weapons. They had also evacuated the area of the fort immediately after the Sauron retaliatory strike.

"As soon as radiation dropped to safe levels, we landed a Pathfinder Team."

The Pathfinders were an elite Cyborg unit, specializing in nuclear attack follow-up. During the state of emergency following the Haveners' strike, Diettinger had released a very few of the Pathfinder Cyborgs from fertility testing to field duty.

Quilland continued. "The Pathfinders reported that the Haveners had buried their dead, disabled surplus equipment, and left the area at least two days ago."

"Are the Pathfinders pursuing?" Koln asked.

"We sent only four. They are setting up an observation post in the Fort Kursk area."

"This should have been done," Koln pointed out, "when we realized that these were a superior variety of cattle, requiring extraordinary measures."

"No doubt," Quilland said. "But by that time, the Fort Kursk area was swarming with guerrillas and bandits. Our small garrison was so busy sending out recon and pacification teams that they didn't fully examine the fort. A larger force would have diverted strength from more important operations."

"From what seemed at the time more important operations," Koln corrected. Abruptly the Deathmaster cut him off.

"A company-strength force of cattle infiltrated the area of Firebase One. Using short-range missiles and infantry weapons, it added considerably to the toll of vehicles and supplies.

"The security troops, reinforced by mobile patrols, have been pursuing these infiltrators for the last two days. We have killed 135 of them. No prisoners were taken."

"Our own casualties?" First Rank asked.

Koln being silent seemed to Boyle, if anything, more sinister than his being loudly insubordinate.

"Three Soldiers killed, twenty-two wounded. Fourteen of the wounded will return to duty within a T-week."

Diettinger kept the reports flowing swiftly from the department heads, then from the Firebase and outpost leaders. Somewhere in the middle of the department heads, Boyle gave his Communications report, although afterwards he couldn't have repeated a word he'd said.

He did remember the faces, though, when he reached one point.

"Our Sauron capabilities free us from dependence on computers. We are not so fortunate where radio and radar are concerned. We and the cattle both need them."

Unhappy faces, and in Koln's case outright unfriendly.

Diettinger summarized the whole stack of reports in a few sentences, then went to the map display. A few more sentences summarized his strategy.

"The haven Militia is to be destroyed as a fighting unit. All other actions against Havener forces are to be downgraded to defensive holding actions. I don't want any crucial positions surrendered, but we aren't trying to serve a whole planet all at once. This—Militia—is a rallying point for the planetary forces. "It is effective and well-led. It is to be hunted down and destroyed within the month."

For once, even Cyborg Koln seemed to agree with the First Rank. But turning this strategy into a series of tactical moves took longer than Boyle had expected. It was the ancient problem: if you cannot defend everything, what are your priorities?

Priority, Diettinger decreed, would go to the Citadel and the breeding stock—the female cattle already rounded up. They could lose nearly everything else and still survive.

In more than the very short run, they would need more space for breeding creches than the Citadel could provide. But meanwhile the breeders could be crammed into the Citadel, and all the Soldiers who would otherwise be tied down defending isolated camps and firebases would be free to fight Cummings.

Once Cummings was broken, there would be defensible creche sites for the asking, and the Engineers and Breedmasters would come into their own. Right now, even the Cyborgs would be assigned to the duty of driving the breeding stock to the Citadel!

Cyborg Rank Koln's face was a study when Diettinger announced that assignment. Koln had been displeased over lack of combat duty for his Cyborgs, so he could hardly refuse outright. But assigning those who represented the future of the Sauron race to cattle-herding—!

"The Haveners will go berserk at the sight of their women being driven off as breeding stock, First Rank," Quilland put in.

Diettinger nodded. "Yes. I know. Twenty percent losses among the captive women will be acceptable if a Haven trooper-to-female kill ratio of ten-to-one is maintained. All captives are expendable if Cummings' Haven Militia can be drawn out."

Boyle's intake of breath was noticed by the other officers. Only Quilland reacted, however. The Death-master gave the young Fourth Ranker a look that said: *"That is why he is First Rank."*

Boyle was beginning to understand at last what being a Sauron was all about.

From a distant escarpment, a tamerlane called. The horses and muskylopes whickered, hissed, and moaned.

General Cummings dismounted to rest his mount. Colonel Leung did the same, even though he'd been swaying in the saddle all night.

"Is he calling his mate, or calling up all his friends for dinner?" Leung wondered half in jest.

"We won't be going his way," Cummings said, as he unfolded the map. Even the so-called flatlands of Haven were filled with small mountains and patches of rugged terrain.

Cummings lit the shrouded candle-lantern he was using to save the flashlights for the medics. With one dark finger, he traced a route looping south and west around Redemption.

"That's taking us close to the Hamilton barony."

"I know. I need to talk to the Baron. We owe him."

Leung nodded. He'd been a company commander when Baron Hamilton made his deal with Cummings, during the days when paper money had been devalued to less than the cost of printing it. Hamilton had traded gold and grain for working durasteel up into suits of armor. The gold filled the Brigade's paychests and the grain filled its men's bellies.

When troops were not paid and fed they perforce turned bandit or at best mercenary. With Hamilton's help, Cummings had kept the First Haven Volunteers in existence as an organized militia. They had even kept a semblance of order in the Shangri-La Valley, when the rest of Haven had slipped into chaos even before the Saurons arrived.

"I agree that we owe him for keeping us alive, but that was ten years ago," Leung said. "Sure, he's helped us since, but what are we going to pay him with?

"Not armor this time," Cummings said. Baron Hamilton had done well with his new-model knights. They'd made him a power in the Valley almost as effective as Enoch Redfield on the other side of the Miracle Mountains. Unlike Redfield, Hamilton was respected as well as feared. Even now, the Barony was as peaceful as anyone could hope for, this close to Sauron territory.

"We pay with intelligence," Cummings said. "Not just about the Saurons, either. Remember the scout we captured, from the Redfield Rifles?"

Leung nodded. The man had been looking for ammunition dumps—for his leader's forces, he said. But the militia recognized a paper he carried as a Sauron safe-conduct. Any ammunition hoard he found would be confiscated by the Saurons, the nearest village leveled, the inhabitants enslaved or killed—the whole ghastly tale they'd seen a dozen times and heard twenty more.

The more merciful of the troopers had wanted the man staked out for tamerlanes. Others had proposed more ingenious entertainments, such as tying a bucket with a drillbit in it upside down over the man's groin.

Cummings had provoked universal outrage by simply shooting him outright.

"You're right, General," Leung admitted. "Redfield's always been one to play up both sides, as long as they'll leave him in power. Remember the deal he struck with

King Steele the First and Last. Now, if he thinks the
Saurons are winning—"

"Our friends ought to know."

Darkness was almost complete now, but fortunately
the next stretch of the journey was over nearly open
ground. They couldn't make it all the way in and out of
Hamilton territory during truenight, but they could
get in and go to ground before dawn.

Then the Saurons might miss them altogether, so
close to the holdings of a man who'd given them neither
allegiance nor opposition. If the strike force was discovered and had to fight its last battle, the Hamiltons
would still have a plausible excuse for not knowing that
it had ever been there.

The tamerlane called again, and this time several
more replied. The pack was on the prowl, and Cummings posted an experienced hunter with a night-scoped
rifle at either end of the column before they moved out.

The half-ruined village had been overrun by bandits
ten years ago, when Baron Hamilton was still settling
the affairs of Castell and "King David" Steele. Its survivors had joined the Castle Whitehall garrison, women,
or labor force, depending on their age, abilities, and
inclinations.

Herdsmen and peddlers still used the few windproof
buildings as a waystation. So even the most paranoid
Sauron would find nothing suspicious in an occasional
light or a few tethered muskylopes with saddlebags.

One of those lights was a candle, burning in the
middle of a camp table set on a dusty floor. On camp
stools to either side of the table sat Baron Hamilton of
Greensward and General Cummings. Hamilton was bent
over a sheaf of papers, squinting at them with eyes that
had many more wrinkles around them than two years
ago.

"Thanks for putting it all on paper, Gary," the Baron
said finally. He straightened up, then winced and put a

hand to the small of his back. "We're going to be back to abacuses and wax tablets in another generation if things go on this way."

"Be sure you've got a reliable scribe to copy this on something more durable," Cummings said. "This is from our last batch of flash paper. We didn't want anybody caught with it, ourselves included."

"I understand. I'll have Mattie do it. She's only five weeks to term, but she's going to climb walls if I can't find something for her to do."

"How many great-grandchildren does this make?" Cummings knew he should remember how many children Matilda Hamilton and Captain Aram Mazurin had produced, but he was too tired.

"This is the fourth, and the other three are all alive so far." The Baron looked around for some wood to knock, then compromised by thumping his own forehead. Cummings grinned.

The sound of scuffling outside the hut wiped the grin right off his face. A few moments later, Sergeant Major Slater entered with a disheveled John Hamilton in tow.

Slater had been Cummings' driver when they were both with the Land Gators in '21, and close to retirement age even during the war against David Steele. He still managed a firm grip on a man half his age and half again his size.

"I found this one skulking outside, sir."

"It's all right. You can let him go."

Slater released Hamilton from the hammerlock, saluted, and stepped out.

The Baron spoke first. "John, what the bloody hell do you think you're doing, violating the general's hospitality—?"

Cummings silenced the Baron with a slicing gesture. The two Hamiltons were peas from the same pod. If they had a set-to, he'd never find out what this was all about without alerting every Sauron from here to the Citadel.

John took the reprieve to roughly finger-comb his tangled hair. It had some streaks of gray in it now, Cummings noticed, but John still had those holo-star looks that seemed to improve with age. It wasn't by accident that he'd been the rake of Castell.

He'd settled down, though, when he had to. He'd been his father's right hand in turning the barony into a feudal domain, and done as much as most to bring down the late unlamented David Steele.

"I want to fight the Saurons. I'm tired of waiting things out at Whitehall, waiting for the other boot to drop. One of these days—maybe not for another twenty years, but it *will* happen—the Saurons are going to want our little backwoods portion of Shangri-La.

"Then they'll be our problem. Before that, someone from Greensward has to learn how to deal with them, negotiate with them, or fight them. We can't go on living in a fool's paradise of They'll Never Come Here.

"They're coming. It's only a question of when!"

Cummings could see that this was an old argument. He could almost hear what his friend had asked before.

"Haven't I given enough to the Empire? My favorite grandson, my father, two brothers, an uncle—where does it end? Here and now with the last of the Hamiltons? Our name may not be a great one, but it's good. Our banners fly in Imperial Hall. Colin Hamilton was the first commander of the 77th Marines, the Land Gators.

"Do we owe the last drop of our blood?"

As silently, Cummings gave his reply.

"I'm sorry, my old friend, but the answer is yes."

Fathers, sons, daughters, children were dying all over Haven thanks to the Saurons. And the red harvest had just begun.

It was still summer, but the Saurons had bombed all the food factories and power plants. The Shangri-La Valley, with the most temperate climate on Haven, grew only about half its own food. With fields bombed and burnt and food stocks carted off by Sauron raiding parties, what would happen when winter blew in?

Hunger, then famine, and then how many dead? Half a million, a million, two million, four million dead?

What about the rest of Haven, where life was already on a knife's edge? The Saurons didn't need to sweep Haven clean of resistance. In far too many areas, winter would do it for them.

On top of it all, John Hamilton was *right*. Whitehall needed to know more about the Saurons—good, if there was any, and bad, which there was a lot of. Otherwise the Baron's legacy would be no more than bleached bones behind crumbling walls.

"Albert, listen to your grandson. He's making sense. The Saurons aren't going away. They're here for the duration. And don't count on any help from the Empire. If the Saurons haven't won, they've done the next worst thing. Driven the Empire back to defending its heartworlds, and hang the frontiers!"

The old Baron flinched at each word. *True. Damn it.*

"As for you, young man, I'm appointing you an acting captain in the First Haven Volunteers—"

"I thought it was Cummings' Brigade?"

"Over my dead body. When I'm gone, it can call itself anything it damned well pleases. Meanwhile, you have a lot to learn about the military. Lesson one: you never interrupt a superior officer, even if he's blathering.

"Lesson two: you do not disobey orders, the way you did with your grandfather here tonight. Your job with me is to observe and survive, not die leading the Charge of the Light Brigade.

"Are you with me so far, Captain Hamilton?"

"Yes, sir."

"Good, because I don't have much time. If the Saurons find anything or anyone from Greensward with my command, their patience with you will evaporate. Right now you're tolerated. As long as you're tolerated, there's hope for non-Sauron civilization on Haven.

"Give them an excuse to strike you, and that chance vanishes. So does Whitehall."

"I thought you took out the last of their nukes?"

"So did I, until they laid ten megatons on Fort Kursk. Understand this, our intelligence of the Saurons is somewhere between negligible and zero. All we know is what we see.

"That may have been the last of their ready weapons. Even if it was, I wouldn't bet against their scraping up enough fissionables for a pony bomb. There's only one commander on Haven who's sure he's out of nukes, and you're looking at him."

John Hamilton frowned. "Would they risk their own people assembling a pony bomb?"

"If they were desperate, yes. Or they might ask Enoch Redfield to 'volunteer' some technicians."

The Baron frowned. "The satrapy's that far into their pockets?"

"It might be. What we know is all down there." Cummings tapped the sheaf of flash paper.

"Now, John, I want you to give your grandfather *everything* that might link you to Whitehall. That means your university ring and your underwear, if necessary.

"While under my command, you'll use the name John Hall. That should reduce the confusion and obscure your past.

"Past—you're too young to be a former Imperial officer. So—let's make you a former officer of the Navy Krakow Second Militia. You ran into me and decided to re-up to fight the Saurons. Can you speak Polish?"

"I can do a sort of generic Slavic that should fool a Sauron, at least."

"Good. That's your cover."

"Yes, sir."

"You're learning. Now, Captain Hall, say goodbye to your grandfather. I'll be outside with the horses."

A dark-haired, large-featured head rose over the rim

of the landing pad. Roger Boyle advanced to greet Cyborg Sargun.

Today was the high point of Boyle's military career so far. He'd just been appointed second-in-command of the patrol searching for Cummings' strike force. Death-master Quillan himself had given Boyle a field promotion to Fourth Rank, ostensibly for initiative. Boyle knew better. There simply wasn't anyone left.

Davis was back on duty, and two Third Ranks had come down from the Citadel. Boyle was now free to go into the field. His announced objective was to find Cummings's strike force.

He also had another mission, one Diettinger had given him in person this morning. "I'd have promoted you to Third Rank if you had more combat experience," the First Rank said. "You will have that, after this mission."

He handed Boyle a sealed envelope. "It has been brought to my attention that there is some question about Cyborg Sargun's loyalty to the present command system. He will still be senior commander of the patrol. But if his leadership—*suffers*—during the expedition, these orders will put you in full command, by my authority."

That was all Diettinger had said on the subject, but even the hints took away much of Boyle's enthusiasm for his first combat command. Everyone knew about the faction among the Cyborgs led by Koln and Zold.

Still—Boyle ran his fingers over the two opposing silver pips on his chevron. His spirits began to lift.

Fourth Rank, and a combat command to go with it. That has to be worth putting up with a few Cyborgs!

Boyle squatted at the edge off the pad and waited while the Cyborg finished hauling himself up the forty-meter cliff face. Soldiers would die if their leaders disagreed. So be it. No arguments.

Sargun stood, looked down at Boyle from his full two and a half meters.

"All squadron Soldiers present or accounted for?"

"Yes, Cyborg."

"Status of our transport?"

Boyle looked behind him at the three big-tilt rotors with improvised armor. Both the machines and their armor had been scavenged at Fort Fornova.

"Fully fueled and inspected, Cyborg."

"Call the Soldiers for a briefing."

"With respect, Cyborg, I gave the basic tactical briefing while we were waiting for you." *Which was twenty minutes longer than it would have been if you hadn't decided to play climbing vine.*

"Without my orders?"

"You gave no orders against the briefing. Our orders from the Deathmaster were to lift out at 0820."

Sargun looked at the sky. Roger doubted that the Cyborg could tell time by the position of Cat's Eye yet, so the gesture merely annoyed him. He remained at attention, and if he could have willed the dirty butter-colored hair on his head to stand upright as well, he'd have done it.

"Very well," Sargun said finally. "You have done your duty as you saw it. Perhaps you will not need as much instruction as I feared a Tech might."

Boyle won the battle to keep a burning flush from rising above his jaw. *I probably won't, war machine. But I'm not making bets on you.*

Cat's Eye's waning orange light was more sinister than usual, or perhaps it was just in Roger's mind as the troop carrier ran the ridges along the Miracle Mountains.

Boyle had gone ridge-running before, in training. Now it was real. *And I am not really a Soldier.*

Nor was his state of mind helped by the knowledge that one of the pilot's arms was a prostheses. The med techs claimed the prostheses were every bit as good as flesh and blood, yet one heard stories—

"Heat signature," the copilot shouted. He rattled off a string of coordinates.

"Ignore it," Sargun said. "That's not where the report said the camp was."

Boyle saw the pilot shake his head very slightly, almost to himself.

"There was an error factor in the report," Boyle reminded the Cyborg. "That heat signature is well within the limits of error."

"A big signature, too," the pilot added. "Could be fifty campfires, maybe more."

"All the more reason to ignore it, then. Nobody unfriendly would be lighting that many fires in Sauron territory."

"Not unless it was a decoy," Boyle said. "My estimate is this is a group of campfires left burning to attract our attention. I see no animal signatures."

"They might be lost in the spillover effect from the fires," the pilot said.

"Possibly," Sargun replied. "But the cattle could have simply run off and left their fires burning when they heard us coming."

"Or—" Boyle began.

"Or what?"

"Or left the fires burning to draw us into an ambush."

Sargun didn't smile. By temperament, if not by heredity, Cyborgs were almost incapable of the act. But his face looked less stern.

"Land on the ridge running west from Hill 1367, about halfway along. That will give us good command of the camp. If they want to come back to it, the cattle will have to run the guantlet of our fire."

The pilot began turning the tilt-rotor toward the ridge, while the other two ships followed. They stayed a thousand meters above the ground, out of range of most small-arms fire.

"Bandits!" the pilot called. "Two missiles."

The ship lurched in evasive action. The flare launchers popped as the computers analyzed the attack. One missile soared past the transports, wobbled, started to turn to track the heat pulse of the last tilt-rotor, then ran out of thrust and began to tumble.

Before Boyle could see where it landed, the second missile exploded just under the left wing. Windows shattered, gouging skins with flying plastic. Lights flickered and dimmed, and the note of the left engine changed sharply.

"We're going straight down before we lose her," the pilot shouted. He was using one arm on the stick, the prosthesis was bent at an unnatural angle below the elbow.

Boyle had just tightened his shoulder harness when the transport landed, hard.

The landing sent everything and everyone not strapped down flying toward the overhead, then crashing down. A squad of cattle would have lost half its strength to fractures and concussions. The Soldiers had only one man hurt, a Soldier who took a full ammunition box on the knee.

The wounded Soldier was half-carried, half-dragged out, as the squad swarmed out of every door and hatch, and a couple of the shattered windows as well. Boyle smelled leaking fuel and felt the ground squish under his boots.

As the pilot lurched out beside him, Boyle asked, "Anything I can do to help?"

The pilot looked down at his oddly bent arm and said, "I was scheduled for the regeneration tanks a week ago, but there was a schedule foul-up." He grinned. "Must have been my lucky day."

Boyle pointed to the ground. "You've got a fuel leak somewhere. You might want to start evacuating the transport."

"We're down to less than a dozen of these rotors," the pilot said as he patted the side of the transport like a woman's flank. "I'd sooner leave my good arm."

"Boyle! Deploy security around these transports," Sargun ordered. Then the Cyborg led the other two squads from the undamaged craft uphill. Boyle's night vision and the distant glow from the campfire let him see the Soldiers alternately creeping and rushing, using every bit of cover while maintaining silence and fire discipline.

A quick check showed they had a secure perimeter.

"With permission, I will examine the ship," the pilot said.

A look into the pilot's eyes told Boyle he was going to examine his ship, permission or not. "Go ahead, but be careful. No lights. We're leaking fuel, and I don't know if that missile team was the only cattle around."

A quick jerk of the pilot's thumb on his good arm told Boyle whose fault the pilot thought that was. Then the two crewmen climbed uphill toward their disabled craft.

The two pilots had just disappeared through the cockpit when rifles spattered the transport's armor with bullets. The security Soldiers promptly imitated drillbits, burrowing deeper into the ground than ever. Like their comrades uphill, their fire discipline held.

The other two tilt-rotors lifted off in clouds of dust. They quickly vanished in the inky darkness of truenight. All that remained of Cat's Eye was a smudge of orange behind the distant peaks.

Boyle scanned the darkness, wincing every time bullets punched out another window or struck sparks from metal. Sparks and leaking fuel were a bad combination.

He heard an asthmatic cough from someone's rifle, then watched in helpless frustration as a grenade detonated on the troop carrier's right wing. An almost full tank ignited. A huge ball of fire swallowed the transport, igniting what was left in the other tanks and on the ground as well.

For a moment his night vision was blinded by the intense light, then his eyes adjusted and he could see again. The tilt-rotor was nothing but a pile of burning wreckage; Boyle felt a pang of regret for the one-armed pilot who would never live to see his prosthesis replaced. Then he knew he was one step closer to being a Soldier and that it was not going to be anything he had expected.

"Take out that grenade launcher!" Boyle shouted, through the gunfire as the ammunition for the belly gun cooked off.

The cattle didn't run. They even got off two more grenades, but the blazing transport seemed to dazzle them. Both grenades went wide and the Soldiers' return fire cut the grenadiers down where they stood.

They died in silence, as the pilots had.

Sargun led the charge up the side of the hill. The burning fuel illuminated the slope of the ridge, giving both sides clear targets. The Soldiers' superior marksmanship and firepower gave them a quick victory, but not a bloodless one.

When Boyle joined Sargun on the ridge line, the first thing he saw was two Soldiers dressing each other's wounds. "How many cattle were up here?" Boyle asked.

"Eighteen, with two launchers. We killed them all, captured one launcher and two spare missiles, and are ready to move on the camp."

Boyle turned and looked down hill at the burning wreckage until he could control his face. "Attack the camp?"

"Of course," Sargun said, a flicker of annoyance creasing his face. "These cattle can hardly be the only ones, from a camp that size. If we hold it when the other cattle return, they will be walking into the kind of trap they set for us."

Boyle decided that Sargun's plan would be keeping the tactical initiative, not committing suicide. It also might allow the strike team an opportunity to replenish supplies lost with the transport.

And, if Sargun was right, any cattle in the area probably would have to come back to the camp. Then they could be fought on ground of the Soldiers' choosing, instead of being chased all over the Miracle Mountains to be fought only when the cattle chose.

Gary Cummings could swear that he felt the cold lance right through the stone walls into his temporary office in the town of Last Chance. He pulled on his lightest gloves, then turned back to the map showing the deployment of his brigade.

Most of one regiment, the Fighting First, was scattered all over the Miracles and their foothills. The other, Falkenberg's Irregulars under Colonel Harrington Cahill, was deployed all through the Atlas Mountains, north near the Citadel.

Technically the Irregulars were still under Cummings' command, but in practice, communication with them was too sporadic to make his control effective. This was beginning to cause trouble. Lately Cahill seemed to believe that he was going to execute a major counterattack, with Cummings' support. Together they would drive the Saurons out of the Citadel itself.

The secret to fighting the Saurons had to be *never* to concentrate against them, Cummings knew. Snipe at them instead, in guerrilla ambushes, local uprisings, the whole repertoire of the weaker force.

Who are you fooling, old man? came the bitter thought. *The only reason the Brigade still exists is that you haven't yet got the Saurons pissed off enough to do anything serious to you! This could change any day, and your first notice that it has could be a squad of Cyborgs coming through your CP door.*

Loud knocking jerked Cummings back to reality.

"Come in."

Instead of a Cyborg, Major "John Hall" entered. It took a conscious effort now for Cummings to think of him as John Hamilton.

"Sir, we've made contact with the enemy."

Cummings wished he could share the enthusiasm of his new chief of staff. Hamilton had replaced Colonel

Leung after the former chief's death in an ambush outside New Salem. With the post came a temporary promotion to major.

Cummings knew there'd been grumbling, but Hamilton's appointment was making the best of a bad job. In close combat against Saurons, Hamilton might last a T-week. At Headquarters, he'd be under Cummings' eye, with time for a little on-the-job training.

He might not even need that much training. He'd done a good report on the ambush that killed Leung, one that impressed Cummings almost as much as the ambush itself.

No doubt about it, the bandits were getting bolder, or at least controlling more ground suitable for ambushes. They'd cost Cummings thirty-five men, then retreated when the reserves got around their rear, without taking many casualties themselves *and* with the weapons they'd captured. Saurons in front, bandits to the rear, local potentates on either flank—the whole planet seemed to have overdosed on borloi weed!

"Where are the Saurons?" he asked Hamilton.

"They landed about fifteen klicks north of Ranjapar village. Captain Morales reports three squads of Soldiers. His missile teams took out one of the tilt-rotors during the landing."

"Good. What would three Sauron squads have?"

Hamilton rose to the test. "At full strength, each squad has nine Soldiers, one Under Assault Leader, and one Assault Leader. That's the equivalent of nine privates, a corporal, and a sergeant."

"Right as far as it goes. But remember that a typical Sauron Soldier, not common enhancements, has as much training and skill as one of our sergeants. Their Assault Leaders are the equivalent of our Sergeant Majors. Man for man, they're the best combat troops ever to see action."

Hamilton frowned. "Sir, you sound almost as if—you admire them."

"I *respect* their military skill. I only hate their cause and their culture, and what they've done to people who wanted to live in peace.

"The ones I hate personally are the Cyborgs. Those bastards are half-devil, half-homicidal psychopath. They scare the hell out of me and anyone else who's been lucky enough to fight them and survive.

"Lesson's over." Cummings turned back to the map and checked unit pins in the wall map. "Fox Company and Easy Company should join Morales. Able Company should move out of Hatfield and work their way north. They won't join up for a day or two, but they can act as Morales' reserve.

"Meanwhile, general signal to everyone to be ready to move out on an hour's notice. Those bastards have stuck their necks out far enough that maybe this time we can really chop them good and hard!"

Maybe it will work. They can't afford to lose a platoon every time they go outside their controlled area. They can't afford to waste any nukes they have left on dispersed targets, which is all we'll give them.

Maybe we can finally come up with a tactical problem for which that wily old boss tamerlane Diettinger can't come up with a solution!

At first Roger Boyle thought the cattle had a machine gun. Bullets snapped and whizzed around the Soldiers, *spanngged* off rocks, and *wheeted* off into the dawn, half a dozen every second.

Others ended their flight with the solid *chunk* that Roger had learned too well meant striking flesh or bone. Even Sargun leaped and shouted a war cry, as a bullet creased his calf just above the top of his scuffed boot.

Is there no end to these cattle? Boyle thought. After a week of almost continuous attacks and only sporadic communication with Firebase Three, he felt as if his command was facing Cummings' whole Brigade.

As abruptly as it began, the ambush ended. A couple of stray shots echoed around the hillside, but the bullets went nowhere. From either side Boyle heard the scrunch and rattle of Soldiers digging themselves in deeper, mostly with bare hands. In this high country, the ground was so hard that an entrenching tool was useless weight, and the Soldiers were not in the habit of burdening themselves with what *might* be useful.

Certainly not this high on the eastern lip of the Shangri-La Valley. Three thousand meters above what Haven laughingly called "sea level," a Soldier found less oxygen than he did at six thousand meters on Homeworld. The superior physical endowment of the Soldiers largely balanced the superior acclimatization of the Haveners, but balancing was all it did. On Haven, the strategic advantage went to he who held the *low* ground.

Boyle looked uphill, not really expecting to see anything in the tangle of boulders and crevices. They'd been marching too close to the crest for his comfort, but Sargun had insisted on the route.

"Body-heat pulses," the IR detector tech said. "Looks like less than ten men, still within range but moving back over the crest."

"Good work," Boyle said.

Sargun nodded. "Excellent work. You will come with me and two squads. Fourth Rank, you and the other squad and the wounded will maintain a base of fire here. If we are able to pin down the cattle, you can join us for the kill."

"Whose kill?" Boyle asked.

The Cyborg frowned. "What do you mean, Tech Fourth Rank?"

"I mean that the cattle may be using those ten men to set a trap."

"Perhaps. But if we let that fear move us—"

"Who said anything about fear?"

"You interrupt, Communications Tech."

"I need not endure insult, Cyborg Sargun. Nor do we need to endure the risk of being drawn into yet another ambush. Let me take one squad straight up to the crest. If the far side of the hill is open, one squad will be sufficient to detect and pin down the enemy. If it's more rugged ground like the crest, half the Soldiers on Haven could still lose the enemy's trail."

"And if the cattle wait on the crest?"

"Then a squad is all we'll lose."

"My speaking of your fear was inappropriate, Fourth Rank. But we will carry out *my* plan. This discussion is at an end."

Boyle supposed it had been inevitable from the start, but loyalty to his soldiers had forced him to put up as much of a fight as he could.

The messenger practically tumbled down the last fifty meters of slope, went on his hands and knees, and crawled into the thicket of wood ferns. General Cummings went to meet him personally.

The messenger couldn't be more than fifteen T-years old, with a strong trace of Andean Indian in his ancestry. His run and being greeted by a real general left him speechless.

"Catch your breath, son," Cummings said mildly. He uncorked his canteen. "Drink some water, too."

Realizing that the general wasn't going to eat him alive, the boy swallowed a mouthful of water. He reported that the ambush had been successful, and the Havener survivors were withdrawing, taking one wounded man with them. They'd hidden their two dead and left two more men at the observation post with the flare pistol.

Cummings nodded approvingly. "Well done—what's your name?"

"Eric Vrusalko."

Some Finn along with the Indian, it seemed. "All right, Eric. You and your people can go home now. In case the Saurons win the next fight, we don't want you caught with our forces."

"Ah, General, sir—"

"Yes?"

"My father—he says we stay with you in the fight. Make sure we get our share of Sauron weapons and ammunition you capture."

"What are you doing, boy, arguing with the general?" a voice snapped behind Cummings.

"Let him speak, John," Cummings said without turning.

John Hamilton was a technically competent chief of staff. At handling people instead of paperwork, though, Anton Leung had been worth two of him.

Hamilton had spent half of his life disobeying orders and the other half obeying them blindly. Somewhere along the line he—and a lot of the other hereditary nobles Cummings had known—had stopped paying attention to the people factor.

"Are your people planning on setting up a local resistance?" Cummings asked.

"I—well, Pop wouldn't tell me if he was. But I don't think so." Eric frowned. "It's more likely he wants weapons for fighting bandits. We know what Saurons are like—they took away my sister and her little girl. But there's not many Saurons. There's lots of bandits, and Redfielders, and gray shirts, and all kinds of people who say they take what they need to fight the Saurons. But like my father says, mostly they're just taking it for themselves."

The cynicism of a middle-aged man in a boy of fifteen made Cummings wince. On Haven, people always grew up fast or they didn't grow up at all. Yet before the Saurons came, they hadn't grown into intriguers before their voices broke.

Another debt for the Saurons to pay in blood.

"All right, Eric. Drink some more water, then wait

until the messengers leave. Go back to your father with them."

"General—"

"You *will* obey that order, or you'll find I'm not too old or too high-ranking to spank you!"

Eric saluted, then nearly fell on his face trying to click his heels. "Sir!"

As soon as Eric was out of hearing, Hamilton came up and handed Cummings the three outgoing messages for the next stage of the battle. Cummings remembered when a battle involving one-quarter this many soldiers would have meant ten times the communications load. But that was before they had Saurons listening and these blasted mountains interfering.

Hamilton stood awkwardly at attention, as if he had something else on his mind.

"Yes, John?"

"What about having the messengers—ah, hold on to Eric, at least until the fighting is over? He's just a boy. I really don't think he knows what he's up against."

"Maybe you'd like to tell *the boy* that to his face? He's been in at least six firefights since the Saurons landed. Who knows how many before? Would you like to compare battle records?"

Hamilton managed to stay at attention, but he swallowed and his face turned pale.

"Good. While you've been living safe and secure behind Whitehall's walls, these people have been fighting and dying. Eric may not be full-grown yet, but he's a soldier."

From the stricken look on Hamilton's face, Cummings knew he'd overdone it again. Hamilton had seen a fair amount of combat, beginning with the Battle of Whitehall. Not having slugged it out with the Saurons was his fate, not his fault.

Bloody hell, I am getting too old for breaking in new officers!

Hamilton's face was regaining its normal holo-star tan

as he left. Cummings sat down and began a perfunctory
check of the orders. Hamilton wouldn't have made any
serious errors in detail.

It struck Cummings that Haven might be in a race
between the Saurons killing her defenders and the defenders turning into Saurons themselves. Or worse,
into people like Enoch Redfield—using the Saurons to
fuel their own ambitions.

Who would win?

Cummings decided that mere generals were not on
God's need-to-know list for the answer to that one.

From Roger Boyle's right, the almost meticulous rattle of Sauron suppressive fire echoed around the hillside. Straight ahead, the last of Sargun's flanking
movement was vanishing up a ravine.

Boyle tried to wish himself smaller or the rock shield-
ing him larger and more firmly seated. It rocked if he
sneezed, and a nearby explosion could send it rolling
over on to him. Unfortunately, the only position where
it hid him was directly downslope.

Other than that, he was having the time of his life.
Growing up, he'd believed that being a Tech meant he
couldn't be a real Soldier. Now he was finding out that
wasn't true. He was no Cyborg, but even Sargun was
giving him a grudging respect.

He had to complete this mission with honor; the com
bunker would not be home after this.

One of the Soldiers going up the ravine bellowed like
a muskylope twice. That meant they were at the halfway point.

Boyle scanned the slope to both left and right, and
resigned himself to staying put. He had tried his best to
convince Sargun to avoid the ravine. While it was the
quickest way to the crest, it was also the most obvious
site for an ambush.

So Boyle had done the next best thing: set up his
command post where he could keep track of events in

the ravine. Sargun might need either reinforcing or rescuing on very short notice.

A bullet *whnnngged* off the boulder, making it quiver but not roll. "Got a count of our friends up there?" Boyle asked the Under Assault Leader working the scanner.

The Soldier shrugged. "The rock's warming up, along the crest. If they can find cover in the sunny patches, they may not give an IR pulse." He rested a hand on the scanner. "This fellow's due for an overhaul."

For which there are no spare parts within more light-years than even a Soldier wanted to think about.

The Soldier began to make another scan of the crest. This involved exposing himself to possible enemy fire, but none came. Maybe the squad's base of fire was doing some good in return for the ammunition expended. They were scheduled to meet one of the tilt-rotors at Hill 2582, to pick up reinforcements and ammunition. Now, if they could just get past *this* hill—

Somewhere above the ravine, the hillside vomited smoke and rocks. The explosion slammed across Boyle's ears, drowning out the firing. Then the rolling echoes of the explosion were swallowed up by the roar of the landslide sweeping across the hill.

The dust completely obscured the ravine and the hillside for fifty meters on either side. The dust didn't hide the strong IR pulse.

"The cattle are moving, going to hit our people before they recover!" the Under Assault Leader shouted.

"Coordinates?"

They came; Boyle cupped his hands and shouted them out. He heard them relayed, then saw the flare of the rocket launcher.

He also saw dust spurting around the rock, and the Under Assault Leader's head shatter as a ricocheting bullet smashed into the base of his skull, just below the rim of his helmet. A little up, a little to the right or the left, and it would have been no more than a headache.

But it had caught him where a Soldier was as vulnerable as cattle.

Boyle shouted and signaled for more suppressive fire on the crest, then realized that the squad was already generating it. Three generations of warfare had created Soldiers who automatically used tactics based on squad-level initiative.

When Boyle was sure that the Haveners were either dead or pinned down, he sprinted for the foot of the ravine. He'd covered a hundred meters before the crest of the hill came to life again, and the remaining hundred before they got his range. Meanwhile, his squad was hosing the crest with their covering fire.

The survivors of the flanking squads appeared stunned, incapable of either thought or movement. All of them were covered with dust and some of them, including Sargun, oozed blood. Sargun's wound had stripped half the scalp off the right side of his head, and his eyes were barely focused.

"Form up!" Boyle shouted. "Follow me back up the ravine. We need to clear the head, then bring up the other squad and dig out our comrades."

"Dig—?" someone said, his voice creaking like a rusty hatch.

"Of course, dig. It takes more than a few rocks to kill Soldiers."

This was true enough, but neither cattle nor Soldiers could survive being buried under half-ton boulders. Also, anyone too badly hurt to walk was going to present a problem. They were already at the limit of the number of wounded they could carry without abandoning heavy weapons—but without those, they'd be stobor bait.

Boyle looked at the Soldiers again. Words wouldn't reach them. Only actions would register. He slammed a fresh magazine into his assault rifle and shouted, "Follow me!"

He took the ravine at a rush, adrenalin pumping,

slipping and sliding on loose rocks but somehow staying on his feet. He also managed not to look back to see if anyone was following him. If they weren't, tripping and falling because he'd missed his footing wouldn't bring them up.

Boyle was halfway up the ravine before a cattle survivor took a shot at him. He returned fire, a three-round burst, and heard a cry.

He also heard more bursts from behind him, and Sauron war cries. The dusty air seemed to pour into his lungs and blow him up like a balloon, until his feet skimmed the rocks.

He reached the head of the ravine, to find a man with a shattered arm crouched over a body. No, a boy, dark-haired and no more than sixteen T-years old. The boy turned with a hunting rifle in his good hand and tried to fire it.

Boyle and the Soldiers who'd caught up with him fired together. The boy flew five meters and landed sprawling. He did not move.

One of the Soldiers, Boyle saw to his annoyance, was Sargun. He'd somehow managed to dress his wounded scalp, although blood was already soaking through the dressing.

"Well done, Fourth Rank," Sargun said. The words set off a coughing fit. Boyle saw the Cyborg wince at the pain shooting through his skull. A moment later Sargun had composed his face and straightened.

"That should teach the cattle how little they can gain by using cowards' weapons. Now let's search the ravine for salvageable weapons."

Boyle and the other Soldiers looked past Sargun at one another. *Has he forgotten the Soldiers buried under the rocks?* was in everybody's eyes.

Roger shook his head slightly. As long as Sargun was capable of standing and giving orders, removing him from command—even with Diettinger's memo—would be dangerous. The conflict might not stay verbal, and by himself Boyle was no match for even a dazed and wounded Cyborg.

As for enlisting help, Sargun could do the same. That would mean a civil war in their small command, deep in enemy territory, perhaps in the presence of the enemy.

"As you order, Cyborg. If we find any of our comrades, though, could you lend your strength to helping them?"

"Of course."

If Sargun saved anybody's life, it would strengthen his authority all over again. But Boyle would have whistled up a pride of Sauron nightfangs, if he'd thought they would save his men!

More Soldiers had come up the ravine now. Boyle spread the eleven men in a line across the ravine, with himself just out in front of the center and Sargun just to the rear.

"Follow me."

General Cummings stooped as he entered the camouflaged tent. John Hamilton was sitting by the sleeping bag where the last survivor of the patrol lay dying.

"You didn't—need—" the man began, then shook his head. "Thanks, sir."

"I should thank you. Major Hall says you did a good job."

"Wish—we could have got more—but we—we counted their filthy corpses. Three of them. And—I think they took—some wounded with them. Sir."

That was likely enough. Not that Sauron wounded were as much of a liability as ordinary wounded, but they still slowed down a marching column.

"We'll show we have some teeth left," Cummings said. "Well done."

Cummings took Hamilton's notes and read them over. The patrol had gone to check the Sauron graves and give the battlefield a once-over-lightly for any useable equipment that either side might have left. Seven men, mounted but lightly armed, with orders to disengage from any Sauron opposition.

They'd reached the ravine, counted the Sauron graves, then discovered that the Saurons had left a rearguard. At least one machine gun plus assault rifles, and the usual excellent Sauron marksmanship.

Caught in open ground, the patrol hadn't a prayer. The last man survived only because he played dead, and the Saurons didn't make a close inspection.

He might not be dying now, except that the firing had stampeded the ponies. He'd walked home, after using up a good deal of strength moving the bodies.

"I don't understand why he'd do such a stupid thing," Hamilton said. "If this is going to become a habit—"

"Major," Cummings said with deceptive gentleness, then looked at the dying man. His breathing had already faded to where he could no longer talk, but his eyes were open. To Cummings, it seemed that all of his dead looked out from those glassy eyes.

So it wasn't just to "John Hall" that he spoke, when he said, "He didn't want our dead to lie near the Sauron graves. He couldn't bury them, but he had to move them. Any more questions?"

"No, sir."

Roger Boyle watched the tilt-rotor whirl out of the dust and head northeast toward Firebase Three. For a moment he had a most unSoldierly wish to be aboard. Although what would he be returning to? The pilot had unloaded their supplies, loaded their wounded, but brought only six reinforcements instead of the asked-for full squad.

The pilot's answer when questioned had been cryptic indeed. "Trouble at the Citadel." What kind of trouble? The pilot either didn't know or wouldn't say. He only added that there'd be no more reinforcements until the trouble was over.

Boyle wondered briefly if Cummings had mounted an attack on the Citadel. But he doubted that the trouble there came from the outside. The pilot wouldn't have been so close-mouthed if it did. Nor would the Citadel itself. Radio reception the past few days had been rancid even by Haven's standards, but Boyle was sure he would have heard something.

If the trouble was internal, on the other hand, radio silence would be the first thing imposed—possibly by one side or the other seizing the com center.

Boyle allowed himself a second-unSoldierly thought: that it might have been better if the Cyborgs had come to Haven as germ plasm. Germ plasm couldn't fight as well as live Cyborgs, but it couldn't intrigue either.

Rifle fire crackled from the empty village Sargun was searching. Quickly Boyle led his squad plus the reinforcements through the village gate.

He found Sargun with three Soldiers, standing in front of a stone hut. As Boyle approached, Sargun whirled and fired right over his head. Bullets sprayed stone dust and chips all over Boyle. If the Cyborg had aimed a bit lower, it would have been Boyle's blood and brains spraying all over the nearest wall.

"Target?" He had to ask three times before Sargun answered. Then the Cyborg had to speak twice to get through the ringing in Boyle's ears. Most of the Soldiers had backed out of Sargun's line of fire.

Boyle knew the ringing in his ears wasn't just the near-miss by friendly fire or the altitude. It was the strain of watching Sargun stagger toward the edge of madness, until it looked as if he would topple over and finally leave Boyle free to command the survivors.

Each time, though, the Cyborg somehow managed to pull himself back just in time. Just in time to make relieving him of command more dangerous than leaving him alone.

If this went on much longer, one of the able-bodied Soldiers would have to dump *both* the Cyborg and

Boyle, then lead the other twenty survivors out of the highlands. Both officers would be unfit for command.

"Look!" Sargun shouted again, waving an arm at something behind Boyle. Boyle dropped to his hands, whirled around, and came up with his rifle in his hands. He saw nothing but Rock Crest's one stone-paved street.

"She must have gone to cover," Sargun said. He pointed to the two houses on either side of the street. "Search them."

The squad broke up and vanished into the houses.

"She?" Boyle queried.

"An old woman, with a knife in her hand. One of those Tartar daggers, I think."

A woman screamed—not old, from the amount of noise she was making. Two Soldiers hustled her out of the house to the left. A third carried her baby. It was pale, blotchy, and whined pitifully.

"Female, where are the rest of the villagers?" Sargun asked. Apart from the opening word, he sounded almost polite. But Boyle saw him rubbing the bandage over his wounded scalp and battered skull. When they started hurting more than usual, Sargun always drifted toward the edge.

"Where?" Sargun asked again.

"All gone," the woman said. "All gone into the mountains. Word came this morning. You were coming. They went." She spoke Anglic, with an accent Boyle couldn't identify.

"I don't know. They didn't tell. I had to stay behind. My baby's sick. She couldn't be moved." The tears started. "She—"

"Where?" Sargun's politeness was gone.

"I don't know. In the name of God—"

"What about General Cummings? Do you know where he is?"

"Cummings—who's he?" Her voice took on a hysterical note. "I tell you—"

"And I tell you, female." Sargun shook his massive

head. "No, I show you." Before the woman could react, he'd snatched the baby from her arms and flung it against the nearest wall.

"See. Now you can go to your friends, if you tell us where they are."

The woman now seemed incapable of speech. Sargun grabbed her by the hair and twisted. She whimpered. The Cyborg motioned the squad forward. Boyle took advantage of Sargun's attention being elsewhere to join the point of the squad. Torturing cattle was not his idea of sport.

The woman started screaming, and didn't stop for a long time. By the time Sargun realized that she was telling the truth, the damage had been done. There was nothing to be done with the woman but what they'd done in other villages. Put her head on a pole outside the village gate as a warning to the other villagers.

As for the village—

"Burn it," Sargun ordered.

"Burn stone huts?" Boyle asked. He wanted to flinch from Sargun's glare, but he'd already done enough flinching for the day, listening to the woman.

"There's bound to be something in each house that will burn. Pile it all together and start the fire. Now get to work."

Sargun, unfortunately, was right. The stone houses themselves would survive, but they'd be smoke-blackened shells when the villagers returned.

The wind was up, but the smoke cloud from Rock Crest still rose two klicks into the umber sky before it dispersed. Boyle hoped there were not too many around to see it. They already had more enemies than they needed.

Two kilometers above the village, just below oxygen-starvation level for most Haveners, a corporal and two privates of Sherpa descent manned an observation post, untroubled by altitude. They plotted the smoke of the burning village, noted its probable source, and helio-graphed the message back to Cummings' mobile HQ.

Cummings cursed, then decided not to waste the energy. Sauron atrocities were becoming part of life on Haven, and nothing short of a miracle—or the return of the Empire, which amounted to the same thing—was going to change it. His current problem was a new one. Or was it an opportunity?

Cummings swore a solemn oath to himself, that this was the last time he would miss Anton Leung. But why oh why had the man taken a bullet in the head *before* this message arrived?

Colonel Cahill in the Atlas Mountains had thought it worth sending by radio. So Cahill believed it. But, could Cummings believe Cahill? It sounded like a sim-ple case of wish-fulfillment fantasy.

Time to bite the bullet. *Which may be more than an archaic phrase, if we have too many more casualties before we restock on anesthetics.*

"My compliments to Major Hall, and would he come to my quarters."

If the chief of staff hadn't been actually listening at the tent door, he must have been expecting the mes-senger. He poked his head in thirty seconds later. Cummings thrust the message at him.

Hamilton's eyebrows rose.

"Evaluation, sir?"

"Yes."

Hamilton looked at the map. "If there's a real dust-up at the Citadel, it's probably a rebellion against their high command. One or two of the ground commanders disagrees with the first rank to the point of trying to depose him. If enough Soldiers get involved, this could be the answer to our prayers. If one side decides it can't win without allies—"

"They wouldn't ally themselves with 'cattle.' "

"Wouldn't they, sir? If it was their one hope of victory?"

"It wouldn't be a real alliance," Cummings pointed out. "The cattle would be back to the pens the moment they weren't needed."

"Yes, but what they might do while the Saurons' needed them . . ."

"Or at least had their backs turned? You're right. This needs thinking about."

Cummings stepped up to the map. "Are we still reporting caravans headed for the Citadel?"

Hall tapped the map in two places. "There and there, although the first one's three days old. The other message came in this morning."

"Never mind. Try to get a message into one of the caravans as well as to Colonel Cahill. In the event of a civil war among the Saurons, everyone is to try to escape."

"Escape?"

"Yes. The only way they'll be safe is get out of reach of the Saurons while they're busy with each other. Also, if the Saurons seriously try chasing them, the Soldiers will be scattered all over Hell's hectares before they realize it's a lost cause."

"And we'll hit them while they're dispersed?" Hall had good teeth, which helped make his grin all the more diabolical.

"Exactly." Cummings measured distances on the map. "There's no way we can get to the Citadel in time to aid the escape, even if we risk going motorized. But we may be able to get a battalion there in time to cover the escapees' tracks."

"I hope to God we do, sir."

"Good boots and hot meals will do more than God right now. Make certain every body has both."

"Yes, sir. Ah—what about the Sauron patrol that just burned Rock Creek?"

"If we take First Battalion into the Valley, Major, that means we'll only have Second Battalion to cover this entire range. Third Battalion is still based outside New

Survey, where the Miracles turn into the Devil's Heater. They can follow us into the Valley as a reserve."

"But Second Battalion is way understrength. They took the worst of it, both at Fort Kursk and at Firebase One. They're not fit for much more than garrison duty."

"If I want to be told the obvious, I don't need a major to do it. Are you bucking for corporal?"

"No, sir." Hamilton pulled three sheets of paper out of his pocket. "I did a little plotting with a calculator and map. Some of the locals threw in their knowledge too. You'll see that the four villages the Saurons burned are all on a route toward the Shangri-La Valley."

"You think they're trying to get away now, not find us?"

"If they weren't, they will be now. I bet this rebellion isn't news to them. While they're leaving, I believe they're trying to do as much damage as they can, both physically and psychologically.

"I thought I'd hand this plot over to the locals. They don't have our communications, so they can't deploy their forces as fast. But they've got just as many people, they're mad as hell, and they know the ground. If they also know where the Saurons are likely to show up next . . ." This time the grin looked smug rather than diabolical.

Cummings nodded. It made sense. So much sense, that if "Major Hall" pulled something like this two or three more times, he'd be a light colonel. Then John Hamilton would go back to his grandfather a real soldier.

"The cattle have fire superiority," Sargun said. "I did not expect that."

When they outnumber us five to one, and almost every Havener has access to a weapon? Roger Boyle asked himself. *I thought you had more tactical sense. Cyborg Sargun.*

"They don't have clear targets, and we do," Boyle pointed out. He gripped an outcropping and hoisted himself one-handed over a meter of near-vertical pitch.

"That gives me an idea," Sargun said. He plunged upward, covering the last twenty meters to the crest in a single rush. His feet and dislodged stones made enough noise to be heard in the Shangri-La Valley, if the Haveners farther along the ridge hadn't been firing so heavily.

Boyle wondered if they were hitting anything, except by chance, and when their officers would realize that their men were wasting ammunition. Before that happened, the Sauron flankers had to go to work.

Boyle scanned the hillside. The heavy weapons were coming up, a rocket launcher team and a machine gun. They were a thousand meters lower than they'd been while hunting Cummings, but that gave the Haveners as well as the Soldiers more oxygen.

After the Citadel revolt, orders had come to return to Firebase Three. Three days ago they would have gone by air. Now they had to go on foot. Sauron muscles and night vision didn't help much when coping with steep slopes strewn with loose stones. Nor at night when you couldn't see the one stone that turned underfoot, until after it had you tumbling downhill, ass over apex. . . .

At least all the Soldiers who'd started the climb on to the Haveners' flank made it. Boyle saw that Sargun had withdrawn into one of his abstracted moods and took personal charge of placing the weapons.

When Sargun's mood had continued for a good five minutes and the Haveners' fire was beginning to slacken, Boyle began to get uneasy. So far they had the advantage of surprise, and ten Saurons against a hundred cattle needed every advantage they could get. More Cyborgian musing, and the cattle might notice—

"Are the heavy weapons ready to move?" Sargun asked.

Boyle managed to keep surprise out of his voice. "They arrived five minutes ago. They're in position to open fire on your order."

"*Position?*" Sargun made the word sound obscene.

"I thought—"

"You didn't think. You failed in both intellect and courage. From where we are, we can assault along the ridge. The cattle will fall before our weapons."

Boyle couldn't keep the surprise off his face. The plan had been to maneuver the flanking force into a position where the Haveners on the ridge would have to attack it. The heavy weapons should do enough damage to discourage that attack for a while.

During that time the Soldiers below could disengage and withdraw through the pass. Nearly the last pass between them and safety. Probably the last pass the Haveners could defend in force.

"Let's open fire before we risk moving," Boyle suggested, more politely than he felt. "If we draw the cattle on to us—"

"What moral advantage to that? *What*, I ask you?" Sargun almost screamed, as if he'd forgotten the presence of the enemy.

"Dead cattle are dead cattle—"

"Sauron courage cannot die! We must feed it, with our blood if necessary! Tonight it is necessary!" Sargun loomed over the weapons crews. "Prepare to advance on my command. Marching fire."

Boyle swallowed three times before he was sure his stomach was going to stay down.

Even with a surprise flank attack, ten Saurons were at risk, facing more than a hundred Haveners on their chosen ground, at night, with all the potential for confusion darkness gave. At risk—and worse, if the Haveners realized how few Saurons they faced.

All ten Soldiers could die, even if they destroyed the cattle on the ridge. Then the Soldiers below would be in danger, because they would be without more than a third of their strength, their heavy weapons, and their two senior leaders. If the Havener resistance defended any more of the passes to the lowlands, the survivors of the patrol would be lucky to see Firebase Three again.

Boyle wasn't about to risk another squad of Soldiers on the slim chance that the local resistance had exhausted its resources.

"Open fire!" he shouted. He wanted to shock the others into action before Sargun realized what was happening. If the heavy weapons opened up, the assault along the ridge line would lose surprise. Even Sargun would have to see that it was madness.

Or would he?

Little as Cyborgs dealt with emotion, Sargun was for a moment a picture of total surprise. In that moment, the machine gun opened up, and the launcher's loader slapped a round into the tube. The gunner sighted and shouted, "Fire in the hole!"

"Mutiny!" Sargun screamed.

That made the riflemen hesitate, and one man loading his grenade launcher turned to stare at his leaders. Boyle took a step backward. "Only executing previous orders. The tactical situation hasn't changed enough to justify—"

"Mutiny!" Sargun screamed again. He wheeled and aimed a kick at Boyle's knee. If it had landed, the knee would have shattered and the fight ended at once.

Boyle's knee wasn't there to be shattered. He'd wheeled in the opposite direction and sidekicked. Sargun whirled and caught Boyle's leg, but not before the foot caught him in the lower ribs.

Sargun gripped the leg, but Boyle kicked with the other foot. A combat boot drove into Sargun's jaw.

The Cyborg let Boyle fall, and he rolled downhill just far enough to make Sargun think that he was out of control. Then he braked his fall and sprang to his feet again, to meet Sargun coming downhill.

The way the Cyborg moved told Boyle two things, both of them good news. Life-or-death news. The Cyborg wasn't as at home on rough ground as Boyle, who'd grown up on the northern continent of Alberta. Also, the Cyborg's head injury had affected his sense of

balance. The two together might just give Boyle the
edge he needed.

Make that a chance, he amended, as Sargun leaped
three meters and nearly landed on top of his opponent.
Boyle risked a two-handed chop to the side of Sargun's
throat and got away with it, but that wasn't enough to
put the creature down.

*Creature. That's what I call him now. And I was
raised to think of the Cyborgs as the future form of the
Race.*

Then Boyle had to duck, dodge, and weave as Sargun
counterattacked. Any of the blows would have disabled
him, unable to avoid a lethal second blow. He was too
busy to strike back, but not too busy to notice that
Sargun was much slower than a Cyborg ought to be.

The two fighters swung around in a five-meter circle,
now one uphill, now the other. Both were now cautious
about closing, Sargun because he knew he could take
punishment but not deal it out, Boyle because he knew
he couldn't really do either. The Cyborg still had twice
his strength, if not twice his speed.

Not twice his intelligence, either. If he had, he'd
have drawn his sidearm and used it already. Mutiny
was an open-and-shut case for lethal force. If Sargun
was sticking to bare hands, it was either overconfidence
or diplomacy, and if the creature had a diplomatic cell
in his augmented body Boyle had never seen it.

Boyle's feet shot out from under him, as a patch of
scree shifted. He fell rolling downhill, saw Sargun thun-
dering downhill after him, and twisted on his buttocks
to bring his feet up.

Sargun came too fast to stop, and met Boyle's feet
with his abdomen. Breath *wsshhhed* out of him. Boyle
sprang up, gripped the Cyborg's arms, then flipped his
feet up into the creature's belly and flung himself
backward.

Boyle crashed to the ground, but Sargun went flying
over his opponent and came down headfirst. Boyle had

a tense moment wondering if he'd lost his gamble, because he'd knocked all the wind out of himself. If Sargun could so much as crawl—

He managed to reach hands and knees, and crawl downhill himself to where Sargun lay. The Cyborg's skull was a good deal flatter on one side than it had been. His head was also twisted at an impossible angle to his shoulders.

Even with such injuries, Boyle could still feel a slight pulse. The idea of giving him the final stroke barehanded was revolting, but the idea of leaving even a Cyborg for the Haveners to torture was even more so.

He'd just finished strangling Sargun into final death, when he sensed a figure above him. It was a Soldier, the launcher loader. Boyle remembered his obedience, but also remembered that he'd been one of Sargun's loyalists.

I've done my best to get the patrol home. If someone wants to shoot me now—

He thought of pulling out the First Rank's letter. That might keep him from being shot tonight. But it was still a long way to the Shangri-La Valley, plenty of time for "accidents."

Also, Boyle realized that invoking orders from on high would cost him some of the Soldiers' respect. He needed that to get them home, almost as much as he needed a safe back.

The Soldier cleared his throat. "We're out of rockets. Want we should join the firing line?"

Boyle stared. They'd brought twenty rounds uphill —no, thirty. Had they all been shot off in a couple of minutes?

"Fourth Rank, you and the Cyborg were—ah, settling your differences—for a good ten minutes."

That explains why I feel as if I'd fallen off a cliff. It doesn't explain the tactical situation.

"Have the cattle counterattacked?"

"No, Fourth Rank. We saw a bit of firing, toward the

other end of the ridge. Looks like the Soldiers in the valley went up there and made things look like a pincers movement."

Boyle limped to where he could look along the ridge. All the firing that wasn't from his position was at the far end of the ridge. Between the two bands of Saurons, the crest lay dark, silent, and maybe even empty.

The Soldier helped Boyle limp a little farther, to the radio. Assault Leader Lutz came on almost immediately.

"Squad two went up the far end of the ridge with some of those flash grenades we captured, a couple of villages back. Tried to make the cattle think we had men to spare for enveloping them."

"That was a monstrous risk!"

"Worked out all right, didn't it, Fourth Rank? They were too nervous up on the ridge to send a patrol down to count noses in the valley. I think most of them just buggered off. I've sent a patrol up to be sure."

Boyle went cold. "Who's holding the valley?"

"Me."

Boyle closed his eyes, tried to compose a scathing rebuke, then realized that he had no grounds. What did unorthodox tactics compare with killing his legal superior?

Had the killing really been necessary? If the cattle were so ready to live down to their name and shy away at phantoms, might not Sargun's assault have succeeded?

Might have. It also might have led to the disaster Boyle had feared.

There could be no sure answers, in this or anything else about war—and few answers anywhere else. Boyle resolved to remember that. He might have many years of service to the Race ahead of him. The fewer he spent worrying about what couldn't be helped, the better.

"Report!" he called. He thought he was shouting, but he had to call three times before everyone heard. He realized that his throat was too dry to do more than croak like a marshmouth.

"Soldiers. We have the pass clear. Let's take advantage of it."

"And Cyborg Sargun?" one of the riflemen asked.

Boyle stared defiantly at his Soldiers. Now was the time for any of Sargun's friends to shoot, if they wanted revenge.

"Cyborg Sargun died in combat with the enemy. He was severely wounded and flung himself down a cliff to avoid burdening us. All honor to his memory."

Or at least all honor to what he did when he was a good Soldier.

"Hail, Sargun's memory!" the rifleman said, and everyone took it up. Even Boyle joined in, until his dry throat gave him a coughing fit.

A soldier pressed a canteen on him. "Drink up, sir. We can refill at a little spring I noticed on the way up."

"Thanks. Since you know where the spring is, you take point."

"At your command, Fourth Rank."

Boyle wasn't taking point this morning. He felt so fine, with the uncommonly clear weather and the low-altitude oxygen supply, that he kept wanting to run. A patrol with two stretcher cases and five walking wounded could not keep up with a running point.

So he ran the kinks and bruises out of his legs by zigzagging back and forth in the rear of the column. The Under Assault Leader on point was the first to spot the Soldier patrol. Boyle sprinted up to the head of the column as the APC stopped and an Assault Leader climbed out.

Boyle hailed him and identified himself and his patrol. The Assault Leader was too good a Soldier to gape, but his face certainly worked for a moment.

"We thought you all were lost. The cattle claimed the destruction of a Sauron patrol in the Burnt Rock Pass."

"The reports of our death were greatly exaggerated,

but we maintained radio silence after we crossed the pass. I wanted to make the cattle think we were dead."

Boyle looked at the APC. "Improvised" was a kind word for it; it was a local all-terrain six-wheeler with rough appliqué armor and a ring mounting on the roof that looked as if it had been machined in the dark and installed by a drunk.

The Assault Leader was studying the patrol. "Where is Cyborg Sargun? All Cyborgs have been ordered to report to the Citadel at once."

"What for?"

"Didn't you hear about the Revolt?"

"I heard rumors, but no details. That's why we walked out; Firebase Three cut off our air support."

"Let me fill you in, Fourth Rank."

The rest of the patrol gathered around to listen to a brief and—Boyle suspected—garbled account of the Cyborg revolt. Zold was dead, Koln loyal, many breeders dead and some escaped, but one of Cummings' regiments brought to battle and in the end nearly destroyed.

When the Assault Leader was finished, Boyle nodded. "That explains why we fought only local units the last half of the patrol. I suppose we owe the rebel Cyborgs a vote of thanks. But thinking they could rule on Haven . . ." He shook his head.

"That's what comes of getting a superiority complex in your genes, instead of working for it," the Assault Leader said. "By the way, what *did* happen to Sargun?"

Boyle couldn't risk turning his back on the Assault Leader to judge the reactions of his Soldiers. With the Cyborgs clearly disgraced, if nothing worse, nothing would happen to him for telling the truth. Nothing official, anyway.

But again there was the respect of the Soldiers he'd led through so much to think about. Consistency might get him into trouble with the authorities; anything else would lose him hard-earned respect from some fine Soldiers.

"Cyborg Sargun was killed in action at Burnt Rock Pass. He was mortally wounded, and threw himself off a cliff rather than burden us or risk capture."

"Hmmmp. There's courage in the breed, I'll admit. Just don't spread that story around, though. This is no time to get Soldiers thinking of Cyborgs as martyrs."

Boyle wanted to laugh, but coughed instead. Another side of command they didn't teach at school: information as a weapon. Hold it back or spread it out, you needed to give as much thought to information as you did to ammunition.

The Assault Leader was going on, about plans to regularly assign women to Soldiers for breeding. Boyle listened with half his attention, the rest on his Soldiers.

The ones who had the habit of smiling mostly were, except for the wounded or exhausted. The rest—well, approval was hard to judge. But their body language said a good deal, and most of that was:

Well done, Fourth Rank Boyle.

Boyle turned back to the Assault Leader, who was now rambling on about the delights of a harem. Boyle didn't much care whether the new breeding program gave him one woman or fifty. He cared a great deal about whether he could find words to teach this campaign's lessons to the Soldiers those women would bear him.

From *the diary of Martha Rhodes*

Today was a bad day for Willhold. My best friend Kate was killed by the savages. We caught them red-handed stealing our supplies again. This time we were ready. We killed a whole bunch. Poor Kate was reloading crossbows when a stray arrow caught her in the eye—it was horrible!

This is an awful place and I hate my father for bringing us all here!

I was only six when he took us from our home in Castell City, but I keep every precious memory of those days in my mind as though they were shimmer stones. I remember wall screens with voices and moving pictures—my brother Jim says I'm a liar, but he's only ten so what does he know anyhow?

I'm seventeen years old now, but they still treat me like a child. When Willie asked for my hand last spring, Father told him *I* was too young! I'm old enough to remember the good old days—even if *they* won't talk about them.

I can still see boats that fly in the sky, and wagons that float on a bed of air ... Sure the little ones don't believe, but Kate did—she ... remembered ... them too. Now they'll all think I'm crazy! To Hell with them; we'll everyone of us be dead in this horrible place soon enough. I can feel it in my breast. It's always cold here, even when the sun shines your fingers and toes turn blue. What kind of place was this to bring a family?

Stoves that cooked in minutes, with *real* flames. Talking pictures on the wall so I could talk to my friends and Granny. Machines that talked and walked. Most of the elders have forgotten—so *they* say!—or won't admit the truth. Father gets very angry when I bring them up so mostly I just keep them in my head, where no one *here* can touch them.

It was the evil King Steele who convinced my Father to start the hold with six other families. Now there's only four of the original families left. The Stones left the second year after their baby died; the Krenshaws were killed in an ambush this spring while driving the wagons to Morgan Town. Daddy says that's the last trip to Morgan; they're going to have to come here from now on. I just know they won't; who would ever come to this ugly scratch of a village if they didn't have to?

How will I ever see Willie again? If the traders ever come, like Father claims, I'm leaving with them. I won't let this terrible place kill me, too!

There is nothing left here to hold me now. Kate, poor Kate . . . I miss you already. I won't forget you! You'll live in my mind along with all my other precious memories. I promise, Kate. I promise.

STRONG BLOOD

G.C. EDMONDSON

It was during that time of year when wise folk stay in camp and slurp pemmican soup, which can be tasty if the women who pound the dried meat and suet are fortunate enough to find a stand of wild onions. Otherwise, the concentration of fat and protein with barely enough berries to stave off scurvy is nourishing, but with about as much gustatory appeal as wet cardboard.

Ten-year-old Jerôme wished he was in winter camp somewhere enjoying unlimited pemmican but instead, he squatted, incompletely sheltered from the mild but biting wind by a single 'lope hide at his back. The primary was too low and the gas giant too occulted. Defying the faint breeze, an ice mist lay tenaciously over the real ice.

An hour ago the boy had heard the faint, hair-raising howls of a tas-wolf pack on the prowl. But they must have gone the other way for he had heard nothing since. The cold was so severe that he was forced every few minutes to poke his spear down through the yard-thick ice to keep the hole open. He had done this enough times to eradicate the last whiff of blood from his spear, which probably accounted for the tas-wolves' lack of interest. The boy was about to clear ice again when he felt a tug on the line.

He held his breath, praying this one would hook itself instead of just stealing bait. The fish nibbled and played with the bait, seemed to reject it, and finally bit. Jerôme gave a jerk and knew he had it. Hauling hastily, he had the fish halfway up the hole when it jammed against the unbroken ice. From the bony, spearshaped head he knew it was a jack. Not the best eating but the boy was in no position to quibble. Holding the line with one hand, he struggled to chip fresh frozen ice and enlarge the hole with the other.

At first the fish struggled but by the time he had cleared the hole it had frozen into an awkward half moon straining shape that forced him to chip the hole even wider. Finally the foot-long jack lay beside him on the windswept ice, tentacles frozen in mid-writhe like some narcissistic Medusa. Jerôme studied the brighter portion of the sky where Cat's Eye struggled vainly to punch through the mist and knew it would turn colder in another hour. He tossed the fish into his sack along with the other two and began trudging back to camp.

Camp consisted of two *tipis* constructed of oilplant stalks covered with every hide not needed for other purposes. Even multiple layers of muskylope with the hair on could not make a *tipi* warm in this kind of weather. Heat rose in these conical structures, sneaking out the smoke flap and leaving the inhabitants to shiver no matter how high-banked was the snow and earth around the edges of the lodge. Yet the Cree had stuck stubbornly by them for millenia, shivering and muttering over-the-shoulder curses at the Manitou while ignoring their northern neighbors who dressed differently, ate differently, and were warlocks and witches since how, without supernatural help, could those shortbodied, shortlegged folk come down laughing and cheerful from the north where it really got cold? Such were the strangers' disgusting habits that they were called "eats raw meat" which, in Cree, is pronounced *eskimo*.

But Jerôme had learned this all secondhand from tribal legends and campfire tales. The Bureloc had never rounded up any Inuit six hundred years ago when their sweeps removed dissidents and slackers alike from Old Terra. Those hardy hunters had undergone a cultural revival and pulled out of the CoDominium—back into the trackless north as civilization became increasingly unbearable. The Cree had not, so now they were on Haven along with Apaches, Arabs, and anyone whose presence the old CoDominium had found inconvenient. For the last three years they had also shared the planet with the Saurons.

Haven had never been a misprint for heaven. The entire planet had sustained a bare twenty million when the Saurons, on the run from a lost war and seeking whatever bolt hole they could find had settled on Haven. To prepare those twenty million for the new order the Saurons had blown every protein factory and every starch stand off the face of Haven. Five and a half million starved during the first winter of Sauron occupation.

Haveners who thought about such things, which meant everyone still alive, calculated and extrapolated. Without the Empire's daily ration of synthetic swill the planet could, at best, support six million—providing those six million mastered stone age techniques of hunting and gathering since all heavy industry had been taken out in the same strike that put an end to the unfree lunch. By the third year of Sauron occupation Haven's population was down to the projected level. Out in the boondocks, away from the relatively amenable climate of Shangri La the first year brought little change. Nomadic peoples living a marginal life were annoyed by city and farm folk overrunning their trap lines but most of the refugees did not live long enough to disrupt the nomads' lives.

It was during the second winter of the Sauron presence that the survivors were winnowed out and tough enough to push the nomads off into the low-rent districts far north of the Shangri La Valley and beyond the distant range of the Atlas. Which in turn pushed little

Jerôme's band that much farther north—up into the uninhabitable swamps that surrounded the North Sea. The air was so thin at this altitude that it was almost impossible to start a fire. Once ignited, it required constant fanning and infusion of pitch or animal fats to keep the wood burning.

Jerôme flexed a sheen of ice off his mittens and made a snowball which he overhanded against the stiff-frozen skin of the smaller *tipi*. Thus warned, presumably the inhabitants would not spear him before he could finish crawling through the flap. When he got inside his eyes took half an eternity to adjust to the darkness. Why, he wondered, had his mother let the fire die so low? He found a sliver of pitch-kindling and blew the coals into life. And saw why she had let it die so low. Jerôme's *maman* would never cook another meal.

Life wounds. Scar tissue forms and after a while one learns to accept the inevitable. But not at age ten. Fish forgotten, Jerôme rushed from the *tipi* and without pausing traversed the ten meters to the larger *tipi*. "*Oncle* Antoine!" he shrieked as he forced the flap open. Then he saw the dead-cold ashes and remembered that his uncle had already taken the Sky Path. His two aunts, one *Oncle* Antoine's sister and the other the old man's wife, had died over a week ago.

The old man had been too feeble to do what should have been done. There were no large trees handy and even had there been, ten-year-old Jerôme could never have gotten the stiffened corpses in position in a crotch. In the warmth of the *tipi* they had become unbearable after the third day so, with *Oncle* Antoine's reluctant acquiescence Jerôme had rolled and levered the two old ladies onto a toboggan and dragged them a kilometer out onto the ice. The theory was that when spring breakup came the Manitou would give them a decent burial at the bottom of the lake. But of course, the tas-wolves had gotten there first.

Something had gotten to *Oncle* Antoine since Jerôme

had last been in this *tipi*. It did not look like a wolf. But the old man's flint-frozen face had been nibbled at. Eyes were pecked out. Lips had been chewed away to reveal ground-down teeth in an unnatural grin. His nose and earlobes had also been shredded by small teeth. There was a sudden buzz and Jerôme collapsed into a fetal ball of panic as something huge screed and flapped past him and out into thin-aired twilight.

Minutes later the chill brought him to his feet. There would be no help from here. He went back to his mother's *tipi*. In his frantic rush he had left the flap gaping and now it was as cold inside as outside. He looked at the shrinking woodpile and knew tomorrow he would have to do something about that, too. But right now he had to get some food into himself.

Once the fire was reviving he hung his three fish above the tiny flame where they would defrost enough for him to skin and gut them. Meanwhile, he looked to his mother.

It had been a cruel winter. More so because of cruel men driven beyond their limits by Sauron excesses. Although Jerôme's band had never actually encountered a Sauron, their planetary strike had sent a shock rippling round the planet, pushing a rolling wave of starving people ahead of it. At first frost Jerôme's band had numbered twenty-two, of which nine were able-bodied men. Eleven had been women of varying ages and the other two had been ten-year-old Jerôme and his *Oncle* Antoine who could not remember how old he was. After a summer of slim pickings, moving always farther north where it froze even in summer and the air was too thin for parturition, *Oncle* Antoine had been anxious to get past the barrens even if it meant venturing into the near-impossible swamps surrounding the North Sea. It was, at minimum, a place where they could count on being left alone.

But those Sodbusters a day's ride beyond the last

palisaded settlement had been too tempting. This far north they had missed out on the orbital bombing. Whole barnloads of winter forage, *ristras* of tobacco and chiles and onions and other treasures draped from walls and fences, just waited to be taken. Even to ten-year-old Jerôme it had seemed too good to be true.

It was.

When the first raid succeeded beyond *Oncle* Antoine's wildest expectations they came back for seconds. And the Sodbusters were loaded for bear. Lightly armed so they could carry off more, the Lafranche band was first distracted from their looting by an unannounced blizzard of slung stones. Boiled-leather armor immediately demonstrated its inadequacy when three men and a woman went down in the first volley. One man regained his feet just in time to catch the first of the short, heavy crossbow quarrels that next came at the raiders from three sides.

Retreating in the only direction that lay open, the Lafranche band abruptly found themselves thigh-deep in a wild grain bog. The Sodbusters came at them in pirogues, drawing long bows with even longer brush-penetrating arrows whose sectional density was even more demonstrative of the inadequacy of fried-leather armor. One arrow went through Jerôme's father's muskylope breastplate and emerged from that heavy built man's back, stopping only when its leather fletching snagged at his chest. More pirogues came snaking through the grass and women of the Sodbuster colony belabored the surviving raiders with the heavy sticks with which they thrashed wild grain heads into canoes.

Home in camp, ten-year-old Jerôme refused to believe it. Four men and three women had returned, bedraggled, mud-smeared, bloody, bearing neither arms nor loot. Jerôme sat up all night waiting for the others to come home. Those already there did not waste time. They hit the trail at first light, making tracks before the Sodbusters could follow up on their advantage.

Shorthanded and short-rationed was no way to start a winter in even the nicer parts of Haven. Thus, despite his band's ingrained distaste for fish, Jerôme had been fishing. His catch was dripping now, and had relaxed from the agonized shapes into which it had frozen to death. He gutted it and managed a halfhearted job of skinning before letting the three small jacks swing back over the fire. When tentacles began to crackle he snatched the smallest in mittened hands, waved it about for a minute, and began chewing before it could freeze again.

Maman lay relaxed in her half-open blankets, almost as if she were sleeping. But Jerôme knew better. Like the others, one by one, *maman* had starved to death. Jerôme was the last surviving member of this branch of the Lafranche band. He ate the second-largest fish, grumbling at the armored boniness of the jack's huge head. He was eating the last claw when abruptly Jerôme realized he was no longer alone.

Cautiously, he glanced around. The smoke flap was just barely cracked. The door flap was secure and tied behind him. The 'dactyl must have taken refuge from the cold and the rising wind when he had panicked and rushed out, leaving the flap open. It must have been here all this time.

It was a huge 'dactyl, over a meter tall and with a wingspan that could bear away a muskylope calf. This leathery-winged marsupial had claws on its leading edges, and was as savage as most of the local fauna. With ten-year-old hindsight, Jerôme knew this was what had bowled him over in *Oncle* Antoine's *tipi*. He also abruptly guessed that this animal who entered *tipis* and was not shy around humans must once have been someone's pet. "So what do you do here, brother " he asked.

The Lafranche band's usual range was farther north than other nomads, and they had had minimal contact with the more southerly rovers. Little Jerôme had heard the older men speak of spirit-talk but none of the

Lafranches claimed that ability. With the pragmatism that derives from a single decade of existence, little Jérôme's attitude was, "I've never seen it, therefore it does not exist." Thus he was totally unprepared when the 'dactyl replied.

"It's because I'm not used to being alone," Jérôme told himself. "Or maybe I'm going to die of the blood cough like *Tante* Marie. Or maybe if I had another fish or a piece of meat to fill my belly I wouldn't imagine things like this."

"You are not Cree," the 'dactyl spirit-spoke.

"*Métis*," Jérôme said. "*Ma mère fut nettement française.*"

"Then," the 'dactyl said, "the white side of your brain will convince you that you're hallucinating and that none of this really happened."

Jérôme was inclined to agree with this.

"But you will be wrong. Don't you know what all Indians know?"

"Maybe."

"*Jérôme, mon fils, je viens de dire ton nom.*"

"So you have spoken my name. What's yours?"

Lightning flashed briefly in the 'dactyl's eyes as a nictitating membrane closed and opened. With the proto-avian equivalent of a shrug the 'dactyl said, "Weeti."

"All right, Weeti. Now what?"

"Now begins your education—providing you don't freeze to death tonight."

It was already too cold and too dark to think about hunting more firewood. Jérôme found his blankets and began laying himself out as close to the tiny fire as he dared.

"Plan ahead, boy," Weeti spirit-spoke.

"I'm doing my best."

"*Maman's* blankets too, boy. Do you think she still needs them?"

As he buried himself in the robes and slowly began to feel warmer it abruptly occurred to Jérôme that the 'dactyl's spirit-voice sounded just like *Oncle* Antoine.

*   *   *

Hunger almost satisfied, Jerôme fell asleep and dreamed that he had been talking with a 'dactyl. From some reserves of his subconscious he recalled other bits of esoteric Cree knowledge. The 'dactyl had spoken his name. Of course he knew what that meant. Everybody knew that! Yet, despite his desperate situation Jerôme was calmly certain that he was not going to die. Other people sickened. Others were struck down by arrow or blade. Not Jerôme. He'd been around for ten years and it hadn't happened yet. Therefore it was never going to happen.

The faint growing light cast a glow through the upper part of the *tipi* where the greased skins were only one layer thick. Jerôme stretched and heard the tinkle as frozen breath shattered off the outer side of his tas-wolf robe. To the uninitiated these robes of inch-wide twisted strips of winter fur seemed useless. Woven so loosely that a finger could be poked through at any point, they seemed totally incapable of tempering the minus sixty of this prairie. Yet, unlike blankets, a wolf robe never absorbed perspiration, never became soggy, did not hold dirt, and was inhospitable to vermin.

Without conscious thought, Jerôme stepped out of the tipi and spread his robe to the morning air. Immediately the moisture of a night's sleeping turned to frost which fluttered to the ground like a miniature snowstorm when he shook the robe. Freeze-dried and clean of all vermin, he rolled it and took it back inside the *tipi*.

Weeti—funny how he remembered that name. Had the 'dactyl really spoken to him? The 'dactyl was eating. It took Jerôme an instant to realize what the beast was eating. Then he realized there was only one piece of flesh in this *tipi*.

This morning the carnivorous marsupial did not spirit-talk him, leaving Jerôme sure that it had never happened. But what was a 'dactyl doing inside a *tipi*? Then he knew. Tight-tied flaps and the smoke of fires kept most predators away. The fire had been out for days in *Oncle* Antoine's *tipi*. With game scarce, the 'dactyl was no respector of persons. Now that the fire had gone out in this *tipi* too, the 'dactyl was having breakfast from *Maman*'s marble-hard corpse.

"No time to be delicate, boy. The dead are dead. If she were alive she'd want you to live."

It had to be hunger. He was dizzy and starting to see double. But whether the message was coming from a 'dactyl or his own subconscious, Jerôme knew it was simple truth. He had been warm as long as he slept wrapped in enough coverings for two people but now the cold was getting to him. Before he could muster energy to go hunt firewood or more fish, Jerôme had to get something into his stomach. In the dim light of the *tipi* he found the axe and began hacking.

Frozen raw liver is of the crunchy consistency of a popsicle, less difficult to chew than plain ice. It is also infinitely more nourishing. Without further comment, the 'dactyl cleaned up the bits and pieces left where Jerôme's hasty ill-aimed axe had failed to hit twice in the same groove. The meter-high carnivorous marsupial still roosted atop a berrying basket hung from the sloping *tipi* wall when Jerôme had rested and felt strength returning. He took the flesh-fouled axe and went to look for dry wood.

Among the extraordinary fantasies which humans are capable of believing, the myth of a balanced diet is right in there with other true whoppers. Explorers starved on ancient Earth, lost teeth and skin from scurvy, had expedition after expedition fail for lack of supplies before one white man asked what, in hind sight, seemed an obvious question: if vitamins and lime juice and green vegetables are all necessary to sustain health, how do Eskimos, who've never seen a green vegetable, manage to live long, happy lives and die with a mouthful of teeth?

When Vilhjalmur Stefansson who, despite his Icelandic name was an American, considered this question he went native and learned the secret, which is no secret at all to any Argentine gaucho.

When primitive hunters made a kill the cuts normally found in a supermarket—steaks, chops, roasts, and other muscle-meat were given to the dogs. Organ meats had higher and better flavor. Liver, kidneys, lungs and spleen, brains, guts, reproductive organs, and other items not normally on civilized menus contained all the vitamins necessary for a balanced diet. Thus Jerôme survived the winter by eating first his mother, then his uncle—from the inside out.

It was not easy. Gathering firewood took the greater part of each short day. And his people had all died of hunger, leaving lean stringy bodies without an ounce of fat.

Fat in Haven's clime is essential. In winter the overlong, folded-back sleeve of a parka forms a pocket always stocked with whatever fat is available. Those who have not endured a Haven winter forget that, though it is possible to wear layers of furs and protect one's exterior from cold, no one has yet devised a fur lining for lungs. Each icy breath exits warmed, carrying away calories at such a rate that it is difficult to move in the open without dipping into that parka cuff for a mouthful of fat every ten minutes or so. Finally Jerôme caught a semi-dormant spiny boar and gorged himself on its oozy, juniper-gin-tasting oil which possesses the virtue of not hardening no matter how cold the weather.

But if the short days were hard, the nights were harder. No matter how cold and hungry, it's difficult to remain motionless, wrapped in wolf robes for the nearly week-long stretch of a midwinter night on Haven. Especially at age ten. On the colder clear nights when the wind died and the Kotsnaku took advantage of the interval to threaten Manitou with his fiery war dances, the dry air was so charged with mana that skin prickled and hair stood on end. The gods and demons charged and countercharged across the sky, rattling and shaking fiery blankets at one another until the whole sky rippled with fire and the very air hissed. Night after night the Sky People squabbled, never once paying the slightest heed to men below who lived out their lives unable to fly through the sky or fling shafts of aurora at one another. Nights like this Jerôme would take *Oncle* Antoine's bow and shoot a couple of arrows into the northern sky. "I am here!" he hissed, just as Their light shows hissed and made little balls of fire balance on treetops. "I am alive. Someday I will eat Your liver!"

When the winter was over and game no longer in hibernation the lonely boy speared a pair of bearcat cubs and, while their meat was drying in the smoke of the *tipi* fire he used their hides to patch out his clothing which was falling apart after a winter without *maman* to mend things. With Weeti watching silently from a nearby tree, the boy bundled together the bones and skin that remained of his family and wrapped them in the oldest of his aunts' sleeping robes. Then, seeing Weeti's huge round eyes studying the bundle Jerôme knew he would be barely out of sight before some scavenger had undone his work.

These bits of skin and bone were just that, nothing more. But they had been Jerôme's family, the sole surviving members so far as he knew of the Lafranche band. They deserved some respect. Before breaking camp he put them all into the biggest *tipi* and piled enough wireweed around it to ensure a proper holocaust.

Weeti had not spirit-talked the boy for close to a month now. As his potbelly smoothed from better diet Jerôme was increasingly unable to believe it had ever happened. Starved as he was, he must have just imagined it all. Still, the 'dactyl stuck with him. Together, they had survived the winter. He was not surprised when, ten miles south on his march to get out of here before spring thaw and spring biters turned this region

into a muddy branch office of hell, Jerôme once more
saw the 'dactyl roosting on a scrub hangman bush just
beyond the smoke of his campfire.

Jerôme awoke suddenly in the midst of a nightmare.
Then he realized it was really happening. The 'dactyl
perched on his chest, claws locked in the boy's buck-
skin shirt. Saucer-round eyes stared unblinking into
Jerôme's.

The boy did not know whether it was spirit-talk or
just common sense. He rolled away from the fire, snatching robe and spear as he oozed away from the faintly
glowing coals. From the phase of the Cat's Eye, he had
been sleeping about six hours, which meant at least
three more hours before full daylight. Whoever or whatever was out there in the semi-dark . . .

Jerôme willed his mind blank and receptive. Nothing. What good was spirit-talk if it did not work when
he needed it? There wasn't any such thing anyhow; he
was sure of that now. Breathing shallow, lest he send
too far a scent, Jerôme was sure he smelled something
familiar. An instant later when a muskylope trumpeted
through blubbery lips he knew what that smell was. If
Jerôme could just slip around and get that muskylope
while somebody was out there in the brush still creeping up on his fire . . .

Then came the answering trumpeting of another
muskylope in the opposite direction. Jerôme froze. They
were all around him. He could not remember the route
too well but Jerôme thought he was fairly close to that
place where the Lafranche band had come to grief
against the Sodbusters. Should have circled well around
it. But it was too late now for afterthoughts.

"*Personne.*" The voice was low but Jerôme recognized the overly nasalized *joual* that had been native to
the Lafranche band. He swallowed his sudden hopes
and waited.

"Only one, no muskylope. Short fellow. Maybe a

woman." These observations came from a second voice. In the distance light flared and Jerôme realized someone had ignited a torch from his dying fire.

"One of ours?" the first voice asked.

"Who else? Would a Sodbuster be out here alone? *Hey ami!*" he called in a soft voice. "You out there in the bush. *Est ce que vous êtez des Lafranche?*"

"Who wants to know?" Jerôme called.

"Marc-Antoine, chef-Lafranche."

"Over here, Uncle."

"Weetigo!" an old woman muttered when the dozen Lafranches in Marc-Antoine's group learned how Jerôme had survived the winter. Cannibalism was an everpresent spectre in a country where flesh freezes and corpses are an eternal temptation in lean times. Every tribe had its own repertory of horror stories, of supernatural anthropophagous monsters. To preserve sanity at the sight of a camp full of half-eaten corpses it was necessary to create monsters, legends, devils—anything but admit that humans just like ourselves had done this, done it so often that someday surely we might do it too.

Next winter was just as bad. Worse, since Marc-Antoine had not reduced the number of mouths in his group with some disastrous battle. They had been shot at several times by muskylope-mounted militia but no one had been hit and the cavalry were unwilling to mire their beasts in the mud which became a refuge for the Lafranche.

After solstice it was obvious that Marc-Antoine's dozen, plus Jerôme added up to an unlucky number. They had accepted the boy. He was, after all, a Lafranche, and his parents had been close kin. But there was always a certain reserve. That boyish, innocent face had eaten forbidden things. That he was doggedly followed by an ill-omened carnivorous marsupial did not enhance the boy's status. It was possible that the boy might grow up to be a warrior. More probable, most agreed, that Jerôme would become a warlock.

But as winter turned the ice flinty and game disappeared the boy increasingly took over. Old Gisèle, who had pronounced him *weetigo*, was first to succumb. Quietly, as befitted an old lady, she had expired in her sleep. After the wake Marc-Antoine had supervised the wrapping and her pall had been lifted into the fork of the nearest winter-bare backstabber bush. A week later her husband, an ancient with abundant silvery hair also named Jerôme, had grown weary of life without her.

Over the next month Marc-Antoine had eyed eleven-year-old Jerôme quietly, studiously, without pronouncing judgment. The others grew thin; short of breath, hectic of cheek. Young Jerôme remained cheerful and healthy, managing always to do more than an eleven-year-old's share of the work of breaking ice to bring water, sweeping snow aside to hunt for dry wood, and the constant round of the traps looking both for furs and edible animals. There were not enough of either.

"You've been eating well and steadily, haven't you?" Marc-Antoine asked one night when the others had fallen into the restless sleep of hunger.

Jerôme made no effort to deny it.

"Who?"

"*N'importe pas.* When you're ready you'll all fight over my leavin's."

"I hope it doesn't come to that," Marc-Antoine said.

"So did I. But it did and I did and I'm alive. I plan on stayin' that way."

"Can you really spirit-talk that 'dactyl?"

The eleven-year-old shrugged. "You really believe that kind of stuff?"

Marc-Antoine was not sure what he believed. Once years ago an itinerant priest had described heaven and hell. In spite of the priest's badmouthing, the latter seemed possessed of a more amenable climate and more interesting companions. Someone else had once told Marc-Antoine that a true mark of leadership was to believe three impossible things before breakfast. But there had been no breakfast today. "I wouldn't go tellin' t'others about it just yet," the *chef* warned.

Jerôme took this warning to heart. He also brought Marc-Antoine a small gift of raw liver a couple of hours later.

A week later the surviving Lafranches grumbled among themselves and found it difficult to look young Jerôme in the face but they all ate of the stew he provided and nobody asked where the meat was coming from. The equinox came with no letup in the sub-zero weather and the daily meat ration turned into a thin, unsalted broth boiled from bones. The older, less active Lafranches studied one another from sidelong eyes. Some wondered why they didn't boil up that damned 'dactyl that hung about the camp but none dared suggest it.

Another month passed and still no hint of thaw. Jerôme was the only survivor strong enough to keep a hole punched through the yard-thick ice but his fishing was not sufficient to keep them all alive. He took to throwing the fish whole in with the bone stew to lend some remembrance of nourishment. Toothless oldsters complained of off flavor as they choked on fish bones.

Marc-Antoine's teeth had loosened badly. In the middle of one night of blustery wind he awoke bent double with a sharp abdominal pain. Jerôme punched up the fire and their eyes met. Each knew what the other was thinking. "You were right," the *chef* told the boy. "Go ahead and do it."

"But *chef*," Jerôme protested, "spring will come. Who then will lead us on the hunt?"

The spasm of acute appendicitis pain passed momentarily and Marc-Antoine relaxed at this reprieve. He was catching a long sighing breath when Jerôme drove the knife into his back.

Spring breakup came about the time Marc-Antoine was finished. Jerôme began to bring home snow lizards, nooraks, spiny boar, and an occasional wild muskylope calf. Within a week the surviving Lafranches had fleshed out enough to pull their weight and hunting began in earnest. And a deep sense of embarrassment settled over the Lafranche band.

They found it difficult to meet their savior's eyes. All were willing to admit that, had it not been for Jerôme they would not be alive. They could admit that his hard young head had seen and clearly distinguished the dreadful choice between *should* and *must*. What they could not admit in so many words—not even to themselves—was that after months of Jerôme' exotic high-flavored meats, the stringy, fat-free spring herbivores they were eating now was pretty poor stuff.

At twelve Jerôme was the acknowledged leader of the Lafranche band. Weeti's position was less clearly defined but no one these days ever thought of eating the 'dactyl. Trekking back south on foot, they moved slowly, putting on fat at about the same rate as the winter-starved animals they hunted. Emerging from the worst of the swamps, the band chanced upon a muskylope.

From its looks and tack Jerôme took the gelding for a survivor from some Sauron battle. The animal was slightly below ideal riding stature and still bore the remains of a bridle it had not quite managed to shuffle off. The saddle marks were prominent. While the band spread out in an effort to surround the beast, Weeti launched himself from a nearby backstabber bush and soared, landing easily on the muskylope's back. Instead of flinching, the animal trotted directly toward Jerôme and nuzzled his shoulder.

Weeti had not spirit-spoken Jerôme for nearly a year, leaving the boy increasingly convinced that it had all been hallucinations and hunger. These days he had other, more pressing concerns. At twelve Jerôme had become abruptly and acutely aware that some parts of his rapidly growing body could be made to serve other than their prosaic tasks of elimination. And the Lafranche women of childbearing age were all of a ferocious determination to bear *his* child. It was heady stuff for a twelve-year-old.

Jerôme tore his mind back to here and now, wondering what had suddenly alarmed him. Then he knew. The thin-aired, barely perceptible breeze was wafting an odor of wood smoke. Mounted on the beast, he signaled his still-afoot clansmen. With no need for detailed instructions, the women took the bulk of the baggage into the midst of a strangleberry thicket, evicting a ground-covering mass of foot-long snapping worms as they burrowed into invisibility.

It was not a town. Three houses with barns, stables and other outbuildings faced inward on a small square. Their heavy-beamed, pointed-topped outer walls of vertical logs formed the palisade. The only entry into the town was through a gate which stood open.

Three houses . . . as few as three men or as many as twenty . . . The able-bodied fighting men in Jerôme's band presently numbered fifteen. All older than Jerôme, of course, but all sufficiently dull and docile to offer his primacy no resistance. It was midmorning. Jerôme decided to sit it out behind this slight rise and see how many came back into the fort for lunch.

The fields seemed deserted. Ryticale was just beginning to straighten after months of "stooling," creeping furtive as strawberry runners along the ground waiting for the snow to melt off. To walk in those fields now would do nothing apart from destroy grain and create knee-deep footprints. Which meant the men were off hunting, off on a trading expedition to the nearest walled town—or manning that stockade just waiting for the Lafranche band to come within range.

The 'dactyl returned from one of its patrol sweeps and flared wings to land on Jerôme's cuir bouilli clad shoulder. The left shoulder of his armor was white from the digging of Weeti's claws and from the 'dactyl's uninhibited droppings. The 'dactyl emitted a grating shriek and for an instant Jerôme's mind gyred and wyvvered as it had during that first awful time. Then he saw what Weeti was looking at.

Coming boldly over the hill, doing what Jerôme would have done if he'd had more men, more muskylopes, and more experience, twelve nomads on midsize mounts moved toward the gate at a smart trot, lances at ready.

There was no outcry from the stockade. Jerôme hunkered down behind his hill and thanked whatever demons saw fit to protect him. He could have been trying to get in there and have these defenders trot in right behind him at the worst possible moment. Then abruptly his perception shattered again. When the dozen nomads were less than a hundred yards away there was an off-key blat of a trumpet or possibly a conch shell and the gates slammed shut just as the first hail of slingstones came whizzing from behind the palisade.

The lightly-armed nomads were totally unprepared. Some bore lightweight targets which they held overhead like hats. Which did not help when stones, peppered increasingly with darts, crossbow quarrels, and arrows converted their unarmored muskylopes into panicked, screaming kicking nightmares that forced the nomads to jump clear and run, some even leaving weapons behind.

"To Kattihaw, *to Kattihaw!*" a foghorn herald's voice roared, and those who could retreated beyond range to re-form. Two men and three muskylopes were still out there under the walls, animals screaming and kicking and the men struggling feebly to crawl out of range of flashing hooves. From the slightly higher palisade alongside the gate an archer pulled a longbow and one man stopped moving. It took three arrows before the defending archer finished off the second raider.

The Lafranche men had no difficulty imagining themselves down there on the killing field instead of these strangers. Jerôme had worried that they might think him too cautious for a leader but he could sense that his stock was rapidly rising. It was nice to be liked.

Abruptly the strangers became aware that they had an audience. Immediately they formed up, wounds forgotten as they faced a new enemy. At a walk, the tiny squadron began advancing toward the knoll behind which the Lafranche band rested. Weeti launched himself from Jerôme's shoulder, swept in a wide arc over the riders and, true as a boomerang, completed his circle with a flared-wing landing on his friend's shoulder. Jerôme suspected any stranger would be at least as awed by a tame 'dactyl as were his own people. He was also the only one mounted. He rode out to meet the nomads.

"What do you here?" the red-mustached nomad leader asked in trade Imperial.

"*Même comme vous*," Jerôme said, then switched to Imperial when it became obvious that the nomad leader did not understand *joual*. "The same as you. We were studying how to learn the strength of the town when you most kindly came along to show us."

"You ain't workin' for theyum Sodbusters, then?"

Jerôme shook his head. Those of the Lafranche band who understood Imperial found this idea hilarious.

The nomad leader's eyes narrowed. "If'n you ain't Sodbusters, then where's your muskylopes?"

"It's a long story that grows no nicer with the telling."

"So you had to eat 'em theyun?"

"Among other things."

Until this moment Jerôme had not realized his talent as a standup comedian. His fellow clansmen were in stitches. He turned and something in his eyes brought the snickers and giggles to an abrupt end.

It was at this moment that Red Mustache first realized he was talking to a fellow chief and not to some twelve-year-old messenger. "Well," he began. "Looks like we'uns bit off a little more'n we could chaw. 'Thout muskylopes I don't reckon you'd be havin' much luck either. What say we throw in together?"

"Who gets what?" Jerôme asked.

"Waal, they's fifteen of you'uns and ten of us. But you ain' got but one gelding and he's gittin long in the tooth. We'uns figger a muskylope is just as good as a man."

"In that case I'll trade you five men for five muskylopes," Jerôme said.

Les Kattihaw laughed, then realized Jerôme was not joking. "How you fixed for women?" he asked.

Too fucking many of them and they all want to do it under my blanket. But Jerôme was leader enough not to voice this opinion in front of his men. "We'll both know that better after we take the farm, won't we?"

"I s'pose you're right," Kattihaw agreed, "and they ain't no use dividing the booty until the battle's won. Y'all in for halves?"

For form's sake Jerôme glanced around at his clansmen before he nodded. They spent the rest of the daylight making fire arrows tipped with packets of dried muskylope dung wrapped in dried willow bark and soaked in a mixture of tallow and pitch.

Under cover of darkness they crept closer to the stockade and the Kattihaws salvaged what gear they could from dead men and dead muskylopes. While a mixed bag of the best archers from the Lafranche band and the best of the Kattihaw circled to concentrate their fire on the rear of the holding where the palisade was slightly lower, Jerôme and Armand, who was the strongest man in the band, manhandled two barrels of the same combustible with which they had tipped the arrows up against the wooden pillars that sustained the single spike-studded gate. To Kattihaw's delight and Jerôme's mild surprise, everything worked out as planned.

Even though the defenders had been expecting just such an attack, the thoroughness of it was overwhelming. With everyone scurrying about in the darkness pulling out fire arrows and beating down flames it was too late before they knew what was really going on. The palisade on each side of the gate was in flames. The fire was too far along to be inconvenienced by a few ill-aimed buckets of water. Still, they had to face the Sodbusters.

"To every man upon this earth
    Death cometh soon or late.
And how can man die better
    Than facing fearful odds,
For the ashes of his fathers,
    And the temples of his gods."

Lafranches and Kattihaws poured through the collapsing gate to a reception of boiling bran which, flung from a ladle, possesses a diabolic ability to stick until skin and flesh are cooked enough to fall from bone. The Kattihaws had mostly swords and hangers, and slightly more cuir bouilli armor than the Lafranche band whose recent hard times were reflected in their relative lack of armor and the wolf spears they carried in lieu of proper arms.

At twelve Jerôme was still a foot short of his full growth and the spear he had appropriated from *Oncle* Antoine was, relatively speaking, more like a short pike in his immature grasp. But his short stature spared him from the worst of those gobs of flung bran and Jerôme managed to slip between fighting, screaming, cursing men to drive a spear into the broadfaced woman who was ladling out woe with such abandon. He got a foot on her supine body and removed the spear from between huge pillowy breasts just in time to drive it into the demon-faced Sodbuster who rushed him with a pitchfork. Jerôme had to drive the foot-long spearhead three times into the man's chest, almost losing it when vertebral musculature spasmed and held the spear fast. Finally the wild-bearded man was down. Eyes glazing, he still clawed at the boy who had killed him.

Without conscious intention Jerôme knelt over the

man's bloody breast and sucked a mouthful of warm gushing blood. Suddenly renewed, he wrenched the spear loose and charged into the stockade intent on his next victim.

But there were no more victims. Men and boys, all dozen of them, were dead. While Kattihaws rounded up women and girls, the Lafranche band patrolled the corpses, driving a spear into any that still moved. Infants and any girls under ten were killed on the spot, as well as all the older women. Which left only two worth consideration as slaves or concubines.

"Which'n you want " Les Kattihaw asked.

The Lafranches were already topheavy with women. And twelve-year-old Jerôme wanted nothing more than to get one night's sleep without some heir-hungry woman crawling under his blankets and rubbing herself against him until the inevitable happened . . . again!

"Tell you what," he offered, "you keep 'em both."

Les Kattihaw stared in disbelief. "What do you want?" he demanded.

"Your folk have better arms than we do. And more muskylopes."

"I can't spare any muskylopes."

"Can you spare us the holding?"

"This little pissant fort? They ain't so much as one good sword in the whole place. All you'll git's a few kitchen knives, maybe a scythe or two and some pitchforks."

Jerôme nodded.

"Is that really all you want—you're willing to let us take the women and whatever we done picked up already?"

Jerôme nodded again.

"Well, I'll be danged! Boy, any time y'all Lafranches need some help you can count on Les Kattihaw." The heavily-mustached man frowned in perplexity. "One thing I can't figger," he said. "I saw you rush the gate. Was you bitin' that bugger after you kilt him?"

Afterward Jerôme never knew why he said it. But once said, he knew the idea must have been germinating within his brain for the last couple of years. Above all, saying it, he knew it was true. "Brave man. Can't let strong blood go to waste."

Kattihaw gave him a doubtful grin and changed the subject. The Kattihaws were awed at the easy way they had gotten the best of the bargain with these unsophisticated Lafranche. So the band had too many women . . . had they never heard how much in trade goods a young woman could fetch down south? Yet the Kattihaws' amusement was tempered by the sly grins of the Lafranche band. It was just as if they had somehow tricked the Kattihaws into the bad end of a bargain.

As the fires died down Cat's Eye began graying the eastern skyline. By the time the sun was up the Kattihaws were on their way back to their main camp. The Lafranche band surveyed the scorched farmstead, licking lips at the sight of all those fat Sodbusters. They turned to with skinning knives. Then the women started cooking.

From *Bar Lev, A Traveler's Tales of Twenty Worlds* (Dayan, 2618)

They don't call it the Outback on Tanith, because for some reason the ubiquitous footloose Aussies missed the ship to Tanith. They do call the wild land beyond the settled areas a great many other things, few of them suitable for print.

And it is wild, make no mistake about that. Almost eerily wild, for a planet that has had not only settlers but cities for five centuries, and escaped the worst of the Formation Wars thanks to being under the Falkenberg Protectorate for most of them.

Part of the problem is that bad flying weather, uncomfortable temperatures, and rugged terrain slow down communications over a large part of Tanith. It's too much trouble to *get* to a good part of the land area, so few people try.

Those hardy souls who do try and survive don't make much of an impact on the land. There aren't very many of them, and what they do cut and clear, the land is constantly trying to take back. They also don't talk with the government, even the local government, more than they have to—and the government usually doesn't find it worthwhile making them talk.

So I came to Tanith wondering why it's so often

the setting for novels of exotic adventure, lost races, and what have you. I left, no longer wondering.

I'd stopped wondering the day I went three klicks into the wilderness from somebody's farm (I won't embarrass my host by giving his name) and it took all of the next day for me to find my way back. I was dry and bug-bitten and thorn-pricked and thanking all the gods of the galaxy that the Weems' Beast isn't as common as it used to be.

The locals say this is because all the ones who survived to breed after the Formation Wars were too smart to hang around human settlements. I said I thought that would make a fine horror novel—the Weems' Beasts secretly developing intelligence.

My host handed me a stiff drink and said that you don't make jokes about some things, even if you've been in the jungle for two days.

BRENDA

LARRY NIVEN

2656 AD, March (Firebee *clock time*)

Human-settled worlds all looked alike from high orbit. Terry thought that the CoDominium explorers must have had it easy.

Alderson Jump. ZZZTT! One white pinpoint among myriads has become a flood of white light. Nerve networks throughout ship and crew are strummed in four dimensions. Wait for the blur to go away. You had a hangover this bad, once. It lasted longer.

Now search the ecliptic a decent distance from the sun. Look for shadows in the neudar screen: planets. Big enough? Small enough? Colors: blue with a white froth of clouds, if men are to breath the air. Is there enough land? How big are the ice caps? Three or four months to move close, and look.

Nuliajuk's ice caps had covered half the surface. If they ever melted, Nuliajuk would be all water. A cold world. Nobody else would settle, but what about Eskimos? So Terry Kakumee's ancestors had found a home, six centuries ago.

Tanith had no ice caps at all, and almost no axial tilt. Tanith had clouds all the time. Hot too. Half land, but plenty of rainfall: the equatorial oceans boiled where they were shallow enough. Salt deserts around the equator. Swamps across both poles. Transportees had settled the north pole.

168

Terry Kakumee floated against the big window at *Firebee*'s nose. It was sixteen years since he'd seen Tanith.

Tanith was a growing crescent, orange with white graffiti, and a blazing highlight across the northern pole. Summer. One serious mountain, the Warden, stood six kilometers tall. It had been white-tipped in winter. Dagon City would be in the foothills, south.

The clouds were sparse for Tanith. The city itself didn't show, but he found a glare-point that had to be the old spaceport.

Brenda's farm would be south of that.

Sharon Hayes drifted up behind him. "I've been talking to the Dagon Port Authority. One George Callahan, no rank given, tells me they don't have much in the way of repair facilities, but we're intensely welcome. I've got a dinner date."

"Good." On a world this far from what civilization was left near Sparta, the population would feel cut off. Ships would be welcome. "What about fuel?"

"They can make liquid hydrogen. There's a tanker. Callahan gave me a course down. Four hours from now, and we'll have to lower *Firebee*'s orbit. Time to move, troops. Are we all going down?"

She meant that for Charley. Charley Laine (Cargo and Purser) was almost covered in burn scars. His face was a smooth mask. There was an unmarred patch along his jaw that he had to shave, and good skin in strips along his back and the backs of his arms and legs, and just enough unburned scalp to grow a decent queue. Sometimes he didn't want to face strangers. He said, "Somebody'd better stay on duty, Captain Sharon. Did you ask about outies?"

"They haven't been raided since the Battle. They do have a couple of high-thrust mining ships. Charley, I think *Firebee*'s safe enough."

Charley let out a breath. "I'll come. I can't be the only war vet on Tanith. There was—I wonder—"

"Brenda," Terry said.

"Yeah. I wonder about Brenda sometimes."

"I wonder too."

2640A, November (Tanith local time):

Lieutenant Kakumee had been Second Engineer aboard the recon ship *Firebee* during the destruction of the Sauron Second Fleet. The enemy's gene-tailored warriors were dead or fled, but they had left their mark. Damaged ships were limping in from everywhere in Tanith system. *Firebee* would orbit Tanith until she could be refitted or rifled for parts.

Firebee's midsection was a blob of metal bubbles where the Langston Field generator had vaporized itself and half melted the hull around it. It was the only hit *Firebee* had taken. Charley Laine had been caught in the flare.

They'd taken him to St. Agnes Hospital in Dagon City.

"The sky's full of ruined ships." Terry told him. "Most of them have damaged Langston Field generators. First thing that goes in a battle. We'll never get replacements."

Charley didn't answer. He might have heard; he might have felt the touch of Terry's hand. He looked like a tremendous pillow stuck with tubes in various places.

"Without a Langston Field we don't have a ship. I'd give *Firebee* a decent burial if I could get her down. You'll be healed a long time before any part of *her* flies again," Terry said. He believed that Charley would heal. He might never look quite human again, and if he walked he'd never run; but his central nervous system wasn't damaged, and his heart beat, and his lungs sucked air through the hole at one end of the pillow, while regeneration went on inside.

Terry heard urgent voices through the door. Patients healthy enough for curiosity stirred restlessly.

"Something's going on." Terry patted the padded hand. "I'll come back and tell you about it."

At first glance she wasn't that badly hurt.

She was slumped in an armchair in the lobby. Half a dozen people swarmed about her: a doctor, two nurses, two MPs and a thick-necked Marine in a full leg cast who was trying to stay out of the way and see too. She was wearing a bantar cloth coverall. It was a mess: sky blue with a green-and-scarlet landscape on the back, barely visible under several pounds of mud and swamp mold.

Bantar cloth had been restricted to Navy use up to eighty years ago. It was nearly indestructible. It wasn't high style, but farmers and others in high-risk jobs wore bantar cloth at half the price of a tractor. Whatever had happened to the woman, it would have been worse without that.

She had black ancestry with some white (skin like good milk chocolate, but weathered by fatigue and the elements) and oriental (the tilt of the eyes.) Thick, tightly coiled black hair formed a cushion around her head. It carried its own share of mud. A nasty gash cut through the hair. It ran from above her left eye back to the crown of her head. A nurse had cleaned it with alcohol; it was bleeding.

She drained a paper cup of water. A doctor— Charley's doctor, Lex Hartner—handed her another and she drained that too. "No more," Hartner said. "We'll get you some broth."

She nodded and said, "Uh." Her lip curled way up on the left. She tried to say something else. Stroke? Nonsense, she couldn't be past thirty. The head wound—

Poor woman.

Hartner said, "We'll get that soup into you before we look you over. How long were you out there?"

"Wumble." Her lips curled up; then half her face

wrinkled in frustration. The other half remained slack.
She held up one finger, then lifted another.

"A week or two?"

She nodded vigorously. Her eyes met Terry's. He
smiled and turned away, feeling like an intruder. He
went back to talk to Charley.

2656 AD, June, Tanith local time

The wrecked ships that had haloed the planet after
the Battle of Tanith were long gone. Shuttle #1 descended through a sky that seemed curiously empty.

What had been the Tanith spaceport still glared like a
polished steel dish. Seen from low angle the crater
became a glowing eye with a bright pupil.

The big Langston Field dome had protected Dagon
City during the battle. The smaller dome at the spaceport had absorbed a stream of guided meteors, then
given all of the energy back as the field collapsed.

A new port had grown around the crater's eastern
rim. Terry and Charley, riding as passengers while
Sharon flew, picked out a dozen big aircraft, then a
horde of lighter craft. The crater must make a convenient airfield. The gleaming center was a small lake.
Have to avoid that.

Both of *Firebee's* shuttles had lost their hover capability. They'd been looking for repair facilities for six
years now. Shuttle #1 came in a little fast because of
the way the crater dipped, coasted across and braked to
a stop at the rim.

Tanith was hot and humid, with a smell of alien
vegetation. The sun was low. Big autumn-colored
flutterbys formed a cloud around them as they emerged.
These were new to Terry. He'd never seen a Tanith
summer.

They had drawn a crowd of twenty-odd, still growing.
Terry noticed how good they looked: shorter than aver-
age, but all well muscled, none obtrusively fat. A year

in Tanith's 1.14 gravity made anyone look good. The early strokes and heart attacks didn't show.

Terry was a round man; he felt rounder by contrast. Sharon Hayes fit right in. She was past fifty, and it showed in the deep wrinkle patterns around eyes and mouth; but regular exercise and a childhood in Tanith gravity had kept her body tight and muscular.

The airport bar was cool and dry, and crowded now.

George Callahan was a burly man in his forties, red hair going gray, red fur along his thick arms. He and Sharon seemed to like each other on sight. They settled at a smaller table, and there they dealt with entry forms on Callahan's pocket computer. (Cargo: a Langston Field generator big enough to shield a small city. Purpose of entry: trade.)

Terry and Charley drank at the crowd's expense and tried to describe sixteen years of interstellar trading.

Terry let Charley do most of the talking. Let him forget the fright mask he wore. "*Yes* we are heroes, by damn! We saved Phoenix from famine two years ago." He'd tried to hold his breath when *Firebee*'s Langston Field generator blew up, but his voice still had a gravelly texture. "We'd just come from Hitchhiker's Rest. They've got a gene-tailored crop called kudzu grain. We went back and filled *Firebee* with kudzu grain, we were *living* in the stuff all the way back, and we strewed it across the Phoenix croplands. It came up before twenty-two million people quite ran out of stores. Then it died off, of course, because it isn't designed for Phoenix conditions, but by then they had their crops growing again. I never felt that good before or since."

The barmaids were setting out a free lunch, and someone brought them plates. Fresh food! Charley had his mouth full, so Terry said, "It's Hitchhiker's Rest that's in trouble. That kudzu grain is taking over everything. It really is wonderful stuff, but it eats the houses."

He bit into a sandwich: cheese and mystery meat and

tomatoes and chili leaf between thick slices of bread.
Sharon was working on another. She'd have little room
for dinner . . . or was this lunch? The sun had looked
like late afternoon. He asked somebody, "What time is
it local?"

"Ten. Just short of noon." The woman grinned. "And
nights are four hours long."

He'd forgotten: Dagon City was seven hundred kilometers short of the north pole. "Okay. I need to use a
phone."

"I'll show you." She was a small brunette, wide at
hips and shoulders. When she took his arm she was
about Terry's height.

Charley was saying, "We don't expect to get rich.
There aren't any rich worlds. The war hurt everybody,
and some are a long time recovering. We don't try to
stop outies. We just go away, and I guess everyone else
does too. That means a lot of worlds are cut off."

The brunette led him down a hall to a bank of computer screens. He asked, "How do I get Information?"

"You don't have a card? No, of course not. Here."
She pushed plastic into a slot. The screen lit with data,
and Terry noticed her name: Maria Montez. She tapped
QQQ.

The operator had a look of bony Spartan aristocracy:
pale skin, high cheekbones and a small, pursed mouth.
"What region?"

"I don't know the region. Brenda Curtis."

The small mouth pursed in irritation. (Not a recording?) He said, "Try south-south. Then west." Brenda
had inherited the farm. She might have returned there,
or she might still be working at the hospital.

"South-south, Brenda Curtis." The operator tapped
at her own keyboard. "Six-two-one-one-six-eight. Do
you have that?"

She was alive! "Yes. Thank you." He jotted it on his
pocket computer.

Maria was still there . . . naturally she'd want her

card back. Did he care what she heard? He took his courage in both hands and tapped out the number.

A girl answered: ten years old, very curly blond hair, cute, with a serious look. "Brenda's."

"Can I talk to Brenda Curtis?"

"She's on the roof."

"Will you get her, please?"

"No, we don't bother her when she's on the roof."

"Oh. Okay. Tell her I called. Terry Kakumee. When should I call back?"

"After dinner. About eighteen."

"Thanks." Something about the girl . . . "Is Brenda your mother?"

"Yes. I'm Reseda Anderssen." The girl hung up.

Maria was looking at him. "You know Brenda Curtis?"

"I used to. How do you know her?"

"She runs the orphanage. I know one of her boys. Not hers, I mean, but one of the boys she raised."

"Tell me about her."

Maria shrug-sniffed. Maybe talking about another woman wasn't what she'd had in mind. "She moved to a swamp farm after the Battle of Tanith. The City paid her money to keep orphans, and I guess there were a lot of them. Not so many now. Lots of teenagers. They've got their own skewball team, and they've had the pennant two years running."

"She was in bad shape when I knew her. Head wound. Does her lip pull up on one side when she talks?"

"Not that I noticed."

"Well," he said, "I'm glad she's doing okay."

Thinking of her as a patient might have put a different light on things. Maria took his arm again. They made an interesting match, Terry thought. Same height, both rounded in the body, and almost the same shade of hair and skin. She asked, "Was she in the Navy? Like Mr. Laine—"

"No."

"How did she get hurt?"

"Maria, I'm not sure that's been declassified. She wasn't in the Navy, but she got involved with the Sauron thing anyway." And he wouldn't tell her any more.

2640A, November (Tanith local time):

He'd taken Dr. Hartner to dinner partly because he felt sorry for him, partly to get him talking.

Lex Hartner was thin all over, with a long, narrow face and wispy blond hair. Terry would always remember him as tired . . . but that was unfair. Every doctor on Tanith lived at the edge of exhaustion after the battle of Tanith.

"Your friend'll heal," he told Terry. "He was lucky. One of the first patients in after the battle. We still had eyes in stock, and we had a regeneration sleeve. His real problem is, we'll have to take it off him as soon as he can live without it."

"Scars be damned?"

"Oh, he'll scar. They wouldn't be as bad if we left the sleeve on him longer. But *Napoleon*'s coming in with burn cases—"

"Yeah. I wouldn't want your job."

"This is the hardest part."

It was clear to Terry: there was no way to talk Lex into leaving Charley in the sleeve for a little longer. So he changed the subject. "That woman in the hall this morning—"

Lex didn't ask who he meant. "We don't have a name yet. She appeared at a swamp farm south of here. Mrs. Maddox called the hospital. We sent an ambulance. She must have come out of the swamps. From the look of her, she was there for some time."

"She didn't look good."

"She's malnourished. There's fungus all over here. Bantar cloth doesn't let air through. You have to wear net underwear, and hers was rotted to shreds. That head wound gouged her skull almost through the bone. Beyond that I just can't tell, Terry. I don't have the instruments."

Terry nodded; he didn't have to ask about that.

There had been one massive burn-through during the Battle of Tanith. Raw plasma had washed across several city blocks for three or four seconds. A hotel had been slagged, and shops and houses, and a stream of flame had rolled up the dome and hovered at the apex while it died. The hospital had lost most of its windows . . . and every piece of equipment that could be ruined by an electromagnetic pulse.

"There's just no way to look inside her head. I don't want to open her up. She's coming along nicely, she can say a few words, and she can draw and use sign language. And she tries so hard."

All of which Terry told to Charley the next day. They'd told him Charley wasn't conscious most of the time; but Terry pictured him going nuts from boredom inside that pillow.

2656, June (Tanith local time)

The bar had turned noisy. At the big table you could still hear Charley. "Boredom. You spend months getting to and from the Jump points. We've played every game program in ship's memory half to death. I think any one of us could beat anyone on Tanith at Rollerball, Chance, the Mirror Game—"

"We've got a Mirror Game," someone said. "It's in the Library."

"Great!"

Someone pushed two chairs into the pattern for Maria and Terry. Charley was saying, "We did find something interesting this trip. There's a Sauron ship in orbit around EST 1310. We knew it was there, we could hear it every time we used the Jump Points, but EST 1310 is a flare star. We didn't dare go after it. But this trip we're carrying a mucking great Langston Field generator in the cargo hold . . ."

Captain Sharon looked dubious. Charley was talking a lot. They'd pulled valuable data from the Sauron wreck, saleable data. But so what? Tanith couldn't reach the ship, and maybe they should be considered customers. And Brenda might hear. Let him talk.

"It was *Morningstar*, a Sauron hornet ship. The Saurons must have gutted it for anything they could use on other ships, then turned it into a signaling beacon. They'd left the computer. They had to have that to work the message sender. We disarmed some booby traps and managed to get into the programming. . . ."

People drifted away, presumably to run the airport. Others came in. The party was shaping up as a long one. Terry was minded to stay. He'd maintained a pleasant buzz, and Brenda had waited for sixteen years. She'd wait longer.

At seven he spoke into Maria's ear. "I'd be pleased to take you to dinner, if you can guide me to a restaurant."

She said, "Good! But don't you like parties?"

"Oh, hell yes. Stick with the crowd?"

"Good. Till later."

"I still have to make that phone call."

She nodded vigorously and fished her card out of a pocket. He got up and went back to the public phones.

2640A, November (Tanith local time):

When *Firebee*'s Shuttle #2 came down, there had been no repair facilities left on Tanith. There was little for a Second Engineer to do.

Napoleon changed that. *Napoleon* was an old Spartan troopship arriving in the wake of the Battle of Tanith. Word had it that it was loaded with repair equipment. Now *Napoleon*'s shuttles were bringing stuff down, and *Napoleon*'s Purser was hearing requests from other ships in need of repairs.

Captain Shu and the others would be cutting their

own deals in orbit. Terry and Charley were the only ones on the ground. Terry spent four days going through Shuttle #2, listing everything the little GO craft would need. When he went begging to *Napoleon*'s Spartan officers, he wanted to know exactly what to ask for. He made three lists: maximum repairs if he could get them, the minimum he could settle for, and a third list no other plaintiff would have made. He hoped.

He hadn't visited Charley in four days.

The tall dark woman in the corridor caught his attention. He would have remembered her. She was eight inches taller than Terry, in a dressing gown too short for her and a puffy shower cap. She was more striking than beautiful: square-jawed and lean enough to show ribs and hip bones where the cloth pulled taut.

She caught him looking and smiled with one side of her face. "He'o! I member you!" Her lip tugged way up on the left.

"Oh, it's you," Terry said. Six days ago: the head wound case. "Hey, you can talk! That's good. I'm Terry Kakumee."

"Benda Curris."

It was an odd name. "Benda?"

"Br, renda. Cur, tiss."

"Brenda. Sorry. What were you doing out there in the swamps?" He instantly added, "Does it tire you to talk?"

She spoke slowly and carefully. "Yes. I told my story to the Marines and Navy officers and Doctor Hartner. I don't like it. You wo—wouldn't like it. They smiled a lot when we all knew I wasn't pregnant." She didn't seem to see Terry's bewilderment. "You're Charley's friend. He's out of the regeneration sleeve."

"Can he have visitors?"

"Ssure. I'll take you."

Charley wasn't a pillow any more. He didn't look good, either. Wasted. Burned. He didn't move much on the water bed. His lips weren't quite mobile enough;

he sounded a bit like Brenda. "There are four regeneration sleeves on Tanith, and one tank to make the goo,
and when they wear out there's nothing. My sleeve is
on a Marine from Tabletop. Burn patient, like me. I
asked. I see you've met Brenda?"

"Yeah."

"She went through a hell of an experience. We don't
talk about it. So how's the work coming?"

"I'll go to the Purser tomorrow. I want all my ducks
in a row, but I don't want everyone getting their requests in ahead of me either. I made a list of things we
could give up to other ships. That might help."

"Good idea. Very Eskimo."

"Charley, it isn't really. The old traditions have us
giving a stranger what he needs whether we need it or
not."

He noticed Brenda staring at him. She said, "How
strange."

He laughed a little uncomfortably. "I suppose a
stranger wouldn't ask for what the village had to have.
Anyway, those days are almost gone."

Brenda listened while they talked about the ship.
She wouldn't understand much of it, though both men
tried to explain from time to time. "The Langston Field
is your reentry shield and your weapons shield and
your true hull. We'll never get it repaired, but *Firebee*
could still function in the outer system. I'm trying to
get the shuttles rebuilt. Maybe we can make her a
trader. She sure isn't part of a Navy any more."

Charley said, "The Tanith asteroids aren't mined out."

"So?"

"Asteroids. Metal. Build a metal shell around *Firebee*
for a hull."

"Charley, you'd double her mass!"

"We could still run her around the inner system. If
we could get a tank from some wrecked ship, a detacha-
ble fuel tank, we'd be interstellar again." His eyes
flicked to Brenda and he said, "With more fuel we could

still get to the Jump points and back. Everything'd be slower, we couldn't outrun anything . . . have to stay away from bandits . . ."

"You're onto something. Charley, we don't really want to be asteroid miners for five years. But if we could find *two* good tanks—"

"Ahhh! One for a hull. Big. Off a battleship, say."

"Yeah."

"Terry, I'm tired," Charley said suddenly, plaintively. "Take Brenda to dinner? They let her out."

"Brenda? I'd be honored."

She smiled one-sided.

November was twelve days long on Tanith, and there wasn't any December. Every so often they put the same number on two consecutive years, to stay even with Spartan time.

In November Dagon City was dark eighteen hours out of twenty-one-plus. The street lighting was back, but snatchers were still a problem. Maybe Terry's uniform protected him; and he went armed, of course.

He took her to a place that was still passable despite the shortages.

He did most of the talking. She'd never heard of the Nuliajuk migration. He told her how the CoDominium had moved twenty thousand Eskimos, tribes all mixed together, to a world too cold for the comfort of other peoples.

They'd settled the equator, where the edges of the ice caps almost met. They'd named the world for a myth-figure common to all the tribes, though names differed: the old woman at the bottom of the sea who brought game or withheld it. There was native sea life, and the imported seals and walruses and bears throve too. Various tribes taught each other their secrets. Some had never seen a seal, some had never built an igloo.

The colony throve; but the men studied fusion and Langston Field engineering, and many wound up on

Navy and merchant ships. Eskimos don't really like to
freeze. The engine room of a Navy ship is a better
place, and Eskimos of all tribes have a knack with tools.

Nuliajuk was near Sol and Sparta. It might still be
part of the shrinking Empire, but Terry had never seen
it. He was a half-breed, born in a Libertarian merchant
ship. What he knew of Nuliajuk came from his father.

And Brenda had lived all her life on a Tanith farm. "I
took my education from a TV wall. No hands-on, but I
learned enough to fix our machines. We had a fusion
plant and some Gaineses and Tofflers. Those are special tractors. Maybe the Saurons left them alone."

"Saurons?"

"Sorry." Her grimace twisted her whole face around.
"I spent the last four days talking about nothing else. I
own that farm now. I don't own anything else." She
studied him thoughtfully. Her face in repose was sym-
metrical enough, square-jawed, strong even by Tanith
standards. "Would you like to see it?"

"What?"

"Would you like to see my farm? Can you borrow a
plane?"

They set it up for two days hence.

2656, June (Tanith local time)

Brenda's face lit when she saw him. "Terry! Have
you gotten rich? Have you saved civilization? Have you
had fun?"

"No, yes, yes. How are you?"

"You can see, can't you? It's all over, Terry. No more
nightmares." He'd never seen her bubble like this. There
was no slur in her voice . . . but he could see the twitch
at the left side of her mouth. Her face was animated on
the right, calmer on the left. Her hair bloomed around
her head like a great black dandelion, teased, nearly a
foot across. The scar must have healed completely.
She'd gained some weight.

He remembered that he had loved her. (But he didn't remember her having nightmares.)

"They tell me you opened an orphanage."

"Yeah, I had twenty kids in one schlumph," she said. "The city gave me financing to put the farm back on its legs, and there were plenty of workmen to hire, but I thought I'd go nuts taking care of the children and the farm both. It's easier now. The older kids are my farmers, and they learn to take care of the younger ones. Two of them got married and went off to start their own farm. Three are in college, and the oldest boy's in the Navy. I'm back down to twenty kids."

"How many of your own? I met Reseda."

"Four. She's the youngest. And one who died."

"I guess I'm surprised you moved back to the farm."

She shook her head. "I did it right. The children took the curse off the memories. So how are you? You must have stories to tell. What are you doing now?"

"There's a party at the spaceport and we're the stars. Want to join us?"

"No. Busy."

"Can I come out there? Like tomorrow, noon or thereabouts?"

He was watching for hesitation, but it was too quick to be sure. "Good. Come. Noon is fine. You remember how to get here? And noon is just past eleven?"

"And midnight is twenty-two-twenty."

"Right. See you then."

He hung up. Now: summon the Library function on the computer? He wondered how much of the Sauron story was still classified. But a party was running, and a spaceman learned to differentiate: there was a time for urgency and a time to hang loose.

When he pushed back into the crowd, Maria grabbed his arm and shouted in his ear. "Mayor Anderssen!" She pointed.

The Mayor nodded and smiled. He was tall, in his late thirties, with pale skin and ash-blond hair and a

wispy beard. Terry reached across the table to offer his
hand. The Mayor put something in it. "Card," he
shouted. "Temporary."

"Thanks."

The Mayor circled the table and pulled up a chair
next to him. "You're the city's guest while you're down.
Restaurants, hotels, taxis, rentals."

"Very generous. How can we repay you?"

"Your Captain has already agreed to some interviews.
Will you do the same? We're starved for news. I talked
Purser Laine into speaking on radio."

"Fine by me. I'm busy tomorrow, though."

"I got a call from a friend of mine, a Brenda Curtis.
She says she used to know you—"

"I just called her a minute ago. Hey, one of her
kids—"

"Reseda. My daughter. Brenda isn't married, but
she's had four children, and she's got something going
with a neighbor, Bob Maddox. Anyway, she called to
find out if I was getting you cards, which I already
was."

Terry's memory told him that nuclear families were
the rule on Tanith. "An unusual life style," he said.

"Not so unusual. We've got more men than women.
Four hundred ships wrecked in the Battle. Lots of
rescue action. Some of the crews reached Tanith and
never went any further. We tend to be generous with
child support, and there are specialized marriage contracts. Can you picture the crime rate if every woman
thought she had to get married?"

Tanith had changed.

Maria handed Terry a drink, something with fruit
and rum. He sipped, and wondered.

Brenda must have called the Mayor as soon as the
little girl told her about his first call. He remembered
an injured woman trying to put her life back together.
She'd been in no position to do spur-of-the-moment
favors for others. Brenda had changed too.

* * *

2640, November (Tanith local time):

"We're trying to save civilization. *Napoleon*'s Purser lectured Terry. "Not individual ships. If Tanith doesn't have *some* working spacecraft, it won't survive until the Empire gets things straightened out. So. We're giving you—*Firebee?*—if you want it. The terms say that you have to run it as a merchant ship or lose it. That's if we decide it's worth repairing. Otherwise—well. We'll have to give any working parts to someone else."

Arrogant, harassed, defensive. He was dispensing other people's property as charity. The way he used the word *give*—

They discussed details. Terry's third list surprised him. He studied it. "Your drives are intact? Alderson and fusion both?"

"Running like new. They are new, almost." Terry knew the danger here. *Firebee* was alive if her drives were alive . . . and some other ship might want those drives.

"Well. I don't know anyone who needs these spares, offhand, except . . . we'll record these diagnostic programs. Very bright of you to list these. Some of our ships lost most of their data to EMPs. Can I copy this list?"

"Yessir."

"I can give you a rebuilt fusion zap. You'd never leave orbit without that, would you? We can recore the hover motors on your #2 boat. Spinner for the air plant if you can mount it. *Don't* tell me you can if you can't. Someone else might need it. You could ruin it trying to make it fit."

"I can fit it."

"I dare say. Nuliajuk?"

"Half-breed. Libertarian mother."

"Look, our engineers aren't Esks *or* Scots, but they've been with us for years. So we can't hire you ourselves, but some other ship—"

"I'd rather make *Firebee* fly again."

"Good luck. I can't give you any more."

From the temporary port he went directly to the hospital. Lex Hartner was in surgery. Terry visited with Charley until Lex came out.

"Brenda Curtis invited me to visit her farm with her. Anything I should know? What's likely to upset her?"

Lex stared at him in astonishment. He said, "Take a gun. A big gun."

"For what?"

"Man, you missed some excitement here. Brenda said something to a nurse a couple of days after she got here. You know what happened to her?"

"She doesn't want to talk about it."

"She sure doesn't, and I don't blame her, but the more she said the more the Navy wanted. She'd have died of exhaustion if I hadn't dragged her away a couple of times. She was kidnapped by two Saurons! They killed the whole family."

"On Tanith itself?"

"Yeah, a landing craft got down. More like a two-seater escape pod, I guess. I haven't seen pictures. It came down near an outback farm, way south. The Saurons killed off her family from ambush. They stayed on the farm for a month. She . . . belonged to one of them." Lex was wringing his hands. Likely he didn't know it. "We looked her over to see if she was pregnant."

"I should think you bloody would! Can they still breed with human beings?" Rumor had it that some of the Sauron genes had been borrowed from animals.

"We won't find out from Brenda. She's had a child though. It probably died at the farm. She won't talk about that either."

"Lord. How did she get away?"

"One went off by himself. Maybe they fought over Brenda. The other one stayed. One day a Weem's Beast came out of the water and attacked them in the rice paddy. It clawed her; that's how she got the head wound. When she got the blood out of her eyes the Sauron was dead and so was the Weem's Beast. So she started walking. She had to live for two weeks in the swamps, with that wound. Hell of a woman."

"Yeah. You're telling me there's a Sauron loose on Tanith."

"Yup. They're hunting for him. She took the Marines to the farm, and they found the escape pod and the corpse. I've been doing the autopsy. You can see where they got the traits—"

"Animal?"

"No, that's just a rumor. It's all human, but the way it's put together . . . think of Frankenstein's monster. A bit here, a bit there, the shape changes a little. Maybe add an extra Y gene to turn it mean. I'm guessing there. The high-power microscope's down."

"The other one?"

"Could be anywhere. He's had almost a month."

"Not likely he'd stick around. Okay, I'll take a big gun. Anything else I should know?"

"I don't know how she'll react. Terry, I'll give you a trank spray. Put her out if she gets hysterical and get her back here fast. Other than that . . . watch her. See if you think she can live on that farm. Bad memories there. I think she should sell the place."

2656, June, (Tanith local time)

Dinner expeditions formed and went off in three directions. The cluster that took Terry along still crowded the restaurant. A blackboard offered a single meal of several courses, Spartan cooking strangely mutated by local ingredients.

The time change caught up with him as desserts arrived. "I'm running out of steam," he told Maria Montez.

"Okay." She led him out and waved at a taxi. The gray-haired driver recognized him for what he was. She kept him talking all the way to Maria's apartment house.

She wasn't interested in planets; it was the space between that held her imagination.

On the doorstep Maria carefully explained that Terry
couldn't possibly presume on an acquaintanceship of
one afternoon (though he hadn't asked yet.) She kissed
him quickly and went inside.

Terry started down the steps, grinning. Customs dif-
fer. Now where the hell was he, and where was a taxi
likely to be hiding?

So Brenda was alive and doing well. Friend of the
Mayor. Running an orphanage. Four children. Well,
well.

Maria came out running. "I forgot, you don't have a
place to stay! Terry, you can come in and sleep on the
couch if you promise to behave yourself."

"I can't really do that, Maria, but if you'll call me a
taxi?"

She was affronted. "Why not?"

He went back up the steps. "I haven't set foot on a
world for four months. I haven't held a woman in my
arms in longer than that. Now, we heroes have infinite
self-control—"

"But—"

"I could probably leave you alone all night. But I
wouldn't sleep and I'd wake up depressed and frustrated. So what I want is a hotel."

She thought it over. "Come in. Have some coffee."

"Were you listening?"

"Come in."

They entered. The place was low-tech but roomy. He
asked, "Was I supposed to lie?"

"It's not a lie, exactly. It just, just leaves things open.
Like I could be telling you we could have some coffee
and then get you a taxi, and we could wind up sniffing
some borloi, and . . . you could be persuasive?"

"Nuliajuks lie. It's called tact. My mother made sure
I knew how to keep a promise. She wasn't just a Libertarian. She was a Randist."

Maria smiled at him, much amused. "Four months, hey? But you should learn to play the game, Terry."

He shook his head. "There's a different game on every world, almost in every city. I can't sniff borloi with you either. I tried it once. That stuff could hook me fast. I just have to depend on charisma."

She had found a small bottle. "Take a couple of these. Vitamins, hangover formula. Take lots of water. Does wonders for the charisma."

Maria made scrambled eggs with sausage and fungus, wrapped in chili leaves. It woke him up fast and made him forget his hangover. He'd been looking forward to Tanith cooking.

There were calls registered on his pocket computer. He used Maria's phone. Nobody answered at Polar Datafile or Other Worlds. When he looked at his watch it was just seven o'clock.

No wonder Maria was yawning. She'd woken when he did, and that must have been about six. "Hey, I'm sorry. It's the time change."

"No sweat, Terry. I'll sleep after you leave. Want to go back to bed?"

He tried again later. Polar Datafile wanted him tomorrow, five o'clock news. An interviewer for Other Worlds wanted all three astronauts for two days, maybe more. Good payment, half in gold, for exclusive rights. "How exclusive?" he asked. She reassured him: radio and TV spots would be considered as publicity. What she wanted was depth, and no other vidtapes competing. He set it up.

He called Information. "I need to rent a plane."

Maria watched him with big dark eyes. "Brenda Curtis?"

"Right." The number answered, and he dealt with it. A hoverplane would pick him up at the door. He was expected to return the pilot to the airport and then go about his business. How far did he expect to fly? About forty miles round trip.

Maria asked, "Were you in love with her?"

"For about two months."

"Are you going to tell her about us?"

"That might put both women in danger. "No. In fact, I'm going to get a hotel room——"

"Damn your eyes, Terry Kakumee!"

"I'll be back tonight, Maria. I've got my reasons. No, I can't tell you what they are."

"All right. Are they honest?"

"I . . . dammit. They're right on the edge."

She studied his face. "Can you tell me after it's over?"

". . . No." Either way, he wouldn't be able to do that.

"Okay. Come back tonight." She wasn't happy. He didn't blame her.

The land had more color than he remembered. Fields of strange flowers bloomed in the swampland. Huge dark purple petals crowned plants the size of trees. A field of sunlovers, silver ahead of him, turned green in his rear view camera.

Farms were sparse pale patches in all that color. In the wake of the Battle of Tanith they had had a scruffy look. They were neater now, with more rice and fewer orange plots of borloi. The outworld market for the drug had disintegrated, of course.

He should be getting close. He took the plane higher. Farms all looked alike, but the crater wouldn't have disappeared.

It was there, several miles south, a perfect circle of lake. . . .

2640B, January (Tanith local time)

. . . A perfect circle of lake surrounded by blasted trees lying radially outward. "A big ship made a big bang when it fell," Brenda said. She was wearing dark glasses, slacks and a chamois shirt. Her diction was as precise as she could make it, but he still had to listen hard. A Tanith farm girl's accent probably slurred it further. "We were on the roof. We wanted to watch the battle."

"Sauron or Empire ship?"

"We never knew. It was only a light. Bright enough to fry the eyeballs. It gave us enough warning. We threw ourselves flat. We would have been blown off the roof."

They turned east. Presently he asked, "Is that your farm?"

"No. There, beyond."

Four miles east of the fresh crater, a wide stretch of rice paddies. The other farm was miles closer. The Saurons must have gone around it. Why?

They'd passed other farms. Here the paddies seemed to be going back to the wild. The house nestled on a rise of ground. The roof was flat, furnished with tables and chairs and a swimming pool in the shape of a bloobby eagle. The walls sloped inward.

"You don't like windows?"

"No. It rains. When it doesn't, we work outside. On a good day we all went up on the roof."

The door showed signs of damage. It might have been blasted from its hinges, then rehung.

Lights came on as they entered. Terry trailed Brenda as she moved through the house.

Pantry shelves were in neat array, but depleted. The fridge was empty. The freezer was working, but it stank. He told her, "There've been power failures. You'll have to throw all this out." She sniffed; half her face wrinkled.

He found few obvious signs of damage. Missing furniture had left its marks on the living room floor, and the walls had been freshly painted.

There were muddy footprints everywhere. "The Marines did that," Brenda said.

"Did they find anything?"

"Not here. Not even dry blood. Horatius made me clean up. They found the escape pod three miles away."

Beds in the master bedroom were neatly made. Brenda turned on the TV wall and got Dagon City's single station, and a picture of Boat #1 floating gracefully toward the landing field. "This works too."

Terry shook his head. "What did these Saurons look like?"

"Randus was bizarre. Horatius was more human—"

"It looks like he was ready to stay here. To pass himself off as a man, an ordinary farmer."

She paused. "He could have done that. It may be why he left. We never saw a Sauron on Tanith. He was muscular. His bones were heavy. He looked . . . round shoulders. His eyes had an epicanthic fold, and the pupils were black, jet black." Pause. "He made sex like an attack."

The smiling faces of *Firebee*'s crew flashed and died. The lights died too. Terry said, "Foo."

"Never mind." Brenda took his arm and led him two steps backward through the dark. The bed touched his knees and he sat.

"What did Randus look like?"

"A monster. I hated Horatius, but I wanted him to protect me from Randus."

Could he pass as a farmer? He'd have to hide Randus the monster and Brenda the prisoner, or kill them. But he hadn't. Honor among Saurons? Or . . . leave the monster to guard his woman. Find or carve a safe house. Come back later, see if it worked. The risk would not be to Horatius. So.

"Did Horatius think you were pregnant?"

"Maybe. Terry, I would like to take the taste of Horatius out of my mind."

"Time will do that."

"Sex will do that."

He tried to look at her. He saw nothing. They were sitting on a water bed in darkness like a womb.

"I haven't been with a woman in over a year. Brenda, are you sure you're ready for this?" He hadn't thought to ask Lex about *this!*

She pulled him to his feet, hands on his upper arms. Strong! "You're a good man, Terry. I've watched you. I couldn't do better. Do you maybe think I'm too tall for you?" She pulled him against her, and his cheek was against her breasts. "You can't do this with a short woman."

"Not standing up." His arms went around her, but how could he help that?

"Is it my face? We're in the dark." He could hear her amusement.

"Brenda, I'm not exactly fighting. It's just that I still think of you as a patient."

"So be patient."

She didn't need patience. She had none herself. He'd expected the aftereffects of the head wound to make her clumsy. She was, a little. She came on as if she would swallow him up and go looking for dessert. He was apalled, then delighted, then . . . exhausted, but she wouldn't let him go. . . .

He woke in darkness. He wasn't tempted to move. The water bed was kind to his gravity-abused muscles. He felt the warmth of the woman in his arms, and presently knew that she was awake.

No warning: she attacked.

She disappeared into the dark like a vampire leaving her victim. She draped his clothes over him and dropped the heavy flechette gun on his belly. He giggled, and presently dressed.

She led him stumbling through a black maze and out into the dusk of a winter morning. "There. After all, I know the house."

"This is the trouble with not having windows," he groused.

"Weem's Beasts like windows too. In rain they can come this far."

The graveyard was eight stone markers cut with a vari-saw, letters and numbers cut with a laser. "The names and dates are wrong, except these old ones," she said. "Horatius hoped it would look like they all died many years ago. I'll get a chisel or a laser to fix it."

There was no *small* grave. "Lex told me you had a child."

"Miranda. He took her with him."

"God." He took her in his arms. "Did you tell the Marines?"

"No. I . . . try not to think about Miranda."

There was nothing more to see. She told him that the Navy men had found Randus' skeleton and taken that, and sent out a big copter for the rescue pod. When the lights came on around noon, Terry helped Brenda clean up the mudstains and empty the freezer and fridge.

"I need money to run the farm," Brenda said. "Maybe someone will hire me for work in Dagon."

"Why not sell the place?"

"It was ours for too long. It won't be bad. You can see for yourself, the Saurons left no trace. No trace at all."

2656, June (Tanith local time)

Four miles east of the crater. He should be near. He was crossing extensive fields of rice. A dozen men and women worked knee-deep in water that glinted through the stalks like fragments of a shattered mirror. A man stood by with a gun. Terry swooped low, lowered his flaps, hovered. Several figures waved.

They were all children.

He set the plane down. The gun-carrier broke off work and came toward him. Terry waded to meet him; what the hell. "Brenda Curtis's?"

The boy had an oriental look despite the black, kinky hair. He grinned and said. "Where else would you find all these kids? I'm Tarzan Kakumee."

"Terry Kakumee. I'm visiting. You'd be about sixteen?"

The boy's jaw dropped. "Seventeen, but that's Tanith time. Kakumee? Astronaut? You'd be my father!"

"Yeah. Can I stare a little?"

They examined each other. Tarzan was an inch or two taller than Terry, narrower in the hips and face and chest, and his square jaw was definitely Brenda's. Black eyes with an oriental slant: Terry and Brenda both had that. The foolish grins felt identical.

"I'm on duty," Tarzan said. "I'll see you later?"

"Can't you come with me? I'm due for lunch."

"No, I've got my orders. There are Weem's Beasts and other things around here. I once shot a tax collector the size of my arm. It had its suckers in Gerard's leg and Gerard was screaming bloody murder." Tarzan grinned. "I blew it right off him."

Smaller fields of different colors surrounded a sprawling structure. If that was the farmhouse it had doubled in size . . . right. He could make out the original farmhouse in the center. The additions had windows.

Fields of melons, breadfruit, and sugar cane surrounded the house. Three children in a mango grove broke off work to watch him land.

Brenda came through the door with a man beside her.

He knew her at once. (But was it her?) She waved both arms and ran to meet him. (She'd changed.) "Terry, I'm so glad to see you! The way you went off—my fault, of course, but I kept wondering what had happened to you out there and why you didn't come back!" Her dress looked like current Tanith style, cut above the knee and high at the neck. Her grip on his arm was farmhand-strong. "You wouldn't have had to see me, it just would have been good to know— Well, it *is* good to know you're alive and doing all right! Bob, this is Terry Kakumee the astronaut. Terry, Bob Maddox is my neighbor three miles southeast."

"Pleased to meet you." Bob Maddox was a brown-haired white man, freckled and tanned. He was large all over, and his hand was huge, big-knuckled and rough with work. "Brenda's told me about you. How's your ship?"

"Truth? *Firebee* is gradually and gracefully disintegrating. There's a double hull instead of a Langston Field, and we have to patch it every so often. We got Boat #1 repaired on Phoenix. Maybe we can hold it all together till the Empire gets back out there. You interested in spaceflight?"

Maddox hesitated. "Not really. I mean, it's surprising more of us don't want to build rocket ships, considering. We weren't all transportees, our ancestors."

Brenda turned at the door. She clapped her hands twice and jerked her thumb. The children who had been climbing over Terry's rental plane, dropped off and scampered happily back toward the mangoes.

They went in. Reseda Anderssen, busy at a samovar, smiled at them and went out through another door. There was new furniture, couches and small tables and piles of pillows, enough to leave the living room quite cluttered. Brenda saw him looking and said, "Some of the kids sleep in here."

It didn't look it. "You keep them neat." He noticed noises coming from what he remembered as the kitchen.

"I've got a real knack for teaching. Have some tea?"

"Borloi tea? I'd better not."

"I made Earl Grey." She poured three cups. She'd always had grace, even with the head injury to scramble the signals. He could see just a trace of her lip pulling up on the left when she spoke. She settled him and Bob on a couch and faced them. "Now talk. Where've you been?"

"Phoenix. Gafia. Hitchhiker's Rest. Medea. Uhura. We commute. We tried Lenin, but three outie ships came after us. We ran and didn't come back, and that

cuts us off from the planets beyond. And we found a
Sauron ship at EST 1310."

It was Maddox who stared. "Well, go on! What's left
of it? Were there Saurons?"

"Bob, we were clever. We knew there was a ship
there because we caught the signal every time we used
the Jump Points to get to Medea. We couldn't get down
there because the star's a flare star and we don't have a
Langston Field.

"Only, this time we do. Phoenix sold us—actually
they *gave* us a mucking great Langston Field generator.
We left it on. We moved in and matched orbit with the
signal ship, and we expanded the field to put both ships
inside."

"Clever, right. Terry, we Taniths are a little twitchy
about Saurons—"

"Just one. Dead. They rifled it and left it for a message beacon. They left a Sauron on duty. Maybe a flare
got him." The corpse had been a skewed man-shape, a
bogie man. Like Randus? "I managed to get into the
programming. Now we're thinking of going on to Sparta.
We learned some things they might want to know."

"Let me just check on lunch," Brenda said, and she
went.

It left Terry feeling awkward. Maddox said, "So there
are still Sauron supermen out there?"

"Just maybe. The beacon was set to direct Saurons to
a Jump point in that system. Maybe nobody ever got
the message. If they did, I don't know where they
went. I ran the record into *Firebee*'s memory and ran a
translation program on it, but I didn't look at the result.
I'd have to go back to *Firebee*, then come back here."

Maddox grimaced. "We don't have ships to do anything about it. Sparta might. I'd be inclined to leave
them the hell alone."

"Did they ever catch—"

"Nope. Lot of excitement. Every so often some nut
comes screaming that he saw a Sauron in the marshes.

The Mayor's got descriptions of a Sauron officer, and he says they don't check out. How the hell could that thing still be hiding?"

"Those two must have gone right past your place to get here."

"Yeah. Brenda had to backtrack to get to my place. Weeks in the wild, fungus and tax collectors, polluted water, God knows what she ate . . . Well, yeah, I've wondered. Maybe they saw we had guns."

"That's not it."

Bob hesitated. "Okay, why?"

He'd spoken without thinking. "You'd think I'm crazy. Anyway, I could be wrong."

"Kakumee, everyone knows more about Saurons than the guy he's talking to. It's like skewball scores. What I want to know about is, I never saw Brenda's lip curl up like that when she talks."

"Old head injury."

"I haven't seen her face do that since the day she staggered through my gate. I wonder if meeting you again might be upsetting her."

Bob Maddox was coming on like a protective husband. Terry asked, "Have you thought of marriage?"

"That's none of your business, Kakumee—"

"Brenda's—"

"—But I've asked, and she won't." His voice was still low and reasonably calm. "She'd rather live alone, and I don't know why. Ventura's mine."

"I haven't met her."

"I guess I don't mind you worrying over Brenda. Have you met any of the kids?"

"Yeah—"

Brenda was back. "We can serve any time you get hungry. Terry, can you stay for dinner? You could meet the rest of the children. They'll be coming in around five."

"I'd like that. Bob, feel like lunchtime?"

"Yeah."

The men hung back for a moment. "I'll leave after dinner," Terry said. "I tell you, though, I don't think anything's bothering Brenda. She's tougher than that."

Bob nodded. "Tough lady. Kakumee, I think she's working on how to tell you one of the kids is yours."

2640B, January to March (Tanith local time)

Their idyll lasted two months.

They made an odd couple. Tall and lean; short and round. He could see it in the mirror, he could see the amusement in strangers and friends too.

Terry's rented room was large enough for both. Brenda began buying clothes and other things after she had a job, but she never crowded the closets. Brenda cleaned. Terry did all the cooking. It was the only task he'd ever seen her fail at.

He was busy much of the time. In a week the work on Boat #2 was finished. There were parts for Boat #1, and he carried them to orbit to work. Boat #1 still wouldn't be able to make a reentry.

He talked *Napoleon*'s Purser out of a ruined battleship's hydrogen tank. Over a period of three weeks (with two two-day leaves in Dagon) Terry and the rest of the crew moved *Firebee* into it. Had Charley been thinking in terms of a regeneration sleeve for the ship?

Firebee was now the silliest-looking ship since the original Space Shuttle, and too massive for interstellar capability. Without an auxiliary tank she couldn't even use a Jump point with any hope of reaching a planet on the far side.

Captain Shu had done something about that. *Firebee* now owned a small H2 tank aboard *Armadillo*, but they'd have to wait for it to arrive. Terry went back down to Dagon City.

Brenda was still attending the clinic every two days. She was working there too, and trying to arrange something with the local government. She wouldn't talk about that; she wasn't sure it would work.

He made her a different offer. "Four of our crew want to stay. Cropland doesn't cost much on Tanith. But you've got a knack for machines. Let me teach you how to make repairs on *Firebee*. Come as my apprentice."

"Terry—'

"And wife."

"I get motion sickness."

"*Damn.*" There had never been a lover like Brenda. She could play his nervous system like a violin. She knew his moods. She maintained civilization around him. The thought of leaving her made him queasy.

Armadillo had won an expensive victory in the outer Tanith system. The hulk was just capable of thrust, and it didn't reach Tanith until months after the battle. Then crews from other ships swarmed over it and took it apart. *Firebee*'s crew came back with an intact tank and fuel feed system. Terry had to tear that apart and put it together different, in vacuum. It would ride outside the second hull.

Firebee was fragile now, fit to be a trader, but never a warship or a miner.

Charley was in decent shape by then and working out in a local gym. He came up to help weld the fuel tank. He seemed fit for space. "Captain Shu wants to go home, but we've got you and me and Sharon Hayes and that kid off *Napoleon*, Murray Weiss. I say we go interstellar."

"I know you do, but think about it, Charley. No defenses. We can haul cargo back and forth between the mining asteroids, and if outies ever come to take over we'd have someplace to run to."

"And you could see Brenda every couple of months."

The argument terminated when Terry returned to Dagon.

Brenda was gone. Brenda's clothes were gone. There was a phone message from Lex Hartner; he looked grim and embarrassed.

Phoning him felt almost superfluous, but Terry did it.

"We've been seeing each other," Lex said. "I think she's carrying my child. Terry, I want to marry her."

"Good luck to you." The days in which an Ihalmiut hunter might gather up a band of friends and hunt down a bride were long ago, far away. He considered it anyway. And went to the stars instead.

2656, June (Tanith local time)

Reseda and three younger children served lunch, then joined them at the table. Three more came in from the fields. There was considerable chatter. Terry found he was doing a lot of the talking.

Dessert was mangoes still hot from the sun.

Brenda went away and came back wearing a bantar cloth coverall. It was the garment she'd worn the day she reached the hospital, like as not, but much cleaner. The three adults spent the afternoon pulling weeds in the sugar cane. Brenda and Bob Maddox instructed him by turns.

Terry had never done field work. He found he was enjoying himself, sweating in the sun.

The sun arced around the horizon, dropping gradually. Other children came flocking from the rice fields shortly after five. The adults pulled weeds for a little longer, then joined the children in the courtyard. He could smell his own sweat, and Bob's, different by race or by diet.

Twenty children all grinned at some shared joke. Brenda must have briefed them. When?

"Brenda, I can sort them out," Terry said.

"Go ahead."

"The Mayor already told me Reseda was his. The freckled girl must be Ventura Maddox. Hello, Ventura!" She was big for twelve, tanned dark despite the freckles, and round in the face, like Bob himself. A tall girl, older, had Brenda's tightly kinked black hair, pale skin and a pointed chin. "I don't know her name, but she's . . . Lex's?" Lex's face, but it would still be a remarkable thing.

"Yes, that's Sepulveda."

"Hello, Sepulveda. And the boy—" Tarzan grinned at him but didn't wave. Tactful: he didn't know whether they were supposed to have met "—is mine."

"Right again. Terry, meet Tarzan."

"Hello, Tarzan. Brenda, I set down in the rice field before I got here."

She laughed. "Dammit, Terry! I had it all planned."

"And they're named for suburbs of some city on Earth."

"I never thought you'd see *that*."

A different crew served dinner. Bob and Brenda took one end of the table. Terry and Tarzan talked as if nobody else was present, but every so often he noticed how the other children were listening.

But tracks in his mind ran beneath what he was saying. *They look good together. He's spent time with these children, probably watched them grow up. She should marry him.*

She can't! Unless I'm all wrong from beginning to end.

Wouldn't that be nice? "We've been carrying kudzu grain in the cargo ever since. Someday we'll find another famine—"

She must have been carrying Tarzan when she took up with Lex. She held his attention while she carried Tarzan to term, and she held him after Lex knew Tarzan wasn't his, and *then* she had Sepulveda. She could have held him if she'd married him, but she didn't. Held him anyway.

Quite a woman. And then she gave him up. Why?

Terry took the car up into the orange sunset glow and headed north. En route he used his card and the car phone to get a hotel room. By nine he had checked into the Arco-Elsewhere and was calling Maria.

"Want to see the best hotel on the planet? Or shall I get a cab and come to you?"

"I guess I'll come there. Hey, why not? It's close to work."

He used an operator to track down Charley and Sharon, and wasn't surprised to find they had rooms in the same hotel. "Call me for breakfast," Sharon said groggily. "I'm not on Dagon time yet."

Charley seemed alert. "Terry! How's Brenda?"

"Brenda's running the planet, or at least twenty kids' worth of planet. One of the boys is mine. She looks wonderful. Got a burly protector, likeable guy. Wants to be her fiancé but isn't."

"You've got a kid! What's he like?"

Terry had to sort out his impressions. "She raised 'em all well. He's self-confident, delighted to see me, taller than me . . . if he saves civilization I'll take half the credit."

"That good, huh?"

"Easily."

"I've been working. We've sold the big Langston Field generator. Farmer, lots of land, he may be thinking about becoming a suburb for the wealthy. I got a good price, Terry. He thought he could beat me at the Mirror Game—"

"He bet you?"

"He did. And I've signed up for eight tons of borloi, but I'll have to see how much bulk that is before—"

"Borloi!"

"Sure, Terry, borloi has medical uses too. We'll deal with a government at our next stop, give it plenty of publicity too. That way it'll be used right."

"I'm glad to see you've put some brain sweat into this. What occurs to me is—"

The door went *bingbong*.

"Company." Terry went to open the door. Maria was in daytime dress, with a large handbag. "Come on in. Check out the bathroom, it's really sybaritic. I'm on the phone." He returned. "Borloi, right? It's not worth stealing on the way out, but after we Jump we tell the whole population of Gaea about it? Shrewd. We'll be a target for any thief who wants to *sell* eight tons of borloi on the black market."

"Good point. What do you think?"

"Oh, I think we raise the subject with Sharon, and then I think we'll do it anyway."

"Let's meet for breakfast. Eight? Someone I want you to meet."

"Good." He hung up. He called, "I can offer you three astronauts for breakfast."

Maria came out to the sound of bathwater running. "Sounds delicious. It has to be early, Terry. Tomorrow's a working day."

"Oh, it'll be early. Early to bed?" He'd wanted to use the city computer files, but he was tired too. It wasn't the time change; the shorter days would have caught him up by now. It was stoop labor in high G.

Maria said, "I want to try that spa. Come with me? You look like you need it. And tell me about your day."

They all met for breakfast in Charlie's suite.

Charley had a groupie. Andrea Soucek was a university student, stunningly beautiful, given to cliches. She was goshwowed-out by the presence of *three* star-travellers. Sharon had George Callahan. Terry had Maria.

The conversation stayed general for awhile. Then George had to leave, and so did Maria. Over coffee it degenerated into shop talk, while Andrea Soucek listened in half-comprehending awe.

Eight tons of dry borloi (they'd freeze-dry it by opening the airlock) would fill more than half the cargo hold. Not much mass, though. The rest of the cargo space could go to heavy machinery. Their next stop, Gaea, had a small population unlikely to produce much for export, unlikely to buy much of the borloi. Most of it would be with them on two legs of their route.

Sharon asked, "Tanith doesn't manufacture much heavy machinery, do they?"

"I haven't found any I can buy. I'm working on it," Charley said.

Terry had an idea. "We want to freeze-dry the borloi anyway. We could pack it between the hull and the sleeve. Plenty of room for light stuff in the cargo hold."

"Hmm. Yeah! Any drug-running raider attacks us, his first shot would blow the borloi all across the sky! No addicts on our conscience."

"Rape the addicts. Evolution in action," Sharon said. "What kind of idiot would hook himself on borloi when the source is light years away? Get 'em out of the gene pool."

Andrea began to give her an argument. All humans were worthwhile, all could be saved. And borloi was a harmless vice—

Terry returned to his room carrying a mug of coffee.

The aristocratic phone operator recognized him by now. "Mr. Kakumee! Who may I track down for you?"

"Lex Hartner, MD, surgeon. Lived in Dagon City, Dryland sector, fifteen years ago."

"Fifteen years? Thanks a lot." But she'd stopped showing irritation. "Mmm. Not Dryland . . . he doesn't appear to be anywhere in Dagon."

"Try some other cities, please. He won't be outside a city."

Almost a minute crawled by. "I have a Lex Hartner in Coral Beach."

"I'll try that. Thanks."

It was Lex. He was older, grayer; his cheeks sagged in Tanith gravity. "Terry Kakumee?"

"Hello. I met your daughter yesterday."

The sagging disappeared. "How is she?"

"She's wonderful. All of Brenda's kids are wonderful. Are you wondering whether to tell me I've got a boy?"

"Yeah."

"He's wonderful too."

"Of course he is." Lex smiled at last. "How's Brenda?"

"She's wonderful. I asked her to marry me too, Lex. I mean sixteen years ago."

"Who else has she turned down?"

"Brawny farmer type named Maddox. Lex, I don't think she needs a man."

"How are you?"

"I'm fine. Would you believe Charley Laine is fine too? He looks like you'd expect, but his groupie is prettier than mine if not as smart."

"I did a good job there, didn't I?"

"That's what I'm telling you."

"Is it too late to say I'm sorry?"

"No, forget that. She didn't need me. Lex, have you got a moment? I've got some questions."

"About Brenda?"

"No. Lex, you did an autopsy on the corpse of a Sauron superman. Remember?"

"A man isn't likely to forget that. They rot fast in the swamps. It was pretty well chewed, too."

"Was there enough left for a gene analysis?"

"Some. Not enough to make me famous. It matched what the Navy already knew. I didn't find anything inhuman, anything borrowed from animals."

"Yeah. Anything startling?"

"Nope. It's all in the records."

"A Sauron and a Weem's Beast, you don't expect them to go to a photo finish."

"It must have been something to see. From a distance, that is. Brenda never wanted to talk about it, but that was a long time ago. Maybe she'd talk now."

"Okay, thanks. Lex, I still think of you as a friend. I won't be on Tanith very long. Everything I do is on the city account for awhile—"

"Maybe I'll come into town."

"Call me when and if, and everything goes on the card. I'm at the Arco-Elsewhere."

Next he linked into the Dagon City computer files.

Matters relating to Saurons had been declassified. Navy ships had transferred much of their data to city computers on Tanith and other worlds. Terry found a picture he'd seen before: a Sauron, no visible wounds, gassed in an attack on Medea. It rotated before him, a monster out of a nightmare. Randus?

An XYY, the text said. All of the Sauron soldiers, any who had left enough meat to be analyzed, had had freaky gene patterns—males with an extra Y gene, where XY was male and XX was female—until the Battle of Tanith. There they'd found some officers.

Those pictures were of slides and electron-microscope photographs. No officer's corpse had survived unshredded. Their gene patterns included the XY pair, but otherwise resembled those of the XYY berserkers.

Results of that gene pattern were known. Eyes that saw deep into the infrared; the altered eye structure could be recognized. Blood that clotted fast to block a wound. Rapid production of endorphins to block pain. Stronger bones. Bigger adrenal glands. Powerful muscles. Skin that changed color fast, from near-white (to make vitamin D in cold, cloudy conditions, where a soldier had to cover most of his skin or die) to near black (to prevent lethal sunburn in field conditions under a hotter sun.) Officers would have those traits too.

Nothing new yet.

Ah, here was Lex Hartner's autopsy report on Randus himself. XYY genes. Six-times-lethal damage from a Weem's Beast's teeth, and one wound . . . one narrow wound up through the base of the skull into the cerebellum, that must have paralyzed or killed him at once.

A Sauron superman working in a rice paddy might not expect something to come at him out of the water.

Terry studied some detail pictures of a Weem's Beast. It was something like a squat crocodile, with huge pads for front paws, claws inward-pointing to hold prey, a single dagger of a front tooth . . . That might have made the brain puncture if the thing was biting Randus'

head. Wouldn't the lower teeth have left other marks
on, say, the forehead?

So.

And a stranger, human-looking but with big bones and
funny eyes, had run loose on Tanith for sixteen years.
Had a man with a small daughter appeared somewhere,
set up a business, married perhaps? By now he would
have an identify and perhaps a position of power.

Saurons were popularly supposed to have been exter-
minated. Terry had never found any record of an attack
on whatever world had bred the monsters, and he
didn't now, though it must have happened. No mention
of further attempts to track down fleets that might have
fled across the sky. The Navy had left some stuff
classified.

Early files on the Curtis family had been scrambled.
He found a blurred family picture: a dark man, a darker
woman, five children; he picked out a gawky eleven-
year-old (the file said) who might have grown to be
Brenda. The file on the Maddoxes was bigger, with
several photographs. The men all looked like Bob
Maddox, all muscle and confidence and freckled tans.
The women were not much smaller and tended to be
freckled and burly.

So.

An XY officer, a male, might have wanted children.
Might have had children. They were gene-tailored, but
the doctors had used mostly human genes; maybe all-
human, despite the tales. They weren't a different species, after all. What would such children look like? How
would they grow up?

The Polar Datafile interview was fun. The Other
Worlds interview the next day felt more like work.
Charley's voice gave out, so they called it off for a few
days.

The borloi arrived in several planeloads. Terry didn't
notice any special attempts at security. On many worlds

there would have been a police raid followed by world-wide publicity. Memo: call all possible listeners in Gaea system *immediately* after Jump. Sell to government only. Run if anything looks funny.

They flew half the borloi to orbit and packed it into *Firebee's* outer hull, with no objection from Sharon. The work went fast. The next step was taken slowly, carefully.

The Langston Field generator from Phoenix system was too big for either boat.

Sharon put *Firebee* in an orbit that would intersect the atmosphere. With an hour to play with, they moved the beast out of the cargo hold with an armchair-type pusher frame and let it get a good distance away. They all watched as Terry beamed the signal that turned it on.

The generator became a black sphere five hundred meters across.

Charley and Terry boarded Shuttle #1. Sharon set *Firebee* accelerating back to orbit.

When the black sphere intersected the atmosphere there was little in the way of reentry flame. Despite the massive machine at the center, the huge sphere was a near-vacuum. It slowed rapidly and drifted like a balloon. Boat #1 overshot, then circled back.

Air seeped through the black force field to fill the vacuum inside. It ceased to be a balloon.

It touched down in the marshes south and east of Dagon City, more or less as planned. No signal would penetrate the field. Terry and Charley had to go into the Field with a big inflatable cargo raft, mount it beneath the generator and turn it off.

At that point it became the owner's problem. He'd arranged for two heavy-lift aircraft. *Firebee's* crew waited until the planes had landed, then took Boat #1 back to Dagon.

They were back at the hotel thirty-six hours after they'd left. Maria found the door open and Terry lolling in the spa. "I think I'm almost dissolved," he told her.

*   *   *

Lex didn't call. Brenda didn't call.

They ferried the rest of the borloi up a day later. Some went into the outer hull. The rest they packed around the cargo hold, leaving racks open in the center. Dried borloi for padding, to shield whatever else Charley found to carry.

It was morning when they landed, with time for sightseeing. Andrea and Charley opted to rent equipment and do some semiserious mountain climbing in the foothills of the Warden. Terry called Maria, but she couldn't get off work, and couldn't see him tonight either. That made mountain climbing less attractive. Terry hiked around Dagon City for awhile, looked through the major shopping mall, then went back to the hotel.

He was half-asleep with his shoes off when the phone chimed.

The face was Brenda's. Terry rubbed his palms together and tapped the answer pad.

"Hi, Terry. I'm in the lobby. Can I come up?"

"Sure, Brenda. Can I order you a drink? Lunch?"

"Get me a rum collins."

Terry rang off, then ordered from room service. His palms were sweating.

I ran the record into Firebee's *memory and ran a translation program on it, but I didn't look at the results. I'd have to go back to* Firebee, *then come back here. Had Bob Maddox told her? Probably not.*

She walked in like she owned the hotel, smiling as if nobody was supposed to know. Her dress was vivid orange; it went well with her color. The drink trolley followed her in. When it had rolled out she asked, "How long are you going to be on Tanith?"

"Two weeks, give or take a week. Charley has to find us something to sell. Besides borloi, that is."

"Have you tried bantar cloth? It's just about the only

hi-tech stuff we make enough of. Don't take clothing. Styles change. Get bolts, and be sure you've got the tools to shape it."

"Yeah . . . Brenda, is there anything you can't do?"

"Cook. And I'm not the marrying type."

"I know that now."

"But I have children. Do you like Tarzan?"

He smiled and relaxed a little. "Good job there. I'm glad I met him."

"Let's do it again."

His drink slopped. Somehow he hadn't expected this. "Hold it, Brenda. I'm with another woman this trip."

"Maria? Terry, Maria's with Fritz Marsden tonight and all tomorrow. Fritz is one of mine. He works at the fusion plant at Randall's Point, and he only gets into town every couple of weeks. Maria isn't going to give *him* up for a, well, a transient."

He sipped his drink to give himself time to think. When he took the glass from his lips, she pulled it out of his hand without spilling it and set it down. She pulled him to his feet with a fist in his belt. "I'm not asking for very much, am I?"

"Ah, no. Child support? We'll be leaving funds behind us anyway. Are you young enough?" Was she *serious*?

"I don't know. What's the worst that can happen?" She had unzipped his shirt and was pulling it loose. And with wild hope he thought, *It could be*!

She stripped him naked, then stepped back to examine him. "I don't think you've gained or lost an ounce. Same muscle tone too. You people don't even wrinkle."

"We wrinkle all at once. You've changed incredibly."

"I wanted to. I needed to. Terry, am I coming on too strong? You're tense. Let me show you something else I learned. Face down on the bed—" She helped him irresistibly. "I'll keep my dress on. Okay? And if you've got anything like massage oil around, tell me now."

"I've never had a massage of any kind."

The next hour was a revelation. She kept telling him to relax, and somehow he did that, while she tenderized muscles he'd strained moving borloi bags in free fall. He wondered if he'd been wrong; he wondered if he was going to die; he wondered why he'd never tried this before.

"I took massage training after you left. I used it at the hospital. I never had to work through a Nuliajuk's fat padding before . . . no sweat. I can reach the muscle underneath."

"Hell, you could reach through the ribs!"

"Is this too hard? Were you having trouble in orbit?"

"Nope. Everything went fine."

"Then why the tension? Turn over." She rolled him over and resumed work on his legs, then his arms and shoulders. "You didn't used to be shy with me."

"Am I shy now?"

"You keep tensing up." Her skirt was hiked up and she straddled his hips to work on his belly. "Good muscle here. Ease up— Well."

He had a respectable erection.

She caressed him. "I was afraid you'd changed." She slid forward and, hell, she didn't have panties.

"I kept my promise," she gloated.

"True," he croaked. "Take it off."

She pulled her dress over her head. There was still a brassiere; no woman would go without one in Tanith gravity. She took that off too.

She was smoothly dark, with no pale area anywhere. His hands remembered her breasts as smaller. Four kids—and it had been too long, far too long. He cried out, and it might have been ecstasy or grief or both.

She rolled away, then slid up along the length of him. "And that was a massage."

"Well, I've been missing something."

"I did you wrong all those years ago. Did you hate me? Is that why you're so tense?"

"That wasn't it." He felt good: relaxed, uncaring.

She'd come here only to seduce him, to mend fences, to revive memories. Or she already knew, and he might as well learn. "There's a Sauron message sender, galactic south of the Coal Sack. It was there to send Sauron ships to a certain Jump point."

"So?"

"Would you like to know where they were supposed to go? I could find out."

"No."

"Flat-out no? Suppose they come back?"

"Cut the crap, Terry. Hints and secrets. You never did *that* to me before."

"I'm sorry, love—"

"Why did two Saurons go around the Maddox farm and straight to us? You told Bob you knew."

"Because they were white."

Brenda's face went uncannily blank. Then she laughed. "Poor Bob! He'd think you were absolutely looney."

"He sure would. I didn't *want* to know this, Brenda. Why don't you want to find the Saurons?"

"What would I want with them? I want to see my children safe—"

"Send them."

"Not likely! Terry, how much have you figured out?"

"I think I've got it all. I keep testing it, Brenda, and it fits every time."

She waited, her nose four centimeters from his, her breath on his face. The scent of her was very faint.

He said, "You saw to it that three of your own children were out in the rice paddy, including Tarzan. The girl you kept at the house was Reseda, the blond, the girl with the least obvious of Sauron genes. You invited Bob over. Maybe he'd get rid of me before the kids came back."

"Just my luck. He likes you."

"They took away your scent. No enemy could smell you out. They gave you an epicanthic fold to protect your eyes. The flat, wide nose is less vulnerable and pulls in more air." He pushed his fingers into her hair. Spongy, resilient, thick. She didn't flinch; she smiled in pleasure. "And this kind of hair to protect your skulls. It'll take an impact. You grow your own skewball helmets!"

"How gracefully you put it."

"But it looks like a black woman's hair, so you want black skin. So you spend an hour on the roof every afternoon. Naked?" There were no white areas.

"Sure."

"There was a burn-through over Dagon City, and the EMP destroyed most of the records, but maybe not all. Whatever was left had to say that the Curtis family was mostly black."

"Whereas the Maddoxes are white," she said.

"That burn-through was important. You had to be sure. I'm betting you caused it yourself. It didn't have any serious military importance, did it? The pulse wiped out hospital equipment too, so they couldn't look inside you. Couldn't see that you aren't built—"

"If you say, 'Not quite like a woman,' I'll turn you upside down." She reached down to grip his ankle.

"You came down in a two-man escape pod. One XYY Sauron, and you. There wasn't any Horatius loose for fifteen years. Miranda either."

"Only an XX," she said. Oh, she felt good lying alongside him. The Saurons weren't different species. Gene-tailored, but human, quite human.

He said, "But you didn't speak Anglic. Here you were on Tanith with some chance of passing for a . . . citizen. But you couldn't speak a word, and you were with a Sauron berserker—"

"We say Soldier. Soldiers and officers. We don't say Sauron."

"Okay."

"We killed a family and took over the house. It was still war, Terry. We cleaned up as best we could. Hid one body, a girl about my size, and buried the rest. I painted our bantar cloth armor. Turned on the TV wall and left it on. It didn't tell me what they were talking about, but I got the accents. Worked naked in the fields, but that didn't help. It left my feet white up to the knees!"

"The Soldier couldn't hide, so you had to kill him. Lex found the knife wound. He wouldn't tell me about it, Brenda."

"Lex knows. He delivered Van, our second. Van was a Soldier."

He couldn't think of anything to say. Brenda said, "I killed Randus. I found a Weem's Beast and gave him to it. We don't think much of the soldiers, Terry. I cut a claw off the Weem's Beast and made the wound—"

"Almost through your skull."

"It had to be done in one stroke. And kept septic. And in the jungle I had to climb a tree when I had daylight and take off all my clothes to keep the tan. I waved at a plane once. Too late to hide. If the pilot saw me he must have thought he was hallucinating."

"What'd you eat out there?"

"Everything! What good is a Soldier who gets food poisoning? Anything a De Lap's Ghoul can eat, I can eat."

"*That's* not in the records."

"That's why I can't cook. I can't tell when it tastes wrong, I can't tell when meat's rotten. I used recipes till I could teach some of the kids to cook."

"You couldn't talk, but you could fake the symptoms of a stroke. That's the part I just couldn't believe—Goddamn!"

"The left side of her face had gone slack as a rubber mask. She grinned with the other side. "Brenda Curris," she said.

"Don't do that."

She reached across him and finished the Collins in two swallows. "How long have you known?"

"Maybe fifteen years, but I didn't *know*, Brenda. I

was still angry. There's a lot of time to think between the stars. I made up this tale. And worked on the kinks, and then I started thinking I must be crazy, because I couldn't pick a hole in it. You told the Marines about the Saurons to make them talk to you. They wouldn't notice how fast your speech improved. They were hanging on every word, trying to get a line on the escaped Sauron, and chattering away to each other. They taught you Anglic.

"I used to wonder what you saw in me. I'm an outworlder. I couldn't recognize a Tanith accent. You made love to me in the dark because you'd lost too much of your tan in the hospital—"

He stopped because her hand had closed hard on his arm. "I wanted your child! I wanted children, and Tarzan would *look* like he was half outworlder. I didn't plan the power failure, Terry. Hell, it probably tipped you off."

"Yeah, you moved like you could almost see in the dark. And wore dark glasses in daylight. The Tanith sun doesn't get that bright, love."

"Bright enough."

"Tanith must have been perfect for you. The sun never gets high. In this gravity *everybody's* got muscles."

"True, but I didn't pick Tanith. Tanith was where the ships went. What else did you notice?"

"Nothing you could have covered up. I talked marriage at you so you switched to Lex. While you were carrying my child."

"But I *can't* get married. In winter the tan goes away. I have to use tanning lotion and do everything by phone."

"What was it like for . . . you? Before?"

Brenda sat up. "For Sauron women? All right. I'm second generation. Test tube children, all of us. Women are kept in . . . it's like a laboratory and a harem both. The first generation didn't work out. The women didn't like being brood mares, so to speak, and one day they killed half the doctors and ran loose."

"Good."

"There's nothing good about any of this. They were hunted down and shot, and I got all of this by rumor. Maybe it's true and maybe it isn't."

"They made you a brood mare too, didn't they?"

"Oh, sure. The second generation Sauron women, we like having children. I don't know if they fiddled with our genes or if they just kept the survivors for, for breeding after the revolt. They gave us a TV wall and let us learn. I think the first group was suffering from sensory deprivation. Most of the children were bottled, but we tended them, and every so often they'd let us carry a child to term, after they were sure it'd survive. I had two. One was Miranda."

"Survive?" He was sitting up now too, with the remains of his Collins.

"Mating two Saurons is a bad idea. The doctor's don't give a shit about side effects. Out of ten children you get a couple of Soldiers and an officer and a couple of girls. They're the heterozygotes. The homozygotes die. Paired genes for infrared eyes give blindness. Paired genes for fast blood clotting gets you strokes and heart attacks in your teens. You get albinos. You get freaks who die of shock just because the adrenal glands got too big."

"Yuk."

"Can you see why I don't want to find the Saurons? But these are good genes—" Her hands moved down her body, inviting him to witness: good genes, yes. "As long as you don't backbreed. My children are an asset to the human race, Terry."

"I—"

"Six of us escaped. We killed some doctors on the way. Once we reached the barracks it was easy. The XYYs will do anything for us. They smuggled us into four of the troop ships. I don't know what happened to the others. I got aboard *Deimos* as a Soldier. None of the officers ever saw me. We were part of the attack on

Tanith. When I saw we had a good burn-through in the Dagon City shield, the whole plan just popped into my mind. I grabbed a Soldier and we took an escape pod and ran it from there."

"You're incredible." He pulled back to look at her. Not quite a woman . . . not quite *his* woman, ever.

"Terry, did you wonder if I might kill you?"

"Yeah. I thought you'd want to know where the Saurons went first."

"You bet your life on that?"

"I bet on you."

"Fool."

"I'm not dead yet," he pointed out.

"Bad bet, love. When I knew you knew, I assumed you'd made a record somewhere, somehow, that would spill it all if you died. I couldn't find it in the city records. But suppose I decided to wipe out everyone who might know? Everyone you might have talked to. Charley, Sharon, Maria—"

Oh my God.

"—Lex, Bob because you might have talked to him, George Callahan in case Sharon talked, maybe a random lawyer; do you think I can't trace your phone calls? Okay, calm down now." Hands where his neck joined his shoulders, fingers behind the shoulder blades, rubbing smooth and hard. The effort distorted her voice. "We Saurons . . . we have to decide . . . *not* to kill. I've decided. But you've got a . . . real blind spot there, Terry. You put some people in danger."

"I guess I just don't think that way. I had to *know* whether you'd kill me, before I told you anything useful. I had to know what you are."

"What am I?" she asked.

"I'm not dead. Nobody's dead since you reached the hospital."

"Except Van."

"Yeah. Van. But if any of this got out, you'd be dead and Tarzan would be dead and, hell, they'd probably kill every kid who ever lived with you, just in case you trained them somehow. So."

"So," she said. "Now what?"

2656 AD, April (Firebee *clock time*)

Firebee approached the Alderson Jump Point with a load of borloi and bantar cloth.

Tanith's sun had turned small. Terry searched the sky near that hurtingly bright point for some sign of Tanith itself. But stars don't waver outside an atmosphere, and he couldn't find the one point among many.

"We made some good memories there," Sharon said. "Another two minutes . . . Troops, are we really going to try to reach Sparta?"

Charley called from aft. "Sparta's a long way away. See what they buy on Gaea first."

Terry said, "I'm against it. Sparta's got six Alderson points. If they're not at war they'll be the center of all local trade. This beloved wreck won't be worth two kroner against that competition. We might have to join a guild too, if they let us."

"Isn't there a chance the Emperor would buy the data we got from *Morningstar*?"

"I'll run through those records, Captain, but my guess is we've got nothing to sell. There won't be anything Sparta doesn't have."

She nodded. "Okay. Jumping *now*."

And *Firebee* was gone.

The following transcript was discovered among the papers of the late Henry Blaine Barton, Commander, Imperial Navy Reserve. Between the time of his retirement from active duty and his death at the age of seventy-nine, Commander Barton added to his military honors by distinguishing himself as the Empire's foremost expert on Sauron Phenomena.

Critics have pointed to a certain lack of objectivity (some say fanaticism) on the part of Commander Barton regarding Sauron "survivors" that might have escaped the destruction at the Second Battle of Tanith and the following Sack of Sauron, spreading throughout the Empire as sort of a "genetic fifth column," claiming that Barton's wartime defense experiences clouded his judgment. In Commander Barton's defense, it must be pointed out that his knowledge and expertise concerning the Saurons, gained though it was by sifting through the ruins of their society on Sauron, was far superior to that of any of his critics; a point conceded by the more honest of that breed.

Thus, while his warnings of a resurgent Sauron can be seen (in the light of today's problems throughout the Empire) to be somewhat strident, it would be a mistake to dismiss them out of hand. Perhaps the danger is less from a reborn Sauron than from twisted individuals and degenerate societies seeking to emulate them, but it might be a danger, nevertheless.

This transcript was previously unknown to Imperial research teams, and seems to have generated significant interest, though no official comment has been issued regarding it.

TIME: 1423/SAURON INVESTITURE
UNIT: 97th Imperial Fighter Squadron (Jolly Rogers), INSS Centurion (CV/Ald.)
ELEMENT: Red Flight, Captain Serling commanding:
Lieutenants De Tar, Vogel, Willoughby, Stewart and Gold accompanying.
Gunners and Co-Pilots: Ensigns Sullivan, Hassan, Yermakov, Walsh, Obata and Valladares.

(At this time Red Flight was intact, consisting of six heavy fighters of the "Morgan" class (AF-7), two-seat assault craft.)

SERLING: Form up, Red Flight, I have visual on target. Field status.

VOGEL: Enemy's field shows no burn-throughs, Captain.

SERLING: I make ship engaged with target to be the *Lermontov*.

VOGEL: Affirm that, Captain.

SERLING: Well somebody tell 'em to pour it on, for chrissakes! De Tar.

DE TAR: Roger.

SERLING: Take your half in a rake down the target's side, I'll bring my half across her bow. And make sure the *Lermontov* knows we're coming.

SULLIVAN: Burn-throughs, sir ... multiples, looks like the *Lermontov*'s waking up and decided to play.

SERLING: Belay that, Sully. You never know who's listening, De Tar.

DE TAR: (Lt. De Tar's transmission is severely garbled, presumably due to his close proximity to the enemy ship's overloaded Langston Field) Close in . . . Gold firing . . all missiles . . .

SERLINGS: Say again, De Tar . . . ah, shit, bring us over the Sauron's back, link up with De Tar's element and—

VOGEL: Break, break, target moving, target may be attempting to disengage.

DE TAR: . . . confirm . . . firing maneuvering . . . coming about (?) to . . . five.

SERLING: De Tar, break off your element, repeat, break off your element.

VOGEL: Sauron firing . . . De Tar's hit, Captain, looks like a lucky main battery shot.

SERLING: Anything left?

WILLOUGHBY: Christ, they're angel dust.

SERLING: Match accelerations and close with target, coordinate *Lermontov*.

VOGEL: *Lermontov* says she's not pursuing, Captain; says there's other ships vectoring now.

SERLING: Maintain pursuit.

VOGEL: Sauron at five Gs accel.

SERLING: Squadron to six Gs.

VOGEL: He's headed for the Alderson, Captain.

SERLING: He'll never hit it at this speed.

VOGEL: Sauron at eight Gs.

SERLING: Godammit, go to nine!

WILLOUGHBY: Losing . . . thrust . . . line feed . . . fracture.

(Severe distortion here due to acceleration effects on inboard recording equipment. Transcripts are estimates.)

SULLIVAN (inboard): VST (Vital Signs Telemetry) show Stewart and Gold unconscious. Willoughby going, I don't feel so hot . . . myself.

SERLING: Vogel; where's the Sauron?

VOGEL: Coming up on Point at eleven Gs.

SERLING: He can't make a Jump at eleven Gs. Impossible. Hold us at nine; we'll catch him.

OBATA: Three-F! Three-F! (Fuel Feed Failure, a common danger at high G acceleration, particularly in the *Morgans*.)

SERLING: Break off, Obata.

SULLIVAN: He's gone, Captain; engine blew. VST shows him and Stewart ejected safely and drifting.

VOGEL: Sauron's coming up on the point . . . Jeez, he's firing his Alderson Drives . . .

SERLING: I don't (expletive deleted) believe it.

SULLIVAN: Captain . . .

SERLING: Red Flight, intercept Obata and Stewart for pickup, drop to three Gs ASAP. Vogel, what have you got on that Sauron?

VOGEL: Fragmentary, Captain. Sounds like they were trying for a Random Jump. No way to tell if they made it at the other end.

SERLING: (Expletive) They're gone either way. Sully, download everything we got out of this fiasco to FleetOps.

SULLIVAN: Think anybody'll care?

SERLING: Somebody sure as hell ought to.

SOME THINGS SURVIVE

JOHN LAVALLEY

". . . All of which brings me to this, gentlemen," said
retired admiral Hawthorne. "Whether that cruiser got
where it was going in one piece or in many pieces is not
as important as the fact that we don't *know* if it made it
in one piece."

The half-dozen other men sitting around a warm,
old-style hearth fire in the admiral's home were quiet.
It had been a long night, just discussing the generalities
of the Assault on Sauron, the last and most furious
battle of the Secession Wars.

The admiral had dominated the conversation partly by
his personality but mostly because the others felt he
was right. One of the particulars of the battle made it
possible that the most expensive victory of the war
would be the most useless. Something would have to
be done.

Hawthorne paused to sip the carefully-aged whiskey
he shared with his guests. "You've all heard my plan.
Marcus and Philip, I'll need you both to pull whatever
strings you can with the Council. Call in every favor
anyone owes you and then some. Be sure not to mention my name. Much as it pleasures me to be hated by
Councilor Campbelson, I'd hate to see this fall apart
because of an old grudge."

Philip Daybridge shook his head. "I don't think Councilor Pedorakis will help, no matter what he owes me.

224

He has opposed fleet refurbishment and all other military spending—"

"True, but I know of a situation developing with a certain young female officer who works as his attaché. The situation could be embarrassing for him in about six months. I think we could use it."

"I like that," said Daybridge, musing. "I like that."

"As much as I admire the idea," said Captain Ezio Sanchez. At age forty-two he was by far the youngest of those present. "I don't see how you are going to get it past Campbelson. He's very much against the old military lobby and he knows each of you well."

"Funny you should say that, Ezio. Because I don't think he knows you that well at all," said Hawthorne with a chummy grin.

Sanchez's shoulders fell. Oh shit, he thought.

Captain Sanchez stood at ease before the panel of Councilors. He shifted his weight slightly as he answered a question from Hyron Campbelson, the High Councilor to the Imperial Viceroy of Sector Twenty-Eight. "Yes, sir. There is an official reference to a Sauron warship making an Alderson Jump. A log entry from the *Centurion* describes a large Sauron ship making for the Alderson point at top acceleration. The *Centurion*'s log goes further, sir. Their fighters had just broken off from engaging the vessel and—"

"Why did they break off?" asked the High Councilor, seeming irritated.

"They were desperately short of fuel, sir, and had hardly enough weapons left to make another attack worthwhile."

"You mean to say that they didn't fight to the last bullet?"

The High Councilor seemed to have romantic notions on how to fight a war. Sanchez shook his head. "No, sir. If they had tried, they'd not have had sufficient fuel to return to the *Centurion*. As it was, only two were lost in the engagement. If they had run out of fuel, the whole strike force would have been lost."

"Still, if they hadn't let the Sauron ship get away, you wouldn't be here making this request, now would you?"

Come within arm's length of me and ask that again, you chicken-necked— "No, sir."

"Any idea where they went, Captain?"

"Sir, it is admittedly unlikely that they would have survived given the damage they'd taken, but if they did survive, there weren't many places they could go. We, that is, my staff and I compiled a list of known worlds that are neither Imperial domain nor known to be under control by Outies."

The High Councilor scanned the documents on the table before him. The list he found filled several pages. He looked at Sanchez over his glasses. "You're kidding."

It was a reaction Sanchez had expected. "Sir, we believe that the Saurons left to accomplish one of two things. First, they would want to hole up and repair the ship. We consider this to be unlikely because they were so badly damaged that only a good-sized shipyard could serve the purpose. They'd have to avoid the Empire. There's nowhere they could go for repairs."

"All right," conceded the High Councilor.

"The other possibility, sir," said Sanchez, steeling himself against the Council's stares, "is that they wanted a system with a human population but completely isolated from any Imperial contact or contact with any of the Outies. That reduces possible planets to fewer than one hundred, sir."

"Well," the High Councilor was punctilious, "as long as they're gone and out of our hair, I see no reason why we should expend ships hunting them down when we're having enough trouble holding things together here."

Captain Sanchez suppressed an inward sigh. Were all Imperial politicians this myopic? "Sir, any planet that forgotten and isolated would probably not have kept up the technology to defend themselves from a Talon class heavy cruiser."

"So the Saurons beat them up. What of it?"

"That is most certainly what they did. The problem is what they may be doing now."

"Which is?"

"Breeding, sir. That ship had a large enough crew for a core breeding stock. It is my guess that they augment this stock with the best of the local gene pool, probably by force."

"Your guess, Captain?"

"There are historical precedents for it, sir."

"Well, you would know about that, right, Professor?"

The High Councilor's contempt for historians was more than evident now, which made Captain Sanchez, as a professor of history at New Annapolis, feel less than confident. He felt that politicians' almost universal disregard for the past was the reason so much of it was repeated. "It is possible, however unlikely sir, that in another few hundred years, we may be faced with a Sauron invasion."

"Which makes it hardly our problem now, does it? Still, we'd hate to go down in history," Campbelson looked at the other councilors, then smiled condescendingly at Sanchez, "as the men who let it happen. The Council will recess for two hours to discuss your proposal, Captain."

Hyron Campbelson sat hunched in his chair at the end of the long conference table, enjoying the massage a young servant girl was giving him. "That's enough," he said, rotating his shoulders and leaning back.

Campbelson watched the girl quietly leave, tracing the curve of her hips with his eyes, and decided to retain her for other services in the evening.

"I'm not sure we should take this Captain Sanchez too seriously," one of the Councilors said. "He's asking for more than half the capital ship strength in this sector to chase ghosts with."

"The Viceroy would take our heads if—"

"I think we should send three squadrons." Councilor Mendell was the only Frystaater on the Viceroyal Council. His lone presence on a sixteen-member council was fair indication of his world's control over sector affairs. He, along with Councilor Pedorakis, presented the only arguments in favor of Sanchez's proposal. His statement silenced the others in the room only for a second.

"You're a fool, suggesting—"

"We don't even have three squadrons—"

"They'd never return—"

"Exactly," Campbelson said, smiling confidently. He tilted back in his chair and interlocked his fingers behind his head, showing the casual control with which he dominated the Council. "You don't seem to realize what an opportunity this is."

The others waited out the pause. Campbelson enjoyed their confusion. Simple things which muddled the Councilors or escaped their notice entirely were small problems to him. There was little doubt as to who would succeed the Viceroy, whose health was in noticeable decline.

"In recent years," he began, sounding almost bored, "we've been getting a lot of trouble from certain naval officers. I can think of five in particular, who don't seem to agree with the way we run the sector. I think we should let them see the galaxy for themselves. Then we can function a little more smoothly."

"But three cruisers—!"

"No," Campbelson raised a hand, chuckling. "No, not three cruisers."

It was close to four hours before Captain Sanchez was summoned to the Council Audience Chamber. The Council's decision left him bitter and angry.

"Captain Sanchez, the Council agrees to a modification of your plan," the High Council began. "Instead of the three large cruisers you asked for, we authorized a destroyer to be used—"

"Sir—!"

"No protests, Captain! We're having the devil's own time maintaining order with what's left of the fleet as it is. All resources are at a premium. We just can't spare you the cruisers to pursue these wild geese of yours."

The High Councilor took a theatrically deep breath. "Again, we authorize a destroyer to be used for the purpose of reconnoitering these designated planets for any sign of Sauron activity. This destroyer will not be equipped with nuclear or other planetary bombardment weapons. It can have ship-to-ship weapons and short-range defenses but nothing more.

"If you find anything important you are not, repeat, not to take any direct action. Instead, you are to return immediately and show us what you find.

"And, Captain?"

"Yes, sir?"

High Councilor Campbelson smiled his tight, imperial smile. "You are the expert on the history of the wars and since we've no use for that anymore, you may go hunt wild geese with the ship, but only as an advisor. You will have no place in the chain of command. You will have no authority.

"So entered in the Council Record." He tapped the small gavel. "This Audience Session is adjourned."

Captain Sanchez exited the airlock of the drydock station and propelled himself along the gangway tube to the ship.

The vessel was perhaps three hundred meters long and cylindrical in design. To Sanchez it looked like a length of pipe, slightly swollen in the middle. The ship was built on the design of a ramjet, with the interior diameter of the tube narrowing from both ends to pinch point at the center, like an hourglass.

On the outside, Sanchez could see the thick region in the middle, ringed with the ship's main weapons' batteries and sensor arrays, as he slowly moved through the access tube. He shook his head sadly when he noticed one of the missile arrays being removed from its barbette. A large telescope was tethered nearby, waiting to be slid into place. Scattered over the hull, several work crews were busy painting the ship a dull, light-absorbing black.

"Captain, Imperial Fleet, arriving." The airlock guard's words were the first sound Sanchez heard as the lock opened into the ship. He noticed that the young sailor's face had the look of hard wood or chiseled granite common to natives of the planet Frystaat.

He showed his identification to the guard. "Is the Captain on board?"

"Right here," said a tall uniformed man emerging from a corridor. "You must be Captain Sanchez. Welcome aboard the *Fledermaus*. I'm Kattinger, Hans Kattinger, Commanding Officer."

"Call me Ezio." Sanchez took the proffered hand. It was like shaking hands with a living statue. The ship's captain was from Frystaat as well.

"Ezio, you're the last of the new arrivals. Glad to have you aboard."

As he and Kattinger floated down the corridor, Sanchez noted two things. First, each of the crewmen they encountered had the same hewn-from-rock features of their captain and the airlock sentry. And second, when passing others in the corridor, crewmen would salute Sanchez, the stranger, with sharp perfection, while salutes given Kattinger were more relaxed, not sloppy but with respect shared by confident familiarity. Usually, the salute accompanied a cheery "Good morning, Captain." Or even, "Hello, Skipper."

There seems to be, thought Sanchez, *a closeness, a tightness to this crew, like a family. Good.*

"Captain Sanchez," Kattinger spoke, stopping by a closed door, "here is your stateroom. I've had your things put inside already. I'll be in my cabin just around the corner. If you'd like to get rid of that pressure suit and put on some real clothes, then join me for some coffee, I'd be grateful."

"Be a pleasure, sir."

"Please, call me Hans."

Sanchez did feel comfortable in the shipboard uniform. He felt even more so upon entering the C.O.'s stateroom. The ship being a destroyer, the Captain's cabin was not very spacious, but Kattinger had made room for a three-tiered bookshelf. And what books! *Hitler and The Third Reich*, *The American Revolution*, and *The Rise and Fall of The Roman Empire* were some of the titles Sanchez recognized. "May I?" he said, tentatively reaching for one of the books.

"Go right ahead."

"The *Rise and Fall of The Roman Empire*," Sanchez breathed, carefully opening the book. "My father's copy was lost during the war and I haven't been able to find one. It's out of print."

"Not aboard this ship," Kattinger smiled. "Watch."

Below the shelves, against the bulkhead was a small personal computer and printbinder. Kattinger's fingers beat a quick, delicate tattoo over the small console. Within seconds, a pile of printed pages accumulated in the bin. A double-creased board appeared under the stack then folded over it. A darting red beam stitched along the edge, making holes for the small composite pins that slid into place. A press flattened the ends of the pins, then a printed cover was snapped and pressed onto the spine. The finished book then slid into a wire tray on the side of the binder. The whole process took less then thirty seconds.

"That's impressive," said Sanchez. He saw that the book in the tray was identical to the one in his hands.

"Now go ahead," said Kattinger, "and tear the title page in half."

"What? This is—"

"Go on, try it."

Sanchez opened Kattinger's book and carefully tried

to rip the first page down the middle. It resisted. He glanced at Kattinger, who simply nodded. He pulled mightily for several seconds, then gave up. The paper showed only the slightest wrinkle which rapidly smoothed out.

Sanchez shook his head slowly. "Is it that harsh on your world?"

Kattinger burst out laughing. "No, no, it's not our weather. It's our children!"

Sanchez thought for a moment, then had to agree. It made sense that a small child with nearly the strength of a normal human adult could wreak havoc in a library.

"The paper is high-memory polymer impregnated with composite fiber. The nice thing is, you could lose that book in the Kraggerian jungle, find it fifty years later and you'd only have to wash the mud off to make it look new."

"Now that *is* impressive," said Sanchez, returning Kattinger's book to the self. He noticed that many of the books therein were similarly bound.

Kattinger gestured to the new book in the tray. "You might want to let it cool down for a bit. The ink has to be heat-fused to the paper. Here, have some coffee."

All thoughts of books vanished from his mind as Sanchez took the insulated bulb. He popped the vent open for a second, then smelled the aroma. His eyebrows arched in surprise. "Is this real coffee?"

Kattinger nodded.

Sanchez drew from the bulb, smiling in sublime pleasure. "Mmm."

Kattinger chuckled. "Has it been that long?"

"Too long," said Sanchez, carefully drawing more of the hot liquid. "Much too long." He swallowed then looked at Kattinger. "I've got to ask, how did you get this?"

The destroyer's captain grinned again, his blue eyes sparkling with remembered mischief. "Last month we stopped over New Colombia and I gave a plantation owner and his family a ride in one of the ship's longboats. For an hour and a half they goggle-eyed at the blue boulder hanging over us. Then, I treated them to a reentry burn with the viewports open. Senor Aldonado said that he knew he was going to Heaven because he'd seen the fires of Hell.

"It was illegal, but so what? They loved the ride and we got about eleven tons of his best coffee. It's filling up number three hold right now, all packed in nitrogen." Kattinger winked slightly. "Stays fresher that way."

"Well Hans," said Sanchez, "I guess we should get down to business. Have you been briefed about the mission?"

"Just that we were handpicked to check on a possible renegade Sauron ship in the remote systems. We look around, see what we can find, then go home. What I don't understand is why you wanted a destroyer to hunt for a heavy cruiser. Not that I mind—"

"Hans, I didn't want a destroyer!" Sanchez said in exasperation. "I wanted three cruisers. Dear God, I wanted the whole fleet." He sighed, feeling the futility of his anger. "Hans, please do not misunderstand me. From what I can see, the *Fledermaus* is a fine ship, but against that cruiser I wanted—"

"Ezio," said Kattinger, his face softening such as it could, "I know what the Council can be like. You should have asked for the whole fleet, they'd given you a squadron of cruisers. Don't worry, we'll do our best."

"I know," said Sanchez, drawing from the bulb again.

Feeling awkward, he changed the subject. "That brings me to something I wanted to ask. Are you all from Frystaat, your whole crew?"

Kattinger nodded. "There aren't many of us left, all—Frystaat crews, that is."

Sanchez knew why. The Sauron attacks on Frystaat had been beaten back by the Imperial Fleet but the planet did not go unharmed. Centers of industry and culture were destroyed leaving a disrupted and fractioning civilization to be picked at by off-world vultures clad in the robes of the Imperial State.

"There is not a man or woman in this ship," said Kattinger, "who hasn't lost many of those who were close, even our new crewmembers. Many were orphaned in the attacks.

"I just hope that if we find Saurons, that *Fledermaus* is part of the attack force sent me to kill them."

For a moment the merriment left Kattinger's eyes. It was replaced by something else, something which sent a cold feeling along the back of Sanchez's neck. It was gone in an instant, but had been there. Sanchez noticed a small, framed picture on the desk, a picture of an attractive Frystaat woman and two little girls. "I'm sorry, Hans."

Kattinger blinked, some of the sparkle returning to his eyes. "Can I ask about you, Ezio? I mean, did you volunteer to join this expedition?"

"Well, sort of," said Sanchez, hesitating. "I was assigned by the Council."

Kattinger nodded to himself, knowingly. "I thought New Annapolis staff had immunity from space duty."

"I didn't want to use it. Besides, the Academy is phasing out the History Department. They were going to retire me. What then? Who in the Empire wants a used history teacher?"

Sanchez could see from the patient look on Kattinger's face that the man was not yet convinced.

"All right, do you want the real reason? Look at those books, Hans." He gestured to the shelves. "Think of the minds that made them—not just the histories but the literature, the philosophy and science. Look, you've got the Shakespearean plays, the works of S.L. Clemens. Do you think the Saurons could write that? Could they produce a Socrates, or—or a Darwin or a Franklin? No! And I'll tell you why. It's because the very things that bring out those qualities in men were gene-altered out of them by people who forgot that a perfect soldier will resent taking orders from those less capable than he!"

Sanchez caught his breath. "I'm sorry, Captain. Sometimes I forget that I'm not in a classroom anymore."

Kattinger sat, quietly listening.

Sanchez spoke again. "Hans, when I first read the entry in the *Centurion*'s log of a Sauron ship escaping, my heart froze. I could almost hear a sound, like a drumbeat and voice telling me that all that I live for, my whole civilization, was going to die.

"No sir. No. I'll fight them. I'll fight them with guns, rocks. Break my naked teeth on them if I—"

Sanchez felt a warm, strong hand on his shoulder. It was Kattinger's. "Ezio," the Frystaater said softly, "I understand. You're among friends. Welcome aboard the *Fledermaus*, sir."

Sanchez gave a weak smile, regaining his composure. "Thank you, Captain. I should get my stateroom ready to get underway."

"Good idea. Be sure to get in touch with the Engineer and ask him for a set of piping and electrical tab books and get a qual-card from the X.O."

"Qual-card?"

"Yes," said Kattinger, "you and the other new officers will have to learn how to stand watches—"

"But Hans, I'm not even certified in basic navigation. I've never been assigned to a ship—"

"I know. I was ordered to have you do nothing while we were underway, that you would not be a member of the crew.

"That's a lot of bullshit, Ezio. You'd be climbing the walls with boredom. When I said 'Welcome aboard,' I meant it. You are now a part of the ship's crew."

"Well, yes," said Sanchez, looking doubtful. "I should certainly pull my own weight, but is it wise? I mean two full captains?"

Kattinger waved the problem away. "Don't worry about it. You'll be under myself, the X.O, the Eng and the Navigator but you will still be given the respect due a captain.

"Let's face it, Ezio. You may as well keep the title because you've endorsed your last paycheck."

"What!" Sanchez's dark eyes flared.

Kattinger considered the man before him. A bespectacled college professor in a captain's uniform. An historian with a sense of the past but one who lost sight of the forest when a tree got in the way. "You don't understand, do you?"

"No, I don't think so." Sanchez tried not to appear ruffled.

"Did you ever read about a certain 'hand-picked' Roman Legion that was ordered to march east until they reached the end of the world?"

As the destroyer's captain watched, Sanchez caught sight of the forest. He looked at Kattinger. "That's us, isn't it?"

"You, me, my crew, the five other 'troublesome' officers, the Council doesn't *want* us to come back, let alone expect us."

Both men remained silent, Sanchez wrestling with his doubts and questions. He could find no answers.

At last Kattinger broke the stillness of the room. "Ezio, the Empire is going to Hell at high-gee, and for years I've watched the Viceroy rape my planet. Not a goddamn thing I can do about it.

"But let me tell you something. If there are Saurons out there, we'll find them. Sooner or later, we'll find them. What happens then is entirely up to us. There really isn't going to be any attack force."

"I see," said Sanchez, his voice a dry whisper. "Thanks for the coffee," he said, moving toward the door. His stateroom was only one of the things he now had to prepare for the voyage.

"We limit ourselves to two cups a day, to make it last," Kattinger said as he opened the cabin door. "But feel free to come by any time."

Captain Sanchez had almost reached his own cabin

when Kattinger called him back. "Ezio, you almost forgot your book."

"Oh, yes. Thank you."

"In a few minutes they'll be serving lunch on the mess deck," said Kattinger. "I think it's veal cutlets today. Genuine veal."

Sanchez stared at him.

Kattinger just smiled. "No, don't ask."

Later, making his way to the mess area, Sanchez thought about the ship's captain. On the one hand, he seemed very resourceful and cared for the well-being of his crew. On the other hand, such skippers were becoming rare in the fleet.

Something else nagged at him. In his father's time, things like coffee and veal were common staples throughout the fleet. After the war, however, they were unheard of. The Fleet's telling its captains that they were "free to provision their own vessels as they see fit" was only a tacit admission that the Fleet was unable to provide proper logistic support for its units, even in peacetime.

The Empire of Man was going the way of the Romans, only this time there were more than just new versions of Goths and Vandals. There were Saurons.

Sanchez felt his appetite begin to wane. He shook his head to clear his thoughts. He refused to be cheated out of the enjoyment of good food by a distant and probably nonexistent enemy.

In the mess area, Sanchez found not only genuine veal, but real spices as well. The usual glutamates were absent. In their place were parsley, basil, rosemary and garlic.

Hans Kattinger floated near his acceleration chair on the bridge, feeling none of the excitement he usually felt just prior to getting underway. He listened calmly as Carl Hansen, the Maneuvering Watch Officer-of-the-

Deck, gave him the final routine message. "Sir, the ship is stowed for maneuvering and acceleration. The Maneuvering Watch is set with all hands accounted for, and we have Dock Control's permission to get underway."

"Very well. Take us out." Kattinger and Hansen strapped themselves into their chairs. Kattinger noticed a monitor screen which showed the curved surfaces of the planet below. Beneath the patterns of cloud were various greens, blues and browns, mostly browns. Frystaat.

He reached out to touch the screen, tracing the length of coastline where he lived.

"Now all hands brace for pitch maneuver," came over the announcing system.

Slowly, with barely perceptible movement, the planet's image began to rotate on the screen. Kattinger barely heard the voice of Sigmund Besmann, the Chief-of-the-Watch, speaking to Hansen. "Sir, Dock Control reports the dry-dock has reached safe distance. The tugs have completed the pitch maneuver and are ready to detach."

"Very well, detach tugs," said Hansen, following Kattinger's gaze to the monitor.

Outside the ship, eight tugs, each basically a large fuel tank with a rocket cluster and cockpit, released their mechanical hold on the grip flanges near the ends of the ship and turned on small maneuvering jets. Within minutes they had grouped up and followed the dry-dock to safe distance from the *Fledermaus*.

On the bridge, Hansen waited until the tugs signaled their arrival with the dock, then called the communications center. "Radio, Bridge. Inform Dock Control that we are commencing the five-minute countdown to departure burn."

"Bridge, Radio. Aye."

In the ensuing quiet on the bridge, Chief Besmann saw his captain staring at one of the screens. The look in Kattinger's eyes confirmed what the chief and most of the crew suspected. That something about this mission was wrong, very wrong. "Captain," he said at last. "This is it. Isn't is?"

For several seconds the only sound was the vent fan whirring in the corner. Kattinger twisted a knob by the screen, fading the picture to black. His voice was a choked sigh. "Yes."

Sanchez crouched with his ear to a sixty-millimeter pipe labeled 'D I WATER.' He pulled a spoon from his pocket and tapped the pipe three times. He was soon answered by three faint taps from further down the line. "That's it," he said, opening the door to the next compartment, "I think that's the whole system, Lieutenant."

Lieutenant Johanna Dettering was one of the new officers sent by the Viceroyal Council to exile aboard *Fledermaus*. She and Sanchez had just finished tracing the ship's deionized water system. "Do you think we're ready to get this signed off, sir?" she asked.

"Well, I think the only ones who can sign it are on watch or asleep, so we'll have to wait. I'm going to the hydroponic section. How about you?"

"Oh, no sir," said Dettering. "I've been chasing quals all day. I've got to get some sleep before I go on watch. Good night, sir."

"Good night."

Sanchez could not help looking at Dettering as she left the compartment. Only on Frystaat could rock hard muscles look so good on a woman.

It's too late for you, old fellow, he told himself. *About ten years too late. Besides, she could probably twist you into a pretzel.*

Still, Sanchez had to admire her. Dettering was the only one of the new officers who did not grumble at her new assignment. She seemed very adaptable and openly enjoyed the challenge of ship qualification.

Sanchez wondered how many times people like her

had been robbed of their futures, their dreams, by the shortsighted but powerful. *As many as the days Captain*, he thought, *since the monkeys started throwing rocks*.

In the hydroponic gardens, Sanchez enjoyed a rare moment's solitude. It was here that one could almost forget one was on a ship. With piped-in sounds of birds and running water one could easily imagine a paradise on some other world. Even if the feeling lasted only a moment.

Another reason Sanchez enjoyed the gardens were the things grown there. In addition to the oxygen-producing algae vats and fibrous plants consumed by the crew, all the spices the cooks used to season the meals with were grown and tended in the gardens. There were anise, rosemary, mint, thyme, sage, several kinds of pepper. There were rows of onions, potatoes and garlic. Foods, spices and flavorings too numerous for Sanchez to remember at once, all cared for by the ship's hydroponic techs and the Chief Cook.

In one section, Sanchez found something truly wondrous. Several citrus trees including lemon and mandarin orange. A smaller tree provided cinnamon bark and another—nutmeg! Lastly, he discovered the source of the delicious dessert he'd enjoyed earlier. The ice cream itself had been artificial but the vanilla flavor came from the beans produced by the vanilla orchids hanging in the gardens.

It's no wonder the crew loves and respects their captain, thought Sanchez, *he cares enough to feed them well. These men and women eat better then most people in the empire*.

From Hans Kattinger's private log aboard *Fledermaus*:
". . .After searching only seventeen habitable systems, we have good news. There is strong evidence of recent Sauron presence in this, the Byers System. The bad news for us is the nature of the evidence. . . ."

*   *   *

"All class-D electrical equipment is shut down, sir." The ODD's report informed Kattinger that computers, electro-magnetic sensors, and other complex electrical gear had been deactivated for the Alderson Jump.

"Very well," said Kattinger, turning to the navigation plotting party. "Mr. Rossbaum, are your scopes ready?"

"Yes, sir," said the Navigator. He had set three of the ship's telescopes to the known positions of three fixed stars in relation to the system they were about to enter. "ETA to Alderson Point in twenty-seven seconds."

"Very well. Test the comm circuit."

"Aye aye, sir. Maneuvering, Bridge. This is the Navigator, how do you read?"

"Bridge, Maneuvering. We read you loud and clear."

"Maneuvering, Bridge. Stand by to activate Alderson Drive on my mark. Stand by at five. Four. Three. Two. One. MARK!"

One of the last vessels to enter the Byers System had left twenty devices in position to monitor the Alderson Point and render a particular greeting to any who might follow.

Since then, only one ship had arrived in the system before *Fledermaus*. An Outie freighter had come looking for new markets and products for trade. The silent, guarding machines forced the merchant and his crew into a kind of early retirement. Pieces of the destroyed freighter still drifted in scattered orbits throughout the Byers System.

With the passage of time, twelve of the devices had run out of fuel needed to keep station with the Point and drifted into long, elliptical orbits around the primary. Eight of them remained.

One of the peculiarities of the Alderson drives was the way it played havoc with complex electrical systems, including biological ones. After a Jump, crewmen, would feel drunk or dizzy for as long as several minutes. The older the crewman, the longer the effect generally lasted. For this reason many spacers found a place to settle and refrained from interstellar travel. For some, felling the lengthening effect of each successive Jump was like watching a clock whose hands moved inexorably toward the hour of death.

In Maneuvering, the room where *Fledermaus*'s power and drive equipment were controlled, Chief Petty Officer Gartner had a simple but vital post during Jump Watch. After the Jump he would pull a small, three-position switch to the "ON" position, activating the circuits that energized and controlled the ship's Langston Field.

Normally, a ship's protective Langston Field could be left on during a Jump, but sometimes one or more of the more delicate components of the control circuitry would be damaged by the momentary dip and surge in the electrical current. Because of this, Kattinger had ordered the Field to be energized only after a Jump was complete. *Fledermaus* could afford to risk very little on the voyage.

Gartner always worried slightly about Alderson Jumps. He was one of those who listened to that imaginary but terrible clock. With this Jump, the clock would tick again for him. It would tick very loud.

On the bridge, Kattinger felt the familiar dazed confusion that always followed a Jump. He watched the sudden shift of background stars from one pattern to another on a screen. His smile was almost childlike as his imagination began to work out constellations in the starfield. The stars were so beautiful. Yes, beautiful and—visible! With a Field on, the screen should have been blank.

He shook his head as awareness returned. "Maneuvering, Bridge. Where the hell's that Langston Field?!"

In Maneuvering, the Engineering-Officer-of-the-Watch answered the call and glanced questioningly at Chief Gartner.

Startled, Gartner spun around to find a horrifying

sight. The switch for Langston Field was only in the neutral position. He quickly snapped it on, then spoke apologetically, "Switch on, sir." Gartner kept staring at the switch. He could feel the eyes of the others upon him and could not bear to look back.

"Bridge, Maneuvering. The Field switch was in neutral," said the EOW. He knew what Gartner was feeling. His words would stab but the report had to be made. "Jump Effect, sir."

Kattinger knew that Gartner had made dozens of Alderson Jumps in *Fledermaus* and that he was usually one of the first among the crew to fully recover. But changes happened and there was nothing for it. "Maneuvering, Bridge. Very well."

Kattinger glanced again at the star-filled screen. It would be a few more seconds till the Field came up. The control circuitry for the Langston generator was deliberately made simple in design to speed recovery after a Jump. It was as simple as possible, but no simpler.

A telescoping mast with a sensor cluster had extended beyond the known reach of the Langston Field.

Rossbaum looked into one of the scopes and turned a mechanical dial. "I have one, two stars. Wait a second," he adjusted a vernier crank. The third star had moved a bit from its previously charted position. "Three stars and," he turned to another scope and turned the dial again. "Spectro readings match. We're in the Byers System, sir."

The eight sentinels awakened. Something had entered the space they were guarding. The newly arrived object was immediately scanned and recognized as to type and class. Small computers made decisions according to instructions given many years before.

"Very well," said Kattinger. "Officer-of-the-Deck, secure from Alderson Jump Watch. Return to underway watch, section five and tell Maneuvering to reenergize the four-hundred cycle switchboards."

With that, Kattinger prepared to settle into the routine of system reconnaissance.

A technician in Maneuvering, whose hull monitoring station had one of the first computer systems to reactivate, changed all that.

"Bridge, Maneuvering. Hull monitor registers rapid temperature increase at eight points along the Mid-Ship bulge!"

One of the bridge screens came on, showing the locations of the heat buildup.

On the hull, along the ringed arrays of exterior equipment circling the destroyer's middle section, eight separate areas began to glow. Just small points of red, at first, but rapidly expanding and becoming a bright, incandescent white. Black paint blistered and outgassed. Hull plates and equipment began to melt.

Kattinger's reaction was immediate. "Chief-of-the-Watch, sound General Quarters. All hands on the bridge, this is the Captain, I have the Deck and the Conn." He growled into a microphone. "Maneuvering, Bridge. What's the matter with that goddamn Field? It should be up by now!"

As the relieved OOD raced from the bridge, the Chief-of-the-Watch grabbed a microphone. "General Quarters! General Quarters! All hands man your Battle Stations!" A repeated gong sounded throughout the ship for several seconds.

The EOW watched the Langston Field control panel tensely. The green light he expected didn't appear. In its place blinked one red light, then another. He fought to keep the fear out of his voice. "Bridge, M-Maneuvering. We've got critical fault indications on the Langston panel. I've got to take it off-line!"

"Shit!" snarled Kattinger. "Maneuvering, Bridge. Very well. Get a DC and repair party at the generator on-the-double!" Angrily, he switched the mike to another circuit. "All hands, this is the Captain. The ship has just entered the Byers System. The Langston Field is down and we're taking energy hits. This not a drill. Man Battle Stations *now!*"

All over the ship people were leaping, flying and otherwise propelling themselves in the zero gravity to reach their assigned posts. For most, however, their Jump station and Battle station were the same. It took only a few seconds for everyone to find their places.

But seconds were precious.

"I want Auto-Response!" said Kattinger to Will Kreigler, the Weapons Officer.

"It's on line, sir, but I don't have a sensor or weapons for it!"

"You do now, sir," said voice from across the bridge. "Number Two Field Coil, on line."

"It'll have to do," said Kattinger. "What do we have for weapons?"

"Just the close-ins, they—"

"Tie them in and activate, now!"

"Aye, sir. Activated."

One of *Fledermaus*'s field coils energized, generating a torus-shaped magnetic field which rotated with the array. Several kinetic energy and short-range laser weapons fired, selecting and reselecting ferrous anomalies as targets.

Kattinger fell into a pattern of short, brief commands. "Target analysis."

"Targets were," Kreigler looked at the readout display, "missiles, conventional, possible multi-warhead. Seven distinct salvoes. We are now tracing trajectories to likely points of origin."

"Very well."

"Sir," said the Chief-of-the-Watch. "All compartments report manned for Battle Stations."

"Very good. Set ship's airtight condition One-Alpha."

All ship's airtight doors and airlocks were shut to reduce possible atmosphere loss in battle. Only the ventilation lines remained open, but ready to be closed.

"Maneuvering, Bridge," said Kattinger. "What's the status of the energy hits?"

"Bridge, Maneuvering. Hit points still active. Temperature increase has slowed down, however."

"Maneuvering, Bridge. Aye." Kattinger switched comm mikes. "Radar, Bridge. Ship's sensor status."

"Bridge, Radar. Number Two Main Radar is down. Telescopes One, Three and Four are down. Number Two Maser is down. All other sensors are on line, sir."

"Well, finally some good news. Weps, what have you got for the Main Battery?"

Kreigler gave a wry smile. "I've got turrets Two and Three on line. Number One is gone. Indicates red across the board, Captain."

"Bridge, Radar," spoke a voice from the wall speaker. "We finished our sweep of those missile bearings from Fire Control, sir, and they show seven stationary contacts at one five zero thousand kilometers and one stationary contact at two seven zero thousand."

"Radar, Bridge. Good work. Send the bearings to Fire Control."

"Bridge, Maneuvering. DC party reports Langston generator housing has been breached and the generator appear to be melting. Petty Officer Schmidt reports that she can see stars through the three levels of deck out from the generator room and the airlock door is getting hotter."

"Maneuvering Bridge. Aye. Get your DC party into pressure suits and get everyone out of the compartment and shut the compartment ventilation valves."

In Maneuvering, the EOW acknowledged then relayed the orders to the DC party.

On the bridge, Kriegler looked up at his captain. "Sir, Fire Control has target acquisition. Main Battery tracking."

Kattinger wasted no time. "Good. Open Fire."

Two of *Fledermaus*'s main laser turrets swiveled in conjunction with the remaining large radar dish. Rapid-pulsed invisible beams left eight expanding clouds of gas and debris where the devices had been. A full, active sensor sweep showed no other hostiles in space.

"Something doesn't make sense," Kattinger muttered under his breath. "Eight contacts, eight energy hits, Where's the eighth missile salvo?" His eyes flashed accusingly at the tech monitoring the Auto-Response system. "Dammit! Where's that other salvo?"

"I've nothing, sir, no indication!"

Kattinger checked the readout himself and saw that the petty officer was correct. "I'm sorry, son." The incident was immediately forgotten. "Maybe it didn't launch any . . . or—"

Kattinger and Kreigler locked eyes in mutual realization —"Non-ferrous vehicles!"

Kattinger spun, grabbing his mike. "Maneuvering, Bridge. Have you got any drive control at all?"

"Bridge, Maneuvering. Not yet. We should have local control in just a few—"

"Engineer, we better get some right now, or we won't—"

"Sir! Sir, we just got local control on line right now—"

"All right, I want a full, twenty-second burn along the yaw axis. Ascend ship, ninety degrees—zenith. Do it now!"

"Aye aye sir!"

Kattinger got halfway through "Brace for acceleration" when the ship trembled with the power of the sub-ramspeed drives pushing the vessel ninety degrees from its line of motion.

The sudden change in direction caught some crew-members unaware. The point-two-gee acceleration resulted in a number of sprained limbs and one crewman was knocked unconscious.

Twenty seconds later, the shaking subsided, as zero gravity returned.

Thirty-nine seconds later, two of the ship's enhanced optical monitors burned out with a flash.

"Bridge, Radar. We just recorded six pulses, three

gamma and three neutron. Mild EMPs detected indicated thermo-nuclear detonations in the one-to-two kiloton range." Kattinger heard the hiss of static. Radar still had their mike keyed. The same voice quietly spoke. "Thank you, sir."

"Radar, Bridge . . . . Radar, Bridge. Aye. Maneuvering, Bridge. Damn good work." Looking around the bridge, Kattinger was met with looks of admiration, of thanks for deliverance and of lingering fear for the nearness of the escape.

He broke the tension by reaching for the PA mike. "Now all hands make reports to Damage Control Central. Secure from General Quarters."

"Superficial hull and armor damage in the Midship Bulge area—"

"Langston Field generator and control guides fused—"

"Waste Heat Exchangers Twelve through Seventeen ruptured due to coolant expansion—"

"Number One Main Turret, laser crystal firing and feed-rack system beyond repair—"

"Telescopes One and Three destroyed. Number Four under repair—"

"Twelve minor injuries and one concussion due to evasive maneuver. No deaths."

Sensors, weapons, auxiliary equipment all destroyed or damaged beyond hope of repair. These the officers and senior enlisted crew of the *Fledermaus* took calmly. The ship and crew had been through worse.

When all damage reports were in, there were only two that seemed to affect anyone at all. The effect was devastating. The ship's three hydrogen scoop field generators had been slagged by the energy weapons.

And fuel bunkers were down to 7.89 percent capacity.

The Engineer's face was like red coral. "They knew right where to fucking hit us!"

"Can't we repair one of the scoop generators?" asked Sanchez.

"With what?!—Sir? All our big spares were off-loaded before we left. What are we supposed to do, rub two—"

"Eng," said Kattinger. "That's enough."

"Ezio, as I said, the Council was very thorough." Kattinger paused to rub sore neck muscles. "There is supposed to be an automated repair and fueling station in orbit over Cat's Eye, which is that big gas ball we're headed to. Perhaps we can do something there."

Kattinger hovered over one of the scopes in the radar room, just aft of the bridge. In the room were more than just radar equipment. All manner of ship's sensors were controlled from what was simply called "radar room."

Kattinger swore at the monitor. "Nothing. All right, let's go active. Hartmann, set Number One Maser for a one-second pulse. Oscillate at one hundred cycles, set arc radius point oh-two degrees around prime location."

"Aye aye, sir," said one of the three petty-officers on watch.

On top of the ship, behind the bridge, one of the new sensors, a large microwave laser, swiveled and tilted. A small resonator activated and the laser element began to vibrate..

Seconds later, "Ready, Captain."

"Okay, go active."

The tech touched a control. In one second the beam from the array washed back and forth over the prime location one hundred times, then stopped, while a radar antenna passively listened.

"Pulse sent, sir."

"Very well." They waited. And waited.

"No echo, sir."

"All right. Go ahead and secure the array."

"Aye aye, sir."

At the other end of the room, Lieutenant Dettering, Officer-of-the-Watch in Radar, spoke up. "Captain, I just finished the orbit run on those metal objects we've been tracking."

"Yes, Johanna?"

"Well, they all have rather eccentric orbits which do intersect the known orbit of the station."

"And?"

"I ran the orbit paths back until they converged, accounting for perturbations from all the moons. They do converge together with the prime orbit, sir."

Kattinger caught his breath. "Let me guess, thirty years ago, right?"

The woman nodded solemnly.

"Well, that ties it up then. Good work. Just keep a lid on it for a while." Kattinger turned and left the radar room.

"What?" said a disbelieving Sanchez when he heard the news.

"It seems," said Kattinger, "that the Saurons or whoever was in this system thirty years ago blew up the refueling station when they got here. We can't scoop gas off a giant, we can't ram, and now there's no way to repair the generators. And we don't have the fuel to get back to Alderson Point.

"Ezio, I think we're here to stay."

Sanchez seemed more angry than surprised. " 'Resources at a premium' the motherless dog said. The lives of men are cheap but spare parts they had to squeeze." Then the full reality of it hit him. "Is there nothing we can do?"

"Not much, nothing in the way of fuel, anyway. I'm going to call a meeting of the wardroom in one hour. You're welcome to put forth any ideas."

Sanchez nodded absently as Kattinger left.

Coffee bulbs bobbed gently at the ends of wrist tethers or were motionless, gripped in officers' hands as the meeting progressed. Captain Kattinger had almost finished speaking. "So that's where it stands. We're stuck in the system, we're low on fuel and there's no way for us to get more. We are currently on course for Haven, our low consumption trajectory will bring us there in just over nine hours. Once there, we'll achieve a low orbit from which to observe the surface.

"Officers-of-the-deck will from here on refrain from using attitude thrusters or any other rockets for maneuvers unless we are on the daylight side of Haven—which reminds me."

Kattinger spoke into a bulkhead panel. "Bridge, Wardroom. This is the captain."

A voice came in from the speaker. "Wardroom, Bridge. Officer-of-the-deck here."

"Bridge, Wardroom. Set exterior lighting for darken ship. De-energize all outside lights and secure all port windows. I don't want so much as a photon of visible light leaving the ship."

"Wardroom, Bridge. Aye. Does that mean I can still dump heat?"

"Bridge, Wardroom. Yes, use the radiators as necessary, but try to use those that are on the opposite side of the ship from Haven."

"Wardroom, Bridge. Aye."

Kattinger turned back to those in the room. "Did you all get that?" There was a general "yessir, ayeaye" and nodding of heads.

"Sir, we might was well march right in. When those nukes went off, anyone in the system could have seen them, no matter how far away they were," said the Lieutenant Commander Hansen.

"No," the Navigator gently corrected, "Haven was deeply occluded by Cat's Eye when that happened."

"Oh."

"All right," the captain continued, "that's it. I'll make the announcement to the crew. Pretty soon you'll be inundated with questions. I've told everything I know, which is damn little. We'll have to wait till we reach Haven to get any more answers."

Haven yielded answers—in spades. Satellites placed in low orbit and the ship's own special sensors revealed a strong Sauron influence. The Sauron stronghold was located, as were the perimeters of Sauron influence and probable contact, which were distressingly widespread after only thirty years.

Satellite pictures played back on the Wardroom screen told much of Haven's last decades; of the nuclear destruction stitched across the Shangri-La Valley.

"Look at this one." Sanchez had a blastpoint shown in freeze-frame. "When they hit Falkenburg, they aimed one directly at the University, directly! Why?" He shook his head. The others remained silent. They had seen things before, up close and personal, on their own world.

Next, they were shown a series of satellite images showing recent Sauron activity. They nearly all shared a common theme; the taking of prisoners. Whether it was the raiding of a village or the waylaying of travelers the end was the same. The native Haveners would fight bravely (most of the time), and the Saurons would round up the women. Sometimes gently, sometimes not.

At the comparatively rare times that a satellite caught the image of a Sauron being killed or injured, an enthusiastic roar of approval would issue from the assemblage in the Wardroom. Captain Kattinger had to strain from joining the shouting, as his own emotions boiled from what he was seeing.

His reserve crumbled when, on the screen, having rounded up some fifteen women from a northern tribe and locked them in a wagon, a Sauron Soldier appeared to argue with a superior for several seconds. The superior turned away, leaving the Soldier, who then shrugged and proceeded to burn the wagon with a flame thrower, calmly hosing the stream directly into the prisoners.

"*No!*" shouted Kattinger, at the top of his lungs. His

huge fist impacted the bulkhead, putting a large dent in it.

"For the love of God!!" He turned to the young officer operating the monitor. "That's enough! Shut it off, now!" The officer almost broke his hand hurrying to comply. Kattinger immediately was silent. His face hardened and crimson with rage, his eyes moist.

The Wardroom was quiet as well. The officers had never seen their captain so angry. They had never seen him this close to tears.

"Any ideas," said Kattinger, barely winning the fight for control, "will be welcome. Just remember that whatever we do, we are committed to it. There is no going back."

The wardroom emptied slowly, quietly. Totally absent was the earlier enthusiasm. *Fledermaus*'s mission profile had changed.

Three hours later, a knock on Kattinger's door broke his reverie. "Come in."

It was Sanchez. "Hans, you wanted ideas?"

"Yes, come in. Shut the door, would you?"

Sanchez handed one of the coffee bulbs he was holding to Kattinger, who drank immediately.

It tasted different. "Ah, a bit of the Irish this time."

"I think you'll need it," said Sanchez, "when you hear what I'm going to say."

"I think the whole crew could use it after my command performance in the wardroom."

"Hans, considering what we saw that Sauron doing—"

"No," said Kattinger, shaking his head. "It's more than that."

He looked up at Sanchez. "When I was in school, I was walking home when a Sauron bomber attacked the city. A firebomb hit our house just as I had come around the street. I saw my mother trying to carry my sister out of the house. They were covered with fire."

In his hands was the picture from the desk. "This is all I have left."

Kattinger then nodded to some papers on his desk. "You should read some of these," he said, changing the subject. "Johanna, God bless her. She wants to mount our remaining weapons on the longboats and 'strafe the living shit out of them.' X.O. wants to take everything we can to an isolated spot then drop the *Fledermaus* on their stronghold." Kattinger shrugged. "That one has merit, but the rest of these, I don't know. They're brave suggestions, all, but more the product of emotion than reason. Nothing that would eliminate enough of the Sauron gene pool."

Sanchez leaned forward. "Captain, if we drop the ship on them, we give them metal and reveal our presence. If we try to shoot them, they may still have heavy enough weapons to shoot down the longboats. These are things we cannot allow, sir."

"I've been thinking the same thing and you're right. What do you suggest?"

Sanchez sipped his coffee for a moment. "We have to beat the Saurons at their own game, Hans. We find a spot that is isolated from Sauron and Havener populations, but still on the main continent. Then we put down with everything we can take in longboats, and bring the ship down nearby."

"I'm afraid that bringing the ship down is ruled out. The entry burn for something this big would circle the planet at least once. As you said, we can't let anyone know we're here."

"There's something else, Hans. If there is an accident in bringing down the longboats we'll lose the genes of anyone killed. How many women are aboard?"

"Forty-seven," said Kattinger, grinning slightly, "So you think we should get them pregnant before anything else begins?"

Sanchez nodded.

"Well," said Kattinger, "It's a rough job but I think the men will be 'up' to it."

The shared laughter eased some of the earlier tension.

"Ah, yes. The men," said Sanchez, grinning broadly. "What about yourself?"

"What do you mean?" asked Kattinger, trying to look innocent.

Sanchez's manner softened to one of friendly understanding. "You like Lieutenant Dettering, don't you?"

"Is it all over the ship?"

"Mm, I have ears. Apparently, you made the mistake of calling her by her first name while on watch."

"Oh. That's right, I did," said Kattinger, regretfully.

"Don't worry about it, no seems to mind." Sanchez paused, smiling. "Least of all, young Miss Dettering."

Kattinger didn't speak but he didn't have to. The light returning to his eyes gave him away.

"But," said Sanchez, "we'll need a very tight breeding program. No two children from the same parents for the first few generations. We'll have to give up a few customs if we're to survive."

"Yes, you are right, of course. The program will be Dr. Gettmann's job." Kattinger's thoughts returned to the immediate problem. "All we need is a suitable location."

"I've got one," said Sanchez, producing a map of Haven's principal continent. "This part here, the Eden Valley shows no sign of recent habitation and does not appear low enough for having babies. But this region here," he pointed southeast of Shangri-La Valley, "is a wide plateau that's low enough to live on."

"But not low enough to have babies on."

"No. That is why we must keep the longboats. They can be pressurized and used as maternity wards."

Kattinger brows slowly arched. "Hmm."

The previously cramped spaces of the *Fledermaus* appeared gaunt and empty as the crew stripped anything that could be used on the planet below. All available scrap metal along with the tools in the small machine shop and the various sizes of bar stock. It would be precious little but vital to survival. Several spools of copper wire for making generators were put down. All manner of dry goods, medical supplies, emergency fresh water. And just about everything in the hydroponic labs. Everything left the ship on daylight burns along the uninhabited side of the planet.

Several officers and enlisted crewmembers were enjoying a last bulb of coffee in the docking bay before riding the last of the deliveries to the surface.

The door to the C.O.'s stateroom was open as Sanchez approached. Inside, Kattinger worked the printbinder rapidly. Some ninety books, representing the last of his special paper supply, were floating in three sacks near the binder.

Sanchez saw some of the titles. Different fields of science and mathematics, mining and metallurgy, high-altitude agricultural theory, medicine, anatomy and other subjects were there.

Kattinger sensed Sanchez in the room. "Ezio, we're going to need this. Some of the knowledge here took humanity thousands of years to acquire. We are about to join a very barbaric world. This planet is going to see many years—generations—of banditry, war, slavery and who knows what else. It will be a long time before Haven can produce what's written in these books. I think we should see that these things survive."

"Absolutely," said Sanchez looking at the indicator on the printbinder's feed tray. "You have only one sheet left. May I have it?"

"Sure. I've got to take these down to the bay. I made redundant copies, one for each boat. Careful, they're hot."

Sanchez moved back from the sacks as Kattinger carried them out of the stateroom, leaving Sanchez alone with the printbinder.

He touched the console and called up the file of documents. Searching down the list, he stopped suddenly. "Yes, Hans," he spoke softly as he brought up the item he'd found. "Some things must survive." He entered the command to print then reached for the tongs as the hot paper slid into the tray.

After waving the sheet in the air several seconds to cool, he rolled it into a small chart tube and put it in his pocket.

"Gracias," he said to the little machine as he shut it off, then turned and left the stateroom.

"Ezio," said Kattinger, calling across the ship's loading bay, "we almost threw away our key to the future down there." Sanchez could see a certain excitement, almost joy, on the Captain's normally unchanging features.

"Our decedents could become very rich and influential!"

"What are you talking about?"

"This!" said the Chief Engineer, who floated toward Sanchez with Kattinger. He held a drinking bulb over his head. "Coffee!"

"We will be the only coffee growers on the whole planet," said Kattinger. "Others will start, eventually of course, but we'll be the first and our people will control the market for generations!"

Sanchez seemed doubtful. "Can we carry it?"

"Yes, we can take about two tons apiece in each boat. The chief has a working party on it now."

"It could work," said Sanchez, nodding slowly. "We'll have to experiment on growing it."

"Anything to save the drink of the gods."

Kattinger was the last to board a longboat. The others waited while he floated near the far bulkhead. His lips moved slowly but no one heard his words. After a moment, he gently stroked the bulkhead. No one needed to hear to know what he said. "Goodbye."

Haven was known to have few species of flying vertebrates. The new arrivals to the planet discovered one that had not been mentioned in the references. Its mottled color and long, thin wings served to make it nearly invisible to the pilot of the last longboat to descend from the ship. He saw it just as it shot past the cockpit window.

"—The fuck? Shit!" were all he could say as the creature was sucked into the craft's port ramjet engine. The rotor disintegrated, sending pieces of itself and its pulverized victim into the fuselage and port fuel tank.

The pilots of the other two craft saw the longboat disappear in a bright fireball, taking its cargo, crew and Hans Kattinger with it.

Fledermaus did as her computer was told. With Shangri-La Valley on the night side, she accelerated away from Haven and Cat's Eye. Having left the gas giant and its moons, *Fledermaus* shed her solar orbital velocity and began to fall toward the system's primary.

On her new course, she spent her remaining fuel as miserly as possible, making slight corrections.

Weeks later, *Fledermaus* added her tiny, vaporizing mass to that of the sun shining in Haven's sky.

Children did grow on the plateau, called "Acropolis" by Sanchez.

Coffee, however, did not. All attempts to grow it ended in complete failure. The agricultural text provided no answers. Frustration mounted as bean after bean refused to germinate or did germinate but died soon after.

With regret and more than a few tears, attempts to grow coffee were halted. The remaining stores of the precious beans were reserved for the community's celebrations, to run out when it would.

But where coffee didn't grow, many of the herbs and spices did. Nutmeg, cinnamon, dill weed, even some of the vanilla orchids grew in one of the greenhouses built on the southern foothills of Acropolis.

Haven would never see the dreamed-of coffee trade. But the spice trade would soon make the new colony rich when it finally made contract with the native Haveners in the southeast region of the Shangri-La Valley. Very rich, indeed.

And very, very influential.

The colony atop the mountain was less than twelve Terran years old when Haven claimed Ezio Sanchez. A cancer had spread through his lymphatic system, leaving him months instead of years. Dr. Gettmann was helpless. The pharmaceuticals she could have saved his life with were lost with Kattinger and the two others when their longboat was destroyed.

"Heidi," Sanchez spoke softly to the daughter of Johanna and Hans Kattinger as he lay, barely breathing. Heidi had her mother's red hair and her father's gentle blue eyes.

"Heidi, my time is over. On the shelf there is a wooden box. Please take it."

The young girl did as he said and began to open it.

"No, not yet," said Sanchez. "Wait until you go to sleep tonight, please. There are two things—" he paused, trying to catch his shallow breath. "Inside. One is for you. The other is for your children to give—" another breath—"to Haven."

"Which one—"

"Shh." He lifted a finger to Heidi's lips, softly. "You will know."

"Thank you, Uncle Easy."

Sanchez smiled weakly. Heidi was the only child who could call him that pet name.

"Now go, child. I wish to say goodbye to your mother."

Heidi reached over Sanchez to hug him. "Vaya con Dios, Señor," she said through tears.

"Gracias, mi paloma blanca. Gracias."

Heidi picked up the box and slowly walked from the room as her mother entered. She had almost reached the top of the stairs when her heart gave in and she sat down to cry.

It had been difficult, waiting so long to open the box, but Heidi waited out of respect for her dying teacher.

"Don't be up late, now," said Johanna, seeing her daughter to bed, then returned down the stairs.

Heidi lit the small reading lamp on the table near her bed. Then, with eager curiosity, she reached under her pillow and lifted the box. Carefully, she opened it.

Inside was a book. She read the title, "The Rise and Fall of the Roman Empire." Opening the book she found an inscription on the inside cover:

> To Captain Ezio Sanchez,
> A good book, like a good friend,
> is a terrible thing to lose.
> Hans Kattinger

Heidi cried again for several minutes. She had lost her teacher and the only father she'd known.

And the closest friend she ever had.

Gently, she closed the book and put it on the bed beside her. Inside the box was one more item, a small plastic tube with a rolled, printed paper inside. She carefully removed the paper and placed the tube in the box.

Slowly, the paper unrolled until it was flat. Heidi's eyes were drawn to some bold print near the top. She read aloud to herself, her voice echoing softly down the stairs. "We hold these truths to be self evident . . ."

In rare disobedience to her mother's orders, Heidi's little reading lamp burned long into the night.

From "The Frontal Assault and Other Tactical Pathologies," in *The Way of the Soldier* (traditionally attributed to First Lady/Second Soldier Althene Diettinger)

The hardest thing to fight is a Tradition. And every valley, every town and village, and sometimes every farm or even farmer on Haven has at least one Tradition that folk will die for. Never mind that the Folk are cattle—cattle willing to die can always kill more Saurons than we can afford to lose.

So remember that not all of Haven's defenses are visible to the senses, even the enhanced senses of Saurons. Some of our new home's defense in depth exists only in the minds of its folk—but as tenaciously rooted there as the mountains are in the crust of the planet.

NO SUCH THING AS A
NON-LETHAL WEAPON

James A. Landau

I was eating a sandwich when the professional killer walked up to me.

"You're Mr. Herrero, foreman of the Millvale lumberyard?" he asked.

"Thomas Herrero, at your service," I said, as sarcastically as I could. "Acting foreman."

He offered his hand. "Major Andreadis, of the Cumming Brigade."

Rather than shake hands with him, I took a bite of my sandwich. He didn't seem annoyed at my rudeness, so I said, "Your kind doesn't deserve good manners."

He replied in a friendly tone, "As one soldier to another, there are certain courtesies. But you don't have to salute me."

"Since I'm not going to stand up for you, either, have a seat," I said, pointing to a nearby pile of trash. Anyway, who could look military rising from a rolled-up tarpaulin? "Or get lost. But don't call me a soldier."

He knelt to face me, not on the trashpile but in front of it. "You went into battle with Cross's militia," he said.

Cross was the real foreman as well as part-owner, on office duty now with a broken leg. He also commanded the town militia, two dozen friends of mine with romantic illusions and a liking to hear guns go bang. "Fine," I said. "So I'm a soldier. That doesn't mean I have to be polite to you just because you have pine cones on your shoulders."

"Oak leaves," he said, smiling, "and yes, they mean I'm a career soldier. Or a mercenary, same difference. You might be polite to me since we are allies. I'm liaison to Cross's militia today."

"Then go talk to *Captain* Cross."

"I did. He said to talk to you."

"And I say go talk to yourself. What do you want?"

"There's a band of nomads headed this way to attack Millvale. The Cummings Brigade sent me to help the militia stop them."

"You shoot them, I'll bandage them. But I don't see what else I can do. Or the militia either, except pray the nomads go somewhere else."

"I'm told you're a pacifist."

"I am."

"Yet you rode into battle with the town militia."

"They needed a medic, and I know first aid."

"That makes you part of a combat unit."

"You want me to let my friends die because I wasn't there? War, unfortunately, is a human activity, and the militia are all friends of mine." What was he trying to say?

"Mr. Herrero, there are pacifists whose pacifism makes them refuse to have anything to do with war, under any circumstances."

"So what?"

"Being a combat medic, even if you never shoot anyone, is as bad as fighting. Or, if not as bad, it is still unacceptable."

Why was this professional killer preaching pacifism at me? "That kind of hairsplitting neither prevents war nor helps those who get shot," I said. "I am not about to change my beliefs and I will thank you to stop preaching in *my* lumberyard."

"I wasn't preaching. I am a soldier, a killer by trade. I am asking you a serious question: are you willing to go into combat, provided that you don't have to kill anyone?"

"I am and I have done so. But on my initiative, not yours. Get to the point, Mr. Andreadis, before you get to the lockup for being crazy."

"There is a battle coming up. The militia will be in it."

"And why should I care about a battle, if I'm not going to fight?"

"You've heard of the nomad chief who calls himself 'Suleiman the Magnificent'?"

"Yes. He was threatening to do something obscene to us if we didn't lower the tolls on the Bridge for him."

"Mr. Herrero, he gave your Mayor an ultimatum that he would take the Bridge by force if Millvale didn't *eliminate* the tolls for him. The ultimatum expires at noon today. Your Mayor asked for help from the Cummings Brigade, which I'm afraid amounts to me.

"As you know, Millvale keeps independent by playing everyone off against each other, one nomad tribe against another, the Sauron Breedmasters against their Deathmasters, the wind against the rain.

"This time it's the nomads against the Cummings Brigade. The militia and I are suppose to do something obscene to an entire tribe of nomads."

"So the militia will be fighting. I'll be there as their medic, nothing more. Why are you wasting my time?" I asked.

"Because I want you to take charge of a non-lethal weapon."

"There's no such thing as a non-lethal weapon," I said, pointing to a nearby sledgehammer.

"Point well taken. As weapons go, however, this weapon is exceptionally non-lethal."

"Mr. Andreadis, I never touch a weapon of any kind, including the one you are talking about."

"On the contrary, Mr. Herrero. You are sitting on it."

"The tarpaulin? How can it be a weapon?" I asked.

He told me.

"It's the dumbest thing I ever heard of," I told him.

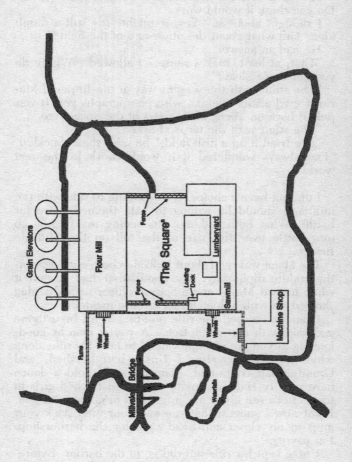

"You ride with the militia, therefore you know horses. Do you think it would work?"

I thought about it. "Yes, it might. It's still a dumb idea. And what about the other end of the field?"

He had an answer.

"That, at least, makes sense," I allowed. "Where do you get these ideas?"

"The stunt with the wagons was in the Imperial Marines' civil affairs manual, with photographs yet. It was pulled back on Terra, early years of the Space Age."

"The stunt with the tarp?" I asked.

"I've tried it on a drill field," he said, then chuckled. "I've always wondered if it would work in the real world."

I did not have a choice. If I'm willing to ride with the militia, I should be willing to help them prepare for battle. What bothered me was seeing my friends go into battle over the size of the toll on the Millvale Bridge.

The Major was right about Millvale's both-ends-against-the-middle diplomacy. My grandfather had started it when he was Mayor and a Sauron officer named Untag showed up with a demand for tribute maidens.

Grandpa ignored the rifle pointing at his breastbone and said with a straight face, "A young man as good-looking as you are shouldn't need to take his rifle along when he goes courting." Untag had blushed, and Grandpa had continued, "Tonight we'll hold a dance here in City Hall and invite all the unattached girls in town. Let's see if any are interested in going with you. Right now I suggest that you and your men stack your guns in my closet and head right for the barbershop. I'm paying."

Untag kept his rifle but did go to the barber. Before-and-after photos hanging in the mayor's office show that he was long overdue for a haircut.

At the dance four girls, including Grandpa's niece

Juanita, volunteered to go with the Saurons. Untag was beaming, since Millvale's quota for tribute maidens was three.

"Just one thing before you leave," Grandpa told Untag. "These girls are going with you to start families. As their elected Mayor, I must insist on conducting wedding ceremonies for them." Untag, not seeing any harm in a formality, agreed, and the dance ended with a quadruple wedding.

Poor Untag the Unsubtle, as Grandpa always called him. He had created a Precedent. When the next Sauron showed up with a demand for tribute maidens, Grandpa told him that there was a Tradition to be followed, and after a brief but stubborn argument the Citadel capitulated. As the Sauron training manual now says, the hardest thing to fight is a Tradition.

Millvale still supplies women to the Citadel, but every single one has been courted by the Saurons and has agreed to go with them. Most come back to visit and show off their Sauronettes, and a few have been allowed to leave the Citadel and return to Millvale permanently.

My cousin Juanita is not about to leave. She produced a complete squad of Saurons on her own and became a childbirth instructor. I now have more cousins in the Citadel than I do in town.

The river runs fast and deep past Millvale, too fast to ferry, too deep to ford. The only way to cross is by bridge, and the Millvale Bridge is the only one for many kilometers in either direction.

I know the Bridge well. It gave me my first job, as a carpenter's apprentice. I worked my way up to boss of a repair gang. One day, while I was at the lumberyard selecting timber for repair, Cross fired his assistant yard foreman for drinking on the job and offered me the position.

The "Square" is the open area between the lumberyard and the flour mill, used as a corral and a loading area. At either end there is a low stone fence to keep draft animals from wandering off. You can ride through the Square on a horse, jumping both fences easily or going through the gates. It makes a good shortcut to the bridge, if you don't mind riding down a steep hillside and jumping the flume. The main road takes a long detour around the lumberyard to have a gentle grade.

"This nomad leader Suleiman, he's familiar with the town?" Andreadis asked.

"Yes. He was here last week to buy from the lumberyard."

"Good. We can use his own knowledge of the town layout against him. What was he buying?"

"Hardware. Lots of fasteners—bolts, treenails, tape, glue. Carbon fiber. Hand tools—hammers, axes, wrenches. All the battery-powered drills we had in stock. Fire extinguishers and a portable water pump with hose. He loaded up two pack mules."

"Any lumber?"

"No. He didn't bring any wagons with him."

"What was he planning to do with the hardware?"

"I have no idea. Build another bridge?"

"How did he pay?"

"Barter. He haggled with Cross, not with me."

"Did he stop anywhere else in town?"

"Probably. He had four more pack mules that he didn't need for what he bought here."

"Has he been back? And have any other nomads shown up?"

"No."

Andreadis was silent for a minute, then said, "If I were trying to capture the bridge, I'd stock up on small items that would be lost if Millvale caught fire. I'd also make sure I could keep the bridge from burning down.

"Mr. Herrero, my comrade in arms, if you'll pardon

the term, I think it's time to get started on the tarp. I'll
arrange about the wagons."

Cross hobbled over on his crutches to ask for volunteers. My entire yard crew agreed to help me, as did
two clerks and a curious customer. How Cross does it I
don't know. I would never have the hubris to ask my
own people to go into danger.

First we stretched the tarp out on the ground along
the fence. It was five meters short. Then I put the crew
to work planting a row of 5X10's vertically into the
ground. The idea was to have a row of stakes parallel to
and behind the fence. I personally nailed a hook into
the near side of each stake.

When the stakes were ready, Andreadis returned to
inspect. "Perfect," he told me. "As for the space between the tarp and the flour mill, stack up some lumber
or bricks or flour sacks to fill the gap. About your height
will do."

"What about the gate?"

"Leave it open."

The five-meter gap was easy to fill. I put empty
lumber racks in it and weighted them down with stone
blocks.

"Is there a doctor in this town?" Andreadis asked.

"My father. He's out in the backwoods somewhere,
delivering a baby."

"Then you and I are the entire medical corps. Do
you have your first aid kit with you?"

I slapped my hip pocket to show where it was. He
pulled his out of an ammo pouch on his pistol belt.

It was half an hour before noon. I told my crew to break
for lunch but not to leave the Square. The two women
in the crew produced sandwiches from home. Most of
the men headed for the bake shop in the flour mill.

"We have an old saying in the Brigade about that,"

said Andreadis, gesturing at the line forming for the bake shop. " 'They also serve who only wait at the refreshment stand.' "

Come noon I had my crew take their positions. I told each crewperson individually, "Remember this. You are not armed. Your job ends when the tarp goes up. Then the shooting will start. Stay below the level of the stone fence and crawl to the safety of the flour mill or the lumberyard."

We saw the militia, first as a dust cloud, then as heads appearing over a hilltop. As they reached the Square, they were bunched together but hardly in formation. Every so often a rider in the rear would turn around in his saddle and fire a shot, at what I couldn't tell.

As they came closer I could see they were at less than a full gallop. That had been Andreadis's orders, to keep a constant distance from their pursuers. Most jumped the stone fence into the Square; three riders chose to go through the gate.

Suddenly there was fireworks overhead. Long thin parallel lines appeared in the air—tracer bullets. The galloping horses made too much noise for us to hear the guns that had fired them. Not all the rounds were too high. I saw the rearmost rider, too far away to be recognizable, throw up his hands and fall out of his saddle. His horse slowed down and started trotting aimlessly around the Square. Another horse fell, pinning his rider underneath.

The rest of the militia were across the Square now and starting to jump the second stone fence onto the tarp. One horse refused the jump; his rider turned him to ride into the lumberyard.

As soon as the militia were clear of the fence I yelled to my crew, "Raise the tarp!" It went up with no trouble, the tie-strings on the tarp slipping easily over the hooks on the stakes. We now had a three-meter wide tarpaulin raised at a forty-five-degree angle, its lower edge touching the base of the fence.

"Everybody duck, crawl to safety!" I yelled. Most did not duck. Being on the underside of the tarpaulin, they could not tell how low the fence was. But all made it to cover in either the mill or the lumberyard. I found out later one woman had twisted her ankle but no one else was hurt.

I didn't crawl, I ran, crouching low, trying to remember the height of the fence. The thin red line of a tracer bullet suddenly emerged from a hole in the tarp several meters in front of me. I crouched lower and tried to run faster.

And then I was on the loading dock of the sawmill building. I could see that the militia were down the hillside and at the foot of the bridge before they could stop, and they had knocked down the toll barrier. One rider—it was my cousin John—had his horse turned around and was waving to the rest to do the same.

Major Andreadis grabbed his arm. "All your people safe?"

"Two militia down. You can't do anything to help them right now, but keep your kit handy." He pulled me to a stack of lumber. "Keep your head down and you should be able to see safely." Yes, there were wide-enough gaps between the boards to get a good view of the Square.

I could see the nomads. How many there were I couldn't say, but it seemed like hundreds. Horses were jumping the fence now. the leading rider was standing up in his saddle, holding one of our bright red fire extinguishers in his right hand. I heard myself saying, "Yes, they must really be worried we're going to burn down the bridge."

The nomads were galloping across the yard in a ragged formation, as if some men had gotten impatient and tried to pass their leaders. The ones in front had sub-machine guns out but were not firing. No targets?

"Now look," said the Major. The front of the formation became a confused mass of horses swerving or sliding to a halt. "The horses can see the tarp now."

Horses galloping from the rear were beginning to collide with milling horses in front. I saw two steeds go down together with high-pitched screams and another horse buck, throwing its rider.

Andreadis had been right. "A horse will not jump an obstacle unless he's confident his rider knows what the two of them are doing. If the rider hesitates, the horse will refuse to jump."

The entire front rank of horses had refused, and the following horses, even had they wanted to jump, were caught in a traffic jam.

The rearmost riders, seeing the crowd ahead, were reining in. Shortly all the nomads were in the Square, milling around aimlessly.

A mule broke loose from the mob and calmly trotted up to the cashier's window. Our portable water pump was tied to his packsaddle. I could hear someone yell, "Give him a refund!"

Andreadis told me "Cover your ears." I did. He pointed his automatic rifle to the sky and fired off an entire magazine in one burst.

"What was that for?" I asked, when his gun was finally quiet.

"To distract them. Look," he said, pointing. Cross had his wagons moving across the far end of the Square. Yes, there seemed to be enough wagons to block off the end. As each driver parked his wagon touching the one ahead of him, he yanked the emergency brake, nailed the brake lever in place, and ran for cover.

The nomads were neatly boxed in, with buildings to either side, a solid line of wagons blocking the rear exit, and the tarpaulin baffling them in front.

"Now let's see if cavalrymen are as dumb as advertised," said Andreadis.

"They can escape, can't they?" I asked.

"Of course. Hop off the horse, cut down the tarp with a knife, then the horse can step over the fence and go where he wishes. Or walk the horse through the lumberyard and out the side door. But cavalrymen are strange. They don't dismount except to get laid, and they'd do that in the saddle if they could."

One of the nomads shouted an order and the leading horsemen fired their submachine guns at the tarp. They succeeded in turning the tarpaulin into a fishnet but it stayed in place. A 5X10 is five centimeters wide and ten centimeters thick and that is more wood than a submachine gun bullet can cut through.

"I need a white flag so I can hold a parley with their commander," said Andreadis. "What do you have?"

I gave him the largest bandage in my medical kit.

Sixty-two nomads surrendered; two had been killed falling from their horses. Half a dozen nomads were injured. I was to spend the afternoon setting broken bones.

Both of the militiamen who had fallen in the square— Scott Panden, a blacksmith from the town, and David Older, a local farmer—had been trampled to death. Was I responsible for their deaths? Or had they honestly known they were risking their lives when they led the nomads into the trap? And had they agreed to do so, for the sake of nothing more than the toll on the Bridge?

I asked Andreadis about it. he said," How could you be responsible? *Your* working with the tarp meant *they* were risking their lives for something *they* thought valuable, and since the livelihood of your town depends on that damn bridge, I would say it *was* valuable. And if you had refused, I would have put someone else in your place, and your friends would be just as dead." I'll have to think about that.

*   *   *

A very subdued and unmagnificent Suleiman was now standing in the Square, discussing terms with the Mayor.

Andreadis asked me, "Do you still think it was a dumb plan?"

"Yes. I don't see how it worked."

"The tarp was just to keep the horses from seeing the ground, so that they would hesitate," he answered. "The wagons—once, back on Terra*, some farmers marched on their capital to protest something. They drove their tractors into a square, like this one except a couple kilometers long. Once the farmers were distracted by their own speeches, the authorities quietly blocked off all the entrances to the square with buses, trucks, wagons, anything they had."

"Then what? The farmers surrendered?"

"No. They spent days plowing up the square, then went home, so much a laughingstock that the authorities didn't bother to arrest them."

"But a horse and rider isn't a tractor."

"A cavalryman's a strange beast, Mr. Herrero. No longer human, he is animal with two arms and six legs. And two brains, one human, one equine. The human brain is willing to charge into gunfire or jump blind into a tarpaulin. The equine brain knows better, knows enough to demand assurance from the human brain.

"As you said earlier, war is a human activity, and charging through the Square in the face of an armed enemy is war. Humans will do it on their own, but horses are too smart."

*Washington DC, February 5, 1979

From *The Wisdom of Breedmaster Caius* (traditional)

Men and women will come to care for each other beyond the bedchamber's doors, no matter what.

I have heard some unSoldierly lamentation about this, when the man is Sauron and the woman cattle. I think I have heard fools.

These bonds grow, and grow as close as they do, because the cattle of Haven are as close to the level of Saurons as it is in cattle to be. Are those who lament such closeness wishing that we breed up our sons from worthless mothers?

I say again, I have heard fools.

LOVED I NOT HONOR MORE

MARTIN TAYS

It was the face that drew him first, a face carved of steel and ice, untouchable. Of all the extraordinary women in this extraordinary tribute, she was the most beautiful, the most arresting, the most distant. She captured his heart in an uncontested battle.

Not, of course, that he could ever admit it, to her, to his followers, or most of all, to himself. He, after all, had an example to set. He was the grandson of Galen Diettinger and the Lady Althene. He was the First Soldier.

He was a Sauron.

With an effort, Hel Diettinger tore his eyes away from her, back to the Nomad waiting patiently for audience before him. As different as the females were from the normal group of Tribute Maidens, so this Nomad and his—the only word to describe it would be troops—were to the Maidens' normal escort. He carried himself with an ageless dignity and bearing that attracted attention as a magnet does steel. Most of the ones who came as escort came shamed, performing what was to them an onerous duty, as distasteful as it was necessary. Diettinger had once seen a Nomad shoot his muskylope after it had broken it's leg in a twenty-meter sliding fall down a spalled cliff face. He always thought of the look on that Nomad's face when he saw the Tribute group approach.

But this group was different. Vastly different. If he didn't know better, he would almost say they carried themselves with a certain quiet pride. But that would be senseless.

Still, this was what his grandmother would have dubbed "wool gathering" and it was accomplishing nothing. There was much to do today, as every day, and never enough time. He turned to face the Nomad leader.

"You're a day early."

"Better thus than a day late."

Hel blinked. "True. But you have managed to upset our schedules to no end."

"If it is your desire, sir, I'm sure we can round up our goats, and muskylopes and," with a glance at the women waiting with patient indifference, "other tributes, and leave. We can return tomorrow as your schedule dictates." He could have sworn the Nomad was laughing at him.

Impossible.

"And put up with this circus all over again?" He glanced around at the barely controlled chaos of the caravan and shook his head in disgust. "There is no possibility of that. Show me your lists."

The Nomad leader produced a handwritten list from inside his robes. He looked up at the Sauron for a long moment. Just when Diettinger was about to make an issue of it, the Nomad looked back down at the paper and began to read out loud in a monotone.

It was an impressive tribute. There were more meat animals than in the last two tributes combined. The muskylopes were of prime breeding stock, rather than the marginally acceptable animals they usually tried to pawn off on them. There was a decent amount of Earth—seeded food grain, not the wagon loads of acorn squash and, even worse, heart fruit that was the norm. The Soldiers privately referred to the heart fruit as "Nomad's Heart" because of its bitter taste.

Diettinger didn't think his Soldiers knew that this

practice had been picked up by the Nomads themselves, for much the same reason.

As the voice of the Nomad leader droned on, Hel felt
his eyes drawn once again to look at her.

She was standing as before, straight, unmoving. Her
shoulders were thrown back, her head was held high,
her legs apart and braced. The thin cold wind blowing
down out of the pass whipped her cloak back and plas-
tered the thin cloth of her dress to her, outlining her
muscular legs, her flat stomach, her small, firm breasts.
She seemed completely indifferent. She stared off into
the distance, then lowered her head and slowly turned
it to look the First Soldier in the eye.

Whatever he expected to find in the depths of those
eyes, it was not what he actually encountered. There
was determination there, a fierceness as unexpected as
it was disconcerting. A gauntlet thrown. The challenge
of one soldier to another. It was damned unnerving,
even more so when he realized that he had been the
one forced to break eye contact. He shook his head
slightly to clear it, then realized the Nomad leader had
been silent for some time, his list completed. He was
standing there staring at the Sauron leader with a look
of amusement.

Hel was startled by the dryness in his mouth. He had
to swallow before he spoke. " . . . Acceptable. All seems
to be in order."

"Silva. Her name is Silva."

Knowing the answer, he asked anyway. "What do
you mean? Whose name?"

"She is for you."

He looked sharply over at the woman. She was staring at him intently, a look that cut through to the desire
that had been growing steadily over the past hour. He
slowly turned his head back toward the Nomad. Before
the denial could form on his lips, the Nomad spoke
again.

"She is my daughter."

His nostrils flared as he drew a sharp breath. He reached out, gathered a fistful of robe, and lifted the Nomad up to eye level. In a dangerously quiet voice, he said, "An explanation appears to be in order, here."

The Nomad leader seemed undisturbed by the treatment and the accompanying unspoken threat. "There have been hostilities, ill will, bloodshed, between our people for too long. As the leader of our council of tribes, I have decided to try to put an end to it. I have convinced my brothers that if we present our best to you, you and your people may come to realize our true intentions. As a token of my feeling toward this goal, I have given over my daughter to the Tribute Maidens, hoping she would be worthy for you. Do you find her . . . satisfactory?"

Diettinger stared at the Nomad, groping for his name. K . . . Kar? . . . Karn! He realized he had been bobbing him up and down, as if testing the Nomad's weight before throwing him. He opened his fist abruptly and was slightly disappointed when the Nomad didn't collapse. "Tribe Leader Karn, your tribute is accepted. Take your people and animals and get out. And Karn?" The Nomad cocked his head expectantly. "Next time, send someone else to present the lists. Your attitude leaves something to be desired."

"In some people's opinion, sir, it contains something to be desired. May your days be filled with interest."

The First Soldier of the last bastion of the Sauron Empire stood staring at the back of the departing Nomad, wondering why he had not had him killed.

He could not for the life of him come up with an answer.

There had never been any question, really, of his not taking her to wife. The death of his father in a landslide in the High Pass region had been painfully unexpected, more because of his sudden unprepared rise to leadership at the relatively young age of seventeen T-years than to any actual grief. When he thought of his father at all, he merely felt a bit embarrassed that he had failed to die a warrior's death.

His mother had been dead for most of his life, and his father had claimed he was too busy to worry about taking another one now. Hel knew the real reason was that he would have had to choose a local. Deep in his cups one night, his father had confessed revulsion at the prospect of, as he put it, "humanizing cattle" with a Sauron child.

Therefore, Hel was the only heir to the first leaders of Haven. When that leadership fell on his barely adult shoulders, he knew, at least, two things. He would have to father an heir, and he would have to do so with a Havenite.

There were two reasons for this. The first was simple genetics. Long study sessions with successive Breed-masters over the years had aquainted him with the rather precarious situation he and his people were in. Breeding for the attributes of a Soldier was a chancy business to begin with, and although it had succeeded to an extraordinary degree with the Sauron Soldier, the price was high.

Deformities and obvious non-Sauron traits could be, and were, dealt with in the Breedmaster's domain. The child was normally never seen by the mother. The less obvious variances could only appear through regular genetic testing. This was easy enough on Sauron itself, where a gene pool of billions served as a leveling of the effects to begin with.

Not so on Haven. Even the best made equipment, Sauron made equipment, wears out over the years. Although the current Breedmaster was at least two hundred years advanced medically over anything else on Haven, this was due more to procedure and training rather than to technology. The ability to do a genetic scan at birth had vanished before Hel had been born.

This moved inbreeding from a clinical possibility to

an active menace. His grandfather had had the foresight
to realize this. Thus had begun the Tribute Maidens.
The idea was a leavening of the Sauron gene pool with
the better of the non-Sauron stock. After all, as his first
teacher had put it, "Even Sauron evolved from cattle."
Hel had always, then, considered it a duty to the race
for him to take a Havenite bride when the appropriate
time came.

The second, and greater, reason had to do with his
newly acquired followers. Though given all appropriate
courtesy due his rank, he knew he had yet to prove
himself, in battle or in progeny. Fathering an impressive child, a soldier, by a non-Sauron, would show not
only that he was an adult and a Sauron, but that he was
independent of his father and capable of choosing a
path that the old man was known to disapprove of.

Like any good Soldier, Hel Diettinger knew his duty,
and knew he would be able to perform it despite his
desire for a real woman. The good of the race came
first.

Though unnecessary, he still consulted the command
staff on his decision. His justification to them was that
the woman was presented directly to him as a peace
offering from the Nomad tribes. To refuse her would be
to deliberately insult them by slapping aside their gift.
After a minor amount of waffling, they concurred. So
after medical examinations and delousing, the marriage
was recorded by the personnel officer and the Nomad
woman was brought to him.

She was dressed in an ill-fitting set of fatigues, used
gear returned by a Soldier to central issue and given to
her to replace the clothing of her people. These had
been burned as a precautionary measure. The oversize
shirt was tied at her midriff, exposing a chain around
her stomach bearing a steel medallion. Her hair was
bound back in a tail, and her face was scrubbed raw

from the caustic soap. Tucked in her hair over her ear, incongruous, was a bright colored clown fruit blossom.

Her eyes. He has never seen a black as intense. They held him for a small eternity. With an effort, he broke the spell and spoke.

"Come inside. There's no reason to be afraid."

She stepped inside and shut the door. After a moment of puzzling, she turned the lock bolt. Straightening, she lithly stepped over to the startled Soldier and kissed him full on the lips. Just as he broke from his paralysis and began to respond, she drew back, hands on his hips, and said "Are you sure?"

She smiled at the expression on his face and drew his unresisting form toward the bed.

He had always thought his life was complex. Field exercises with the Survivalmaster, session after endless session with the Deathmaster, classes for everything from weapons construction to planetary economics. He was being groomed for leadership, and every thing he did for seventeen T-years reflected this. His every waking moment was filled with something intended to further his training toward his eventual acceptance of the First Soldier's Baton, all interweaving and locking like a mason's wall.

Hel realized now that his life before Silva (that's how he had taken to dividing it— Before Silva; After Silva) had been childishly simple. Get up, attend class, learn, listen, live. No worries, no problems. No wife.

He found his life inordinately complex now. Not that any aspect of it had changed other than her. Just that that was enough.

It was bad enough that he seemed to think of her nearly constantly. That his staff had reached the point of routinely explaining something to him twice, just to make certain he was catching the gist of it. That his list of deferred projects grew longer as he put off anything that would separate him from her even for one night.

What was worse was that he could see the changes

occurring, hated them, and seemed to be powerless to do anything about them. He would decide that he must do something, go somewhere. His mind would be firmly decided, unswayable. Then he would return to their (his!) quarters to tell her. And she would look at him, and smile, and begin to tell him of her day with the other women in the weaver's pit. She would tell of Martil's practical joke on her sister, of the way the light fell on Jorda's loom in the late afternoon, of the fine new wool traded to them by the Redfielders.

And the world would quietly fade away.

It was night time, in fact truenight. The stars gleamed cold and distant outside the sleeproom window. Hel's grandmother, the Lady Althene, had always asserted that she could just make out Sol, Earth's sun, at times like this. Hel had never allowed her to show him where it was.

He had woke suddenly from third-level sleep to find the other half of the bed empty. A light gleamed around the barely open common door. There was a sound . . . some sound . . . coming through it.

He rose and walked noiselessly (naturally) through the door. Silva was sitting at his work carrel, one of his grandmother's books open before her. The sound he had heard had been her quietly crying.

He gently eased up behind her and peered over her shoulder. It was open to a poem by an Englishman named Richard Lovelace. He realized she was reading the poem out in a whisper. Her shoulders gave a start, but only a slight one, when he joined her on the last two lines.

> ". . . I could not love thee, dear, so much
> Loved I not honor more."

She turned abruptly and buried her face in his chest, sobbing. He stroked her hair and made soothing noises and wondered what the hell he was supposed to do to help.

He was lying on his side, pleasantly exhausted and idly running his left hand down over her sweat-sheened stomach. The swell was barely detectable. He ran a finger under the chain, still fastened, though a bit tighter than before. The pendant, he noticed for the first time, was not really featureless, but was lightly engraved with an eye. A lidded eye. He puzzled over it for a second, then shrugged it off.

"You'll have to take this off soon. In another two months it will be too tight for him to breathe."

Her eyes widened momentarily in what could almost have been panic, then her normal calm returned, and she said "First off, silly, he's not born yet. I'll handle his breathing, thank you very much. Secondly, my father made this, and my father is a clever man." Something washed over her eyes, an expression Hel could not begin to fathom. "A very clever man. See?" She unfastened a hidden clasp, and the chain expanded. "If I decided to have six babies at once, he made it to fit me."

"You mean he designed it to fit you even while you were pregnant?"

"I told you," she said, the smile starting to slip, "my father is a very clever man."

He lay there and stared at her as she gazed off in the distance. After a long time, he spoke. "I love you."

She looked slowly over at him with a bittersweet smile. "I know."

A hand that could leave fingerprints in soft steel reached out to gently brush her lips. "You love me, too." It was a flat statement.

She clenched her eyes shut convulsively. A single tear appeared. Shuddering, she drew in a breath and whispered, "I know. You son of a bitch, I know."

Stunned, he watched her leap from the bed to run crying from the room.

The Breedmaster looked at him indulgently as he paced, nervous. "I have been doing this job for nearly ten years now and haven't . . ."

"If you tell me you 'haven't lost a father yet' I'm going to transfer you to muskylope breeding."

"Ahem. I don't, ahem, believe there will be any difficulty with the procedure, but the necessity of the Cesarian precludes your being present for the actual birthing. I would actually recommend you leave. Waiting will do you no good, and doing some work should take your mind off it."

"And get me out from underfoot?"

The Breedmaster barely succeeded in not smiling. "You know sir, that you are always welcome here. But the waiting room is a little crowded . . ."

" . . . and having the First Soldier camped in it would play hell with your routine. I can understand. The Engineering Officer has been after me to come by for a briefing. Now seems as good a time as any."

The Breedmaster was holding out something that glittered. Hel held out his hand and the Breedmaster dropped the chain and medallion into it. The lidded eye gleamed. Hel looked up, slightly surprised.

"We kept her clothing, of course, but we try to give the jewelery to someone like yourself, the father, that is, if we can. It seems to make the mother feel better knowing who has it."

"I would be willing to bet you had a hard time getting her to give this up."

The Breedmaster looked puzzled. "It was actually rather strange. She fought my assistant, at first, then relaxed and said 'It's alright. It doesn't matter anymore.' Then she told me to throw it away. I just assumed it was disorientation and brought it to you."

Diettinger stood, rubbing the teardrop-shaped pendant between thumb and forefinger. It was slick, and still slightly warm from her body heat.

With an effort, he dismissed it from his mind, dropped the medallion into his tunic pocket, and walked off to the Engineering labs.

Surprisingly, the Breedmaster was right. The Engineer had been working on a project for clearing fields of debris from the *Dol Gulder*. To accomplish this, he had been designing and building an entirely Haven-built radiation detector.

Hel had always had a secret fascination with the *Dol Gulder*, the ship his grandfather had called to its dying day its commissioning name, the *Fomoria*. As far as the crew knew, the *Fomoria* had been the only survivor of the Empire's fatal strike at the Sauron home world. A blind Jump through the Alderson point brought them with destroyed stardrive to the system of Byer's Star, where Haven was located. Making such a jump to an inhabitable system had been sheer luck, and Hel's grandfather intended to exploit that luck to the extreme.

Galen Diettinger knew beyond any reasonable doubt that he and his crew were the last free Saurons. In fact, possibly the last Saurons, period. He decided, along with his second in command and future wife, that he and his crew had stopped being a strike force and become a colonizing force.

Choosing a cover from the ancient Terran legend that had given them their name, they had presented themselves as mercenaries of a ship named the *Dol Gulder*. As insignia they chose the lidless, flaming eye.

The first Diettinger had known that they needed all the edge they could get. Therefore, they did not just land. They subjugated. They used kinetic energy weapons from orbit on every tactical and industrial target they could find. If any of the civilian cattle were injured, well, it was a pity. Still, after all, this was war.

Afterward, they chose a pass in the east end of the

major inhabited valley for their Citadel. Using the ship's shuttles, the Saurons shipped down everything even remotely removable from the *Dol Gulder*, leaving only a barely operable shell. Sauron ships were designed for planet landing capability in extreme emergency, once. Once. Knowing how badly they would need the processed metal richness the hull represented, they brought the ship in to land.

And discovered they had, to a great extent, underestimated their enemies. A small group of volunteers, knowing they would die, climbed to an exposed rock face high above the Sauron landing site and, with the *Dol Gulder* only a hundred meters above the valley floor, fired a small surface to air missile with a tactical nuclear warhead at the descending starship. The resulting explosion scattered radioactive debris over a hundred square kilometers of the east end of the valley. Hel's people were still suffering from the loss.

The Engineer was holding up a fifteen-centimeter transparent tube. "Now that we are consistently making decent glass, we were able to blow a tube strong enough to pull a vacuum in. This enabled us to build a Geiger-Mueller tube for the first time. After that, it was simple to build the proportioning circuits and metering systems." The short, solidly built Lead Engineer was almost bouncing in excitement.

"So. Show me how it works,"

"Well, we have these graduated sources, here, that are of decreasing amounts of activity. As we increase the sensitivity of the device, we decrease the amount of radioactive material. See, we are trying to see . . . see just how . . . sensitive . . . now, that's odd. . . ."

"What's wrong?"

"I can't get the level to go down. I don't think it is the meter. I just finished calibrating it. It's like a background source. It's almost as if there were another radioactive source in the . . ." He trailed off as he saw the expression on the First Soldier's face.

Diettinger silently, slowly raised his arm, the shiny metal of the medallion gleaming in the Cat's Eye light streaming in through the window. The Engineer silently raised the probe of his device up to hold its side against the engraved eye. He stared at the meter, then up at Hel's face.

He then stepped quickly backward.

Hel could never remember, later, the actual run back to the Breedmasters domain. The first thing he could recall was the expression of the assistant as he stood, ashen-faced in the hall. As he came running up, the assistant saw him coming and avoided looking into his eyes.

The First Soldier bypassed him completely and ran into the offices. He never slowed as he plowed down two orderlies in his path and rounded a corner to the delivery wards. The Breedmaster was waiting for him.

"Stop!" I don't know what you were told, but it will do you no good to go in there. We normally use a general anesthetic, but she convinced us to use a saddle block for the procedure so that she could watch. When, when . . . it . . . came out of the incision, she insisted we let her have it." The Breedmaster, looking drawn and withered, shook slightly as he spoke. "It's as she expected it. I didn't know what to . . . I mean, I don't know why I let her . . ."

The Soldier reached out and put a hand gently on the aging Breedmaster's shoulder. "She, I have discovered, is an extremely difficult person to refuse. Excuse me." He stepped through the partially opened doorway past the Breedmaster and shut it behind him.

There was a curtain drawn around the bed. Behind it, he could see the shadow of Silva holding . . . something. She seemed to be looking out at him.

"It was debris from the *Dol Gulder*, wasn't it? Your Father found it, melted it, cast it, and engraved it." He discovered he was using the medallion to gesture with, its lidded eye mocking him. He threw it furiously against the wall. "Why?" His voice shrunk, threw off the fury for its underlying pain. Again quietly, "Why?"

The curtain whipped abruptly back. Silva was propped up in bed, the bundle hidden in the blankets in her lap. "Your grandfather was responsible for killing half of the people on the planet." Her voice was tired, filled with pain, resigned. "After which he went on to set the survivors back technologically by five hundred years. To establish his dynasty," here Diettinger flinched, "he killed civilization. For all we know, we may be the last humans left alive in the Universe. After all, I understand we're not the only ones dead set anxious at committing suicide. It's possible everyone else succeeded. And First Soldier Galen Deittinger, out of a vague possibility of being attacked by a group whose air power was composed of biplanes, destroyed everything we had that might have helped keep this one small pocket of idiots alive.

"You really want to know why? Revenge. Pure and simple. Revenge."

"But, what did he lose? His wife? His family? His home?"

"His books."

"*What!?*"

"My father was the librarian at Falkenberg. It was quite literally his whole life. Karn O'Malley was twenty-nine years old when your people came. Of those twenty-nine years, he had spent the previous seventeen at the library, first as helper, then in control. He eventually wanted to bring together, in one place, every book on Haven. He thought of them as idiot savants, you see, capable of great deeds and thought and unable to come in out of the rain. They were his children, Hel Diettinger, and he saw it as his duty to protect them and keep them available for Haven's eventual renaissance. He was on a buying trip to an outlying farm for some family heirloom books someone wanted to sell when your people struck. By the time he got back, there was nothing he could do. The whole library, the only one on Haven, had been destroyed. You want to know what you grandfather destroyed that was so important to my father?

"It was knowledge. Your grandfather wantonly and callously murdered knowledge. And that is why I'm here today."

"But you . . ."

"Are dying. The doctors told me, back when they first dreamed this up, that it would probably be uterine cancer. I knew all along. I volunteered. I trained for this. And because I did, your grandfather's line is finished. Your people will never accept you, now. Now that you've fathered this." She pointed downward with her chin.

He walked slowly up, staring fixedly into her face. "The poem. I thought it was supposed to be about me. But it was you." She nodded. "You know, I still love you?"

Her head dropped back on the pillow as the tears began. Her "thank you" was almost, but not quite, inaudible.

Hel Diettinger, former First Soldier of the last bastion of the Sauron Empire, kissed his wife gently on the forehead and looked down for the first time at his son.

—and McFarland came back the next morning, with Kubei and a cage that was tough enough, if not big enough, for tamerlanes.

I asked if we needed to hump something that heavy for drillbits. McFarland gave me one of his "you oughta be in a zoo yourself" looks, then translated what I'd said for Kubei.

Kubei laughed himself silly. By the time he'd recovered, McFarland explained.

"Thing about drillbits, they grow a lot bigger out where we're going than they do around here. I've seen them a meter long."

I mentally took twenty centimeters off that figure, but that still made a beast twice the size of any I'd seen around Halliburton. "Does that make a difference?"

"Sure as hell does. The big ones—they can eat through anything but alloy steel, give 'em enough time or make 'em hungry enough."

"God! What are their insides made of?"

"Don't know what you boffins'd call it—"

"I'm no scientist, McFarland. I'm just a horny-handed animal collector."

"Sorry." He didn't sound sorry, but then, he never did. "Anyway, you gut one, you've got good rope, shock cord, canteens, slingshots, anything that's gotta be tough and bouncy. Thing is, though, you can wear out a good knife makin' anything out of the beasties' guts."

"Is that why those plains have never been settled?"

"Oh, it's settled, all right, if you call herdsmen settlers. But you gotta be careful with anything that can't run away. That incudes babies, by the way."

The mental picture that conjured up made me instinctively reach for my pistol butt. McFarland's pale blue eyes followed the gesture.

"What bore?"

"Standard 9-mm."

"Let me loan you one of my 11.7m-mm SMG's. A big drillbit's as tough outside as inside. I've seen people make football helmets out of the hides. A 9-mm won't even give a big drillbit a headache, unless you hit him in the eye."

Since drillbits' eye were just this side of vestigial— they tracked food by scent and vibration—I decided to accept McFarland's offer.

I also decided that I now understood why the Imperial Zoo had sent its junior collector to Haven.

THE FIELD OF DOUBLE SOWING

HARRY TURTLEDOVE

The fluorescent panels in the delivery room flickered, almost died. The Sauron fortress at the mouth of the Tallinn Valley was half a continent away from the Citadel. The last supply shipment had reached Angband Base six Haven years—46 T-years—before. Outside the Citadel, Saurons were Soldiers, and Soldiers only, not engineers. When the panels finally quit for good, they would do without.

This time, though, the silvery light came back. The woman—girl, really; she could not have had more than fourteen T-years—writhing in the stirrups noticed neither dimming nor return. Eyes screwed shut, she pushed with all her might.

Her partner, a Chief Assault Leader named Dagor, touched her cheek. "Soon now, Badri," he murmured. "Soon it will be done."

Angband Base's Breedmaster stood between Badri's legs, ready to receive the baby when it came. "Don't worry. This is what the cattle women are for," he told the Chief Assault Leader. "And if she dies giving birth to a Soldier, well, fair exchange."

The scar under Dagor's left eye went pale. Almost, he grabbed for the Breedmaster's throat. "Shut up Grima," he growled. He made himself subside. They were far from friends, but he needed Grima's skill to bring Badri through safe. On Haven, no birth was ever

293

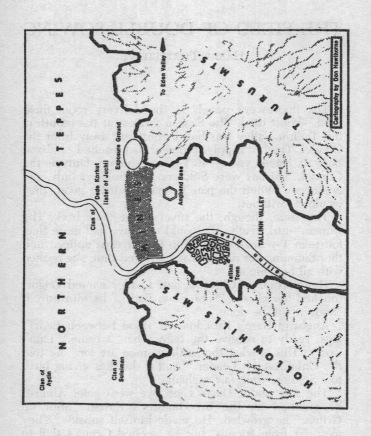

NORTHERN STEPPES

Clan of Aydin

Clan of Suleiman

Clan of Dede Korkut (later of Juchi)

Exposure Ground

To Eden Valley

TAURUS MTS.

M I N E S

Angband Base

Tallinn Town

Tallinn River

TALLINN VALLEY

HOLLOW HILLS MTS.

Cartography by Don Hawthorne

easy. And despite his harsh words, the Breedmaster knew his obstetrics. He would not let a successful breeder die if he could prevent it.

Badri shrieked. Dagor squeezed her hand, willing himself not to use his enhanced strength to crush it.

Grima grunted in satisfaction. "Here we are." His hands reached where, Dagor thought, only himself had any business touching. The Breedmaster knew what he was doing, though. He guided the baby out, sponged mucus from its mouth. It began to cry. "A girl," Grima said, with a faint sneer Dagor's way.

The Chief Assault Leader's iron shoulders sagged. Soldiers always wanted—Soldiers always needed—to breed more Soldiers. Dagor knew the chromosome that decided the baby's sex came from him. He could not help frowning at Badri even so.

Grima delivered the raw-liver horror of the afterbirth. Dagor expected his woman's travail to end then, but her belly still rippled with contractions. Grima palpated it, stared, palpated again. "There's another baby in there," he exclaimed, startled out of his usual air of omniscience.

Badri's struggle to give birth began again. She was close to exhaustion now; Dagor learned at firsthand why the process was called labor. "You should have known she was carrying twins," he snarled at Grima.

Above a linen mask, the Breedmaster's eyes were harassed. "More than half the time, the first indication of twins is birth," he said. "If this were the Citadel, with the technology they still have there, maybe. As is, keep quiet and let me—and your woman—work. Just be thankful I hadn't started sewing up the episiotomy yet." Dagor scowled, but nodded.

Not too much later, as the Chief Assault Leader reckoned time—an age went by for Badri—another baby let out its first indignant cry. "A boy this time," Grima said. "Now I sew."

"Well done," Dagor told Badri. Glancing down at

her, he doubted she heard. Her head lolled, her eyes were half-closed, her breath came slow and deep. She was, the Chief Assault Leader thought, falling asleep. He did not blame her a bit.

First one newborn, then the other squalled as Grima stabbed tiny heels to draw blood. "Don't let your woman get too attached to them yet," he warned. "The genetics have to check out."

"Get on with it, then," Dagor growled, though the Breedmaster outranked him, Scowling, Grima stalked out of the delivery room. Dagor shouted for a servant to see to the twins.

Back in the laboratory where only he was allowed to go, Grima frowned as he ran his checks. The babies' blood clotted Soldier-fast, that was certain. The rest of his test had to be more indirect. Some—too many—reagents were not changing color as they should when they found Soldier genes.

But almost all his reagents were *old*. For some, his predecessors had found equivalents brewed from Haven's plant life. For most, there were none. And so he made do with tiny driblets of the chemicals the last shipment from the Citadel had brought, hoping the driblets were enough to react to genes whose presence they were suppose to mark, hoping also that the complex chemicals had not decayed too much over the decades.

His frown deepened. If the reagents told the truth—if—these two twins were marginal Soldiers at best. He suspected some of the chemicals were too far gone to be useful any more, but what were his suspicions against the hard evidence of the test tubes?

"Marginal, marginal, marginal," he said under his breath. That meant the decision lay in his hands. He enjoyed the strength accruing to him from this power of life and death, but with power went risks. Chief Assault Leader Dagor, for instance, was up and coming, and would not take kindly to having two of his children ordered set out for stobor.

On the other hand, Brigade Leader Azog, Warlord of Angband Base, had been looking askance at the rising young Chief Assault Leader lately. Subordinates with too much ambition could be dangerous; every senior officer knew that.

Grima pondered, rubbing his chin. Breedmasters, by the nature of things, had to be conservative; conserving genes was their job. Given the choice between displeasing Dagor and displeasing Brigade Leader Azog, Grima hesitated only a moment.

"There is no choice," he told the hard-faced Chief Assault Leader a few minutes later. There *was* a choice, he knew, but he had already made it. He spoke so not to salve his own conscience but Dagor's anger. "The newborns do not meet our standards. They must be exposed."

Badri wept helplessly. Dagor soothed her as best he could, which was none too well: "They have only cattle genes in them. They could never serve the Base, serve the Race, as they must."

"They are my children!" Badri screamed. She clawed at his face. He seized her wrist with the thoughtless, automatic speed his enhanced reflexes gave him. She wept louder, turned her nails against her own cheeks.

Dagor offered the only promise he could: "Maybe some woman of the cattle will take them in."

Badri stared, hope wild in her eyes. Better than she, Dagor knew how forlorn it was. Stobor, cliff lions, and cold claimed exposed babies, not cattle women. But every Base's exposure ground was unpatrolled, to give each mother the chance to think her infant might be the lucky one, rescued by people instead of death.

Dagor had once thought that weakness: simple euthanasia of unacceptable infants would have been quicker and cleaner. Now he saw for himself the wisdom of the scheme. Even Soldiers had to be able to live at peace with their women.

Second cycle night at Angband Base: black and freezing, with neither Byers' Sun nor Cat's Eye in the sky for light and warmth. Two tiny voices cried in the frigid darkness. Both were weaker than they had been an hour before. Soon both would be still forever, unless . . .

Kisirja came stumbling, drawn by the sound, but not drawn enough to dare show a torch. Aye, Saurons were not known to shoot at skulkers on the exposure ground, but no one on Haven ever felt easy putting Saurons and mercy in the same thought.

Kisirja stooped by the abandoned infants, scooped one up in firewalker-fur gloves, pressed it against her. Warmth and softness made the baby quiet. "Mine now," Kisirja crooned. "Mine." She held it inside her sheepskin coat.

Then she reached for the second baby. Her gloved hand touched another glove. She gasped and jerked backwards, snatching for the knife that hung from her belt. The sudden motion made the baby she had taken squall in protest. "Who are you?" she whispered harshly to the other shape in the blackness. "What do you want?"

A ghost of a chuckle answered her, and a woman's voice using her own Turkic speech, though strangely accented: "The same as you, child of the steppe. The Bandari hate the Saurons no less than you, but we need their genes if we ever hope to meet them on equal terms. And there are two babes here, so we need not even fight. Go in peace."

"Allah and the spirits grant you the same, haBandari," Kisirja said. She knew nothing but relief that they could share. The Bandari were farmers, a couple of valleys over, but they were also warriors. She hadn't heard this one approach, while she'd made enough noise on the exposure ground to wake a gorged tamerlane.

The other baby quieted as the Bandari woman picked it up. Somewhere not far away, a stobor started yowling, then another and another, until a whole pack was at cry. Kisirja hurried toward her muskylope, which was tethered to a Finnegan's fig out of sight of Angband Base.

If the Bandari woman had a mount, it was nowhere near Kisirja's. She untied her muskylope and climbed onto its broad, flat back. She tugged on its ears to send it back toward the clan's yurts. She wanted to gallop, but not during second cycle night.

Not much later, the stobor pack trotted through the exposure ground. The nasty little predators soon left, hungry still.

The baby nursed and nursed, as if there were no tomorrow. "Hungrier than mine, he is," said the woman who held him at one breast and her own, much bigger, daughter at the other. She did not sound angry, but rather indulgent, motherly, almost proud.

"He has every reason to be," Kisirja answered. Under her, the yurt swayed and rolled, as if at sea. Horses snorted, muskylopes grunted. Kisirja was only glad Nilufer had given birth three T-months before, and so had milk to spare. Otherwise they would have lost the child she rescued.

"What will you call him?" Nilufer asked.

Kisirja had thought about that all through the long, cold journey home. "His name will be Juchi."

" 'The Guest,' " Nilufer smiled. "Yes, that is very good. Juchi he shall be."

When at last he'd drunk his fill, Juchi burped lustily against his wetnurse's shoulder. His head stayed steady and upright on his shoulders, instead of wobbling like a normal newborn's.

He had some Sauron genes in him, then, Kisirja thought. But the Saurons did not cull just babies in whom their strain was too weak. If it was too strong, an infant could die of a heart attack like an old man or spasm to death when overenhanced reflexes sent it into convulsions at the slightest sound. Whether Juchi was a permanent guest remained to be seen.

"May Allah and the spirits make it so," Kisirja murmured. Nilufer nodded, understanding her perfectly.

Juchi burped again, sighed in contentment. The wet-nurse handed him to Kisirja. He looked up at her. Even baby-round, his face was longer than those of children born in the yurts, and his eyes had no folds of skin to narrow them. Kisirja did not care. He was hers now, for however long she had him.

Brigade Leader Azog thumbed on the Threat Analysis Computer. As the screen lit, he smiled at the machine. It was one of the last pieces of high-tech gear the Base had that still worked.

Azog punched in the first of his usual questions: THREAT TO ANGBAND BASE—RANK ORDER. His typing was one-fingered but rapid, a curious blend of lack of practice and Sauron speed.

The TAC muttered to itself. Words appeared on the screen: THREATS TO ANGBAND BASE: 1. THE CITADEL; 2. THE BANDARI; 3. STEPPE NOMADS, CLAN OF DEDE KORKUT; 4. TOWN OF TALLINN; 5. RIVER PIRATE BARTON'S BAND. OTHERS TOO LOW A PROBABILITY TO BE EVALUATED.

Azog eyed the screen, frowning a little. The Citadel and haBandari were always one and two on the TAC's list. But the last time he'd checked, ten or twelve cycles before, the nomads had been fifth. The time before that, no clan had even been named. He wondered what this Dede Korkut was up to. Maybe one of his shamans had tried cooking up smokeless powder and not blown himself sky-high in the attempt.

Frowning still, the Brigade Leader cleared the screen. He typed his second ritual question: THREATS TO CO, ANGBAND BASE, RANK ORDER. Again the TAC went into what seemed its own private ritual of thought. It took so long to come out that Azog wondered if it was working as it should.

Just as he began to worry in earnest, he got his answer: THREATS TO CO, ANGBAND BASE; 1. SENIOR ASSAULT GROUP LEADER DAGOR; 2. STEPPE NOMADS, CLAN OF DEDE KORKUT; 3. BREEDMASTER GRIMA. OTHERS TOO LOW A PROBABILITY TO BE EVALUATED.

Now Azog was frankly scowling. END, he typed, and the screen went blank and dark. His own thoughts cleared more slowly. He'd commanded Angband Base for close to twenty T-years, far longer than any other CO since the *Dol Guldur* landed on Haven. In all that time, he'd never seen anything but one of his fellow Soldiers listed as a threat to him personally. What *were* those cursed nomads up to?"

The Brigade Leader's eyes lit. Had he been a man who laughed, he would have chortled. Instead, he nodded in slow satisfaction. This was what the battle manuals called an elegant solution.

"Why you?" Badri demanded.

Dagor shrugged. "Because I am ordered." He went on checking his combat kit, methodical as a good Soldier ought to be. He was especially careful examining his ammunition; most of the pistol cartridges were reloads. He set aside a couple that did not satisfy him.

He was leaving his assault rifle behind, heading out as a man who could be anyone rather than a Soldier. Since many Haveners tried to kill Soldiers on sight, that might prove useful. It made him feel very vulnerable, but, he told himself, a lone raider ought to feel that way. And he was his own best weapon, always.

"You are too senior for a seek-and-destroy mission," Badri insisted. The two Haven years—fifteen T-years—that had passed since her first breeding had refined young-girl prettiness in a dangerous beauty. Black eyes sparked above a proud scimitar of a nose; her cheekbones seemed high and unconquerable as the cliffs that walled off Tallinn Valley.

The years had refined her wits, too, making her in all ways a fit companion for the Soldier who, folk whispered, would next wear Brigade Leader's leaves. Quietly, quietly, she fed those whispers.

Dagor shrugged again. "I know. But I am not senior enough to refuse." To rebel, he meant, and they both knew it. In that as in all things, timing was critical. If he moved against Azog now, he would fail. "Once I return, though, with the added prestige of having ended a threat to the Base—"

"—when Azog has not gone into the field in a Haven year or more," Badri finished for him. It was not cowardice that kept the Brigade Leader at his desk, only good sense—combat stress killed more middle-aged Soldiers than any foe. And for a Soldier, Azog was downright elderly. Troopers noticed, though, and also noticed that Dagor was still of an age to lead from the front.

"Aye," he said. "Once I return, I think the time will have come at last to settle accounts with him."

"And with Grima." Badri's voice was flat, determined. Since the twins the Breedmaster had forced her to expose, she'd given Dagor two more sons, neither of whom Grima had dared condemn. Neither still lived. One had died in hand-to-hand combat training, the other from a fall.

The Breedmaster had had no part in their deaths. She blamed him for them anyway, for ruining her children's luck. And even were that nonsense, without him she would have had two children who lived.

Dagor had his own reasons for wanting Grima dead. "Aye, he's Azog's toady, sure enough. When I come back, I'll set the base to rights. The risk to me, I'm certain, is less than Azog hopes."

"It had better be." Badri clasped him with almost Soldier's strength, kissed him fiercely.

Reluctantly, he pulled away. "Duty," he said, reminding himself as much as her. Her genes were not enhanced, he thought, but she was almost Soldier all the same. The thought ran against indoctrination. He believed it even so.

Still, once he was out on the steppe, trotting north fast and tireless as a muskylope, he found himself eager to meet these nomads who had the presumption to menace Angband Base. Time to remind the barbarous cattle, it seemed, just what the cost of facing Soldiers was. He smiled, an expression that had as much to do with good humor as a tamerlane's reptilian grin. He would enjoy administering the lesson.

Juchi rode along, every now and then shouting from muskylope-back to keep the sheep going in the direction they were supposed to. He wondered which were stupider, sheep or muskylopes. It was one of the endless arguments that kept the clan amused through the long, cold second cycle nights.

A flicker of motion, far off the steppe. Without his willing it, Juchi's eyes leaped the intervening distance. The flicker expanded into a man, a man wearing a shaggy sheepskin cape much like his own. Whoever the stranger was, though, he did not move like a nomad—he was far too self-assured on foot.

Juchi tilted up his fur hat so he could scratch his head. He glanced at the sheep. They were, for a wonder, going in the right direction. If they did start fouling up, Salur on the other side of the flock could deal with them for a while. Anyone alone and afoot on the steppe needed checking out.

Sometimes Juchi's extraordinary vision made him underestimate how far away things were. The muskylope's steady amble also helped deceive him. Not until he looked back at the flock did he realize he had ridden close to three kilometers.

He grew uneasily aware that he had only a knife at his belt. He slowed his mount, thought about heading

back to Salur. Pride forbade it. In any case, Salur had
no gun either. He rode on.

Dagor waited for the nomad to approach. His feet
ached inside his boots. Just because he could run like a
muskylope did not mean he enjoyed it. And here came
a muskylope for him to ride. That the beast belonged to
the young man lying on it never entered his mind.

The youth asked formally, "Who comes seeking the
yurts of Dede Korkut?"

Dagor grinned: the very clan he'd been looking for!
And here was a lovely way to start making life miserable for them. He produced his pistol, watched the
cattle lad's eyes get round. "I require your muskylope.
Kindly climb down."

"No," the youth said, as if not believing his ears.

Dagor gestured with the pistol. "Mind your tongue,
boy, and I may decide to let you live. Now climb
down!" He put some crack in his voice, as if dressing
down one of his troopers.

As the youth descended, his hand went halfway to
the hilt of his knife. Then he thought better of it, and
stood very still. "Thief," he whispered.

"Robber," Dagon corrected genially. He gestured
with the pistol again, more sharply this time. "Now
move away from that muskylope."

The nomad went red; he had, Dagor thought, more
caucasoid genes than most steppe-rovers. But he did
not stand aside. "He's mine," he protested with the
innocence of the young. "You can't just come and take
him away from me."

"Can't I?" The Senior Assault Group Leader had all
he could do not to burst out laughing. "How do you
suppose to stop me?"

The plainsboy surprised—almost stunned—him by
blurting, "I'll fight you for him."

"Why shouldn't I just shoot you and save myself the
trouble?" As Dagor spoke, though, he lowered the pis-

tol. Man to man, hand to hand—that was what Soldiers were bred for. Let this upstart piece of cattle learn—briefly—who and what he faced. "Knives, or just hands?"

"Hands." The young man took the knife from his belt and tossed it in back of him. He fell into a crouch that said he knew something of what he was about.

Dagor shrugged off his cape, then his pack. He threw his pistol twenty meters behind him. If the nomad wanted it, he would have to go through Dagor to get it. The Soldier took off his own knife and, as he did, his foe jumped him.

He'd expected that. Indeed, he'd been ostentatiously slow disarming himself, to lure the nomad in. His foot lashed out to break the youth's knee. After that, he thought with grim enjoyment, he would finish him at leisure.

But the nomad's knee was not there. Dagor was almost too slow to skip aside from his rush, and still took a buffet that made his ear ring. He shook his head to clear it, stared in amazement at the plainsboy. "You're quick," he said with grudging respect. "Very quick."

"So are you," said the nomad, who sounded as disconcerted as Dagor.

They circled, each of them more wary now. Another flurry of arms and legs, a brief thrashing on the ground, and they broke free from each other once more. Dagor felt a dagger when he breathed—one of his foe's flailing feet must have racked a rib. Blood ran from the steppe-rover's nose; a couple of fingers on his right hand stuck out at an unnatural angle, broken or dislocated.

Dagor willed his pain to unimportance. He had to be getting old, he thought, to let a puppy—and a puppy from the cattle, at that—lay a finger on him, let alone hurt him. Old? He had to be getting senile! All right, the fellow was fast and strong for an unaltered man, but that was all he was, all he could be. It did not suffice.

No more play now, Dagor thought, and waded back into the fight.

Even when he lay on the ground with the nomad's arm like a steel bar at the back of his neck, he could not believe what had happened to him. "I will spare you if you yield," his opponent panted.

Instead, as any Soldier would, Dagor tried once more to twist free. That steel bar came down. He felt—he heard—his vertebrae crack apart, then felt nothing at all. "Badri," he whispered, and died.

"More kavass, my son?" Before Juchi could answer, Kisirja handed him the leather flask. He drank, belched with nomad politeness, drank again. The fermented mares' milk mounted to his head, helped blur the hurts he had taken in the fight with the outlaw.

He belched again, touched the pistol on his belt. After endless searching, he'd found it and the ammunition the outlaw had carried for it. Better than either had been the awe on Salur's face when he brought his prizes back to the flock.

"Who was the bandit?" Kisirja asked, for about the tenth time. "Who could he have been?"

Juchi shrugged, as he had each time she'd asked. "By his gear, he could have been anymore. He was very fast and strong, stronger than anybody I've wrestled in the clan."

"Could he have been—a Sauron?" Kisirja knew a sudden spasm of fear, remembering what she had drilled herself never to think of: how Juchi had come to her, come to the clan.

He stared at her. "How could I hope to best a Sauron, my mother? No, I think he must have been a bandit of some sort, perhaps exiled from the Bandari. They have Frystaat blood, many of them, which makes them fast and tough. But as I say, I can't be sure. I'll never be sure, just glad that I'm here."

"As am I, my son." A haBandari outlaw, Kisirja mused.

That was possible, maybe even probable. For the first time in years, she wondered what had become of the exposed Sauron babe the Bandari woman had taken when she found Juchi.

And, for the first time in even more years, she found herself feeling odd to hear Juchi call her "mother." No one in the clan had ever told him he was not theirs by birth. The nomads stole babes from Bases' exposure grounds now and again, aye, but they feared the Saurons too much to let those babes learn their heritage. The genes were valuable. Everything that went with them . . . Kisirja shivered.

Juchi hugged her, tight enough to make her bones creak. "Don't worry, my mother. There was but the one of him, and he is not coming back to rob honest men any more."

"Good." Kisirja smiled and did all the things she needed to do to reassure him. Even his embrace, though, somehow only made her own worries worse. That effortless, casual strength—She felt like a filebeak that had hatched a land gator's egg.

The land gator named Juchi was, for the moment, quite nicely tame. "I have to go now, my mother. The clan chief himself invited me to his yurt, to see the pistol and hear my story." He puffed out his chest and did his best to strut in the cramped confines of the yurt, then kissed Kisirja and hurried off to guest with Dede Korkut.

Kisirja should have been proud. She *was* proud, and all her forebodings, she told herself, were merely the fright of any mother at her son's brush with danger. After a while, she made herself believe it.

"He is not coming back," the Breedmaster said.

"How can you be sure?" Badri wanted to scream it at him. Ice rode her words instead. Ice was better for dealing with the likes of Grima. "He's only been gone twenty cycles."

"Only?" Grima twisted words; his tongue writhed like a worm, Badri thought. The Breedmaster went on. "Twenty cycles is more than a quarter of a T-year. He should have returned in half that time, or less. No, we have to conclude the cursed cattle got lucky this time."

"I don't believe it," Badri said flatly. She spoke simple truth: Dagor was too fine a soldier, and too much a Soldier, for her to imagine any mere human vanquishing him.

"I fear I do." The Breedmaster did not sound as though he feared it; he sounded glad. "And not only do I believe it, so does Brigade Leader Azog. He has ordered me to put your name on the reassignment list. You are not as young as you once were, but you have at least a Haven year's worth of fertility left to give to the Race, maybe close to two. You may yet bear many children, many Soldiers."

Badri fought panic, felt herself losing. She had seen this happen to other women at Angband Base, but had never thought it could be her fate. Dagor, dying in combat against cattle? As well imagine Byers's Sun going out. Without thinking, she looked up to see if the star still shone. It did, of course. But Dagor was gone.

"Children." She forced the word out through the lips that did not want to shape it. "Children by whom?"

Grima smiled. Badri wished he hadn't; the expression stretched his face in directions it was not meant to go. "By me," he said. "Our genetic compatibility index is very high." His eyes slowly traveled the length of her body, stripping her naked—no, worse, spread and exposed—under her gray tunic and trousers.

"No," she whispered.

"Why not?" That smile returned; suddenly Badri preferred it to the—hungry—expression it replaced. "I am Breedmaster, no mere Trooper to despise. One day, who can say, I may rank higher yet. As my consort, you will be a person of consequence. If you refuse me, do you think another would risk my anger by choosing you?"

Numbly, Badri shook her head. The Breedmaster could do too much harm to a Soldier who opposed him. She thought again of her twins, more than half a lifetime gone now. He could she lie with the man who had ordered them set out for stobor? But even Dagor had accepted that, reluctantly, for the good of the Race. Now, though, Grima was as much as saying that he might twist birth analyses for his own purposes.

Through her confusion, his voice pursued her, tying off her future as inexorably as a hangman bush's noose: "Shall I visit you after mainmeal, then?"

She felt the noose's spikes sink into her neck as she muttered, "Yes."

Much, much later, after Grima finally left the cubicle she had shared so long with Dagor, she lay alone on the bed, huddled and shivering. The breedmaster had been worse even than she'd imagined, cruel, selfish, caring nothing about her save as a receptacle—several receptacles—for his lust, and, almost worst of all, with his Soldier's strength utterly tireless. Had he not had work to do, he might have been here with her yet.

He'd enjoyed himself, too, she thought furiously, no matter how still and unresponsive she lay. "We'll do this many more times," he'd promised as he was dressing.

"I'll kill him," she said into her pillow. But how? How could she, of mere human stock, kill an enhanced Soldier? Grima never relaxed, not even in the moments just after he spent. And if she tried and failed, he would only relish punishing her. The thought of giving him pleasure in any way made her want to retch.

Instead she washed herself, again and again and again, as if soap and hot water could scrub away the feel of his mouth chewing at her breast, his hands rough on her most secret places. "I'll kill him. One day, somehow, I will," she vowed.

Brigade Leader Azog typed in his first question: THREATS TO ANGBAND BASE—RANK ORDER.

The TAC performed its electronic equivalent of thought, replied, THREATS TO ANGBAND BASE: 1. THE CITA-DEL; 2. STEPPE NOMADS, CLAN OF DEDE KORKUT; 3. THE BANDARI. OTHERS TOO LOW A PROBABILITY TO BE EVALUATED.

The Brigade Leader scowled. He understood why the rankings had changed, but could not remember a time when nomads represented a greater danger to the Base than the Bandari. How had they taken out Dagor? That was a good man gone, even if a rival; had Azog known the Senior Assault Group Leader would perish without accomplishing anything at all, he might not have sent him out alone.

Azog put his second question to the TAC: THREATS TO CO, ANGBAND BASE, RANK ORDER.

This time the machine's reply was prompt: THREATS TO CO, ANGBAND BASE: 1. BREEDMASTER GRIMA. OTHERS TOO LOW A PROBABILITY TO BE EVALUATED.

The Brigade Leader stared. Only one threat? The others that dogged his tracks had not disappeared. That meant one of two things: either the TAC had malfunctioned at last, or Grima's threat was so overwhelming that it made all others pale beside it.

Azog could not afford, did not intend, to take a chance. Just as his finger stabbed for the button to summon the Breedmaster, the intercom buzzed. "Who is it?" the Brigade Leader snarled.

"Breedmaster Grima, Brigade Leader," came the reply.

Azog's grin was all teeth, like that of a cliff lion about to pounce. "Come in, Breedmaster. I was thinking of you." He made sure his sidearm was loose in his holster. "Well, Grima," he said as the other Soldier sat across the desk from him, "what can I do for you?"

Grima steepled his fingertips. "I came"—he glanced at his wrist chrono—"to say goodbye, Brigade Leader."

"Odd," Azog said, "for I was just about to summon you to give you the same message."

The Breedmaster nodded, unsurprised. "I thought that might be so. Were you less suspicious, you might have been allowed to last another couple of cycles. As is—" He spread his hands in regret.

Azog laughed, or tried to. For some reason, his throat did not work as it should. Full of sudden alarm, he reached for his pistol. At least, he thought he reached for it, but his hand did not move. And when he tried to suck in a deep, furious breath, he found his lungs frozen as well.

The Breedmaster checked his chrono again. "Distillate of oxbane has an *extremely* precise latent period before it manifests itself," he remarked, as if expounding on the poison to one of his assistants. "As I said, I do apologize for having to up the dose to a lethal level so soon, but you left me little choice."

Azog could not even blink now. He felt his heart stutter, beat, stutter again, stop. He watched the office go dark, and knew the lights were not failing. Blackness swallowed all his senses.

"*At* them!" Bugles blared, some of brass, more carved from horns of herdbeasts. Horses, muskylopes, men rushed forward. "Dede Korkut!" the men screamed.

Another line, about as ragtag as the attackers, stood in defense on a low ridge. "Suleiman!" they screamed back.

"Suleiman the sheep-stealer! Suleiman the sheep-bugger!" Dede Korkut's warrior's yelled. The men armed with rifles and bows began to shoot; those who carried pistols or scimitars or lances waited for the fight to come to close quarters.

Suleiman's warriors returned fire. Here and there a man or a beast fell, to lie still or, more often, writhing and shrieking. Had they had more rifles, they could have chewed the attackers to bloody rags. As it was, Dede Korkut's clansmen took casualties, but came on.

At their fore ran Juchi, afoot. Not breathing hard, he stayed even with the mounted men to either side of him. Arrows and bullets sang by. The leading warriors on horses and muskylopes began pulling up at last, waiting for their comrades to reach them and add to their firepower.

Juchi ran on. Suleiman's men shouted and turned more of their weapons on him. But he was no easy target, not running as he did, fast as a horse but with a man's agility. Most bullets flew behind him; his speed made the nomads mistake their aim.

Then, suddenly, he was into the line of defenders. Suleiman's men stopped shooting at him, for fear of hitting their comrades instead. They converged with knives, swords, bayoneted rifles, ready to make an end for this lone madman in their midst. They moved on him in no special order—what need for that, against one?

Quickly they learned. A gray-faced warrior reeled away, clutching the spouting stump of his wrist after Juchi's blade stole hand from arm. Another was down and motionless, half his face sheered away. An instant later another fell, his cheekbone crushed by a left-handed buffet after he thought to rush in on Juchi's unweaponed side.

Worst was that none of their blades would bite on him. Faster than thought, he slipped away, again and again, to stun, to maim, to kill. "Demon!" one of Suleiman's men shrieked as he flopped, hamstrung, somewhere near the middle of Juchi's path of slaughter.

Juchi took no notice. This, to him, was easy as weapons-drill—easier, for his own clansmen had learned to respect, if not always to believe, his speed, and so fought him almost always on the defensive. Suleiman's warriors paid dearly for thinking him no different from one of themselves.

They paid, in fact, with the battle, though Juchi only realized that when he found no more targets to strike. Then Dede Korkut's men were all around him, pounding his back, lifting him off his feet so he could see the last of Suleiman's folk fleeing for their lives.

"We rolled 'em up!" someone bawled in his ear. "Cut 'em in half and rolled 'em up! You threw fifty meters' worth of 'em into confusion, and we poured through and smashed 'em! They won't come sniffing after our sheep again for the next ten Haven years."

Juchi found herself standing before Dede Korkut. The clan chief's hair, he noticed with surprise, was almost entirely white—how had it escaped him till now that Dede Korkut was an old man? To a youth, ever growing and changing, he had seemed eternal as the steppe.

"Bravely, splendidly done!" Dede Korkut told him. As Juchi bowed to acknowledge the praise, the chief raised his voice: "Hail Juchi, new warleader of the clan!"

The clansmen shouted approval. "Juchi!" "Juchi warleader!" "Hail Juchi!" "Hurrah!" They crowded round the new hero to clasp his hand, pound him on the back, and, finally, raise him to their shoulders.

Such praise from his own people—from men, most of them, far older than he—did what the exertion of combat had quite failed to do. Juchi's heart pounded quick in his chest till be thought he would burst with pride.

Another wave of pain washed over Badri. It would have doubled her up on herself had she not been held immobile by the obstetrical table's stirrups. Blood flowed from between her legs, blood and all but formless clumps of tissue.

"Pity," Grima murmured. "It would have been a Soldier." He reached inside Badri with his curette, scraping away the remains of what might have become a life. When at last he was satisfied, he packed her womb with gauze, saying, "I'll monitor your blood pressure round the clock for the next cycle, but I think the risk of hemorrhage is small. Very clean, as miscarriages go."

Badri heard his words as if from very far away. She

was tired, so tired—worse, she thought, than after any of her births, even the lost twins so long ago. She was even too tired to resent Grima's brisk, competent care. But then, she thought, he would have done the same for any of Angband Base's domestic animals.

No sooner had that thought entered her mind than his words confirmed it: "You'll be ready for breeding again as soon as your courses resume."

"As you say," she whispered. She did not argue with him, not any more. But she knew that if she conceived again, she would also miscarry once more. She still had a good supply of the herb one of the other women had brought her from Tallinn Town. Grima would get no sons on her.

And yet—the man she hated, the man she slept with, was no one's fool. One miscarriage might befall anyone. Two, especially from a woman who had always birthed well before, would surely raise his ever-ready suspicions. That made aborting again much more than a physical risk.

He'd been talking, she wasn't sure for how long. Finally some of his words penetrated her exhausted reverie: "—have to meet with the Weaponsmaster again, over the threat of this cursed nomad tribe. The TAC makes it out as more dangerous to us than even the Citadel, which strikes me as insane. I hope the machine isn't finally starting to give out. You rest now. I'll be back presently."

"As you say," Badri repeated. Grima tramped away. For a moment, she was simply glad he had gone. Then she started to think again. Like the Breedmaster-turned-Brigade Leader, she had no idea how a steppe tribe could threaten the might of Angband Base. Unlike him, she had oracular faith in the Threat Analysis Computer. The machine's job was to know everything. If it said Dede Korkut's plainsmen were dangerous, then dangerous they were.

How much more dangerous would they be, she wondered suddenly, if they had an ally inside the Base? When at last she fell asleep, she was smiling at that thought.

Heber, the swordsmith who based himself at Tallinn Town, put aside his scimitars and daggers in their velvet trays. "I thank you for your kindly guesting of me, excellent cham," he said, bowing as he sat crosslegged in Dede Korkut's yurt.

The nomad chief bowed in return. "You are always welcome here—the quality of your edges guarantees it." The prominent clansmen with him, many of whom had just bought new blades from the smith, nodded their agreement.

"Thank you once more." The swordsmith bowed again, hesitated, went on. "Excellent cham, could I but have your ear alone for a brief spell of time, perhaps I could set a weapon in your hands sharper than any scimitar."

Dede Korkut's eyebrows rose. "What would you tell me that my nobles may not hear?" he demanded. The swordsmith sat quietly and did not reply. Dede Korkut frowned, rubbed the few thin white hairs on his chin that he was pleased to call a beard. At last he said, "Very well." He gestured for the rest of the plainsmen to leave the yurt. They filed out, more or less resentfully. "Juchi, you stay," Dede Korkut commanded.

It was Heber's turn to frown. "I would sooner speak to but one pair of ears."

"He is the clan's warleader, and my heir," Dede Korkut said flatly.

The swordsmith still did not yield. "He is young."

"As the ancient *shaykh* Ishaq Asinaf once observed, it is a fault of which everyone is guilty at one time or another," Dede Korkut said. "He does not speak out of turn. If you doubt it, then leave, and take your precious business with you."

For a moment, Juchi thought the swordsmith would do exactly that. In the end, though, the man fixed him with a hard stare, warning, "Lives ride on this, my own not least."

"I hear," Juchi said. "I understand." He visibly composed himself to listen, resolving to show no reaction to whatever wild scheme the smith was about to unfold.

That resolve was at once tested to the utmost, for the fellow asked Dede Korkut, "How would your clan like to seize Tallinn Valley?"

Behind his impassive mask, Juchi had all he could do to keep from shouting. Every band on the plains dreamed of taking a valley for its very own, to make sure all its women's births would be safe. Like the rest of the steppe-rovers, Dede Korkut's clan paid tribute for the privilege of sending its pregnant women to a land of decent air pressure: either to the Saurons for Tallinn Valley or to the Bandari for Eden Valley to the east of it.

By the spark that leaped in Dede Korkut's eye, Juchi was sure the clan chief was dreaming along with him. Dede Korkut's response, though, was dry: "I presume you have this arranged with the Saurons."

"No," the swordsmith said, and Juchi got ready to throw him bodily out of the yurt. Then the man from Tallinn Town went on, "But with one of their women, aye."

"What good will that do?" Dede Korkut said. "Their women are not the folk we have to fight."

"Hold a moment, mighty cham," Juchi said, his mind leaping forward with the agility of youth. "Saurons, from all I've heard, are great fighters, true enough. But there are not many of them, and much of their strength, especially the strength of their fortress, lies in the excellence of its magic."

"Technology," Heber corrected him.

"Whatever it may be," Juchi said impatiently. "If the woman corrupts it so they do not realize we are upon them until the moment, we may accomplish much. If." He let the word hang in the air, stared a challenge at the smith.

The man studied him in return, slowly nodded. "Your chief was right, young warleader, in bidding you stay. You see through to the essence of the scheme. At an hour you pick, the Sauron fort's systems can be made to fail. And when they do, if you strike quick and hard enough—"

"You speak always of *our* striking," Dede Korkut said. "How will the folk of Tallinn Town respond when battle is joined? If they are with us, they will aid us greatly. If they stand with the Saurons, the attack is not worth making."

"Tallinn Town has no love for Angband Base," Heber said after some small pause for thought. "The taxes the Saurons extort far outweigh the protection they give. For now, the town knows nothing of what I discuss with you. Were it otherwise, you may be sure this secret would not stay secret long. But most folk in the town, most in Tallinn Valley, will be for you, come the day."

Dede Korkut rocked back and forth. "*Aiii*, Shaitan could put no greater temptation before me than you dangle now. Victory would make the clan great. But if we fail—" He shuddered. "If we fail, the clan dies."

"How say you, then?" The swordsmith kept his voice steady, even sat relaxed, but Juchi smelled the sharp sweat that sprang forth from him.

The clan chief did not directly answer, turning rather to the warleader he had chosen. "Can this thing be done?"

Juchi had been turning that very question over in his mind. "Perhaps it can," he said. "Perhaps it can."

The swordsmith let out the breath he had been holding. "I shall pass this word back to the one who gave me the message. We go forward, then." He rose, bowed—now to Juchi as well as to Dede Korkut—and left the chief's yurt.

The two nomads were briefly silent. Then Juchi said, "We will have to check further into this before we do in fact go forward. It could be a trick of the Saurons, to lure us to destruction."

"This thought I had also," Dede Korkut nodded. "But if the swordsmith speaks truly . . . oh, if he does!" He clapped Juchi on the shoulder. "If he does, you will lead our warriors."

"Good," Juchi said. "I begin to have some ideas that may help us, come the day. We will be fighting Angband Base as much as the Saurons inside, I think. And the Base cannot run away . . ." All at once, he began to laugh.

"Where is the joke?" Dede Korkut asked.

Juchi told him. After a moment's startlement, the clan chief laughed too.

"This is a filthy sport the boys of the town have," Grima snarled. "Filthy! We should shoot a few, to teach the rest a lesson."

"It does no harm," Badri said, doing her best to soothe the Brigade Leader. He gave her a curious look; usually she cared not a jot for his feelings. She went on, "And shooting children will surely forfeit whatever good will that has managed to grow up over the years between Angband Base and Tallinn Town."

"I have no goodwill toward these rascals." Grima rose, seized Badri's wrist in an unbreakable grip. "Come, see for yourself the mischief they make." He gave Badri no choice, but dragged her along with him as he stamped through the outer court and ascended to the top of the wall. He scowled down at the boys outside. "Look!"

Badri looked. Boys and a few girls frisked about. One reached into the sheepskin bag he carried, drew out a ripe tennis fruit. He hurled it at a friend. The other boy ducked. The tennis fruit splattered against the gray stone of Angband Base's outwall. It slowly slid to the ground, leaving behind a yellow splash of juice.

As if that first throw had been a signal—an opening shot, Badri thought—all the children started flinging fruit at one another. Since they could dodge and the wall could not, it got much messier than they did.

Tennis fruit, red and white clownfruit, purple Finnegan's figs, crimson heartfruit—pulp and juice brought grim stone to bright, even gaudy, life, as if it had become the canvas of some ancient abstract expressionist.

Grima was a Soldier; he had never heard of abstract expressionism. Turning to Badri, he growled, "The little idiots have been at it since first cycle sunrise, close to 120 hours now. The whole wall is smeared with this filth."

"I'm sure they'll give it up soon," she answered mildly, glancing at the small but brilliant point of light that was Byers' Sun. It hung low in the west, slowly sinking toward the jagged horizon. "With both the sun and Cat's Eye gone from the sky, it will be too cold for the boys to play such games—and too dark for them to admire their handiwork."

"Admire!" Grima turned such a dusky shade of purple that Badri wondered if he was about to have a stroke: apoplexy often felled Saurons no longer young. But the Brigade Leader mastered himself, and his woman her disappointment. He ground out, "If it weren't for the waste of ammunition, I *would* order them shot."

"They're only children," Badri said. "They're harmless." She bit down on a giggle as she imagined young Soldiers behaving so. Then the laugh choked itself off. Even young Soldiers were anything but harmless.

Grima shook his fist at the town boys. "Get out of here!" he yelled.

Soldiers' uniforms, from any distance, looked alike regardless of rank. It was easy for the children to assume the Brigade Leader was just another grouchy Trooper. One of them threw a big red heartfruit at him. Luckily for everyone, it missed.

Grima stormed down off the wall. He was as angry as Badri had ever seen him. Considering how the two of them got along, that was saying something. She followed, her face the expressionless mask to which she schooled herself. Behind the shield she held up against the Brigade Leader, she exulted.

Troop Leader Ufthak yawned, poured himself a cup of not-quite-coffee from the insulated flask that hung on his belt. The mild stimulant was welcome, the warmth even more so. Sentry-go was tedious duty, nowhere more so than at the northern edge of Tallinn Valley where it widened out onto the steppe, at no time more than now—second cycle night was extra dark and extra cold.

The sky seemed naked without either Byers' Sun or Cat's Eye to light it, Ufthak thought. Then he laughed at himself—pretty fancy language for a noncom. What would happen next? He'd probably start writing poetry.

"At which point they pension me off," he said aloud. Then he laughed harder. There was no such thing as a pensioned-off Soldier on Haven.

As if to relieve his boredom, a band of nomads came cantering by, closer to his post than they usually dared approach. Some of them drew within a couple of hundred meters. Ufthak frowned, glanced over to the far side of the valley. Sure enough, plainsmen were also making a display in front of the other sentry post. Ufthak glowered. What in the name of bad genes were they up to?

The Troop Leader clicked the change lever of his assault rifle from SAFETY to BURSTS. If the nomads thought they could lull him out of alertness, they were welcome to try. A lot of them would end up dead before they realized they were wrong.

With all of Ufthak's enhanced senses focused on the riders ahead, the tiny noises behind him did not register until someone jumped down into the firing pit in back of him. He started to whirl, too late. Iron-hard fingers jerked his head back. A knife's fiery kiss licked across his throat.

The last thing he felt before he went into the dark was embarrassment at letting cattle trick him so.

Juchi climbed out of the Sauron sentry post, waved his dagger and the dead sentinel's assault rifle to show he had succeeded. His keen ears caught the sound of a struggle in the pit on the opposite side of the valley. He dashed that way, only to see two nomads scrambled out, one supporting the other.

He pursed his lips, silently blew through them. Four men had gone after that other sentry. He just thanked Allah and the spirits that neither Sauron had managed to get off a shot.

The fortress was a couple of kilometers back into the valley. The warriors there might not have heard, or might have assumed the sentries had things under control. But Saurons had enhanced ears and lively suspicions. The last thing Juchi wanted to do was rouse them.

As the plainsmen in the bands that had distracted the sentries realized the way south was open, one of their number galloped away from the mouth of the valley. He soon returned, leading all the fighting men of Dede Korkut's clan.

"Now comes the tricky part," Juchi said softly.

"Aye." One of the nomads nodded. "We'd've had a go at the Saurons in their fort long years ago, were it not for the minefields here."

"Now we know where the mines are, though, with the knowing stolen from Angband Base's own computer," Juchi said. His men murmured in awe; to them as to him, *computer* was but a word to conjure with, as vague and splendid as *demon*. Three centuries had passed since anyone on Haven save Saurons had aught to do with computers.

Juchi studied the map the swordsmith had brought to the clan. "Follow me," he ordered. "Single file, each man walking as best he can in the footsteps of the one ahead. Anyone who steps on a mine, I will punish without mercy." The warriors stared, then chuckled softly.

They made it through without losing a man. Juchi knew nothing but relief, not least for himself. The map was not an actual printout, but the swordsmith's reconstruction of data smuggled out of the base. Even to do so much—Juchi marveled at the courage of the woman who sent the smith what she'd picked from the mechanical brain.

If all went as he hoped, he thought suddenly, he would meet her soon. Now, though, for the one role in the mission he could not play. "Boys forward," he whispered. A couple of dozen lads, all of them with from nine to fifteen T-years, came up to him. "You know your jobs," he told them. They nodded, slipped off toward Angband Base.

Up on the wall, Senior Trooper Shagrat came to alertness at the sound of running feet approaching. Then he heard children laugh, heard an overripe Finnegan's fig splatter off the stone below him.

"Get out of here, you gene-poor cattle bastards!" he shouted. The children took no notice of him. He went back to walking his beat; the Brigade Leader tolerated this nonsense, even if he did not love it.

He heard a couple of other sentries shout challenges, then realize they were just spotting more miserable boys. "For a bottle of beer, I'd blow them all away," he said when he came up to the Soldier on the next stretch of wall.

The other Soldier laughed. "For half a bottle," he said.

Not all the boys were armed with fruit. Most carried drillbits instead, carried them most carefully by the ropes that bound the burrowers' front and hind legs together. They made sure the animals' heads could not

reach anything but air, made especially sure those irre-
sistible teeth came nowhere near their own precious
flesh.

Mustafa's drillbit had a particularly evil temper. It
kept twisting its meter-long ratlike body, kept trying to
jerk its head around so it could bite his hand. As plainly
as it could without words, it told him it was angry and
hungry and wanted its freedom right now, if not sooner.

"Yes, yes," Mustafa muttered, lugging it toward the
wall. He set it down in front of a fruit-besplashed place,
cut its bonds with his beltknife.

The drillbit's teeth sank into the spot where it smelled
fruit. Those diamond-like incisors cared nothing about
stone. As Mustafa watched, the beast started to burrow
into the wall. The youth did not watch long, but turned
and ran.

Shagrat yawned as he came down from his turn at sentry-
go. Sleep would be welcome, sleep and then his woman.
Or maybe, he thought hopefully, the other way round.

He was at the base of the wall when he heard a sound
that did not belong. It reminded him—he frowned at the
image his mind called up—it reminded him of a man
chewing on a mouthful of ball bearings.

He scratched his head. "What the—?" To his amazement, a chunk of wall about the size of his fist suddenly
crumbled to dust. The hole grew larger. A streamlined
head poked through, peered nearsightedly up at him.

Shagrat's precious discipline went south. He was too
horrified to shoot. He screamed instead, as if he were
some rich, pampered Tallinn Town woman watching a
mouse scuttle across her polished floor.

"Drillbit!" he shouted, again and again. "Drillbit!" A
moment later, the same cry rose from another part of
the wall not far away.

Grima cursed his enhanced hearing. He had been
about to mount Badri when the shouting started. He

thought about going ahead regardless—she seemed even more furious about submitting than usual, and that always turned him on.

Then he realized what the troopers were yelling. He cursed again, this time out loud and foully. Wearing only an erection, he dashed for the wall.

His ardor wilted in the chill of second cycle night. The rest of his body ignored the cold. The Soldiers in the courtyard had the good sense not to notice how he was dressed.

Someone had finally decided to kill one of the drillbits. Another one waddled, obscenely fat, close by the wall. The Brigade Leader's bare foot lashed out, slammed the animal into the stone. It twitched and died.

Even as it did, though, a new outcry arose twenty meters away. Another brown bullet head, ridiculous nose twitching, started to emerge from what should have been solid rock.

Grima clapped a hand to his forehead. "The whole frigging wall might be honeycombed with 'em!" he shouted—screamed might be a better word, if screams come in deep, rasping baritone.

"What do we do, sir?" a Soldier asked nervously.

The Brigade Leader snatched the rifle out of the man's hands, fired at the newest drillbit. The unaimed round spanged off stone thirty centimeters from its head. The drillbit squeaked and pulled back into its hole.

"General alert!" Grima yelled back toward the barracks. "Somebody go set off the general alert!"

As soon as Grima dashed away, Badri scrambled out of bed. She grudged the time she needed to throw on a robe, but took it nonetheless. Unlike her lord and master—lips skinned back from teeth in a carnivore grin at that thought—she would draw questions, running through the corridors naked.

As it happened, no one saw her before she got to

Angband Base Command Central. She barred the door behind her—Command Central, she'd learned from the TAC, was intended to be a last redoubt, able to hold out against enemy assault no matter what happened to the rest of the base. And not even Sauron military paranoia, she thought, had imagined an enemy sprung from within.

Too bad for the Saurons. Badri began pulling switches.

"General alert!" Grima cried once more, furious not just at the drillbits now but also at his own men. Was everyone asleep in the second cycle darkness? Red lights should have been flashing, sirens wailing, and Soldiers piling out of the barracks, ready for anything.

Only the Soldiers on the wall rushed toward the Brigade Leader's voice. Then all the lights in the courtyard went out.

Beyond the side of the wall opposite the one where the drillbits had been released, Juchi and his men stood waiting. When Angband Base plunged into blackness, the nomad warleader thumped the plainsman next to him on the shoulder. The whole band dashed forward, scaling ladders at the ready.

The first inkling Grima had of something seriously wrong—as opposed to a monumental fuckup—came when a very junior Assault Leader ran out of the main barracks, shouting, "Sir, sir, Command Central is locked from inside, and whoever's in there won't acknowledge orders!"

While the Brigade Leader was still trying to digest that, the courtyard lights came back on. They showed men on the walls, armed men not in Soldier field-gray. The nomads started shooting down at the troopers by Grima.

The Soldiers returned fire. Stunned, outnumbered, and pinned down as they were, they nonetheless tumbled invaders from their perches. But the plainsmen's guns—they even had a couple of assault rifles, Grima saw with dismay—hosed death through the Brigade Leader's companions.

The din of gunfire did what Grima's shouts had failed to do—it brought Soldiers bouncing out of bed, weapons at the ready. And when the first of them charged out through the doorways, the foes on the wall cut them down before even Soldier's reactions could save them.

"Dede Korkut!" the nomads yelled. "Dede Korkut!"

Grima's heart, already thuttering near panic, almost stopped altogether when he heard that cry. Here was the danger against which the TAC had warned him, the danger that had caught him all too literally naked!

The plainsmen were descending into the courtyard now, and more and more of them were on the walls. This had to be the whole clan, Grima thought, appalled, and all its firepower. Somehow they'd come unscathed through the minefield.

Connecting that improbability with the failure of the general alarm and the Assault Leader's dreadful news, the Bridage Leader groaned, "Treason!" And devastatingly effective treason, too—Grima was almost the only Soldier in the courtyard still standing. Against the guns the nomads had massed, against the surprise and disadvantageous position, genetically enhanced fighting ability did not count enough.

Bullets singing around him, Grima ran for the barracks. Somehow he tumbled through the doorway still unwounded. The Soldiers inside were not trying to come out any more. That, they'd learned, was deadly. Instead they were shooting from loophole windows and, from the screams outside, doing no little damage.

"That's the way!" the Brigade Leader shouted. "They haven't taken us yet!" With the rations stored in its underground cellars, the hall could stand a longer siege than any nomad tribe could afford to undertake. And when the nomads had to withdraw . . . Grima snarled, thinking of the revenge the Soldiers would take.

Then fire-fighting foam gushed from forgotten ceiling fixtures unused since Angband Base was built. The stuff was choking to breathe; worse, when it got in a trooper's eyes, it burned like fire and left him blind for . . . Grima did not know for how long. Long enough. As the shooting from the barracks slackened, the plainsmen, still yelling like their imaginary demons, swarmed into the hall.

What happened next was butchery. It was not all one-sided; even blind, Soldiers could despatch whatever foes came within their reach. But few of the nomads were so unwise. They spent ammunition with such prodigality that Grima wondered whether they would have enough left to hold Angband Base if they took it.

That, however, was not his problem. Getting the traitor out of Command Central was. He could still see out of one eye, after a fashion—and, somewhere back in his quarters, he had a key to a secret entrance to the Base's ultimate strongpoint. (Badri was wrong. In military paranoia if nowhere else, the Soldiers let imagination run free.) He might yet turn the battle against the invaders.

He ran through the corridors, dodging blinded Soldiers and shouting his name over and over so they would not shoot at what they could not see.

Women's screams mingled with warriors'. Some fought side by side with the Soldiers. Others struck at their one-time partners with anything they had. Grima saw one stab a trooper in the back with a pair of scissors. The Brigade Leader broke her neck and ran on.

Badri was not in his cubicle. He did not know whether to be glad—he might have had to kill her too. After frantic rummaging through desk drawers, he snatched the key he needed, then ran for all he was worth toward Command Central.

*   *   *

Silent as a stalking cliff lion, Juchi chased the naked Sauron through the chaos of Angband Base's death throes. He could have shot him more than once, but the officer—he'd heard and seen the fellow giving orders—looked to have some definite purpose in mind. That, Juchi thought, might be worth learning.

So he waited until the Sauron bent to turn a key and swing open a tiny hidden door before he fired a burst from around a corner. He heard the meaty *chunnk* of bullets smacking flesh, peered cautiously to see what he had done.

The Sauron was down but not quite out—he snapped a shot that *craack*ed past Juchi closer than he ever wanted to think about. Juchi returned fire, emptying the assault rifle's magazine. Not even Sauron flesh withstood that second burst. When Juchi looked again, he saw the naked Soldier sprawled in death.

Pausing only to click in a fresh clip (his last, he noted, and reminded himself to make sure someone salvaged the good brass cartridges he'd used), he stepped through the door the Sauron had opened. At the end of a narrow, winding corridor was another door. He opened it.

When Badri saw a piece of the wall of her little fortress within a fortress begin to open inward, she knew she was dead. *So unfair*, she thought, *so unfair*. But then, maybe not. She had had her vengeance on Angband Base; perhaps it was only right that the base have vengeance on her.

She stood, straightened, awaited her fate with a strange calm. Here inside Command Central, she had no weapon. For that matter, how much good was a weapon likely to do against a battle-ready Soldier? She was sure only a Sauron could have sniffed out the hidden way, about which not even she had known.

Thus she gasped when the door revealed instead a

nomad warrior, shaggy in fur cap, sheepskin jacket and boots, heavy wool trousers, and a young man's brown beard sprouting from cheeks and chin.

He swung his rifle toward her, abruptly checked the motion. She realized her robe had fallen open. She made no move to pull it shut. Let the plainsman see all he wanted, if that kept her alive.

He said something in his own language. She shook her head. He tried again, this time in stumbling Russki: "Who—you?"

Russki she could follow; most people in Tallinn Town used it, though the Saurons spoke—*had spoken*, she thought dizzily—Americ among themselves. She gave her name, waved around. "This is Command Central. This is where I fight for you."

His grin was enormous, and looked even more so because of the way his teeth stood out against his unshaven face. "Badri?" he shouted. "You Badri? I Juchi, warleader Dede Korkut's clan. We have Angband Base, Badri. We win! Between you, fighters of clan, we win!" He threw his arms wide.

She sprang forward to hug him. Even the prod of the assault rifle in the small of her back as Juchi's embrace enfolded her was only a brief annoyance. He smelled of stale sweat and smokeless powder. Badri did not care, not now, not in the savage rush, stronger than vodka, of a victory she had never expected to win.

He tilted her chin up. His face felt strange against hers; she had never kissed a bearded man before. Triumph burned as hot in her as in him. The kiss went on and on. She felt her loins turn liquid. Afterwards, she was never sure which of them drew the other down to the floor.

Sitting up in the bed that had once been Grima's, Badri said, not for the first time, "I am too old for you. Soon you will see some maiden you fancy, and tire of me." She kept her tone light, as always when she spoke of such things, but the fear was there, underneath.

Juchi reached out to caress her breast. "You are you, and I am happy," he said, also not for the first time. Then, smiling wickedly, he went on, "And what with Sauron technology and Sauron plunder, you lived better than we did out on the plains. I would never have guessed the age you claim, not within ten T-years."

"You flatter me outrageously." Badri pressed his hand to her. "Don't stop." Half a T-year before, she never could have been so fluent in Russki. Love was a strong incentive.

He grinned at her. "I hadn't planned to." He gave a luxurious stretch; he was not used to sleeping (or rather, at the moment, resting) so soft. But his wits were still alert. "We are a good pair for a whole flock of reasons. This for one—" He squeezed gently; she shivered a little. "And for another, a different sort, what better match to link the clan and Tallinn Valley?"

"None better," she nodded. "But matches made for that sort of reason are more often endured than enjoyed." She leaned toward him. His left hand came up to join his right; he held her breasts as if they were the two balanced pans of a scale.

She might have picked the odd image from his mind, for he said, "I think they're heavier than they were. Are you pregnant?"

She considered that. "We'll have a pretty good idea somewhere around the end of first cycle." Then she threw herself on him. "I hope I am!" She'd never said anything like that before, not even with Dagor. And with Grima, the idea of children had been a nightmare.

"I'm not sure I do," he said. She frowned at him, surprised and hurt, till he went on. "It would mean I'd have to stay away from you for a while, and I don't want to do that."

He rolled her over, pinned her with his greater weight. He was, she thought as he slid into her, rutty as any Sauron she'd ever heard of. Of course, he was also very young. For her part, she knew only joy that their first joining had been followed by so many more.

She knew only joy. . . . Her arms went round his neck, pulling him ever closer to her.

This once, Badri wished the Saurons still held Angband Base. She was used to the attentions of a Breedmaster or his aide, not a nomad midwife dressed in furs and muttering charms. The midwife, though, said, "*Eee*, from the speed of your labor, you've done this a time or three. Have trouble with any of your others?"

"The—" Badri stopped as a contraction washed over her. "The first time was twins. The others, no."

"You probably won't this time either, then. All I'll need do is catch the baby as it falls out, I expect." With the small part of her mind not engaged in birthing her child, Badri hoped the plainswoman was right.

So it proved. After what seemed forever but was less than six hours, the midwife said in satisfied tones, "A fine girl—four kilos, I'd guess. Here, you hold her and I'll go tell Juchi."

Badri took the baby, set it on her breast. "He's not in the fortress building. His mother still stays in her yurt, and she's very ill. Otherwise he'd be here with me."

"Of course he would." The midwife shook her head, annoyed at herself. "Yes. Kisirja. How could I have forgotten?" She shook her head again, not in the same way. "Very ill, aye. May Allah and the spirits be merciful to her, in this world and the next."

Fever wasted Kisirja's face. It had only grown worse through the three days that made up two cycles—two orbits of Haven round Cat's Eye. A hundred thirty hours of fever were plenty to ravage anyone. Juchi held her hand, sponged her brow, did all the other things that made Kisirja more comfortable but did no other good, no real good.

"Juchi," she whispered.

"I'm here, my mother," he said.

She smiled. "Good." She still knew him, then. For the past little while, he had not been sure. But now her hands tightened on his, with more strength than she'd shown in most of a day. "You're a good boy, a fine man, Juchi."

"Thank you, my mother."

"A good boy," Kisirja repeated. "As fine as if I'd borne you myself. A fine man." Her wits were wandering after all, Juchi thought. He took the folded cloth from her forehead, dipped it once more into the bowl of cool water beside her. As the fever grew, he'd had to do that ever more often.

Some time not much later, Kisirja drew in a long, deep breath, as if she were about to say something. Her eyes opened wide, held Juchi's. He watched awareness fade in them. When it was gone, he reached down, eased them shut.

He drew his dagger, slashed each cheek in the nomad style of mourning. The cuts stopped bleeding almost at once.

The folk of Tallinn Town were not used to fighting. These past many years, the Saurons had defended Tallinn Valley. Now the Saurons were five T-years gone from this part of Haven. The clan that had been Dede Korkut's and was now Juchi's needed help, where the Saurons would have scorned it.

"Cover drill!" Juchi shouted. The townsmen dove into foxholes, emerged aiming weapons. Juchi shook his head. "Too slow, too slow. Half of you would have been shot, the rest ridden over. Get out and try it again." His pupils groaned. "Suleiman's men won't have pity on you. Don't expect me to, either."

"Suleiman's men won't know the way through the minefield," one of the bolder men said.

"Mines are like sentries," Juchi told him. "They warn, they slow. They don't stop. We have to have warriors for that. Fear kept people out of this valley, fear of the Saurons. Now that the clan and town hold it instead, folk will test us to see if we are strong enough to keep it. I'm surprised the challenge has taken this long to come."

"But—" The townsman was still not cowed, not quite.

Juchi grinned at him. "Enough words." He tossed aside his knife. "If you want to argue, come do it with hands and feet."

The man from Tallinn Town gulped and shook his head. His folk had not taken long to learn what the nomads already knew: no one bested Juchi in single combat.

"All right, then. You've wasted enough time complaining to catch your breath. So—cover drill!" The raw recruits sprang for their holes again.

Juchi worked them a while longer before he let them go. He walked back to the fortress his warriors now occupied. Badri and their daughter Aisha stood not far outside the bullet-scarred barracks hall. Aisha squealed and sprinted toward her father. He picked her up, flung her high in the air, caught her, flung her again, spun round and round like a top. When he set the little girl down, she took a couple of lurching steps and fell on her bottom. Laughter gushed from her.

More slowly, Badri also came up to Juchi: she was far along with their second child. He leaned forward over her protruding belly to kiss her. "How does it look?" she asked him.

He shrugged. "About as before. The latest scout in says Suleiman's warriors, and maybe another clan's with his, are gathered a few hours' ride north of the mouth of the valley. They have no herds with them; they can't be there for any reason but fighting."

"No." She took his arm. "Come with me. I have something to show you, something of the fortress you have not seen yet."

"Can I come too?" Aisha asked. She was able to stand again.

"No, you play out here for a while," Badri said. Aisha stamped her foot. Badri swatted her on the bottom, just hard enough to let the little girl know she meant what she said. Aisha started throwing pebbles at the wall.

"What is this thing you have to show me?" Juchi asked. He heard the nervousness in his own voice. He sometimes was forced to remember that Badri had lived most of her life at Angband Base, that she took for granted the technology which—where it survived—he still found unnerving.

She did not answer him until they were inside the chamber next to the one they shared. Dust lay thick here; it was not a bedroom, and perhaps had not been entered since the Base fell. The fluorescent ceiling panels came on when Badri flicked a switch, though. Juchi stared with superstitious awe at the screen on the dusty desk. "A—computer?" he whispered.

"A computer," Badri said briskly. She felt around behind it, clicked another switch. The screen lit. She went on, "Grima used it, and all the Brigade Leaders before him. He let me watch sometimes, never thinking I would see how to make it work myself. Most of what I sent to your clan, most of what I did on the night you attacked, I learned here."

"You mean—it can work for us?" Juchi imagined vengeful Saurons somehow stored inside.

But Badri said, "Why not? We hold the Base now. Watch." She typed the first command she had seen Grima use so often: THREATS TO ANGBAND BASE: RANK ORDER.

Juchi stared as the Americ letters appeared one by one on the screen. He stared again, and had to hold himself in place by force of will, when more letters appeared without anyone having typed them: THREATS TO ANGBAND BASE: 1. CLANS OF SULEIMAN AND AYDIN; 2. CLAN LEADER, CLAN OF JUCHI; 3. MOTHER OF CLAN LEADER,

CLAN OF JUCHI; 4. THE CITADEL. OTHERS TOO LOW A PROBA-
BILITY TO BE EVALUATED.

When Badri read the words, Juchi laughed, as anyone will when magic is clearly seen to be fraud. "No
wonder Grima lost, if he put his faith in this thing. My
mother has been dead as long as Aisha's been alive."
He touched the faded scar on each cheek.

But Badri stared at the screen in some perplexity. "It
was always right before. I had to order it not to put me
on any of its lists, or Grima would have caught on to
me." She tapped a fingernail against her teeth. "Let me
try something else."

She typed again: THREATS TO CO, ANGBAND BASE, RANK
ORDER. "I hope it thinks that's you," she said.

"Hush!" He gestured harshly. The answer showed
below the question. THREATS TO CO, ANGBAND BASE, the
TAC wrote: 1. CLAN LEADER, CLAN OF JUCHI; 2. MOTHER
OF CLAN LEADER, CLAN OF JUCHI. OTHERS TOO LOW A PROB-
ABILITY TO BE EVALUATED. "Just read that to me," Juchi
said.

Badri did, then typed END in disgust. "I'm sorry,"
she said, touching Juchi's hand. "I thought it would
help. But then, Grima always worried about how long
the machine would keep working. I suppose it's finally
dead."

"Senile, anyhow." Juchi laughed again. "If the steppe
clans had known this was what Angband Base used for
brains, they would have attacked a hundred T-years ago."

"It really did come up with right answers," Badri
insisted. Even she had to admit, though, "It isn't coming up with them now."

"It certainly isn't." Juchi gave her another cantile-
vered kiss. "I thank you for showing it to me, though.
Were it what it once was"—*What you say it once was*,
he thought—"it could have been valuable."

A few cycles later, Suleiman and his allies attacked.
Juchi's clan and the men of Tallinn Town threw them

back. Among the prisoners they took was a fair-sized contigent from the clan of Aydin.

Juchi wondered about that, a little. He tried to remember whether the scouts had known just who Suleiman's main partner was. He didn't think so. Even clan shamans made lucky guesses every so often, though.

And when the triumphant warriors came back to the fortress, he found that Badri had presented him with a son. That drove all thoughts of the ancient computer from his head.

She wanted to call the boy Dagor. It was a likely enough sounding name. He didn't argue with her.

The clan, Juchi thought, was fat. For some of his men, that was literally true: he watched a couple of middle-aged warriors walking into Tallinn Town to buy something or other, and their bellies hung over their belts. In the old days, out on the steppe, a fat nomad, save maybe a shaman, would have been hard to imagine. Life was too harsh.

The old days . . . Juchi laughed a little, shook his head. Hard to believe more than a dozen T-years had slipped by since Angband Base fell. His own body belied them. It was as firm, hard, and tireless now as then. Just the other day, though, Badri had plucked a white hair from his beard. He shook his head again. Nothing, he thought, lasted forever.

Even that little philosophizing, far from profound, was unlike him. He left off as a horseman rode up. The messenger dismounted, bowed. "Cham, I brought your words to Suleiman. He agrees they hold wisdom."

"Good," Juchi said. "He will meet with me, then?"

"Aye, cham, in two cycles' time. He asks if you would treat with him here or out on the steppe."

"On the steppe," Juchi said at once. "He and his men would only spy if we invited them into the valley—into *our* valley."

"Aye," the messenger said again.

"You need not tell him I said that, though. Tell him . . . hmm . . . tell him that, as we are plainsmen too, the plains are the fitting place to discuss our differences and to settle once for all the boundaries of our clans' grazing lands."

The messenger nodded, mumbled to himself as he memorized the words. Then he grinned. "Shall I also tell him that we'll run his men into the Northern Sea if he doesn't keep within the bounds we set him?"

Juchi grinned back. "He knows that already. If he didn't, he'd still be fighting instead of talking. He's stubborn as a stone."

"He's jealous, is what he is," the messenger said.

"I suppose so. Every nomad cham dreams of taking a valley for himself."

"But you didn't dream—you did it. We did it. And every time Suleiman comes sniffing around, we send him away with a bloody nose."

"I told you—that's why he's finally willing to talk."

"No doubt you're right, cham." The messenger sketched a salute, climbed back on his horse, and headed north at a trot.

Juchi walked into the courtyard of the fortress, and almost got trampled by a mob of boys playing football. That was what his clan called the game, anyhow. To the children from Tallinn Town, it was soccer. He'd never met the odd-sounding word till his people conquered Angband Base; he wondered idly if the locals had borrowed it from Saurons.

His own son was at the head of the yelling pack, running and dodging as fast and lithe as the rest of the boys, though they were anywhere from two to four T-years older. Juchi remembered his own childhood. He'd been more than a match for children his age, too.

As he watched, Dagor booted the ball past the other team's goalie and into the makeshift net. "Good shot, Dagor, lad!" he called. He waved to his son.

Dagor's grin, already enormous, grew even wider as he waved back. The boy's comrades swarmed over him, lifted him onto their shoulders. Again Juchi thought of his own youth—of the day he'd been named warleader. Seeing Dagor get such acclaim so young made him want to burst with pride.

When he found Badri, he spoke of the football game before he mentioned the talks Suleiman had agreed to. "Why meet him on the steppe?" Badri asked.

As he had for the messenger, he explained his reasons.

Badri nodded when he was done. "That makes sense," she agreed. "But remember—and never let Suleiman forget—that you are not *just* of the plains. You hold Tallinn Valley, too. Go out to the steppe, then, but go with all the trappings, all the ceremonial, that shows you to be a lord as well as a cham, if you know what I'm saying."

"Yes, I do." He kissed her. "Your advice is always good. That's one reason I've never looked—well, never more than looked—at anyone else." He kissed her again. "But it's only one reason. There are others."

"Let me shut the door first," she said.

When the time came for Juchi to ride out to meet Suleiman, he remembered what Badri had suggested. He put on a linen tunic instead of the wool he usually wore, to remind the other cham he ruled farmers as well as plainsmen.

And he decided to be lavish when he armed himself. He did not just sling his assault rifle on his back and have done. He put on crisscrossing belts of shiny brass cartridges, too one over each shoulder—let Suleiman see that Angband Base's machine shop could still turn out cartridge cases.

Two knives hung from the left side of his belt. He started to put another on the right, then had a better idea. He rummaged through a leather sack he did not remember opening since he came to the fortress. Sure enough, the pistol he had taken from that arrogant robber on the steppe was inside.

He buckled it on. Since he got his rifle, he'd had no need for the lesser firearm. He was not even sure the rounds would still fire. Today, though, he did not care. He only needed it as one more thing with which to overawe Suleiman.

Feeling quite the fearsome warrior, he swaggered out to Badri. "How do I look?" he asked.

Her lips quirked. "Overwhelming is the word that comes to mind."

He smiled too, but answered, "Good. That's the word I want to come to mind."

Badri noticed the pistol. "You've never worn that before."

"Why bother, when I have the assault rifle?" He reached over his shoulder, patted the Kalashnikov's barrel.

"No reason at all," Badri said. "I just didn't know you had it, that's all. May I see it?"

"Of course." Juchi saw nothing odd in the request. Before she was a plainsman's woman, Badri had been a Sauron's woman. He would have been more surprised were she not interested in weapons. He took the pistol from its holster, showed it to her.

"*Where did you get this?*"

Juchi blinked. The words tumbled out in a harsh whisper, unlike anything he'd ever heard Badri use before. She was staring from him to the pistol and back again. She had gone pale. That alarmed him. In all the time he'd known her, he'd never seen her show fright.

"I took it from a bandit I killed, out on the steppe a couple of T-years before we won Tallinn Valley. He was going to steal my muskylope, but he took me up when I said I'd fight him for it. I broke his neck." The pride the memory put into his voice faltered as he looked at her face. "What's wrong? Tell me, Badri, please."

"This pistol belonged to a Soldier once. A couple of

T-years before Angband Base fell, he went out to the plains to scout a clan that the computer—the computer you don't believe in—said was growing dangerous. It was the clan of Dede Korkut. He never came back."

Badri spoke mechanically, as if by keeping all emotion from her words she could keep it from her heart as well. Then, at last, her voice broke. She looked down at the floor as she went on, "His—his name was Dagor."

"The name you gave our son." Now Juchi's voice too was empty and cold.

"The name I gave my son. Dagor and I had three sons, three sons and a daughter. None of them lived. The girl and one boy were twins, Sauron culls, set out for stobor. I was just a girl myself, then. The other two, later—had accidents. It happens. He was far from a bad man, Juchi—I've known a bad man. His name, at least, deserved—deserves—to go on."

"As you say." After a moment, Juchi found he could bear having a son named for Badri's onetime consort. After all, the man—the Sauron—was fifteen T-years dead and gone, while he and Badri were very much together. He found he could not even blame her for not saying where young Dagor's name came from. The quiet had kept the peace, and with any luck both quiet and peace might have lasted forever.

"You—broke his neck, you said?" Badri asked. Juchi nodded. "How could that be? Dagor was a Soldier, a Sauron."

Juchi understood what she meant. No one, not even a man with Frystaat blood, could match reflexes with a Sauron in unarmed combat. He said slowly, "Maybe I took the pistol from a bandit, one of a band, say, that had ambushed Dagor."

"That must be it!" Badri brightened a little. She had long since known, long since accepted, that Dagor was dead. Thinking the man she loved now was the one who had slain him was something else again. "What did he look like, this bandit you killed?"

"I'll never forget him," Juchi said. "He gave me maybe the toughest fight I ever had. He was a few centimeters taller than I am. He had more reach, too, and knew what to do with it. He was caucasoid, more or less—dark eyes, but fair skin and light brown hair, a little lighter than mine. He had a short white scar, just below one eye—the left one, I think."

"You have painted me Dagor's image in words." Badri shook her head, over and over. "How could that be?" she repeated. Then, fierce, as a tamerlane, she burst out, "Who—what—was your mother, Juchi? Why did the computer call her such a threat to the Base? Why did the computer call *you* such a threat to the Base?"

"Because it's daft," Juchi growled. "Because it's an old, daft piece of junk. I wish someone had put a bullet through it when we took Angband Base. Then it wouldn't be here to worry you."

To his relief, Badri changed the subject. "How old are you, Juchi? Exactly how old, I mean."

He needed to think. "As near as I can reckon it, a bit over four Haven years—say, about thirty-one T-years." He had no idea why she wanted to know, nor did he care. Talking of anything but Dagor—Dagor the elder, he amended—suited him fine. "I hope that satisfies you. Whether or not, though, I have to leave. Suleiman is waiting."

He walked to the door. Behind him, very softly, Badri whispered, "Who was your mother, Juchi? Oh, who?" He did not turn back.

"It is agreed, then." Suleiman's wrinkles arranged themselves into a smile. "We shall not graze our herds east of a line drawn straight north from the fifth ridge to the west of your valley, nor shall your herds graze west of that same line."

"It is agreed, aye." Juchi's voice was hollow. He knew he should have been able to claim grazing lands stretching two or three ridges further west, but his heart was not in the dickering, not today.

He still had no truck with the flashing words Badri had read him from the computer screen. They were too far outside his experience for him to take them seriously. But what his mother said while she was dying came back now to trouble his thoughts. What if her wits had not been caught in fever's grip? What then?

What indeed? he thought. How could he hope to find out? Kisirja was dead. Who else could he hope to ask? He pounded a fist into his thigh. Who better than his wetnurse? He'd had little to do with Nilufer since the clan came to Tallinn Valley, but he knew she still lived.

Fast as politeness allowed, or maybe a little faster, he took leave of Suleiman. The old cham did not seem offended. Compared to grazing land, manners were a trifle.

Riding back to the valley, Juchi wondered if he shouldn't let the whole thing drop. But no, he couldn't, not now, not with Badri so upset. And his own curiosity was roused. He'd always been sure of who he was. Now, suddenly, he doubted. Allah and the spirits willing, Nilufer would set his mind at ease.

Nilufer was a widow these days. She lived in a small yurt close by the larger one that belonged to her eldest son. She poked her head through the door-curtain in surprise when Juchi called from outside, asking leave to enter.

"Honor to the cham! Of course you are welcome!" She held the curtain wide. "Come, come! Will you take tea?"

"Thank you. You are gracious." The rituals of hospitality let Juchi adapt to the gloom inside the black felt yurt. He sat crosslegged on a threadbare rug, sipped Nilufer's tea, nibbled a strip of jerked mutton.

After the polite and pointless small talk that accompanied meat and drink, Nilufer asked, "How may I serve the cham?" Her eyes twinkled. "I fear my breasts are too old to please him now."

Juchi laughed. After so much strain, that felt strange—and good. He said, "As a matter of fact, your breasts are the very reason I came." That made Nilufer giggle, but Juchi went on, "No, no, I speak the truth. I want you to tell me why I needed a wetnurse when I was a baby."

"Why does any baby need a wetnurse?" Nilufer said. "Your mother had no milk to give you." But the sparkle was gone from her face and voice. Something else replaced it—caution, Juchi judged. She was not telling all she knew.

"That I gathered," he said. "Why was it so?"

"I couldn't rightly tell you, cham, not for certain," Nilufer said. She could not meet his eyes, either.

"Why not?" he persisted. "My mother must have given you some reason. Was I perhaps an unusually difficult birth?"

He watched her seize the pretext. "Yes, that's it, that's just what she said, poor thing," she said eagerly.

"You're lying." His voice was a whiplash. Nilufer flinched away from it. "What is it you don't want to tell me? How can it matter, after so long?"

"You won't be angry at me?" she quavered.

"No, not for the truth, by Allah and the spirits. I swear it." He realized he had got up on one knee, had moved toward her as if in threat. No, not as if. He eased himself back to the rug. "I will not be angry at you."

"All right. All right." A little spirit returned to her voice. "As you say, it was long ago, and the Saurons are gone from Angband Base now—all of them but you."

"What? Me? You're mad, old woman." Juchi laughed harshly. "Do you say my mother slipped away from the tents to sleep with a Sauron Soldier?"

"She slipped away from the tents, aye, but not to sleep with the Saurons—rather, to rob them. They cast out infants that did not suit them. Most the beasts took, or the cold, but not all. You were one of the lucky few."

"I don't believe you." *I don't want to believe you*, he

thought. He found a question that had to make a liar of her: "If what you say is true, why has no one ever told me this fable before?"

"At first, cham, it was for fear that if you knew you were of Sauron blood, you might flee the clan and go back to Angband Base. After a while, I suppose, folk had got into the habit of silence. But now that the Saurons are long gone, I don't see what difference it makes whether you know. And if you doubt me, cham Juchi, think on the meaning of your name."

"Guest," Juchi whispered. His world tottered round him. "Juchi."

"The same word," Nilufer nodded. "You've been a cherished guest, an honored guest, and now a great and mighty guest. But always, like I told you, you were a lucky guest. Both babes the Saurons set out that night were lucky."

"*Both* babes?" Juchi stared at her. "What new tale is this?"

"One not everyone knows. But your mother—Kisirja, I mean, Allah and the spirits give her peace—your mother told me that two babies, both newborn, lay exposed by Angband Base then. Just as she picked up the one that was you, a Bandari woman took the other."

His world had tottered. Now it crashed down. "That would have been a girl," he said in a dead voice.

"I really couldn't tell you one way or the other. Your mother never said."

"Yes she did. Just a few hours ago. My mother."

Nilufer scratched her head. "What's that?"

Juchi did not answer. Instead he turned and leaped out through the door-curtain. Nilufer stared after him. He dashed toward the fortress, fast and straight as an arrow from a compound bow.

"Allah!" Nilufer exclaimed. He'd left his horse behind. "I wonder what the poor fellow's trouble is. I hope it's not something I said."

*   *   *

Juchi ran.

His father, dead under his hands. His wife, his mother; his daughter, his sister; his son, his brother.

"What have I done?" he cried. "Allah, what have we done?"

The fortress where he lived—the fortress where he'd been born—was a couple of kilometers away. He ran through fields of ripening barley. As he ran, he thought only of his own field, his field of double sowing, the field in which he'd grown and where he sowed his children. He groaned, and ran on.

Men were working in the fields. They shouted as he trampled the grain. When he did not swerve, they chased him. He outran them. That had always been easy. Now he knew why.

The fortress drew nearer, nearer. He ran inside. Men waved, called out to ask how the parley with Suleiman had gone or simply to greet him. He answered none of them, but sped to the barracks hall.

There at last his way was blocked. The clan's shaman stood in the doorway. Tireshyas had been plump on the steppe. Now he was so fat that any doorway he stood in, he filled. When he saw Juchi, he went white. "Lord cham, your wife—"

"My wife!" Juchi's voice, his eyes, were so terrible that Tireshyas gave back a pace. "My wife! You are one of those who knew I sprang not from the clan but from a Sauron's woman, not so?"

Already agitated and now frightened and confused, the shaman stuttered, "Well, well, yes, lord cham, yes, but—"

"And you knew I took a Sauron's woman to wife." Juchi stepped forward, filling the space from which Tireshyas had retreated. "And you never thought to wonder if the two might be the same. My mother. My wife. Badri."

Horror filled Tireshyas' face. "Lord cham, she is—"

Again Juchi interrupted, this time with a kick that

sank deep into the soft flab of Tireshyas' belly. The shaman flew backwards, crashed to the floor. Juchi sprang over him. "Badri! Where are you? I'm coming for you!" In his own ears, the words sounded more like stobor's howl than speech.

He heard people behind him. Behind did not matter. They could never catch him. Then someone came out into the hall, right in front of him. He did not know if the man would try to stop him. He did not care. He hammered him down and ran on.

The door to the chamber where he and Badri slept, the door to the chamber where their children had begun, the door to the chamber where, for all he knew, he had begun—that door was open. Juchi went in. "Badri!"

No reply. She was not there. He unslung his assault rifle. He'd find her soon, and then . . . half a burst for her and the rest, as much as he could fire before finger slipped from trigger, for him. And even that was not enough. How could one quick instant of pain make amends for—for the twisted thing their lives had proven to be?

"Badri!" Cradling the rifle, he went out to the hall again. The doorway next to his was also ajar, unlocked, as it had not been in a Haven year and more. Through it he saw the dusty glow of the computer screen. He growled, deep in his throat. The cursed computer had seen his doom. He would drag it down to hell with him.

As if it were a human enemy, he wanted to shoot it in the belly at close range and watch it die. He darted into its—its lair, he thought.

He did not fire. The light from the screen let him see a tiny motion, off to one side. He whirled toward it. "Badri," he whispered. He had found her.

She was dead, hanging from some projection from the ceiling, her face dark and distorted. She wore a wool cape, held in place by a heavy golden brooch, steppe work, he had given her. A chair lay overturned behind her.

Juchi let the rifle fall. "Oh, Badri," he cried, half in anguish, half in envy, "You found the truth before me!"

He drew his knife and cut her down. How long he held her, lost and alone in his worse than grief, he never knew. When he looked up, the doorway was full of staring, silent faces.

"Let me by," someone said, her voice small but insistent. "Let me by. I must see."

"No!" Juchi groaned wildly to the unheeding faces. "Not her! Not my—" He choked, could not go on. What word ought he use? Daughter? Sister?

Aisha pushed through the crowd. Juchi watched the color drain from her checks. Her eyes, black and enormous and staring, were Badri's eyes. And his own. "Father?" she whispered. "Mother?"

Seeing her, the sweet child (no, she was almost a woman—and, being what she was, where could she hope to find husband, no matter how great the dowry she brought with her?) who never should have been, Juchi knew he could never face her, not now, not ever again.

He undid Badri's brooch, weighed it in his hand a long moment. With a great shout of pain and fury, he plunged the pin first into one eye, then the other, again and again and again. The last sound he heard before he finally fainted was Aisha's screams.

Blackness. It covered Juchi's vision now, as well as his soul. That, he thought, was as it should be. "I wish someone would slay me," he said.

"Who would dare?" Tireshyas answered, as he had each time Juchi asked for death. "Who could bear the burden of ill-luck taking your life would lay on his shoulders?"

"In all I did, I strove for good," Juchi said.

"And in all you did, you were confounded," the

shaman replied. To that Juchi had no answer. Tireshyas went on, "If still you strive for good, you will do as I have asked, and leave us."

"I will," Juchi said. "Maybe among strangers I can find the end I seek."

"That will be as Allah and the spirits will," Tireshyas said. Juchi heard his tunic rustle, felt air move against his face. No matter how little he wished them to, his senses still told him of the world. He guessed what the shaman was about to say: "Here is your stick."

Juchi took it. He looked to where Tireshyas' voice came from, heard another rustle of cloth: the shaman shifting in unease at his ruined stare. "Care for my children," Juchi said. "Their part in—this—was innocent."

"It shall be done. Would you let them see you one last time? Aisha begs for nothing else."

"No," Juchi said. "If you have any pity, spare me that."

Tireshyas sighed. "As you wish." The shaman opened a door. Juchi raised the stick, afraid Tireshyas was lying to him. But by the sound of his stride, the person who came in was a young man. Tireshyas confirmed that, saying, "Here is Ertoghrul. He will take you past the Valley's minefield."

"I have already been caught in it, and destroyed," Juchi said. Neither Tireshyas nor Ertoghrul replied; neither, Juchi thought, understood. His groping hand found Ertoghrul's shoulder. "If you would guide me, let us go."

Tireshyas turned to watch them leave. Even now, some cycles after Juchi kicked him, the motion made pain shoot through his belly. The shaman's hand began to shape a sign to turn aside evil. *Too late for that*, he thought, *too late*. He finished the sign anyhow. By then, Juchi was gone.

From *The Wisdom of the Breedmaster Caius* (traditional)

In a perfect world, the holes in our genetic
records would matter less. Sauron breeding with
Sauron carries less potential for mischief or
mutation.

But we are not in a perfect world. We are on
Haven, where Sauron breeds with cattle or not at
all.

So the holes in our genetic records matter a
great deal. So do the even greater holes in the
records of the cattle, even when they deserve that
name at all.

Through these double holes, the future of our
race may fall to doom.

Yet where there is peril, there is also opportunity. Two sets of genetic records, each with its
own holes, may be combined to make one set
with few or no holes. We already trade with the
cattle for women, food, iron, and other needs.
Who can say that in some future time we may not
trade with them for genetic records?

No one. Nor can anyone say that from this

trading there may not emerge a single set of genetic records.

And from that single set of records, perhaps in time will emerge a single people—the Haven-born Saurons.

FAR ABOVE RUBIES

Susan Shwartz

They had not been married long, the judge Lapidoth
and Dvora, when they rode beyond the perimeters of
Eden Valley's defenses. Dvora waved at the careful
tumbles of rock, some of which concealed guard em-
placements, as cheerful as if she had won her first case.
Her husband grinned. In a manner of speaking, she had.
The Law allowed that a man who was newly wed might
stay home to cheer his wife, but in these days of Dias-
pora on Haven, when Terra itself became a fainter and
fainter memory, the Law frequently yielded to necessity, especially when necessity involved the Law itself.
Just as well, Lapidoth thought. Had he left Dvora at
home when he went to ride circuit, a cold homecoming—
and death by precedent and brief—would have been
the least he might have expected.

It was a good thing that much of New Eden's law was
tradition, inherited not just from the long-destroyed
settlement at New Vilnus, but from the tough, pragmatic
sabras who had first landed on Haven, wrested a town
from the rock, and survived first its destruction by
nomad, then alliances that were more pragmatic than
agreeable with Frystaat mercenaries and fundamentalist
farmers. What a combination! Lapidoth shook his head,
bemused at and admiring the way the old systems
stretched.

Even in the matter of his wife, who might well become a judge herself. No one knew better than he how much of an innovation that was. When dealing with its women, Eden Valley faced a potentially deadly double bind. Their health and fertility had to be treasured above all else in the community. Yet reducing the tough, wily haBandari, Frystatt-or-farmbred to pampered brood mares was out of the question: Eden needed the strength of their minds as well as, occasionally, the craft of their hands and the strength of their backs. Nothing could be wasted.

At the same time, the distinction of inside versus outside work grew up, where "inside" meant the relative safety of the Valley, and "outside" the steppe, where bandit, warrior, nomad, and Sauron vied with haBandari and villager to survive. Accordingly, women with a taste for field work could be steered toward hydroponics or the building projects that Eden always needed, while women like Dvora were encouraged to become physicians, researchers who labored to extract from Haven's stubborn herbs drugs that could replace Eden's long-vanished high-tech pharmacopeia. Any of those jobs could let a woman exploit her talents while keeping her safely "inside."

In fact, that tradition had become so strong that many farmers regarded any sort of office or lab work as "women's work"—except for administration and law.

So, wouldn't you know it? Lapidoth would not only have to pick a woman who wanted to be a lawyer and ride circuit with him, he'd managed to get her pregnant almost immediately. In his case, the usual backslapping was mixed with a certain amount of irony. "Better you than me" and "Good luck!" were two of the most common responses.

He couldn't have agreed more. Despite his own mixed background, which was betrayed by his broad-backed frame, light hair, and skin ruddy under the weathering, he had wanted a woman of *Ivrit* background. Her quicksilver mind frequently outraced his own steadiness, and if his judgments were uniformly equitable, her intuition frequently led her to suggestions that he privately thought verged on prophetic inspiration.

He turned in his saddle and waved at her. Dvora waved back, the ruby on her left hand glinting in the pallid light of Byer's Sun. He shook his head, wishing that she'd put her glove back on. The ring had been his mother's and her mother's before that. God only knew how many generations of women had treasured it, a surprising vanity for people like themselves. Dvora prized it not just for its beauty, but for the words with which he had accompanied the gift. He smiled, as he remembered: "Who can find a virtuous woman? For her worth is far above rubies."

That had not been part of the ceremony, yet, Dvora had not hesitated to improvise. Her hand had trembled once, convulsively, in his, but then she had spoken without faltering: "I will do you good and not evil all the days of my life." Apparently, she thought that breaking precedent to ride out with him fell into that category. ("It does!" she had insisted. "We're supposed to bring food from afar, not fear the snow, consider a field and buy it, and you can't do that locked up in the Valley.") He had never been so glad to lose a case.

As Dvora's muskylope paused to investigate a knotted patch of ground cover Lapidoth turned to her.

"I want to be off Botha's land before first-cycle night so we don't have to accept any more of his hospitality!"

Eden had a claim against the man, a somewhat sizable matter of three children safely brought to birth in the shelter of the Valley. Living this far out, at this time of year, Botha had claimed that he couldn't make the trip back to the Valley to defend himself. So, Lapidoth the judge simply had to extend his circuit to include Botha's land. And the arrival of a judge was the signal for people from all outlying settlements to crowd in on Botha's land—*paying usurer's rates for campground*, Dvora had noted in disgust.

They had spent several weeks hearing cases and enduring what had to be: enforced hospitality in the home of a man that Lapidoth had had to fine. It wasn't as if he were a bad host, not on the surface. But Lapidoth and Dvora had gotten heartily tired of watching him watch them at mealtimes or hearing him apologize for the necessity of serving *tref* food, which he had probably ordered up on purpose.

The stay had been especially hard on Dvora, who had had to spend a good deal of time with the women of the settlement. At least, though, she had turned up evidence that had enabled Lapidoth to resolve the case: Botha's sister, who had stayed out of the judge's sight, turned out to be pregnant. If she were to carry to term, she would have to be taken to the Valley soon.

They had ridden early, met insincere smiles with smiles of sheer relief, and headed toward Tallinn Town where the old swordsmith was sure to welcome the judge and his new lady. Dvora kept glancing over her shoulder.

"Wouldn't put it past him to ambush us," Lapidoth heard her mutter.

Just because you're paranoid doesn't mean they're not out to get you, she always said. Paranoia was a survival plus on Haven. Lapidoth tugged at the strap of his rifle. He didn't think that Botha would try anything that stupid, but a man who had built his home this far out from safer settlements might suffer from delusions that he could get away with murder, as well as not paying his taxes.

Lapidoth would prove him wrong on both counts.

"Come on, slowpoke!" he cried, his voice carrying too loudly in the thin steppe air.

Dvora's muskylope (a trade from Botha's kraals and about as cantankerous as the man himself) jerked its head forward and yanked with yellowing teeth at a tangle of brownish ground scrub. Dvora pulled at the muskylope's reins, finally leaning forward to wrench its head forward, hand against bridle.

"Ai-yai!" A shriek of bloodthirsty glee cut through the air, and the muskylope leapt forward, pitching her out of the saddle.

Lapidoth swore horribly in Hebrew, Boer, and every other language he had ever learned. Even before the bandits came in range, he had swung his rifle to his shoulder and was firing at the intruders. One . . . two . . . his rifle misfired; a third man was riding at him, laughing, as he steadied his pistol . . . *Yisgadal v'yisgadash* . . . he had time to think before a pistol shot exploded from behind him and the man pitched forward, blood gouting out of the cavity that had been his chest.

Limbs and bladder threatened to give way as he slid from the saddle, but somehow he controlled himself to stumble to his wife's side. Somehow, Dvora had managed to fall as softly as she could—*I'll never say that ground scrub has no reason for existence except to break a muskylope's leg again*, he vowed. God, what a woman! Half dazed as she must have been, she had managed to reach her pistol, aim, and fire in time to save his life.

She still held the pistol. It shook in her hand, and she brought up her wrist to steady herself. Still, the barrel drooped; just as well, Lapidoth thought, seeing his wife's eyes glazed with horror and what he hoped wouldn't be concussion. Her braids tumbled free of her fur hood; one dabbled in the mud and blood that smeared her face.

"Dvora?" he called, making his voice gentle. As far as he knew, she had never killed, never seen violent death before.

"I got him," she announced, her voice faltering. "He would have killed you."

"Killed *us*," Lapidoth assured her, and knelt beside her. "Many daughters have done virtuously, but thou excellest them all," he whispered in *Ivrit* and smoothed back her hair. She let her head sag and allowed him to straighten her, feeling over her limbs for breaks.

"Nothing . . . I think . . . get the muskies . . ." she whispered. "Their horses too. Don't worry . . . about me now."

No one could afford to let a chance to catch and claim horses or muskylopes go by. And the bandits' saddle-bags might hold extra food, some evidence of whether they were outlaws from Dede Korkut's strictly ruled yurts or honored members of a particularly feral tribe. Or Botha's men in disguise.

"Go *on!*" Dvora pushed at his leg. "I'll build a fire. . . ."

Rather than upset her further, he mounted and collected the beasts, who hadn't strayed far. A quick search of their baggage yielded five daggers, a skin of mare's milk, some herbal-smelling smears that he discarded when Dvora grimaced at them, and a *firman*, or letter from the bandit Kemal to Botha.

Ambush, was it? By God, Botha could send his woman to Tallinn Valley and risk losing half of them to Angband Base, where the Sauron's lidless eye was always out for likely breeders. If, after this, the townspeople, tribesmen, and the men of Eden allowed him to claim anything at all, his life, included.

"Kemal," he murmured to Dvora. "And Botha. They were in this together. This proves it."

"A wonder that they can read," she said, her voice acid, though shaky. Then her eyes went wide, and she coiled in on herself, her lips pale and moving in silent protest, oath, or prayer.

"Can you ride?" he asked. Even shaken as she was, she might be better off riding through the night to Tallinn Town than camping here. He tucked the *firman* into her saddlebags and pulled out a blanket to wrap around her as she rode.

But Dvora was shaking her head. Fear clenched in his belly as she tugged at the leather breeches she wore, lowering them in a gesture incongruous this far from the peace of their bedroom. They were stained with blood.

"I'm going to lose it," she whispered, amazed.

"The fall?" Lapidoth was personally going to kill that damned muskylope if it had made her miscarry.

"The fall, maybe. And the altitude. I was told if I were spotting, not to worry too much, just lie down and keep warm. It started yesterday, but we had to get out of there. . . ."

Lie down and keep warm. On the steppe. Wonderful. Their first child. Easy to say that it might never have survived; Lapidoth wanted to howl. Instead, he patted Dvora's hand. He still had a life to worry about. His wife's.

"I'll build a fire, heat water . . ." Damn, he wished that she hadn't ridden out with him.

Dvora's hand was lax, pallid, but the pulse in her wrist, though weak, was steady. Now, Lapidoth thought, if only she didn't hemorrhage, they had every chance of getting her to safety. One more night's rest, he thought. At dawn, they would set out.

"But we have to move," she whispered. "They could come back, see what happened to their friends."

"You can't ride," he told her. "At least sleep till morning."

"No!" She started to rise, and he restrained her. "Tie me to the saddle . . . I'll make it. . . ." Then, with a flicker of her usual wit, "You don't want me to get all upset, do you?"

Caught between the cliff lion and the tamerlane, Lapidoth thought. He took what seemed like an age to lift her to the muskylope's back, settle her in warmly, and tie her to the saddle.

"Horses," she murmured. "I'll lead them; you guide."

Slowly they started off, a tiny, feeble party under the unwinking gaze of the Cat's Eye that provided enough light for Lapidoth to scout out their way. They were nearing Angband's territory now, where the Sauron fortress loomed over the Tallinn Valley. Lapidoth hoped against hope to see riders on the steppe: they might be nomads of Dede Korkut's tribe—but they could be bandits, just as likely.

He turned back toward Dvora, who had drifted into uneasy, muttering sleep. Her forehead was only slightly warm; he tucked the blankets more firmly about her, thankful that childbed fever had not claimed her. Carefully, not to disturb her, he detached the reins of the spare horses from her saddle. If worse came to worst, they would provide a diversion.

For an instant, the shots and screams of Dvora's nightmare blended into reality. She waked, screamed, a huge hand clamped against her mouth. She tried to bring her teeth to bear.

"Quiet!" Lapidoth hissed at her. "We just got unlucky." He stood at her stirrup, adjusting saddlegirth and the ties that bound her. "I'll try to distract them; you get through. Take the *firman* back to the Valley . . . there's proof."

"No!" she cried, despite his muffling fingers. "Don't throw yourself away . . ."

"I'm not a hero, remember? I'll be as careful as I can," he told her. Then he mounted, slapped her muskylope on its rump, sweaty despite the cold, and rode in the opposite direction, leading the captured horses until, with a shout, he could set galloping in a panic.

I'll be as careful as I can. As the muskylope broke into a stumbling run, Dvora realized he had promised her nothing at all. And, as the shouting and shooting rose, then subsided, she realized that he would never tell her anything again.

There being nothing else to do, she rode on, tears freezing on her face. Its skin was growing hotter, more taut, even as she wept. Possibly, she had a fever. If she were fortunate, she would die of it. If she were very fortunate, she might even deliver the evidence, and then die. Dizziness wrapped her in an embrace rougher than Lapidoth had ever dared, and she rode on through the night.

The muskylope's gait slowed to a trot, then to a dispirited stumble. Once or twice it stopped to graze, and she lay dozing, waking when it moved. The last time that happened, she found herself covered with sweat. Her forehead was cooler, and she was shivering, but with honest cold, not with fever.

"Sentenced to life," she muttered to herself, grasping the reins in hands that were disgustingly weak.

Life without Lapidoth—and she had had him for such a short time! She pulled off her glove, wiped her face, then clenched her thighs, numb after the countless hours of riding through the day and early into first-cycle night. The packing between them . . . she should change it, but it lacked the heat and wetness of too-heavy bleeding. *Stronger than I thought. Damn.*

She must be near the town now, unless the muskylope had wandered in circles for most of the night. If she were going to live—and, barring bandits, it looked like she would—she was going to have something to show for it: her vengeance on the people who had robbed her of husband and child-to-be. *I will have justice. Never to forget; never to forgive,* she told herself.

Only one thing would stop her. If the Saurons found her, she had every intention of blowing out her brains with her pistol. Lapidoth's ring winked on her fingers. "Strength and honor are her clothing, and she will rejoice in times to come." Yeah, sure.

Then she heard the wailing, a thin, plaintive noise that forced a shiver up her spine. She glanced around her and saw, in the far distance, the looming, windowless bulk of Angband. Sick and dazed, she had ridden far too close to it! And now she rode across the culling ground that was so much a part of Sauron's bloody history: the blasted land where children who did not meet the standards of . . . "the Master race . . ."—her mind spat out the epithet from hatred that was old before mankind ever soared from Terra—were set out to die. . . .

Or to be taken up, as, she had heard, the nomads sometimes did. Some of the children were too frail to live, the powerful Sauron legacy overstressing tiny bodies, striking them dead just as surely as a plague. But others . . . there was no reason why others might not be claimed, grow up healthy . . .

Grow up hers.

The cries came more and more faintly. Whatever child wailed out there, hungry and abandoned, would not survive until morning; the cold or stobor, drawn to the sound and the smell of a lonely infant, would see to that.

A child to replace the babe I lost. The thought became an obsession, then armor for her weakened body. She reached down and slipped loose the ties that bound her to the saddle. *Lapidoth's knots*, she thought, undoing the familiar tangles. Then she blinked away the tears. She would ride in quickly, quietly, seize the child, and be gone.

A hundred meters from where she thought the child lay, she dismounted and tethered her muskylope, then advanced with all the trailcraft she had ever been permitted to learn. Ahead of her she heard stumbling, and her hand went to her pistol. Did Sauron's stumble? Not with their night sight; and what would it be to them if others took up their discards . . . her baby! Already, she thought of the child lying in her path as hers; that the Saurons could toss it out to die filled her with a rage as hot as what she felt for Lapidoth's killers.

Now she could hear how the cries changed. There were two voices; *two* infants! Children which, if they thrived, would have the Sauron genes, and would grow and raise more children, strengthening the breed. Such children, if they survived exposure, usually thrived. If her own breasts could not produce milk, she would need a very strong wet nurse indeed, she thought. She quickened her pace. *Just a little longer*, she tried to project at the babies ahead. *Your mother's coming!*

"Mine now," she heard another woman croon. "Mine."

A rustle told her that the interloper had placed one of the infinitely precious children inside her heavy coat. Dvora drew closer, saw the woman stoop, her gloved hand touching the second child. . . .

Not both! One is for me! Dvora cried to herself, strode forward, and snatched up the child. How good its tiny body felt in her arms! She could almost believe that this, not whatever it was that Lapidoth had buried (*"Don't look, Dvora; you don't want to see"*) beneath scrub and a few flat rocks, was the child she had borne. Her child . . . and his.

She had to give the other woman credit for speed; she jumped back, ready to fight. Though she tried to keep even her breathing quiet, the infant she held betrayed her location with a squall that already sounded stronger for the warmth it took from her body.

"Who are you?" she whispered in the Turkic of nomads. "What do you want?"

What do you think? Dvora thought, and chuckled faintly, appalled that she could even laugh. She summoned her own knowledge of the speech of the tribe. "The same as you, child of the steppe. The Bandari hate the Saurons no less than you, but we need their genes if we ever hope to meet them on equal terms. And there are two babies here, so we need not even fight. Go in peace."

It was a bluff. Dvora could feel the bleeding start between her legs again. She barely had strength to stand, much less fight a woman of the steppes, hardened by life among the yurts and sheep flocks. Usually, the nomads respected haBandari, left them alone. Perhaps this one . . . *please God* . . .

She heard a faint choke of breath that she identified as a sigh of relief. "Allah and the spirits grant you the same, haBandari," the tribeswoman said and hurried away. Dvora could see her releasing her muskylope from the Finnegan's fig to which it had been tethered. She waited, gathering her strength for the long stagger back to her own beast. Curiously, she seemed to draw strength from the tiny, malodorous bundle that squirmed inside her garments, seeking nourishment from breasts that might never fill.

It took one infinity of struggle to stumble back to the muskylope and another to mount it, to tie herself to the saddle, and, finally to urge it into unwilling movement toward Tallinn Town.

Before she fell into an uneasy sleep, the child resting against her heart, she rehearsed the story she would tell in Tallinn Town. She hadn't miscarried on the steppe, but given birth; despite all odds, the babe had survived, and so had she. That much of the story she would invent. Lapidoth's sacrifice and death—she would die before she would alter the truth of that by so much as a breath.

And the truth of the child's birth would remain for her own people.

Emerging from Eden Valley's small, scrubbed infirmary into the cold of the night and the baleful glare of the Cat's Eye, which reduced Byers' Sun to a gleaming pinpoint, Dvora the judge tensed. The always-pleasant visit to the maternity ward to congratulate the new mothers and admire their sons and daughters faded from her memory, and her hand, on which Lapidoth's ruby gleamed like a gout of blood, dropped to her beltknife.

Children shouting; that was all. If her daughter Chaya were here, doubtless Chaya would put name to every voice and tell her exactly how each child was feeling. Dvora frowned. Eden's children were not brought up to shout like *wildachayim*, like wild little animals or to run into the center of the cluster of houses, outbuildings, and workshops that, three hundred T-years ago, had been called Strong-in-the-Lord.

Just as well that she saw them, rather than one of the Eden farmers with their stern ways and even sterner belts. As the commotion neared her, Dvora shut the door behind her, not wanting to disturb the mothers, whose labors, even in the protection and relatively high air pressure of the Valley, had been long and exhausting. Even given the febrifuges and antibiotics that three T-centuries of ingenious Bandari kitchen chemists had devised from herbs and molds, childbirth on Haven was still a risky business. *I almost died*, Dvora thought, as she did every time she visited the newborn. When she miscarried on the steppe, only her native toughness and *pure Litvak stubbornness* (a phrase her father had often used to describe her mother) had pulled her through. *Dizziness . . . heat pouring down her thighs . . . her body cooling even as she bucked and spasmed to expel what had already died . . . Lapidoth holding her hand, weeping over it as he drew her back from a too-easy death . . . her hand shook, pulsing, the bloodlight in the ruby dancing . . . so cold by the small fire that was all they could kindle . . . the torturous ride, tied to a muskylope, as her strength returned . . . and then the thin, wails of cold hunger . . . weakening even as she neared them . . .*

She had spent months in Tallinn Town, recovering and hiding from the woman-hungry Saurons, until she healed enough to join a merchant train back to the Valley where physicians of her own kind—not the tribal midwives whose skill and cleanliness she profoundly distrusted—observed her, tested her, and warned her against a second pregnancy.

She was almost relieved: if she dared not conceive, she need not remarry, need not risk loss such as Lapidoth's death had caused her. By then, too, she had had her work: the laborious preparation of the case against Botha, followed by the judgeship that had been her husband's. Then Eden Valley and Tallinn Town had ridden out against Kemal, the first time that the two communities had worked together. Lapidoth would have been proud to see that. Now she rode circuit, accompanied by the guards who would now always ride after the Valley's judge.

The running feet pounded closer. She recognized some of her daughter's classmates. "Is it the swordsmith?" she asked, stepping forward into their path. Heber, who had succeeded his father in running the forge, had settled in Tallinn Town, east of Eden. He was very popular among the younger men and (especially) women of the Valley; rumor—which no judge could ever afford to ignore—had it that he was actively looking for a wife. Well, enough, Dvora had thought at the time. A match between the swordsmith and a girl of Eden Valley might be good for trade, unless it drew the lidless eye of Angband Base down upon him.

At the sight of their valley's judge, they jolted to a whispering halt. "Or just a Sauron raid?"

"Here she comes! It's the judge!"

She had sat in judgment over too many of these children's parents not to know what the guilty huddle, the downcast eyes, and thinned mouths meant.

"Sauron . . . Sauron . . . how'd she *know?*" came the whispers, as she stood there, ostentatiously tapping her foot.

"*Laila tov*, Judge," came the voice of her friend Barak's son.

"Using Hebrew to get round me, are you, Avi?" she asked. Her breath wreathed about her like a pale cloud in the night air. "How are you going to get round your teachers if you come in late and have time enough just to do your chores, not your schoolwork?"

That finished Avi. What about the others?

"Well, are you going to explain so we can all go

home, or do we stand in the cold all night?" she demanded, waiting with her arms crossed, as the youths stood there. "And speaking of home, where's my daughter?"

She thought she knew all of the children in Eden Valley, but apparently, she had been wrong. One or two of these were strangers, doubtless from outlying settlements, children who were often pulled out of classes to work in farm, barn, house, or stable when their families decided that chores took precedence over schooling. *Goyische kopf*, she muttered inwardly. Even after 300 T-years of coexistence, haBandari and the original settlers of Eden still had their differences; and, wouldn't you just know it, child-rearing—the most vital and precarious thing on this whole iceball of a planet!— was chief among them.

Muttering and hissing rose from the boys and girls who faced her. Most were near or a little past Eden Valley adulthood of two Haven years, a little past Bar Mitzvah age, but it was the rare haBandari whose child went through that ceremony. Her own daughter had, as she had gone through the *mikveh*, the ritual bath that only the very eldest of haBandari knew how to conduct. There had been need, need to establish clearly that Chaya was hers, Bandari and *Ivrit*, but . . . she shook that thought from her mind. Thirteen or fourteen was the age at which young men and women could own land, sign contracts, bear arms, and marry. And yet they were children to her, and they looked younger each year.

"Well? Do you want to tell me why you're all making more noise than a cliff lion battling for his mate?"

Avi, who sported a fine black eye, looked resigned, opened his mouth, then shut it, clearly reluctant to betray a classmate. Dvora shivered and sighed. "Someone tell me what's going on before I call your parents!" she snapped.

The huddle tightened, then divided, leaving two of

the strangers standing before her. Their heavy clothes
were wrinkled and torn, and dried blood still crusted
the mouth and nose of the boy who stood between her
and the girl, clearly his sister. He tried to stick out
chest and jaw, and quailed as Dvora glared at him. "I'm
Joseph," he said, "and this is my sister Hagar. We came
in for the day. And my father says . . ."

"Tell her!" cried another girl. "Tell the Judge that
you tried to boss her daughter, and when Chaya ignored you, you called her a 'breed' and said she should
have been thrown out at birth like a Sauron cull!"

The boy paled beneath the grime and blood, and
Hagar's eyes widened, her mouth opening in dismay.

Her daughter. Dvora shut her eyes in pain that racked
her heart as badly as the pains of her miscarriage, so
many years ago.

The shoemaker's child goes barefoot, thought Dvora,
the baker's child has no bread, and the judge's daughter
has the story of her birth thrown at her by strangers.

"That's prejudice," Dvora made herself shake her
head. Useless to punish the children, who doubtless
repeated what they heard at home. "Chaya is my daughter and your neighbor." She drew on her memories of
Bible quizzes throughout the years of her schooling.
" 'For ye were strangers in the land of Egypt.' " She
intoned impressively. "Who of us isn't a stranger here?"
she demanded. "Who of us can avoid working together
if we are not all to starve, freeze, or fall to bandits or
Saurons?

"Think about it!" her voice took on the resonant,
lecturing tones that she had learned gave her verdicts
the greatest weight. For this, Ruth bat Boaz hung
from the cross and was lifted down by Piet van Reenan?
For this, a gentle girl had turned general and rebel? So
two young fools on their first visit to town could over-
turn three hundred T-years of work?"

*What did you expect? One lifetime of work isn't
enough—even if it's yours. Or your husband's.* Memo-

ries of Lapidoth, thoughts of how angry this would make him, made her frown even more deeply. Even after three T-centuries of coexistence, such fossil memories still lingered in Eden, as slight, yet as powerful as the Boer or Yiddish oath that some unwary haBandari might snap out, exasperated by the slow speech and conservatism of their neighbors.

As often as not, the Edenites still used Bible names. That much the *Ivrit* among the haBandari shared with them. But where the haBandari raised sons and daughters to study and trade as well, among their neighbors, son followed father into farm or battlefield, while mother raised daughter to tend house, cook for a small army, and—should they be lucky—bear a small army more, three or four of whom might survive to adulthood. Joined by force, they were not yet one people, not wholly—any more than the nomad women forced to wed with the Saurons were one with their appalling mates.

She waited, holding this Joseph's eyes, outglaring the Cat's Eye with her own anger, her own fear, until his eyes fell. "And you, Hagar, do you know the story of your own name? I'd suggest you go home and read about it. And both of you, keep silent, if you cannot speak decently. Whether or not the girl you insulted was my own child or not, your childishness weakens the Valley just as surely as if you sowed a field with salt. Now, get out of here, all of you! I shall talk to you and your father later."

And she would, too. If that kind of bigotry were springing up in the outlying settlements, she would have to. *The black eye and bloody nose that I saw will be nothing. They'll use guns and knives next, and we'll have riots, pogroms, civil war. And if we don't finish each other off, the bandits will.*

Hagar and Joseph fled, Hagar's sobs loud in the night air. To antagonize the judge . . . perhaps she would wait, let the family worry for awhile. That might be the

worst penalty she could impose. She would wait until
the long night was over, then ride out to their farm.
First, though, she would have to find out where it was.
Among the million or so other things that she would
have to do. First of them, though, was to find her
daughter.

The other children dispersed more slowly.

"I think Chaya hid in the bunker." Avi's words floated
behind him in the still air.

Dvora stepped back into the infirmary. "No, no trouble," she told the anxious medic who saw her. "I want
to sign out a sidearm." She caught up the nearest
weapon and headed out. The bunker had been built
when this part of Eden Valley was still named Strong-in-
the-Lord. When, three hundred T-years ago, the exiles
from Frystaat and the New Vilnus refugees who had
made up the Bandari took this valley, the bunker had
been captured without the loss of a single man on
either side. The site of a victory that neither group
wanted to talk about, it had been allowed to fall into
ruins.

A cliff lioness could have made her lair there, birthed
cubs there for all Dvora knew. Or some outcast, more
clever and more desperate than most, could have risked
the Bandari guards to hole up there, waiting his chance
to steal women, drugs, or weapons. It wasn't safe for a
child or a young woman to wander about distressed,
unaccompanied, and unarmed, though Dvora knew that
whatever else her daughter was, she was never without
protection.

The climb to the desolate bunker left Dvora panting,
sweating under her sheepskins despite the cold of the
night. The Cat's Eye winked in the dark sky at her
back, and she set her feet carefully, testing her footing.

A pebble landed in her path.

"You might have warned me what some of the
outbackers might say," Chaya's voice floated over her

head, accusing and too collected for a girl her age.

"Told you what?" Dvora said, guilt sharpening her voice. "That there's always a serpent in Eden? And in *this* Eden, it's fools and bigots. That's life, daughter, and you'd better face it. And face me too, while you're at it."

Anyone else in the Valley would have made a noisy, scrabbling production of climbing down from the fragment of roof that jutted out above Dvora. Chaya managed it in a quick, smooth dismount, her sheepskin jacket flaring open about her. As always, Dvora noted how well suited her daughter was for the stark Haven environment. Sturdy and strong, she carried no extra weight beyond what would keep her warm. She breathed easily in the thin air, but did not display the barrel-chested, hyperdeveloped rib cage of high-altitude dwellers. As the Cat's Eye flashed, she glanced aside. Moisture flickered briefly in her eyes, then dried; her high cheekbones bore no traces of tears.

Conservation of body fluids, Dvora thought, and wondered once again why the Saurons had chosen to discard her daughter. On a planet full of enemies, Saurons were *the* Enemy; but their ways were not so different from those of Eden Valley that they had no need to save alive what girl children they might have to increase the birth rate in the next generation. Why discard a girl? Saurons culled their newborn, she knew, for undesirable traits: blood that clotted in the veins, causing a baby to die of a stroke before his first birthday; night vision that left a child completely blind during the day; reflexes so acute that a child might spasm or die in convulsions if it were startled; and perhaps other, less readily apparent traits that made the mature Sauron warrior not just a fighting machine but a monster, coolly capable of the worst atrocities.

Most of those deformities were latent in women, turning up in boy-children, who were born in greater numbers than Sauron females. Much greater numbers,

Dvora thought, considering the Sauron's demands for "tribute maidens" from the nomad tribes and the way they occasionally carried off the farm girl who strayed, unarmed and unaccompanied, from her family's protection. Thus far, no haBandari woman had been captured. *And none had better be,* Dvora thought.

"You didn't fight," Dvora stated, rather than asked it.

"They're still walking, aren't they? I wish you'd let me join the Scouts," Chaya added. She patted a beltknife in a tooled leather sheath. Both looked new, yet familiar. "I'm quiet, fast, strong; and no one would see me. Doesn't matter, does it, if a half-breed monster keeps you safe so long as you don't have to look at her."

So that was why she had fought the idea of training to be a judge! She feared that defendant and plaintiff alike had already condemned her as an outsider. *Judge then, Judge. The case of Chaya bat Lapidoth versus Eden Valley. Dare I make such a case, even for my own child?*

"And Barak says . . ." Chaya went on.

"Barak talks too much!" Dvora snapped. "All right, so you'd make a fine Scout. But I had to make that rule, and I can't make an exception of it. Stop trying to make me feel guilty." She reached out to her daughter, but the girl stepped back.

"Tell me again," said Chaya. "I know, I grew up knowing that I'm at least half-Sauron. But tell me again."

"This is no place for it," Dvora replied. "Anything could come—a tamerlane, a bandit—" A Sauron, she had almost said, but stopped in time. "Or someone with a complaint. I don't know which would be worse, right now!"

That forced a shaky laugh from Chaya.

"Let's go. We'll go back to the house; I'll make a cup of tea; you'll have something to eat; and then we'll talk. All right?"

Sauron Chaya might be, but she was also a child, glad to have someone to comfort her. *For as long as I*

*can, daughter. And I don't have to be a prophet to
know that that won't be much longer.* She remembered
where she had seen toolwork like that on Chaya's
beltknife: Heber's work. Well, though she had had
dreams of Chaya studying with her, perhaps becoming
judge after her, if the girl were restless, marriage to a
man who lived almost like one of the tribesmen might
suit her better. From all indications, she had steppe
blood as well as the quick-clotting Sauron kind.

The girl agreed with a quick firming of her lips and
led the way down the path, carefully choosing her
footing to protect Dvora, who lacked the nightsight,
speed, and strength of the Sauron-bred, and the energy
of youth.

The eggtree tea was strong and sweet in the large,
crude mugs that Chaya had made years ago in school.
The firelight was dimming, and the lamps had burned
down, almost to extinction. Chaya liked the dimness
because, as she said, "I'm as blind as a drillbit in full
daylight."

She knew that; most of Eden that was acquainted
with the Judge's daughter knew it too. Many, trained to
turn a blind eye to what they did not wish to see, called
it simple nearsightedness and turned deaf ears as well
as blind eyes to the girl's uncanny night sight. Perhaps
the nomads had the right of it; Lapidoth had once told
Dvora that, when they saved a child from the grisly
culling ground outside Angband Base, saving it from
stobor or the subtler fangs of cold, they never revealed
the child's ancestry for fear of Sauron vengeance. *Living
this far away, we must lack practice retrieving children,* Dvora thought. *I can live with being awkward
about such things* . . . yet her awkwardness had caused
her daughter to live as a stranger in a strange land in
what should have been her home.

Was that what drew her to Heber? How could she
bring it up? Was this her daughter's way of punishing

her for her refusal to admit women to the Scouts? *You could be anything else,* she had cried once. *Only don't leave me!*

And was that fair? Was that just?

Here is another case for you, Dvora, she could hear Lapidoth's voice, quizzing her as he had in the days when he was the judge and she a student. *Two people come before you, a parent and child. The child is offered a chance to make a new, rich life; the parent has attempted to restrain the child. What will you decide?*

Put that way, there was no case at all, except between her desires and her conscience. She had spent a lifetime making conscience the victor; and she would not give up now.

The girl doesn't know how to tell you. She needs your help.

Faced with that familiar, beloved need, suddenly Dvora knew how to begin.

Chaya moved slightly, the dusky light gleaming off the bone and metal hilt of that fine new knife.

"Nice beltknife," Dvora said. "What did you pay for it?"

"Heber gave it to me," Chaya replied, her olive coloring suddenly more vivid. "He said he'd come by tonight." Her pupils grew enormous, despite what was, for her, the relative brightness of the house.

To be wife to a swordsmith in Tallinn Town? To scuttle from the menfolk who came to guest and to efface herself? That was no life for her Chaya. And besides, was Heber even *Ivrit* anymore?

"To ask for you? I assume you want me to give my consent. What else do you want me to say?"

"It's not like what you think," Chaya muttered. "I'll travel with him, learn to forge swords myself . . . wear a mask against the glare. And I'll be . . ."

Free of this place. Not for the first time, Dvora could cheerfully have cursed Barak and the other Scouts, all the tough warriors whose honor was expressed in edged steel. There were other ways, other honors, as Chaya must learn in Tallinn, if she did not learn it here in Eden.

"Look at me, girl," Dvora said in her judge-voice. "You asked for the story of your birth. Do you want to hear it again with him, or do you want to tell him?"

Whatever else her daughter was, she was no coward. That was not surprising. Neither were her parents, whichever set.

Chaya raised her head, her eyes flaring like the Cat's Eye that had long sunk into second-cycle night. "I'll do it. Tell me again, so I can make it live for him."

The pregnant woman swayed and fell against the table on which the glass blower had proudly displayed some of his wares. Chaya leaped forward, just in time to thrust between her and the splintering glass. The music of its breaking was akin, though far louder, to the *stamp* and *snap* when Heber had broken the glass underfoot at their wedding.

Only, instead of shouts of *mazel tov* and ribald cheers, there rose the cries of women and children. Someone jerked back a child, who promptly set up a wail, only partially muffled by the hand clapped to his mouth.

"Quiet," ordered a woman. "You are not dying; your chief pain is fear. Master it like a man and a warrior."

Chaya, supporting the pregnant woman, looked around to see which child had been cut and which woman in the fleece and flowered headshawls of the tribe dwellers attempted to console him. She and Heber both knew the importance of good relations with the nomads and had even guested among them.

It was her son, and he hated to be held. In a moment, he would begin to struggle. With his Sauron heritage, he was too strong for a child his age; he must not betray himself! She darted forward, saw him safe, and drew a deep breath, trying to master the adrenaline surge that demanded that she *do something!*

The woman who pulled his hand away from his lips was a handsome woman, hardly into midlife. She wore the gray and the Lidless Eye of Angband Base with distinction and almost as much arrogance as the Sauron-born.

"Your child?" she asked, one brow raised. She had a proud nose and cheekbones like paired daggers. "Ah, Dokuz," she murmured, looking with pity on the woman Chaya supported. "Unlucky the name; unlucky the day." Her voice dropped to a whisper; clearly, she had not expected to be overheard.

"Should we call the Breedmaster?" The woman's face froze into hatred at the question, then relaxed so quickly that Chaya thought she had imagined it. She squinted in what was, for her, the noon light of the crowded store.

She nodded at Chaya. "I shall return her to her quarters. Keep your son safe."

It was a command. Chaya had spent the past T-year or so gaining authority in Tallinn Town; this woman merely lifted her head and spoke: and authority was hers. She walked toward Chaya, her boots crunching fragments of glass underfoot. They were very much of a height and a type: two tall, strong women with sharply marked features—though the elder bore a beauty that Chaya had yet to claim.

The glassblower complained at her elbow, but did not dare even to touch her gray sleeve. With superb unconcern, she dismissed the glassblower's protestations with, "Present your claim to the Brigade Leader."

Take that woman out of the gray, body-hugging Sauron livery, put her in the flowered wools and fleeces of the tribes, and she could walk toward the yurts, free for what might have been the first time since her breasts started to grow, thought Chaya. Why did she not simply disappear?

She knew that she had not spoken, and she had often been told that her face turned blank when she was thinking. But the woman read her with the skill of her own mother Dvora. The elder woman caught her eye.

"No, we are *trusted*," she said, unutterable scorn in that word, "to shop in the town. Where would we go? Home? We were of the tribes; our homes lie—or lay—in our yurts; and who knows where they are? Besides, if we flee, they will but seize other poor women."

"I hope that Dokuz will thrive, khatun," Chaya said, politely using the tribal honorific.

"So do I," the Sauron woman replied. "You were brave to run toward the falling glass."

Brave? I? Rather, she had trusted her speed. Chaya relinquished Dokuz to the elder woman and claimed her son, whose small, grubby hand bore a scratch, clotting long since and already half-healed.

"I am not brave," she repeated aloud. "I merely do what must be done."

"No?" said the woman. "Who are you?"

"I am Chaya, wife to the swordsmith Heber of Tallinn."

"Well enough. I had heard he married one of the Bandari, who has made herself busy in the town. He needed a strong wife. I wish you well." The Sauron woman turned to leave. Abruptly, Chaya wished to hold her there.

"What is your name?" she asked, playing for time.

"Quick! Breedmaster's guards! To me!" The women of Angband Base might not appear to be hostages, but there was no denying that Saurons had appeared with all-too-predictable speed.

"Your name, though?" persisted Chaya.

"I am Badri."

Now Chaya needed all her powers of dissimulation. She bowed her head in acknowledgment. Badri's glance slid toward the door, where three Sauron warriors seemed determined to crash through the frame, take the sick woman off, and interrogate everyone in the shop, all at once. Dropping eyelids in quick acknowledgment, Chaya took her son's hand and led him through the crowd and out the back.

Chaya returned to her home, thinking hard. The Sauron women she had met had all been . . . *been human once*, she began to think. No, that wasn't it. They had belonged to human communities: tribes, towns.

In that case . . . she laughed hoarsely. It was just as well that no haBandari had ever been taken. Mothers carried more than genetic traits; they carried the faith. Imagine sons of a superrace born to an *Ivrit* mother? Imagine *Ivrit* supermen. She chuckled without mirth.

In any case, I'm a cull, she thought. *What are the true Sauron women like?* She shook herself. If she thought along those lines any longer, she'd be wondering if *her* mother had been Sauron or human.

The Sauron's women she had seen had had power and honor—of a sort. They had been demanded or stolen because their fertility was vital to the Saurons. If they fled, other women would be seized to replace those who fled, and examples would be made. Hence, being valued for one thing at least (which was no worse than they might have been treated in the tribes), the women moved with pride. At worst, they were prisoners of their own pride. At best . . . well, Chaya had married for love; but she supposed that some sort of fellow feeling might spring up between a man and the woman who bore his children. Even if the man were Sauron.

And that was the strangest thought of all—except for the one that she dared not think.

Badri. Heber had mentioned a Badri. He had mentioned too damned many stupid things, Chaya thought. Now, when Tallinn Town was peaceful, when her mother ruled Eden Valley, when the Saurons of Angband seemed content, was no time to imitate the Zealots of Terra.

Blood followed the mother . . . Chaya shivered.

A call came from the forge. Time to add fuel to the

fire, was it? No one, not even a woman with light-sensitive eyes, dared let the fire go out or even dim: a weapon's temper depended on constant heat; and lives depended on the weapons that Heber and his family forged.

She rose and seized Heber's last gift to her: a cleverly shaped mask of darkened plastic. She used it whenever she had to enter the forge or stand over a cookfire.

Even wearing the smoked plastic, she squinted against the firelight as she added measured amounts of charcoal. After more than a Cat's Eye year of marriage, she herself was no poor swordsmith. The small steel crucible must be watched, she knew, with especial care. In it, Heber sought to recreate the *wootz* that, thousands of years ago, the ancestors of people like Badri and the chieftain Dede Korkut had wrought into swords and used to conquer half a world.

Filtered by the plastic, the light in the forge was blood red, and the metal would be even bloodier, the cherry red that meant that the *wootz* was ready to pour.

It would be forged, folded, heated, and quenched, over and over. In the old days, it would have been quenched in the body of a slave. Heber, God protect them all for fools, meant to quench these blades and hundreds like them in the bodies of their masters, the Saurons of Angband base.

And he had mentioned a Badri.

You will forget that name, Chaya told herself.

Footsteps sounded outside, Chaya's keen hearing telling her that they approached the forge. She whirled, one hand reaching for the knife hidden in a storage bin. A pistol would have been more sure, but who had ever heard of a swordsmith relying on firearms? Besides, a bullet astray near a crucible . . . Chaya didn't want to think of that either.

"Ho, the forge!" It was Heber's voice, and she relaxed as her husband entered. The doors were doubled.

One let him into the building; the second protected the
forge against gusts of wind or squalls that the outer door
might admit.

Even through the filtered plastic, Chaya found pleasure in watching him. Heber was not especially tall,
either for the Bandari or the townsfolk, but he seemed
bigger, perhaps because his trade had added muscle to
his shoulders. He needed that strength to hammer out
the blades; but it was good, very good for other things
as well. As always, she smiled at the man, and then
smiled more secretly to herself. He shook his head
slightly at her, not needing Sauron sight to know what
she was thinking. "Wife," he said, and the formality of
his voice warned her that he was not alone, "prepare
food for our guests. I go to welcome them."

Wife! Chaya stiffened. As often as she and her husband had had to play the game, she never liked being
relegated to the position of tribal servant. But there
were, God knows, worse roles in life, though; and she
had met women who played them. Deliberately, she
waited until Heber had ushered in his guests, then
made much of dropping her head and scurrying mod-
estly into the kitchens.

But she had seen what she wished to see: one of
Heber's guests was Dede Korkut the chieftan—that
silver hair was unmistakable despite the hat he had
jerked down over as much of it as he could. The other
was a younger man, taller than Heber. The chieftain's
son? Chaya hadn't been aware that Dede Korkut had
one. *His heir*, she concluded as she poured batter on
heated metal to make flat breads and scooped stew into
bowls.

When the trays were loaded, she called her daughter
to help her carry them into the principal guesting room.
It was located, somewhat unconventionally, in the living quarters, and Heber had had her furnish it with
rugs and cushions and leather hangings, so it resembled
the yurt of a prosperous tribesman. Here, he showed

his most favored customers his most expensive swords.

And here they met to discuss what Chaya simultaneously feared and longed for: the downfall of Angband Base.

Chaya flicked a glance at her husband: *stay or leave?* She had been introduced to the cham on several occasions when guesting in the yurts.

"Cham," Heber spoke before the older man could protest, "you brought your heir Juchi into our . . . discussions. My wife, Chaya, must stay."

"A woman?" asked the younger tribesman. He was slightly taller than Chaya herself, with dark eyes and bladelike cheekbones that reminded her of someone she had seen. That was foolishness, she reproved herself, to seek after likenesses when, if they were discovered, others would seek them for slow, painful deaths.

"I greet the guest," Chaya said, low-voiced and polite, in Turkic. The cham chuckled at her words, which were a pun, as she very well knew.

"Khatun Chaya is haBandari, the daughter of the judge of Eden Valley."

"The lady may be a princess among her kind," said Juchi, "but she is no warrior."

"With respect," Heber said, "my wife is a swordsmith and, though she did not join the battle against Suleiman the bandit, in which Juchi became warleader, she is no mean warrior."

I told you I should have fought! Chaya glared at her husband, even as she served food to the men. She had wanted to take part in the battle, but, no, Heber said: bad enough for a woman to join it; but a woman with her speed and strength would rouse more comment than her support would be worth.

"After all," Heber said, "it is a woman among the Saurons who can unlock the secrets of their mine fields to us."

That had been news even to Chaya, when first she heard it. Even more startling had been the revelation that the woman was not Sauron-born, but a woman of the tribes, who had learned, somehow, to compel the Saurons' ancient computer to provide information. Chaya had been astonished; the Eden Valley scientists had sworn that all the computers had crashed years ago.

Dede Korkut nodded. "And if one woman can fight the Saurons, why not another?"

"It is not as a warrior that I can serve," Chaya decided that the time had come to speak for herself. "But as a pledge of support from Eden Valley. Speak the word, and the haBandari will flock to your standard."

"How?" the warleader Juchi demanded. "The time when we had devices for speaking over far distances is long past. Or we are all dead men! Or have haBandari machines that they have not shared with their allies?"

Heber shook his head. "No. They have no *radio*, the word is."

"That is not the question," Juchi answered. "Do the Saurons have such a thing?"

"I think that they cannot," said Heber. "For, if they had, they would have used it long since to summon their fellows from the Citadel half this land away."

"And this," Juchi scoffed, "your woman friend in Angband Base tells you? Would she—or I—know such an instrument if she saw it?"

"She is the Base Commander's woman," said Heber. "Even to whisper of her is to endanger her—and us. Yet, I would trust her as I trust my wife and her mother."

A flick of black eyes, a flash of mature, fierce beauty, and the arrogant words, "*Present your claim to the Base Commander.*" Badri, then, the very woman whom Chaya had spoken with only that day was her husband's mysterious ally. Yes, that Badri was to be trusted.

"Let them call," Chaya interrupted. "I have heard that, even given such a device, the air itself can prevent the words from flying through it. And what if the Saurons at the Citadel hear them? Are they demons or djinn to fly through the air to answer their kin—and would they? That much we must leave to fate."

Dede Korkut nodded. "Truly, we must trust the will of Allah."

"You claim, khatun," Juchi spoke directly to Chaya, "that your word will bring us aid. We do not expect the warriors of Eden to abandon their own. What is it they shall do for us, and how shall you command them from Tallinn Town?"

From her left hand, Chaya stripped her ruby ring and let it clatter onto the low brass table. "Some among your men ride as they will. Let them ride to Eden Valley to give my mother *this*, and our warriors will ride out."

"More women?" Juchi seemed to scoff, but a chuckle underlay the deep, almost familiar rumble of his voice. For a warleader, he was easy to talk to, Chaya thought; their thought processes were curiously alike, even when he felt he had to jeer at her.

"My mother, the judge Dvora, is no warleader. Rather will the warrior Barak lead haBandari out onto the steppes. *If* by some chance, the Citadel sends to these Saurons' aid, Barak's warriors will hold them," Chaya said.

Heber smiled, "I believe you know the man Barak," he remarked. "In a little manner of some sheepstealing— or just the attempt."

The cham shook his head. "My men were young, and have been twice punished, once by defeat, another time by a good beating."

Twice and three times, Chaya retreated to the kitchens to fetch more food and drink. The last time she emerged, she carried a skin of mares' milk, traded for with the tribes against just such a necessity. She stood in what would have been darkness for anyone who lacked her night sight, watching the faces of the other conspirators who had fought and refought in words and maps their way across the battle plain before Angband, but who were, once again, brought up short before the fortress's mighty walls.

"We could encircle Angband with warriors for ten years and never gain entry!" lamented the old man Dede Korkut. Though the night was young—second cycle had not even begun—his eyes were red and he peered as if he had difficulty focusing.

"It is too dim for you, cham," Heber said. "Let me . . ." He threw fuel on the fire, and light flared up.

Chaya, who had chosen that moment to approach holding the skin of mares' milk, stumbled. She regained her balance quickly, managing neither to drop the skin nor to swear.

"When the fire flares up, my sight is no better than a drillbit's," she complained, and sat down a little too rapidly on a heap of cushions. "Drillbits," she repeated.

Juchi raised level brows at her, and even Heber seemed to question.

Drillbits were known for their adamantine teeth and for their greed. Notoriously difficult to control, drillbits could literally chew through walls—assuming you could get them to start.

"Drillbits!" she said, and laughed. Feed a drillbit, and it was yours to command.

"I wish you would explain to me," Juchi said, aggravation plain in his voice.

"When you trade for weapons, do you not ask my husband—too frequently—to 'sweeten the deal'? Well, why should a drillbit not demand the same? Coax drillbits to attack Angband's walls, and they shall speedily fall."

"But how?" demanded Dede Korkut.

Chaya reached into a turquoise bowl that held a garish array of tennis fruit, Finnegan's figs, and red-and-white splotched clownfruit. She caught one up, balanced it in one hand, then tossed it into the air. "Let me speak as a mother," she said. "It has always been hard to restrain the children from insulting the Saurons. How if we do not even try?"

She mimed throwing the tennis fruit at her husband.

"Coat the walls with fruit pulp, and the drillbits will gnaw through them for us."

"And the Saurons? Would they not try to hurt our sons?"

"The Saurons too live with women, who would not see other women's children hurt." *Please God, let that be so!* "And the Saurons are men and warriors, who like being laughed at as little as any other men. What would they have said? That in their pride, they grudge little children a messy game?"

After a moment, all three men began to laugh uproariously. The skin of mares' milk was passed, this time, to her first. She was laughing so hard that the white fluid nearly came out her nose, and she neglected to burp politely.

For once, she forgot to be self-conscious.

In the end, the job of persuading the mothers of Tallinn, town and tribe, to risk their sons and a few of the stronger girls (Chaya's among them) took longer than drawing the maps of Angband's minefields. Dede Korkut's funeral had faded to memories of some memorable hangovers by the time Chaya sheltered herself behind a jutting wall.

It was first-cycle sunrise, and Byers' Sun was still a pinpoint that even Chaya could bear to look at. Today's battle would be long-drawn-out, messy, but (she hoped) bloodless. It might even be amusing.

Two of the smaller children glanced over their shoulders and she shook her head at them. It was a relief when Mustafa ran back to shepherd them and their sheepskin bags toward Angband Base's towering gray walls. Nervous laughter rose and cracked in the cold air as another boy reached into a similar bag, took out a ripe tennis fruit, and threw it at a giggling friend. When he ducked, it smashed against the gray stone, leaving a yellow splash that steamed briefly, then started to freeze.

Chaya bit her lip as she saw several Saurons cluster together on the ramparts. *You lead them*, the other mothers had told her. *You watch them*.

"*On my head be it*," she had promised, finding, as her mother had often said, that persuasion was a harder task than war.

It's their freedom too, she told herself, and brought down her arm in the signal to fire.

The fruit fight broke out. If several children found themselves happily splattered, the walls, unable to dodge, scream shrilly, and run, took on garish life as smears of purple fig, red heartfruit, and yellow tennisfruit exploded on the rough gray stone. *Imagine the heartfruit as Sauron's blood*, Chaya thought. *Let that one be my father, that big one the beast that sent me out into the cold to die*.

Intoxicated by the sweet smell of the juices rising in the air, the children laughed shrilly. Chaya envied them. She saw what she could not help thinking of as a new column of boys bringing sacks filled with reinforcements: the discards of every farmer and fruitstall in Tallinn.

More and more Saurons appeared on the walls, went off-duty, and were replaced. So were the children, shift after shift of them retreating from their gaudy handiwork to their relieved mothers' care. From time to time, Chaya withdrew too, to tend her own hearth and family, to eat (though she had no appetite for fruit!), and to rest. But always she came back to the wall.

Byers' Sun was low in the west, and Cat's Eye was gone from the sky. Soon it would be cold, too cold, for the children to continue the barrage, and too dark for them to see. She herself could watch the figures on the wall tense with fury, especially . . . ah! she recognized that figure, a woman in Sauron gray. It was Badri, and she was being tugged along the wall by a stocky man of middle years. He was almost as purple as a Finnegan's fig, and would have been bright red had the heartfruit that Ahmed boldly tossed up at him hit its mark.

The Brigade Leader, maybe? Just as well that Ahmed had not hit him. The Sauron shook his fist at the children. "Get out of here!" he ordered. His shout was more a scream of rage than a command, and Chaya allowed herself a thin smile.

A moment later, he stormed down from the wall, still dragging Badri by the wrist. Shortly afterward, Byers' Sun went out behind the splintered teeth of the horizon, and the children withdrew,

The battle for Angband Base had just begun.

The boys who were too young to ride with Heber, Juchi, and his warriors to the northern edge of Tallinn Valley yet too old to find fruit-flinging an acceptable substitute, had complained bitterly until they learned their new duty. Then they had laughed, but sobered quickly. Drillbits *could* be handled, but it took care and concentration; because a drillbit could chew through anything at all almost as fast, one boy said, as a musky could lope, a drillbit's bite was no laughing matter.

Fortunately, bright light confused them, rendered it relatively easy for the boys and a few adults to tie the meter-long burrowers' front and hind legs together. Wearing the mask she used at the forge, Chaya cut the last strip of leather and led the boys forward.

Several were slowed by the frantic squirms of the beasts they carried. "Don't let them bite you!" she hissed, and saw the boys' shoulders stiffen: they *knew* that already and didn't need another woman's worry. She could cheerfully have slapped them for that attitude, if she didn't somewhat share it. She too had heard their mothers' protests and the demands—as absurd as they were understandable—that the drillbits be muzzled before the boys carried them out to the walls.

"I'm not putting my hands anywhere *near* a drillbit's

jaws!" Mustafa had cried; and that had been that. A bright lad, Mustafa. Chaya hoped that he came through this. He, and all of the others. Not for the first time, she wished that Heber had allowed her to join the men to the North, but "I'm not letting you anywhere *near* Saurons," he had said. He sounded, she thought, remarkably like Mustafa; and she had to laugh, despite her fears. He might make the swords, but familiarity with their forging wasn't quite the same as daily practice; and many of the Saurons and tribesmen alike had pistols.

Now the boys were setting down the drillbits, whose struggles intensified as the darkness restored their sight and the scent of the slimy fruit pulp on the walls waked their hunger. Darkened knife blades slashed, and the boys ran back, a little breathless, but giggling at the sight of so many drillbits eating into solid rock.

No one even protested when Chaya forbade them to watch until the wall came tumbling down. As they headed back toward what limited safety Tallinn Town could afford, the General Alert shrieked out from Angband Base.

This far from base, not even Chaya could hear the screams and the shooting. *Waiting. That's the hardest task.* She wanted to pace, to shout, even to scream frustration at the men who claimed the work of fighting and left her and their wives to wait and to fear. The women of Tallinn were quiet, though, schooled to waiting while their fates were decided. Even the youngest bride sat calmly, restraining a toddler while its mother nursed a baby.

They were all calm, all quiet. The screaming and lamentations would come later, if they were needed. In the halflight of the shelter, though, Chaya could see the women's eyes. Dark and liquid, their glances shot to the door every time someone thought she heard a sound. Waiting made your ears play tricks on you. She eased

her plastic mask onto the top of her head, glad not to
have to wear it, and exchanged glances with some of
the other women. Each of them had been selected for
her strength and composure; each bore a pistol.

If their menfolk lost, they would not die unavenged.
And, if all went well, the women would follow them,
not to be slaves to Saurons. Chaya wondered how many
of them could hold to that resolve.

She stretched and shifted in her place, trying not to
become stiff with waiting as the night dragged on.

"Quiet!" she hissed to silence a whispered conversation. Moving with as much care as if she sought to avoid
ambush, she edged toward the door.

"Footsteps," she mouthed at the older women and
saw them draw their pistols from their layered clothing.

Then she sagged with relief as a series of taps sounded
on the door. "It's the signal!" she said, speaking aloud
for the first time that night.

Tears rolled down the women's faces, and she would
have wept too . . . but that her tears dried so very
quickly.

Juchi had sent youths to reassure the women and
command them not, the youths repeated, *not* to venture into the base to care for the wounded menfolk.
The injured would be brought out. Repeat: they would
be brought out. Chaya grinned at the very young men,
who bore messily bandaged wounds and their female
relatives' shrill attention with obvious forbearance and
more than a little pride. This might well be their first
time in authority over their mothers and aunts; it was
too much to expect that they would take satisfaction in
the role of returning, victorious warriors. Hurriedly,
they recounted the battle: so many Saurons slain, so
many vanished.

Vanished? Some might try to cross the steppe, make
for the Citadel; and Barak's warriors would be waiting
for them.

Then they saw her, and their jubilation faded.

"Chaya Khatun . . ." one spoke hesitantly.

"We knew there would be dead." Her voice sounded cold and strange. "Who else?"

An odd way to phrase it. But, just from the way they looked at her, she knew. Heber was dead. Somewhere in that thrice-damned fort, her husband lay dead, hacked or torn to pieces, a bullet in his brain . . . it did not matter. The man who had loved her when all around her had called her a freak, lay dead.

The women raised the wail of tribal lamentation until Chaya's too-keen hearing could not bear it. She moved forward, her whole body cold, despite the press of bodies.

"I beg you," she said, still in that lifeless voice. "My work here is done for now. Guard my children. I must go out."

"Where, Khatun?" One of the youths made as if to stand between her and the door. He might never have backed down from the Saurons, but he fell back at her glance.

"The Saurons stole a life from me. They owe me a life in return."

She went out into the night. Briefly, she stopped at the forge to pick up weapons, supplies, and tools. She saddled up a muskylope and rode out of Tallinn Town.

When the muskylope staggered and all but pitched forward onto its knees, Chaya slid from its broad back and made camp. She kindled a tiny fire, sheltering it from the winds that tore across the steppe. She herself might have spotted it from afar, however; and that was good.

She drew her heavy sheepskin coat about her and huddled down by the fire. She did not expect it to warm her; she did not expect anything could warm her since the announcement of Heber's death. They would wonder, those townsfolk, why she did not wail with the other wives, why she would not be present to claim and wash her husband's body.

She did not want to see it.

There would be Saurons wandering the steppe tonight, Saurons and, very probably, her own kinsfolk from Eden Valley. Either way, she would claim a life to replace the life that had been reft from her . . . only she was so weary! It was not a weariness of the flesh, but a draining of the spirit.

Which would come first, she wondered, Saurons or Bandari? And which did she want to see?

At the outermost limits of her hearing sounded a chuckle, surprised and satisfied. Chaya's lips peeled back from her teeth. So. She tensed, listening for footsteps. Only one man, then. Not a man, but a Sauron. She had to hope that the Sauron would be sufficiently demoralized that he would not wonder why one of the "cattle" wandered alone on the steppe during second-cycle night, but would take advantage of whatever he found: shelter, fire, food, a woman, if he were still capable.

She drew out her pistol, looked at it, then laid it aside. That was too quick, too dignified. Moving quickly, but as quietly as she could, she drew out the tools she had taken from the forge and hid them beneath the blankets and furs of her bedroll. The footsteps grew louder, more assured. No trooper, not even one from a beaten Sauron post, could believe himself to be over-matched by cattle.

What would he say if he knew that this "cattle" was a Sauron cull?

Probably the same thing.

Best not threaten him at all, at least at first.

When the Sauron trooper entered the tiny circle cast by Chaya's fire, he found her sitting cross-legged, stirring a fragrant pot of stew. Again, she heard him chuckle, and turned her shudder of revulsion into what she hoped he would think was a shiver of pure terror. So easy, so very easy to reassure himself, faced only with a woman of the "cattle," wasn't it?

"Don't be afraid, girl," the Sauron's voice was hoarse. He used Americ, then, at her carefully blank stare, changed to Turkic. "You're as lost as I am, aren't you? Well, don't worry. We'll join forces. I can use a woman . . ."

She bet he could. She made herself cower back as he hunkered down by the fire, so near to her that her resolve almost failed her.

"Give me some of that," he ordered.

She filled one bowl, then another. Then she emptied the pot and, in a great frenzy of anxiousness to please, brought out a flask of almost coffee. He drank deeply, then belched, a sound that had nothing to do with the courtesies of a tribe. She tried, nonetheless, to look pleased.

"Well-trained are you?" he said as he wiped his greasy mouth on his sleeve. "Whose are you . . . never mind that; you're mine now. What's your name?"

Disdaining a lie, she told him. "And yours?"

"Gorbag. Trooper Gorbag, at your service. As you are at mine," he announced, and lunged at her.

She gasped and held her breath, glad that she had not eaten lest she vomit all over the man who pushed her onto the sheepskins she had spread out. Because the wind was cold, he loosened the minimum possible of his garments and hers. She clenched her fingers into the curls of the fleece on which she lay and wished that he would spend himself quickly. Her body, the body of a woman half-Sauron, adapted to survive in a world that prized fertility, moved to accommodate him. Her mind ranged far away, even as her fingers clutched the shoulders of the instrument of her vengeance.

Make hate to me, Sauron, and then I will make hate to you.

If it had taken that Gorbag . . . *Greasebag,* she

thought, *Scumbag* would have been better names . . .
forever, she would still lie beneath his thrusting, grunt-
ing hulk. But at last he had climaxed, pulled free, and
fallen asleep, exhausted past self-protection by defeat,
the coldness of night on the steppe, and sex.

Chaya forced herself to lie still, his head on her
breasts, until the snoring started. She had not known
that Saurons snored like cattle. Then she reached for
what lay beneath the sheepskins: hammer and spike
from Heber's forge. Reached for them, raised them—
and froze.

*No. Not even if I die for it. I cannot, cannot bear to
kill him as he lies on top of me. I have to move.*

The unnatural calm that had enthralled her since she
had heard of her husband's death broke like a hammer
smashes brittle iron, and she recoiled, shoving Gorbag
onto the sheepskins. He grunted, rolled, and woke.

With an intake of breath that was almost a shriek,
Chaya leapt on him, straddling him with her own Sauron
strength. Gorbag's eyes glowed with awareness. He had
a moment of knowledge and of fear before she thrust
the spike against his temple and hammered it home.
He spasmed like some immensely powerful insect,
kicked, voided, and died.

Knife in hand, Chaya raised herself from where the
dying Sauron had tossed her. He lay face down, and
she was glad of that. A single stroke of Heber's keen
steel severed head from neck; Saurons, she saw, bled
like cattle and died just as easily. She pulled her clothing about herself, grimacing at the moisture on her
thighs.

That too was part of her vengeance. She had always
known when she was ripe to conceive, and she had had
hopes that, after the battle to destroy Angband, she and
Heber . . . *don't think of that*, she told herself. The dry
heaves and the cramps snatched her up, anyway.

At last, she was empty; at least, most of her. She was
sure that she had conceived of this . . . *already, I shall*

forget his name . . . She would take his son, as she had taken his life; and she would bring the boy up as her own husband's son.

She saddled up the muskylope, kicked earth over the dying fire, muffled the Sauron's head in the defiled sheepskin, and tied it to the saddle. She left the tent and the headless corpse behind her as she rode toward Eden Valley.

"Hold! We have you in our sights!"

The sky was paling; the sun would rise at her back, giving her a brief advantage. Then she recognized the voice.

"Avi?" she called, shocked at how plaintive her voice sounded. Mutters from the force ahead of her told her she had guessed right. "It's Chaya bat Lapidoth, who married Heber . . ." her voice was breaking.

A horse—a big one—walked forward. Barak always chose the biggest horses. "Chaya? What are you doing alone out here?" he demanded.

"I wasn't!" she said. "The battle; it's over and we won. I was coming to tell you . . ."

"And Heber . . ."

"Gone. But there is this!" She untied and held up the Sauron's clotted head.

She heard murmurs of pity and sympathy, and Barak rode closer. She forced herself not to recoil when he enveloped her in what he meant to be a comforting hug.

And then, never mind the fact that her tears dried too rapidly, she wept until she was sick.

Screams came from the ruined fortress, and Chaya's youngest son stiffened. With the rapid movements that had made the people of town and valley nickname him Lightning, he was up and running toward the gate.

Her son came running back. "It is the khatun, the

cham, Mother!" he cried. "She is dead, hanged; and he has blinded himself! They are calling for you."

She rose more slowly, sorrow cluching her. Now the truth was revealed, it hurt even worse than she had feared that it might.

The boy's birth, a little more than two Haven years ago, had been harder than she was used to; but the babe had been bigger, stronger, almost preternaturally aware. *The Sauron admixture.* Not quite daring to raise him herself, she had sent him to her mother. If Dvora were past riding circuit, she was not past being a grandmother.

Named Barak in gratitude to the man who had found her on the steppe, the boy soon wore only a translation of that name; Lightning, they called him. Many in the Valley remembered his mother's speed and strength. They even said that he looked like her.

She could not remember what his father looked like. *His father was Heber*, she insisted to herself, and knew it for a lie.

With Barak and his son at her side, Chaya made very sure that no Saurons lingered, disguised as tribal chams or bandits until they could warn their fellows. Increasingly, she took over her mother's duties as judge, riding throughout Eden and Tallinn Valleys. She thought she had repaid Dvora for her earlier unhappiness. And she thought that she was fulfilling her father's and her husband's dream of joining Eden and Tallin Valleys into one people just as, three hundred T-years before, Bandari and Edener had been . . . more or less . . . joined.

Yet, in the last year of her life, Dvora had called to Chaya. "This came to me the night of the battle," Dvora told her daughter, and slipped from her withered hand the ruby Chaya had once used as a sign. "It is time to give it back to you." She lay quietly until Chaya thought that she was sleeping. Quietly, Chaya got up to leave.

But Dvora rose. "Awake, awake, Dvora!" she cried,

more shaman than judge in that moment. "Did you think that I did not know?"

"Know what?"

"As I did with you, giving a dead man the name of father to a Sauron child. Lightning was never Heber's child." The old, filmy eyes flashed with their former cunning.

"A life for a life," Chaya shrugged.

Dvora nodded. "I do not fault you, though I shudder, perhaps, at what you did. But the time when I needed to pass judgement on anything is long gone. Now, I merely *know*; and you must know too. Do you recall, daughter, the night before Heber asked for you, I told you how I found you on the steppe?"

Chaya nodded.

"We've never spoken of that since, yet, seeing Lightning, I have thought about it often." Her ringless hands reached out to clasp her adopted daughter's.

"There were *two* babies left to die, you recall. You, and a boy. A brother."

Chaya shrugged.

"If you are saying that Heber was my brother . . ."

"I am old, girl, but I listen. Who else that you know of has your speed, your strength? Who else has taken power as if it were just his due? He too has made a strange marriage . . ." Dvora's voice had taken on an odd tone, almost chanting intonation, and Chaya remembered that in the most ancient days, judges were often prophets too. "And I tell you, when the field is sowed double, beware!"

Dvora had fallen back, exhausted by her words, and Chaya called her physician. Shortly afterward, the old woman was gone. After the funeral, Chaya rode back to Tallinn.

Though her mother was dead, her words haunted her, and she glanced about Tallinn town, looking for a man much like herself in age and strength and power. . . .

And found him in Juchi, lord and cham of Tallinn Valley.

He was her age, her height, and, in all ways but one, her match. And in that one way . . . he belonged to Badri.

Belonged in two ways, God help them all. Was this God's curse upon them? What had they done? What had any of them done?

Of all the secrets that she heard as a judge, this was the hardest to bear; even harder than the secret of her own son's birth. And she kept it, for the good of the town she served.

They were waiting for her outside her home, the people of town and tribe. "My son has told me," she said, waving aside their explanations and exclamations of horror. "Bring me to them."

"Aisha found her own mother, hanging . . ."

"The poor girl, brought up a princess, and who will wed her now?"

"Son and daughter, accursed, accursed . . ."

"Who will guard us now?"

I must protect my . . . my niece. And my nephew too, if we are to salvage anything from this disaster.

"Quiet!" Chaya snapped. "The girl is guiltless. And it will be a wonder if she is not scared witless."

She will not be. She comes of good stock.

Just as Chaya quickened her pace, two of the elder men came up to her. "Judge," they said, "surely incest is a crime."

"And will you try the dead, the blind for what they did not know?"

"You have always said that ignorance is no escape from the law."

Chaya slipped past the drillbit-gnawed fragments of retaining wall. Hearing the shrill mourning of the women and Juchi's pleas for death, she shivered and quickened her pace.

"Who is it now?" cried Juchi. "Who has come to look upon the monster?"

His head was wrapped in bloody bandages, but it

snapped toward her with the keen hearing they shared. "The judge? Chaya khatun? You have courage beyond the lot of most women . . . all but one, Allah grant her pity! I beg you, kill me."

It would be a mercy. It would be the kindest thing that Chaya could do for her brother. It would be fratricide, the eldest crime. She dared not. And, if she were to save anything at all from this tragedy, she must not even explain why.

"I have told him," the tribe's shaman Tireshyas said, "that, accursed as he is, anyone who slays him will take on an immense burden of ill-luck. Do you agree with me that he must leave this place?"

To wander lost? Better that he had died the night he had been set out. Then Angband Base would still stand; Chaya's children would never have been born; and another generation would have grown up in slavery. She could not wish his life—and hers—undone. They had wrought too long and too well together, even though their lives had been built upon a lie.

Now, because of that lie and the concealments that went with it, their work might easily lie in ruins by tonight. If they had only known—and spoken—the truth! She was at fault there too, having known (or at least suspected) and keeping silence all these years.

Yet Juchi was her brother, her ally, too, for more than half her life. She could not condemn him to death wandering the steppe.

"In all I did, I strove for good," Juchi mourned.

Tireshyas turned to Juchi. "And in all you did, you were confounded." He picked up a stick and handed it to him. "If still you strive for good, you will do as I have asked, and leave us."

Juchi bowed his mutilated head. "I will. Maybe among strangers I can find the end I seek."

"Father, oh father!" That was Aisha's voice, and it broke the former cham, who sobbed dryly, without eyes or tears.

"Care for my children," he said. "Their part in this—was innocent."

Did Chaya imagine that his sightless eyes turned toward her? "I promise," she said, even as the shaman gravely agreed. He looked at her over Juchi's head and nodded. Perhaps away from the tribe, they would have a better chance at some type of decent life.

"Would you let them see you one last time?" the shaman asked Juchi. "Aisha begs for nothing else."

No! Chaya did not know how she kept from screaming.

"If you have any pity," Juchi begged, "spare me that!"

Tireshyas opened a door and admitted a young man who Chaya had seen: Juchi's escort past the Valley's minefield's. It was a hard mercy, not to waste even a mine on an outcast, but Chaya understood. Who knew how Juchi's death might curse the tribe?

Leaning on a stick, Juchi shuffled out the door, one hand on the young man's shoulder. Behind him, Tireshyas made a sign against evil.

A scream went up from the women, and Chaya ran forward. Aisha had broken free of the women who tended her as lovingly as if she had been born of a normal husband and wife, was running toward her father and her guide.

"No!" Juchi screamed, but she flung herself at his feet, the scarf falling off her dark, disheveled braids. Tears sparkled on her high cheekbones, so like her parents'—or Chaya's own; and she sobbed, forgetting calm, forgetting dignity, forgetting modesty of an unwed girl and all else but that her father (and brother) was vanishing from her life.

Again, he shook his head, gestured at his guide, who bent to raise her. Aisha jerked away, and rose on her own. She wiped hands across her face and drew herself up, abruptly cold and dignified.

"Can you deny that you love me? Will you add that to what you have cost me?" she asked. Her eyes were wild with guilt as Juchi flinched under her words, weakening as he had not weakened when she had wept and flung herself at his feet.

"I can see through the minefields as well as you," she told the young man who might, had life been gentler, have offered Juchi riches for the right to wed her. "You may go back now."

Juchi embraced his daughter, hiding his face against her slender shoulder. Head up, she glared at the watchers as she comforted her father. Then she led him away. Their path turned twice, and they were out of sight.

Chaya's eyes filmed with tears, then cleared.

"If this is anyone's fault," she announced, "it lies on the heads of the Saurons and their accursed breeding program."

Cursing your own, are you, girl? she asked wryly.

"I say that we must have the truth," she declared to the shaman. "The truth, the whole truth, and nothing but the truth. And," she took a deep breath, "I shall begin."

She pulled off her glove and worked her ruby ring free.

Beckoning to her son, she handed him the ring.

"Take this . . ." she drew a deep breath. "Take it and give it to your cousin."

She turned to face the town and tribe that she had judged for all these years. It was time that they judge her as they had already judged her family. And more than the fate of a few people hung on their decision. They could separate; they could even swear a blood feud. Or they could all spend their lives trying to repair what had been done.

TAYOK'S BASE

The clouds had piled higher behind the hills while the Sauron patrol dismounted and deployed. A rising wind flecked Assault Group Leader Tayok's cheeks with dust. Fragments of bone, ashes, and bits of dung too small to salvage for fuel danced across the open field in front of what had been Angband Base.

The senior scout, Assault Leader Eney, loped up to his commander. Tayok thought that Eney must walk, or even amble sometimes, but nobody he knew had ever caught him doing it.

"Nobody there but the drillbits, and too many of them for my peace of mind," Eney said. "The cattle've been in and out since the Base fell, but they don't stay long."

Tayok focused his binoculars on the outer wall of the fallen base. Eney was right. Some of the drillbit holes were old and weathered, the ones made when the base fell a Haven year ago. Other parts of the wall were in complete ruin, probably breaches made by the attacking cattle. Even the fallen sections contained holes.

"Too many new holes," Tayok said. "Place is a breeding ground."

"Aye aye, sir. We'd best start distilling assassin weed. Those buggers metabolize so slowly, it'll be halfway to winter before the last of them—"

Tayok held up his hand. The column of pack muskylopes

following the patrol had just come in sight. Ahead of
the column was a stocky man riding on a Chin-bred
tribute pony. As he caught sight of Tayok and Eney, he
drove his heels into its flanks. Despite its mount's weight,
the pony was remarkably quick in bringing him up to
the other Soldiers.

Which was as well. Tayok did not believe in ghosts or
spirits; both Soldiers and cattle who had died here were
dead and gone completely and forever. Even so, the
wind moaning around the ruins of what had once been
a Sauron stronghold made Tayok think of the deathsong
of Dinneh warriors. He had fought against the Dinneh
twice, and had no eagerness for another round.

"Get it over," he muttered. He wanted to work
quickly, either bringing Angband Base back to life or
leaving it to its dead.

The stocky man dismounted and comtemplated the
ruined base with the distance-devouring vision of one
with Cyborg blood. Then he grinned.

"Start unloading the weapons."

Tayok frowned. One did not argue with a Regiment
Leader, especially one who was a legitimate descendant
of Deathmaster Boyle and rumored to be an illegiti-
mate son of Cyborg Rank Koln himself. One could,
however, respectfully request an explanation for orders
that made no sense.

"Regiment Leader, the drillbits—"

"Oh yes, of course. Them. Assassin weed by all means.
I saw a stand of it about two klicks back."

That was more than Tayok had done, and he had won
awards for his fieldcraft. It was one reason he was
second in command of the column, for all that he was
only an Assault Group Leader and the father of a single
son.

"It will take time to clear the whole base, Regiment
Leader. Shouldn't the weapons remain protected from
the weather?"

Regiment Leader Boyle looked up at the younger

commander and smiled. "Dismount and come with me. I think it's time you know why we've ridden a thousand klicks with half of Quilland Base's spare weapons."

So you'll tell me now. Tayok dismounted. "Eney. Cookfires. Get your distillations going." He followed Boyle into the shadow of the Base's gate.

"We had to give it out that we were planning on reoccupying Angband Base," Boyle said. "Otherwise the cattle would never have concentrated in our path. Better a couple of big fights than what we've been having."

"Aye aye." But they both knew the advantage in those fights had not been all to the Soldiers. "Nine dead. Forty-two wounded, Regiment Leader."

"And eight hundred cattle who won't fight us again. We've made worse trades. And we're not done."

"Yes, sir. Now they are well concentrated. And we are a thousand klicks from home."

"True. Which is why, if you thought it over, the idea of reoccupying Angband Base is absurd. We would have to strip Quilland Base of half its strength to hold Angband. And run convoys every season."

"Yes, sir. And we can't do it."

"Exactly. You and I know that. The cattle don't."

"Regiment Leader, I don't understand."

"We'll get out of here as soon as we have cleared a room for the weapons cache and set the boobytraps."

Tayok tried to keep his face from looking as if he'd just sprung one of the boobytraps himself. Then a thought made him frown, and after that smile.

"What are you grinning about, Soldier?"

"Are we putting the boobytraps between the cache and the entrance?"

"Mostly, yes. Why?"

"I need to know to tell the Engineer squad. I was wondering why you were planning to keep the cattle from using the weapons on us. But if the first half-dozen parties trip boobytraps—"

Boyle smiled; it was not the kind of smile even a Sauron would have called *nice*. "Exactly. That will slow the others, if only because they'll have to dig out their friends' bodies."

"It won't keep them away from the cache forever. A load of our weapons is something any tribe of cattle will walk through fire to get. Or take away from those who get it first."

"By the time we're home, the cattle for a hundred klicks in all directions will be killing each other over these weapons. Killing each other, and saving us the trouble. That's the plan, anyway." Boyle gestured at the scarred walls. "Angband Base is dead—for now. But he will reach out from beyond death and strike down those who destroyed him."

Tayok's grin resembled the classic death head. Vengeance for Angband Base's many dead was a pleasant thought. And this scheme could lead to more than vengeance.

By numbers or craft or treachery or all together, the cattle could always destroy any Soldier Base except the Citadel. It had been so for a long time—

Now, perhaps, that time was past. Sauron numbers were now great enough to reach out farther, through the Valley and to every inhabitable part of Haven.

Great enough, that was, if part of it did not need to be spent defending what the Race held already. Keep the cattle busy slaughtering each other, and fewer Soldiers would be needed for the task.

Not to mention that the survivors of those fights would be the best of the cattle, the fittest to add their genes to the next generation of Soldiers.

Every piece of the puzzle fell into place. Tayok let those thoughts fade with his grin of appreciation. Then he unfolded a map.

"If I might make a suggestion, Regiment Leader—"

"I've never known an Assault Group Leader who

didn't think he knew more than most Deathmasters. Including myself, I might add."

"I was thinking of the haBandari. They're the one tribe around here who might find a way around the boobytraps. If they get the weapons and trail us . . ."

The reputation of the haBandari was too well known for Boyle to disagree. "Make your suggestion."

"As we leave, a quick raid on the Eden Valley. Not pressed home, you understand. They have too much firepower and discipline. But enough to make them cautious about leaving the valley for long enough to let other tribes come here first."

They raided the haBandari on the way home, and as always it was a stern fight for both sides. It was also the Assault Group Leader's last battle.

But he had his monument. Regiment Leader Boyle came home to a promotion to Division Leader, which allowed him another woman. He took Tayok's woman to be his, and Tayok's son to rear as his own, and made their lives as honorable as he could. He did not make it easy, because on Haven no life could be easy.

And when in time Boyle rose to the rank of Deathmaster held by his ancestor, he had the naming of new bases in his command. He named one of them Tayok Base, and sent Tayok's son, married to one of the Deathmaster's granddaughters, to command it.

Paksenarrion, a simple sheepfarmer's daughter, yearns for a life of adventure and glory, such as *the heroes in songs* and story. At age seventeen she runs away from home to join a mercenary company, and begins her epic life . . .

ELIZABETH MOON

THE DEED OF PAKSENARRION

"This is the first work of high heroic fantasy I've seen, that has taken the work of Tolkien, assimilated it totally and deeply and absolutely, and produced something altogether new and yet incontestably based on the master. . . . This is the real thing. Worldbuilding in the grand tradition, background thought out to the last detail, by someone who knows absolutely whereof she speaks. . . . Her military knowledge is impressive, her picture of life in a mercenary company most convincing."—**Judith Tarr**

About the author: Elizabeth Moon joined the U.S. Marine Corps in 1968 and completed both Officers Candidate School and Basic School, reaching the rank of 1st Lieutenant during active duty. Her background in military training and discipline imbue The Deed of Paksenarrion with a gritty realism that is all too rare in most current fantasy.

"I thoroughly enjoyed *Deed of Paksenarrion*. A most engrossing, highly readable work."

—**Anne McCaffrey**

"For once the promises are borne out. *Sheepfarmer's Daughter* is an advance in realism. . . . I can only say that I eagerly await whatever Elizabeth Moon chooses to write next."

—Taras Wolansky, *Lan's Lantern*

*   *   *   *

Volume One: Sheepfarmer's Daughter—Paks is trained as a mercenary, blooded, and introduced to the life of a soldier . . . and to the followers of Gird, the soldier's god.

Volume Two: Divided Allegiance—Paks leaves the Duke's company to follow the path of Gird alone—and on her lonely quests encounters the other sentient races of her world.

Volume Three: Oath of Gold—Paks the warrior must learn to live with Paks the human. She undertakes a holy quest for a lost eleven prince that brings the gods' wrath down on her and tests her very limits.

*   *   *   *   *

These books are available at your local bookstore, or you can fill out the coupon and return it to Baen Books, at the address below.

All three books of The Deed of Paksenarrion ____
SHEEPFARMER'S
  DAUGHTER   65416-0 • 506 pages • $3.95 ____
DIVIDED
  ALLEGIANCE   69786-2 • 528 pages • $3.95 ____
OATH OF GOLD 69798-6 • 528 pages • $3.95 ____

Please send the cover price to: Baen Books, Dept. B, 260 Fifth Avenue, New York, NY 10001.

Name_____

Address_____

City_____ State_____ Zip_____